A Holiday of Love

JUDITH McNAUGHT

JUDE DEVERAUX

JILL BARNETT

POCKET STAR BOOKS

New York London Toronto Sydney

A Pocket Star Book published by
POCKET BOOKS, a division of Simon & Schuster, Inc.
1230 Avenue of the Americas, New York, NY 10020

ISBN-13: 978-1-4165-1721-4
ISBN-10:   1-4165-1721-9

This Pocket Star Books paperback edition November 2005

10 9 8 7 6 5 4 3 2

Cover photo by Kazutomo Kawai/Photonica

Manufactured in the United States of America

For information regarding special discounts for bulk purchases, please contact Simon & Schuster Special Sales at
1-800-456-6798 or business@simonandschuster.com.

A HOLIDAY OF LOVE
Four glorious tales of yuletide romance
by celebrated storytellers . . .

Judith McNaught

The *New York Times* bestselling author of
Perfect, Until You, Remember When,
Night Whispers, and *Someone to Watch Over Me.*

Jude Deveraux

The *New York Times* bestselling author of
Temptation, The Summerhouse, The Blessing,
An Angel for Emily, and *Legend.*

Jill Barnett

The *New York Times* bestselling author of
Sentimental Journey, Wicked, Wild, and *Wonderful.*

Arnette Lamb

The *New York Times* bestselling author of
Betrayed, Beguiled, and *True Heart.*

Contents

JUDE DEVERAUX

Change of Heart

1

THE MAN BEHIND THE DESK LOOKED AT THE BOY ACROSS from him with a mixture of envy and admiration. Only twelve years old, yet the kid had a brain that people would kill to have. I mustn't appear too eager, he thought. Must keep calm. We want him at Princeton—preferably chained to a computer and not allowed out for meals.

Ostensibly, he had been sent to Denver to interview several scholarship candidates, but the truth was, this boy was the only one who the admissions office was truly interested in, and the meeting had been set to the boy's convenience. The department dean had arranged with an old friend to borrow office space that was in a part of town close to the boy's very middle-class house so he could get there by bike.

"Ah hem," he said, clearing his throat and frowning at the papers. He deepened his voice. Better not let the kid know that he was only twenty-five and that if he messed up this assignment he could be in serious trouble with his advisers.

"You are quite young," the man said, trying to sound as old as possible, "and there will be difficul-

3

ties, but I think we can handle your special circumstances. Princeton likes to help the young people of America. And—"

"What kind of equipment do you have? What will I have to work with? There are other schools making me offers."

As the man looked at the boy, he thought someone should have strangled him in his crib. Ungrateful little— "I'm sure that you'll find what we have adequate, and if we do not have everything you need we can make it available."

The boy was tall for his age but thin, as though he were growing too fast for his weight to catch up with him. For all that he had one of the great brains of the century, he looked like something out of Tom Sawyer: sandy hair that no comb could tame, freckles across skin that would never tan, dark blue eyes behind glasses big enough to be used as a windshield on a Mack truck.

Elijah J. Harcourt, the file said. IQ over 200. Had made much progress on coming up with a computer that could *think.* Artificial intelligence. You could tell the computer what you wanted to do and the machine could figure out how to do it. As far as anyone could tell, the boy was putting *his* prodigious brain inside a computer. The future uses of such an instrument were beyond comprehension.

Yet here the smug little brat sat, not grateful for what was being offered to him but demanding more. The man knew he was risking his own career, but he couldn't stand the hesitancy of the boy. Standing, he shoved the papers back into his briefcase. "Maybe you should think over our offer," he said with barely controlled anger. "We don't make offers like this very often. Shall we say that you're to make your decision by Christmas?"

As far as the man could tell, the boy showed no

emotion. Cold little bugger, the man thought. Heart as cold as a computer chip. Maybe he wasn't real at all but one of his own creations. Somehow, putting the boy down made him feel better about his own IQ, which was a "mere" 122.

Quickly, he shook the boy's hand, and as he did so he realized that in another year the boy would be taller than he was. "I'll be in touch," he said and left the room.

Eli worked hard to control his inner shaking. Although he seemed so cool on the exterior, inside he was doing cartwheels. Princeton! he thought. Contact with *real* scientists! Talk with people who wanted to know more about life than the latest football scores!

Slowly, he walked out the door, giving the man time to get away. Eli knew that the man hadn't liked him, but he was used to that. A long time ago Eli had learned to be very, very cautious with people. Since he was three he had known he was "different" from other kids. At five his mother had taken him to school to be tested, to see whether he fit into the redbirds or the bluebirds reading group. Busy with other students and parents, the teacher had told Eli to get a book from the shelf and read it to her. She had meant one of the many pretty picture books. Her intention had been to find out which children had been read to by their parents and which had grown up glued to a TV.

Like all children, Eli had wanted to impress his teacher, so he'd climbed on a chair and pulled down a college textbook titled *Learning Disabilities* that the teacher kept on a top shelf, then quietly went to stand beside her and began softly to read from page one. Since Eli was a naturally solitary child and his mother did not push him to do what he didn't want to do, he had spent most of his life in near seclusion. He'd had no idea that reading from a college textbook when he was a mere five years old was unusual. All he'd wanted to do was to pass the reading test and get into the top reading group.

"That's fine, Eli," his mother had said after he'd read half a page. "I think Miss Wilson is going to put you with the redbirds. Aren't you, Miss Wilson?"

Even though he was only five, Eli had recognized the wide-eyed look of horror on the teacher's face. Her expression had said, *What* do I do with this freak?

Since his entry into school, Eli had learned about being "different." He'd learned about jealousy and being excluded and not fitting in with the other children. Only with his mother was he "normal." His mother didn't think he was unusual or strange; he was just *hers.*

Now, years later, when Eli left his meeting with the man from Princeton, he was still shaking, and when he saw Chelsea he gave her one of his rare smiles. When Eli was six he'd met Chelsea Hamilton, who was not as smart as he was, of course, but near enough that he could talk to her. In her way Chelsea was as much a freak as Eli was, for Chelsea was rich—very, very rich—and even by six she'd found that people wanted to know her for what they could get from her rather than her personality. At six the children had taken one look at each other, the two oddities in the boring little classroom, and they'd become eternal friends.

"Well!" Chelsea demanded, bending her head to look into Eli's face. She was six months older than he, and until this year she'd always been taller. But now Eli was rapidly overtaking her.

"What are you doing in this building?" Eli asked. "You aren't supposed to be here." Smugly, he was making her wait for his news.

"You're slipping, brain-o. My father owns this place." She tossed her long, dark, glossy hair. "And he's friends with the dean at Princeton. I've known about the meeting for two weeks." At twelve, Chelsea was already on the way to being a beauty. Her problems in life were going to be the stuff of dreams: too tall, too thin, too smart, too rich. Their houses were only ten minutes apart, but in value, they were miles apart. Eli's house would fit into Chelsea's marble foyer.

When Eli didn't respond, she looked straight ahead. "Dad called last night and I cried so much at missing him that he's buying us a new CD-ROM. Maybe I'll let you see it."

Eli smiled again. Chelsea hadn't realized that she'd said "us," meaning the two of them. She was great at the emotional blackmail of her parents, who spent most of their lives traveling around the world, leaving the family business to Chelsea's older siblings. A few tears of anguish and her parents gave her anything money could buy.

"Princeton wants me," Eli said as they emerged into the almost constant sunshine of Denver, its clean streets stretching before them. The autumn air was crisp and clear.

"I *knew* it!" she said, throwing her head back in exultation. "When? For what?"

"I'm to go in the spring semester, just to get my feet wet, then a summer session. If my work is good enough I can enter full time next fall." For a moment he turned to look at her, and for just that second he let his guard down and Chelsea saw how very much he wanted this. Eli hated passionately the idea of high school, of having to sit through days of classes with a bunch of semiliterate louts who took great pride in their continuing ignorance. This program would give Eli the opportunity to skip all those grades and get on with something useful.

"That gives us the whole rest of the year to work," she said. "I'll get Dad to buy us—"

7

"I can't go," Eli said.

It took a moment for those words to register with Chelsea. "You can't go to Princeton?" she whispered. "Why not?" Chelsea had never considered, if she wanted something—whether to buy it or do it—that she wouldn't be able to.

When Eli looked at her, his face was full of anguish. "Who's going to take care of Mom?" he asked softly.

Chelsea opened her mouth to say that Eli had to think of himself first, but she closed it again. Eli's mom, Randy, *did* need taking care of. She had the softest heart in the world, and if anyone had a problem Randy always had room to listen and love. Chelsea never liked to think that she needed anything as soppy as a mother, but there had been many times over the years when she'd flung herself against the soft bosom of Eli's ever-welcoming mother.

However, it was because of Randy's sweetness that she needed looking after. His mother was like a lamb living in a world of hungry wolves. If it weren't for Eli's constant vigilance . . . Well, Chelsea didn't like to think what would have happened to his mother. Just look at the man she'd married, the horrid man who was Eli's father: a gambler, a con artist, a promiscuous liar.

"When do you have to give them your answer?" Chelsea asked softly.

"My birthday," Eli answered. It was one of his little vanities that he always referred to Christmas as his birthday. Eli's mom said that Eli was her Christmas gift from God, so she was never going to cheat Eli because she'd been lucky enough to have him on Christmas Day. So every Christmas, Eli had a pile of gifts under a tree and another pile on a table with a big, gaudy birthday cake, a cake that had no hint of anything to do with Christmas.

In silence, the two of them walked down Denver's

downtown streets, forgoing the trolley that ran through the middle of town. Chelsea knew that Eli needed to think, and he did that best by walking or riding his bike. She knew without asking that Eli would never abandon his mother. If it came to a choice between Princeton and taking care of his mother, Eli would take care of the person he loved best. For all that Eli managed to appear cool and calculating, Chelsea knew that when it came to the two people he loved the most—her and his mother—inside, Eli was marshmallow cream.

"You know," Chelsea said brightly, "maybe you're overreacting. Maybe your mother can get along without you." "Without us," she almost said. "Who took care of her before you were born?"

Eli gave her a sideways look. "No one, and look what happened to her."

"Your father," Chelsea said heavily. She hesitated as she thought about the matter. "They've been divorced for two years now. Maybe your mother will remarry and her new husband will take care of her."

"Who will she marry? The last man she went out with ended up 'forgetting' his wallet, so Mom paid for dinner and a tank full of gas. A week later *I* found out he was married."

Unfortunately, Randy's generosity didn't just extend to children but to every living creature. Eli said that if it were left up to his mother, there wouldn't need to be a city animal shelter because all the unwanted animals in Denver would live with them. For a moment, Chelsea had an image of sweet Randy surrounded by wounded animals and uneducated men asking her for money. For Chelsea, "uneducated men" was the worst image she could conjure.

"Maybe if you tell her about the offer, she'll come up with a solution," Chelsea said helpfully.

Eli's face became fierce. "My mother would sac-

9

rifice her *life* for me. If she knew about this offer, she'd personally escort me to Princeton. My mother cares only about me and never about herself. My mother—"

Chelsea rolled her eyes skyward. In every other aspect of life Eli had the most purely scientific brain she'd ever encountered, but when it came to his mother there was no reasoning with him. Chelsea also thought Randy was a lovely woman, but she wasn't exactly ready for sainthood. For one thing, she was thoroughly undisciplined. She ate too much, read too many books that did not improve one's mind, and wasted too much time on frivolous things, like making Eli and Chelsea Halloween costumes. Of course, neither of them ever told her that they thought Halloween was a juvenile holiday. Instead of tramping the streets, asking for candy, they would go to Chelsea's house, work on their computers while dripping artificial blood, and send the butler out to purchase candy that they'd later show to Eli's mom so she'd think they were "normal" kids.

Only once had Chelsea dared tell Eli that she thought it was a bit absurd for them to sit at their computers wearing uncomfortable and grotesque costumes while calculating logarithms. Eli had said, "My mother made these for us to wear," and that had been the *final* decree; the matter was never mentioned again.

2

As Eli rode his bike onto the cracked, weedy, concrete drive of his mother's house, he caught a glimpse of the taillights of his father's car as it scurried out of sight.

"Deadbeat!" Eli said under his breath, knowing that his father must have been watching for him so he could run away as soon as he saw his son.

Every time Eli thought of the word "father" his stomach clenched. Leslie Harcourt had never been a father to him, nor a husband to his wife, Miranda. The man had spent his life trying to make his family believe he was "important." Too important to talk to his family; too important to go anywhere with his wife and child; too important to give them any time or attention.

According to Leslie Harcourt, other people were the ones who really counted in life. "My friends *need* me," Eli used to hear his father say over and over. His mother would say "But Leslie, *I* need you too. Eli needs school clothes and there are no groceries in the house and my car has been broken for three weeks. We *need* food and we *need* clothes."

Eli would watch as his father got that look on his face, as though he were being enormously patient with

11

someone who couldn't understand the simplest concepts. "My friend has broken up with his girlfriend and he has to have someone to talk to and I'm the only one. Randy, he's in pain. Don't you understand? Pain! I *must* go to him."

Eli had heard his father say this same sort of thing a thousand times. Sometimes his mother would show a little spunk and say "Maybe if your friends cried on the shoulders of their girlfriends, they wouldn't *be* breaking up."

But Leslie Harcourt never listened to anyone except himself—and he was a master at figuring out how to manipulate other people so he could get as much out of them as possible. Leslie knew that his wife, Randy, was softhearted; it was the reason he'd married her. Randy forgave anyone anything, and all Leslie had to do was say "I love you" every month or so and Randy forgave him whatever.

And in return for those few words, Randy gave Leslie security. She gave him a home that he contributed little or no money to and next to no time; he had no responsibilities either to her or to his son. Most important, she provided him with an excuse to give to all his women as to why he couldn't marry them. He invariably "forgot" to mention that all these "friends" who "needed" him were women—and mostly young, with lots of hair and long legs.

But Eli and Chelsea had put an end to Leslie and all his Helpless Hannahs two years ago. When he was very young, Eli had not known what a "father" was, except that it was a word he heard other children use, as in "My father and I worked on the car this weekend." Eli rarely saw his father, and he never did anything with him.

It was Chelsea who first saw Eli's father with the tall, thin, blonde bimbo as they were slipping into an afternoon matinee at the local mall. And Chelsea, using the invisibility of being a child, sat in front of them, twirling chewing gum (which she hated) and trying to look as young as possible, as she listened avidly to every word Eli's father said.

"I would like to marry you, Heather, you know that. I love you more than life itself, but I'm a married man with a child. If it weren't for that, I'd be running with you to the altar. You're a woman any man would be proud to call his wife. But you don't know what Randy is like. She's utterly helpless without me. She can hardly turn off the faucets without me there to do it for her. And then there's my son. Eli needs me so much. He cries himself to sleep if I'm not there to kiss him goodnight, so you can see why we have to meet during the day."

"Then he started kissing her neck," Chelsea reported.

When Eli heard this account he had to blink a few times to clear his mind. The sheer enormity of this lie of his father's was stunning. As long as he could remember, his father had *never* kissed him goodnight. In fact, Eli wasn't sure his father even knew where his bedroom was located in the little house that needed so much repair.

When Eli recovered himself, he looked at Chelsea. "What are we going to do?"

The smile Chelsea gave him was conspiratorial. "Robin and Marian," she whispered, and he nodded. Years earlier, they called themselves Robin Hoods. Robin Hood righted wrongs and did good deeds and helped the underdog (or at least that's what the legend said).

It was Randy who'd first called them Robin and Marian, after some soppy movie she loved to watch repeatedly on video. Laughingly, she'd called them Robin and Marian Les Jeunes, French for "youths," and they'd kept the name in secret.

13

Only the two of them knew what they did: They collected letterhead stationery from corporations, law firms, doctors' offices, wherever, then used a very expensive publishing computer system to duplicate the type fonts, then sent people letters as though from the offices. They sent letters on law-office stationery to the fathers of children at school who didn't pay child support. They sent letters of thanks to unappreciated employees from the heads of big corporations. They once got back an old woman's $400 from a telephone scammer.

Only once did they nearly get into trouble. A boy at school had teeth that were rotting, but his father was too cheap to take him to the dentist. Chelsea and Eli found out that the father was a gambler, so they wrote to him, offering free tickets to a "secret" (because it was illegal) national dental lottery. He would receive a ticket with every fifty dollars he spent on his children's teeth. So all three of his children had several hundred dollars' worth of work done, and Chelsea and Eli dutifully sent him beautiful red-and-gold, hand-painted lottery tickets. The problem came when they had to write the man a letter saying his tickets did not have the winning numbers. The man went to the dentist, waving the letters and the tickets, and demanded his money back. The poor dentist had had to endure months of the man's winking at him in conspiracy while he'd worked on the children's teeth, and now he was being told he was going to be sued because of some lottery he'd never heard of.

In order to calm the man down, Chelsea and Eli had to reveal themselves to the son who they'd helped in secret and get him to steal the letters from his father's night table. Chelsea then sent the man one of her father's gold watches (he had twelve of them) in order to get him to shut up.

Later, when they weighed the good they had done—

of fixing the children's teeth—against the near exposure, they decided to continue being Robin and Marian Les Jeunes.

"So what are we going to do with your father?" Chelsea asked, and she could see that Eli had no idea.

"I'd like to get rid of him," Eli said. "He makes my mother cry. But—"

"But what?"

"But she says she still loves him."

At that, Chelsea and Eli looked at each other without comprehension. They knew they loved each other, but then they also *liked* each other. How could anyone love a man like Leslie Harcourt? There wasn't anything at all likable about him.

"I would like to give my mother what she wants," Eli said.

"Mel Gibson?" Chelsea asked, without any intent at humor. Randy had once said that what she truly wanted in life was Mel Gibson—because he was a family man, she'd added, and no other reason.

"No," Eli said. "I'd like to give her my father as a real father, the kind she likes."

For a moment they looked at each other in puzzlement. Eli had recently been trying to make a computer think, and they both knew that that would be easier than trying to make Leslie Harcourt stay home and putter in the garage.

"This is a question for the Love Expert," Chelsea said, making Eli nod. "Love Expert" was what they called Eli's mom because she read romantic novels by the thousands. After each one she gave Eli a brief synopsis of the plot, then he fed it into his computer data banks and made charted graphs. He could quote all sorts of statistics, such as that 18 percent of all romances are medieval, then he could break that number down into fifty-year sections. He could also quote about plots, how many had fires and shipwrecks, how many had heroes who'd been hurt by one woman (who always turned out to be a bad person) and so hated all other women. According to Eli the sheer repetition of the books fascinated him, but his mother said that love was wonderful no matter how many times she read about it.

So Eli and Chelsea consulted Randy, telling her that Chelsea's older sister's husband was having an affair with a girl who wanted to marry him. He didn't want to marry her, but neither could he seem to break up with her.

"Ah," Randy said, "I just read a book like that."

Here Eli gave Chelsea an I-knew-she'd-know look.

"The mistress tried to make the husband divorce his wife, so she told him she was going to bear his child. But the ploy backfired and the man went back to his wife, who by that time had been rescued by a tall, dark, and gorgeous man, so the husband was left without either woman." For a moment Randy looked dreamily into the distance. "Anyway, that's what happened in the book, but I'm afraid real life isn't like a romance novel. More's the pity. I'm sorry, Chelsea, that I can't be of more help, but I don't seem to know exactly what to do with men in real life."

Chelsea and Eli didn't say any more, but after a few days of research, they sent a note to Eli's father on the letterhead of a prominent physician, stating that Miss Heather Allbright was pregnant with his child and his office had been directed to send the bills to him, Leslie Harcourt. Sending the bills had been Chelsea's idea, because she believed that all bills on earth should be directed to fathers.

But things did not work out as Chelsea and Eli had planned. When Leslie Harcourt confronted his mistress with the lie that she was expecting his child, the young woman didn't so much as blink an eye, but broke down and told him it was true. From what Eli and Chelsea could find out—and Eli's mother did everything she could to keep Eli from knowing anything—Heather threatened to sue Leslie for everything he had if he didn't divorce Randy and marry her.

Randy, understanding as always, said they should all think of the unborn baby and that she and Eli would be fine, so of course she'd give Leslie the speediest divorce possible. Leslie said it would especially speed up matters if he had to pay only half the court costs and only minimal child support until Eli was eighteen. Generously, he said he'd let Randy have the house if he could have anything inside it that could possibly be of value, and of course she would assume the mortgage payments.

When the dust had settled, Chelsea and Eli were in shock at what they had caused, too afraid to tell anyone the truth—but then if Heather *was* going to have a baby, then they *had* told the truth. One week after Eli's father married Heather, she miscarried and there was no baby.

Eli had been afraid his mother would fall apart at this news, but instead she had laughed. "Imagine that," she'd said. "But Miss Clever Heather *did* get her baby, whether she knows it yet or not."

Eli never could get his mother to explain that remark, but he was so glad she wasn't hurt by the divorce that he didn't mention the "miscarriage" again.

So now Eli had just seen the taillight of his father's car pull away, and he knew without a doubt that his father had been there trying to weasel out of child-support payments. Leslie Harcourt made about seventy-five thousand a year as a car salesman—he could sell anything to anyone—while his mother barely pulled down twenty thousand as a practical nurse. An old candy striper is how Randy described her job. "A glorified bed pan emptier" is what she said she was. "I hold hands and make people feel good. Unfortunately, they don't pay people much for that. Eli, sweetheart, my only realistic dream for the future is to become a private nurse for some very rich, very sweet old man who wants little more than to eat popcorn and watch videos all day."

Eli had pointed out to her that all the heroines in her romance novels were running corporations while still in their twenties, or else they were waitressing and going to law school at night. That had made Randy laugh. "If all women were like that, who'd be buying the romance novels?"

Eli thought that was a very good consideration. His mother had the unusual ability to see right to the heart of a matter.

"What did he want?" Eli asked the moment he opened the door to the house he shared with his mother.

For a moment Randy grimaced, annoyed that her son had caught his father there. Escaping Eli's ever-watchful eye was like trying to escape a pack of watchdogs. "Nothing much," she said evasively.

At those words a chill ran down Eli's back. "How much did you give him?"

Randy rolled her eyes skyward.

"You know I'll find out as soon as I reconcile the bank statement. How much did you give him?"

"Young man, you are getting above yourself. The money I earn—"

Eli did some quick calculations in his head. He always knew to the penny how much money his mother had in her checking account—there was no savings account—and how much was in her purse, even to the change. "Two hundred dollars," he said. "You gave him a check for two hundred dollars." That was the maximum she could afford and still pay the mortgage and groceries.

When Randy remained tight-lipped in silence, he knew he'd hit the amount exactly on the head. He would tell Chelsea later and allow her to congratulate him on his insight.

Eli uttered a curse word under his breath.

"Eli!" Randy said sternly. "I will not allow you to call your father such names." Her face softened. "Sweetheart, you're too young to be so cynical. You must believe in people. I worry that you've been traumatized by your father leaving you without male guidance. And I know you're hiding your true feelings: I know you miss him very much."

Eli, looking very much like an old man, said, "You must be watching TV talk shows again. I do not miss him; I never saw him when you were married to him. My father is a self-centered, selfish bastard."

Randy's mouth tightened into a line that was a mirror of her son's. "Whether that is true or not is irrelevant. He *is* your father."

Eli's expression didn't change. "I'm sure it is too much to hope that you were unfaithful to him and that my real father is actually the king of a small but rich European country."

As always, Randy's face lost its stern look and she laughed. She was as unable to remain angry with Eli as she was to resist the whining and pleading of her ex-husband. She knew Eli would hate for her to say this, but he was very much like his father. Both of them always went after whatever they wanted and allowed nothing to stop them.

No, Eli wouldn't appreciate such an observation in the least.

Eli was so annoyed with his mother for once again allowing Leslie Harcourt to con her out of paying the child support that he couldn't say another word, but turned away and went to his own room. At this moment his father owed six months in back child support. Instead of paying it, he'd come to Randy and shed a few tears, telling her how broke he was, knowing he could get Randy to give him money. Eli knew that his father liked to test his ability to sell at every opportunity. Seeing if he could con Randy was an exercise in salesmanship.

The truth—a truth Randy didn't know—was that Leslie had recently purchased a sixty-thousand-dollar Mercedes, and the payments on that car were indeed stretching him financially. (Eli and Chelsea had been able to tap into a few credit-report data banks and find out all sorts of "confidential" information about people.)

Eli spent thirty minutes in his room, stewing over the perfidy of his father, but when he saw that his mother was outside tending her roses, he went back to the living room and called the man who was his father.

Eli didn't waste time with greetings. "If you don't pay three months' support within twenty-four hours and another three months' within thirty days, I'll put sugar in the gas tank of your new car." He then hung up the phone.

Twenty-two hours later, Leslie appeared at the door of Randy's house with the money. As Eli stood behind his mother, he had to listen to his father give a long, syrupy speech about the goodness of people, about how some people were willing to believe in others, while others had no loyalty in their souls.

Eli stood it for a few minutes, then he looked around his mother and glared at his father until the man quickly left, after loudly telling Randy that he'd have the other three months' support within thirty days. Eli restrained himself from calling out that within thirty days he'd owe not three months' support but four.

When Leslie was gone, Randy turned to her son and smiled. "See, Eli, honey, you must believe in people. I told you your father would come through, and he did. Now, where shall we go for dinner?"

Ten minutes later, Eli was on the phone to Chelsea. "I can*not* go to Princeton," he said softly. "I cannot leave my mother unprotected."

Chelsea didn't hesitate. "Get here fast! We'll meet in Sherwood Forest."

3

WHAT ARE WE GOING TO DO?" CHELSEA WHISPERED. They were sitting side by side on a swing glider in the garden on her parents' twenty-acre estate. It was prime real estate, close to the heart of Denver. Her father had bought four houses and torn down three of them to give himself the acreage. Not that he was ever there to enjoy the land, but he got a lot of joy out of telling people he had twenty acres in the city of Denver.

"I don't know," Eli said. "I can't leave her. I know that. She'd give everything she owned to my father if I weren't there to protect her."

Chelsea had no doubt of this after the story Eli had

21

just told her. And this wasn't the first time Leslie Harcourt had pulled a scam on his sweet ex-wife. "I wish . . ." She trailed off for a moment, then stood up and looked down at Eli, his head bent low as he contemplated what he was giving up by not taking this offer from Princeton. She knew he hated the idea of high school almost as much as he loved the idea of getting on with his computer research.

"I wish we could find a husband for her."

Eli gave a snort. "We've tried, remember? She only likes men like my father, the ones she says 'need' her. They need her money and for her to forgive them."

"I know, but wouldn't it be nice if we could make one of her books she loves so much come true. She would meet a tall, dark billionaire, and he'd—"

"A *billionaire?*"

"Yes," Chelsea said sagely. "My father says that, what with inflation as it is, a millionaire—even a multimillionaire—isn't worth very much."

Sometimes Eli was vividly reminded of how he and Chelsea differed on money. To him and his mother two hundred dollars was a great deal, but the woman who cut Chelsea's hair charged three hundred dollars a visit.

Chelsea smiled. "You don't happen to know any single billionaires, do you?"

She was teasing, but Eli didn't smile. "Actually, I do. He . . . he's my best friend. Male friend, that is."

At that Chelsea's eyes opened wide. One of the things she loved best about Eli was that he always had the ability to surprise her. No matter how much she thought she knew about him, it wasn't all there was to know. "Where did you meet a billionaire and how did he get to be your friend?"

But Eli just looked at her and said nothing, and when he had that expression on his face, she knew she was not going to get another word out of him.

22

But it was two days later that Eli called a meeting for the two of them in Sherwood Forest, their name for her father's garden, and Chelsea had never seen such a light in his eyes before. It was almost as though he had a fever.

"What's wrong?" she whispered, knowing it had to be something awful.

When he handed her a newspaper clipping his hand was shaking. Having no idea what to expect, she read it, then knew less than she did before she'd started. It was a small clipping from a magazine about a man named Franklin Taggert, one of the major heads of Montgomery-Taggert Enterprises. He'd been involved in a small accident and his right arm had been broken in two places. Because he had chosen to seclude himself in a cabin hidden in the Rocky Mountains until his arm healed, several meetings and contract finalizations had been postponed.

When Chelsea finished reading, she looked up at Eli in puzzlement. "So?"

"He's my friend," Eli said, in a voice filled with such awe that Chelsea felt a wave of jealousy shoot through her.

"Your *billionaire?*" she asked disdainfully.

But Eli didn't seem to notice her odd reaction as he began to pace in front of her. "It was your idea," he said. "Sometimes, Chelsea, I forget that you are as much a female as my mother."

Chelsea was not at all sure that she liked this statement.

"You said I should find her a husband, that I should find her a rich man to take care of her. But how can I trust the care of my mother to just any man? He must be a man of insight as well as money."

Chelsea's eyebrows had risen to high up in her hairline. This was a whole new Eli she was seeing.

"The logical problem has been how to introduce my

23

mother to a wealthy man. She is a nurse, and twenty-
one percent of all romance novels at one point or
another have a wounded hero and a heroine who
nurses him back to health, with true love always
following. So it follows that her being a nurse would
give her an introduction to rich, wounded men; but
since she works at a public hospital and rich men tend
to hire private nurses, she has not met them."

"I see. So now you plan to get your mother the job
of nursing this man. But Eli," she said gently, "how do
you get this man to hire your mother? How do you
know he's a good man, not just a wealthy one? And
how do you know they will fall in love if they do meet?
I think falling in love has to do with physical vibra-
tions." She'd read this last somewhere, and it seemed
to explain what her dopey sisters were always talking
about.

Eli raised one eyebrow. "How could any man *not*
fall in love with my mother? My problem has been
keeping men away from her, not the other way
around."

Chelsea knew better than to comment on that.
Making Eli see his mother as a normal human being
was impossible. He seemed to think she had a golden
glow around her. "Then how . . ." She hesitated, then
smiled. "Robin and Marian Les Jeunes."

"Yes. I think Mr. Taggert is at the cabin alone. We
find out where it is, write my mother a letter hiring
her, give her directions, and send her up there. They
will fall in love and he'll take care of her. He is a
proper man."

Chelsea blinked at him for a moment. "A . . .
proper man?" She could see that Eli wasn't going to
tell her another word, but she knew how to handle
him. "If you don't tell me how you know this man, I
won't help you. I won't do a thing."

Eli knew that she was bluffing. Chelsea had too much curiosity not to go along with any of his projects, but he wanted to tell her how he'd met Frank Taggert. "You remember two years ago when my class went on a field trip to see Montgomery-Taggert Enterprises?"

She didn't remember, but she nodded anyway.

"I wasn't going to go, but at the last moment I decided it might be interesting, so I went." Eli then began to tell Chelsea an extraordinary story.

Eli went on the field trip with his class solely for the purpose of stealing letterhead stationery. He didn't have any from the Montgomery-Taggert industries, and he wanted to be prepared in case they needed it.

As he was standing there, bored out of his mind, with a condescending secretary asking the children if they would like to play with the paper clips, Eli looked across the room to see a man sitting on the edge of a desk talking on the telephone. The man had on a denim shirt, jeans, and cowboy boots; he was dressed like the janitor, but to Eli the man radiated power, like a fire generating heat waves.

Quietly moving about the room, Eli got behind him so the man couldn't see him, then listened to his telephone conversation. It took Eli a moment to realize that the man was making a multimillion-dollar deal. When he talked of "five and twenty," he was actually talking of five *million* and twenty *million*. Dollars.

When the man hung up, Eli started to move away.

"Hear what you wanted to, kid?"

Eli froze in his tracks, his breath held. He couldn't believe the man knew he was there. Most people pay no attention to kids. How did this man know he was there? Or see him?

"Are you too cowardly to face me?"

Eli stood straighter, then walked to stand in front of the man.

"Tell me what you heard."

Since adults seemed to like to think that children could hear only what the adults want them to hear, Eli usually found it expedient to lie. But he didn't lie to this man. He told him everything: numbers, names, places. Whatever he could remember of the phone conversation he'd just heard.

The man's face had no discernible expression as he looked at Eli. "I saw you skulking about the office. What were you looking for?"

Eli took a deep breath. He and Chelsea had never told an adult about their collection of letterheads, much less what they did with it. But he told this man the truth.

The man's eyes bore into Eli's. "You know that what you're doing is illegal, don't you?"

Eli looked hard back at him. "Yes sir, I do. But we only write letters to people who are hurting others or ignoring their responsibilities. We've written a number of letters to fathers who don't pay the child support they owe."

The man lifted one eyebrow, studied Eli for a moment, then turned to a passing secretary. "Get this young man's name and send him a complete packet of all stationery from all Montgomery-Taggert enterprises. Get them from Maine and Colorado and Washington State." He looked back at Eli. "And call the foreign offices too. London, Cairo, all of them."

"Yes sir, Mr. Taggert," the secretary said, looking in wonder at Eli. All the employees were terrified of Frank Taggert, yet this child had done something to merit his special consideration.

When Eli got over his momentary shock, he managed to say, "Thank you."

Frank put out his hand to the boy. "My name is

Franklin Taggert. Come see me when you graduate from a university and I'll give you a job."

Shaking his hand, Eli managed to say hoarsely, "What should I study?"

"With your mind, you're going to study everything," Frank said as he got off the desk and turned away, then disappeared through a doorway.

For a moment, Eli just stared, but in that moment, with those few words, he felt that his future had been decided. He knew where he was going and how he was going to get there. And for the first time in his life, Eli had a hero.

4

AND THEN WHAT?" CHELSEA ASKED.

"He sent the copies of letterhead—you've seen them—I wrote to thank him and he wrote back. And we became friends."

Part of Chelsea wanted to scream that he had betrayed her by not telling her of this. *Two years!* He had kept this from her for two years. But she'd learned that it was no good berating Eli. He kept secrets if he wanted to and seemed to think nothing of it.

"So you want your mother to marry this man. Why did you just come up with this idea now?" She meant her words to be rather spiteful, to get him back for hiding something so interesting from her, but she knew the answer as soon as she asked. Until now Eli had wanted his beloved mother to himself. Her eyes widened. If Eli was willing to turn his mother over to the care of this man he must . . .

"Do you really and truly like him?"

"He is like a father to me," Eli said softly.

"Have you told him about me?"

The way Eli said "Of course" mollified her temper somewhat. "Okay, so how do we get them together? Where is this cabin of his?" She didn't have to ask how they would get his mother up there. All they had to do was write her a letter on Montgomery-Taggert stationery and offer her a nursing job.

"I don't know," Eli answered, "but I'm sure we can find out."

Three weeks later, Chelsea was ready to give up. "Eli," she said in exasperation, "you have to give up. We can't find him."

Eli just set his mouth tighter, but his head was propped in his hands in despair. Three weeks they had spent sending faxes and writing letters to people, hinting that they needed to know where Frank Taggert was. Either people didn't know or they weren't telling.

"I don't know what else we can do," Chelsea said. "It's getting closer to Christmas by the day and it's getting colder in the mountains. He'll leave soon, and she won't get to meet him."

The first week she'd asked him why he didn't just introduce his mother to Mr. Taggert, and Eli had looked at her as though she were crazy. "They will be polite to each other because of me, but what can they have in common unless they meet on equal ground? Have you learned nothing from my mother's books?"

But now they'd tried everything and still couldn't get his mother together with Mr. Taggert. "There is one thing we haven't tried yet," Chelsea said.

Eli didn't take his head out of his hands. "There is nothing. I've thought of everything."

"We haven't tried the truth."

Eli turned his head and looked at her. "What truth?"

"My parents were nearly dying for my sister to get married. My mother said my sister was losing her chances because she was getting old. She was nearly thirty. So if this Mr. Taggert is forty, maybe his family is dying to get him married too."

Eli gave her a completely puzzled look.

"Let's make an appointment with one of his brothers and tell him we have a wife for Mr. Taggert and see if he will help us."

When Eli didn't respond, Chelsea frowned. "It's worth a try, isn't it? Come on, stop moping and tell me the name of one of his brothers here in Denver."

"Michael," Eli said. "Michael Taggert."

"Okay, let's make an appointment with him and talk to him."

After a moment's hesitation, Eli turned to his keyboard. "Yes, let's try."

5

MICHAEL TAGGERT LOOKED UP FROM HIS DESK TO SEE HIS secretary, Kathy, at the door wearing a mischievous grin.

"Remember the letter you received from Mr. Elijah J. Harcourt requesting a meeting today?"

Frowning, Mike gave a curt nod. He was to meet his wife for lunch in thirty minutes, and from the look on Kathy's face there might be some complications that would hold him up. "Yes?"

"He brought his secretary with him," Kathy said, breaking into a wide smile.

Mike couldn't see why a man and his secretary would cause such merriment, but then Kathy stepped aside and Mike saw two kids, both about twelve years old, enter the room behind her. The boy was tall, thin, with huge glasses and eyes so intense he reminded Mike of a hawk. The girl had the easy confidence of what promised to be beauty and, unless he missed his guess, money.

I don't have time for this, Mike thought, and he wondered who'd put these kids up to this visit. Silently, he motioned them to take a seat.

"You're busy and so are we, so I'll get right to the point," Eli said.

Mike had to repress a smile. The boy's manner was surprisingly adult, and he reminded him of someone but Mike couldn't think who.

"I want my mother to marry your brother."

"Ah, I see," Mike said, leaning back in his chair. "And which one of my brothers would that be?"

"The oldest one, Frank."

Mike nearly fell out of his chair. "Frank?" he gasped. His eldest brother was a terror, as precise as a measuring device, and about as warm as Maine in February. "Frank? You want your *mother* to marry Frank?" He leaned forward. "Tell me, kid, you got it in for your mother or what?"

At that Eli came out of his seat, his face red. "Mr. Taggert is a *very* nice man, and you can't say anything against him *or* my mother!"

The girl put her hand on Eli's arm and he instantly sat down, but he turned his head away and wouldn't look at Mike.

"Perhaps I might explain," the girl said, and she introduced herself.

Mike was impressed with the girl as she succinctly told their story, of Eli's offer to go to Princeton but his refusal to leave his mother alone. As she spoke, Mike kept looking at Eli, trying to piece everything together. So the kid wanted a billionaire to take care of his mother. Ambitious brat, wasn't he?

But Mike began to have a change of heart when Eli said, "Don't tell him that. He doesn't *like* his brother."

"Tell me what?" Mike encouraged. "And I love my brother. It's just that he's sometimes hard to take. Are you sure you have the right Frank Taggert?"

At that Eli whipped an envelope from the inside of his suit jacket. Right away Mike recognized it as Frank's private stationery, something he reserved for the family only. It was a way the family had of distinguishing private from business mail. His family frequently joked that Frank never used family stationery for anyone who did not bear the same last name as he did. There was even a rumor that on the rare times he'd sent a note to whichever female was waiting for him at the moment, he'd used business letterhead.

Yet Frank had written this boy a letter on his private stationery.

"May I see it?" Mike asked softly, extending his hand.

Eli started to return the letter to his pocket.

"Go on," Chelsea urged. "This is important." Eli reluctantly handed the letter to Mike.

Slowly, Mike took the single sheet of paper from the envelope and read it. It was handwritten, not typed. To Mike's knowledge, Frank had not handwritten anything since he'd left his university.

My dear Eli,

I was so glad to receive your last letter. Your new theories on artificial intelligence sound magnificent. Yes, I'll have someone check what's already been done.

One of my brother's wives had a baby, a little girl, with cheeks as red as roses. I set up a trust fund for her but told no one.

I'm glad you liked your birthday present, and I'll wear the cuff links you sent me next time I see the president.

How are Chelsea and your mother? Let me know if your dad ever again refuses to pay child support. I know a few legal people and I also know a few thugs. Any man who isn't grateful to have a son like you deserves to be taught a lesson.

My love and friendship to you,
Frank

Mike had to read the letter three times, and even though he was sure it was from Frank, he couldn't believe it. Frank's only comment when one of his siblings produced yet another child was "Don't any of you ever stop?" Yet here he was saying his brother's new baby had cheeks like roses—which she did.

Mike carefully refolded the letter and inserted it back into the envelope. Eli nearly snatched it from his hands.

"Eli wants his mother to meet Mr. Frank Taggert in a place where they will be equal," Chelsea said. "She is a nurse, and we thought she could go to this cabin in the mountains where Mr. Taggert is staying, but we can't find it."

Mike was having difficulty figuring out what she was talking about. He looked at his watch. "I'm to meet my wife for lunch in ten minutes—would you two like to join me?"

Forty-five minutes later, with the help of his wife, Samantha, Mike finally understood the whole story. And more important, he'd figured out who Eli reminded him of. Eli was like Frank: cool exterior, intense eyes, brilliant brain, obsessive personality.

As Mike listened, he was somewhat hurt and annoyed that his elder brother had chosen a stranger's child to love, but at least Frank's love for Eli proved he *could* love.

"I think it's wonderfully romantic," Samantha said.

"I think the poor woman's going to meet Frank and be horrified," Mike muttered, but he shut up when Samantha kicked him under the table.

"So how do we arrange this?" Samantha asked. "And what size dress does your mother wear?"

"Twelve petite," Chelsea said. "She's short and f—" She didn't have to turn to feel Eli's glare. He wasn't saying much, as he was extremely hostile toward Mike. "She's, ah, round," Chelsea finished.

"I understand," Samantha said, getting a little notebook from her handbag.

"What difference does her dress size make?" Mike asked.

Chelsea and Samantha looked at him as though he were stupid. "She can't very well arrive at the cabin wearing jeans and a sweatshirt, now can she? Chelsea, shall we go buy some cashmere?"

"Cashmere?!" Eli and Mike said in unison, and it made a bond between them: men versus women.

Samantha ignored her husband's outburst. "Mike, you write a letter to Mrs. Harcourt saying—"

"Stowe," Eli said. "My father's new wife wanted my mother to resume her maiden name, so she did."

At that Samantha gave Mike a hard look, and he knew that all sense of proportion was lost. From now on, anything Eli and Chelsea wanted, they'd get.

6

*R*ANDY GOT OFF THE HORSE GRATEFULLY AND WENT INTO the cabin. Things had happened so quickly in the last few days that she'd had no time to think about them. Yesterday afternoon a man had come to the hospital and asked if she'd please accept a private, live-in nursing job for his client, starting the next morning and lasting for two weeks. At first she started to say no, that she couldn't ask the hospital to let her off, but it seemed that her absence had already been cleared with the chief of staff—a man Randy had never seen, much less met.

She then told the man she couldn't go because she had a son to take care of and she couldn't leave him. As though the whole thing were timed, Randy was called to the phone to be asked—begged, actually—by Eli to be allowed to go with Chelsea's family on an extremely educational yacht trip. Maybe she should have protested that he'd miss too much school, but she knew that Eli could make up any work within a blink of an eye, and he so wanted to go that she couldn't say no.

When she put down the phone, the man was still standing there, waiting for her answer about accepting the job.

"Two weeks only," she said, "then I have to be back."

Only after she agreed was she told that her new patient was staying in a remote cabin high in the Rockies and the only way to get there was by helicopter or horse. Since the idea of being lowered on a rope from a helicopter didn't appeal to her, she said she'd take the horse.

Early the next morning, she hugged and kissed Eli as though she were going to be away from him for a year or more, then got into a car that drove her thirty miles into the mountains, where an old man named Sandy was waiting to take her to the cabin. He had two saddled horses and three mules loaded with goods.

They rode all day and Randy knew she'd be sore from the horse, but the air was heavenly, thin and crisp as they went higher and higher. It was the end of autumn, and she could almost smell the snow that would soon blanket the mountains.

When they reached the cabin, a beautiful structure of logs and stone, she thought they must be in the most isolated place on earth. There were no wires to the cabin, no roads, no sign that it had touch with the outside world.

"Remote, isn't it?"

Sandy looked up from the mule he was unloading. "Frank made sure the place has all the comforts of home. Underground electricity and its own sewage system."

"What's he like?" she asked. Because of the narrow trail, they hadn't been able to talk much on the long ride up. All she knew of her patient was that he'd broken his right arm, was in a cast, and that it was difficult for him to perform everyday tasks.

Sandy took a while to answer. "Frank's not like anybody else. He's his own man. Set in his ways, sort of."

"I'm used to old and weird," she said with a smile. "Does he live here all the time?"

Sandy chuckled. "There's twelve feet of snow up here in the winter. Frank lives wherever he wants to. He just came here to . . . well, maybe to lick his wounds. Frank don't talk much. Why don't you go inside and sit down? I'll get this lot unloaded."

With a smile of gratitude, Randy did as he bid. Without so much as a glance at the interior of the cabin, she went inside, sat down, and fell asleep immediately. When she awoke with a start, about an hour later, she found that Sandy and the animals were gone. Only a huge pile of boxes and sacks on the floor showed that he had been there.

At first she was a bit disconcerted to find herself alone there, but she shrugged and began to look about her.

The cabin looked as though it had been designed by a computer, or at least a human who had no feelings.

It was perfectly functional, an open-plan L-shape, one end with a huge stone fireplace, a couch, and two chairs. It could have been charming, but the three perfectly matched pieces were covered with heavy, serviceable, dark gray fabric that looked as though it had been chosen solely for durability. There were no rugs on the floor, no pictures on the walls, and only one table with a plain gray ceramic lamp on it. The kitchen was in the corner of the L, and it had also been designed for service: cabinets built for use alone, not decorative in any way. At the end of the kitchen were two beds, precisely covered in hard-wearing brown canvas. Through a door was a bathroom with shower, white ceramic toilet, and washbasin. Everything utterly basic. Everything clean and tidy. And no sign of human habitation.

Randy panicked for a moment when she thought that perhaps her patient had packed up and left, that maybe she was here alone with no way down the mountain except for a two-day walk. But then she noticed a set of doors beside one of the beds, one on each side, perfectly symmetrical. Behind one, arranged in military precision, were some pieces of men's clothing: heavy canvas trousers, boots without a bit of mud on them.

"My, my, we are neat, aren't we?" she murmured, smiling, then frowned at the twin bed so near his. No more than three feet separated the beds. She did hope this old man wasn't the type to make childish passes at her. She'd had enough of those in school. "Just give me a little kiss, honey," toothless men had said to her as their aged hands reached for her body.

Laughing at the silliness of her fantasy, Randy went to the kitchen and looked inside. Six pots and pans. Perfectly arranged, spotlessly clean. The drawers contained a matched set of stainless steel cooking utensils that looked as though they'd never been used. "Not much of a cook, are you, Mr. Taggert?" she mumbled as she kept exploring. Other cabinets and drawers were filled with full jars of spices and herbs, their seals unbroken.

"What in the world does this man eat?" she wondered aloud. When she came to the last cabinet, she found the answer. Hidden inside was a microwave, and behind the tall door in the corner was a freezer. It had about a dozen TV dinners in it, and after a moment's consternation, Randy laughed. It looked as though she'd been hired to cook for the missing Mr. Taggert as much as anything else.

"Poor man. He must be starving," she said, and she cheered up at the thought. The beds so close together had worried her, but the empty freezer was reassuring. "So, Miranda, my girl, you weren't brought here for a sex orgy but to cook for some lonely old man with a broken arm. Poor dear, I wonder where he is now."

She didn't waste much time speculating but set to work hauling in supplies. She had no idea what Sandy had brought on those two mules but she soon found out. Packed in dry ice, in insulated containers, were nearly a whole side of prime beef and a couple of dozen chickens. There was lots of fishing gear, bags of flour, packets of yeast, lots of canned goods, and a couple of cookbooks. With every item she unpacked, she felt more sure of what her true purpose here was, and thinking of someone else who needed her made her begin to forget how easily Eli had said he didn't need her for the next two weeks. He very much wanted to travel with Chelsea and her parents to the south of France, then on to Greece aboard some Italian prince's yacht.

With a sigh, Randy put a frozen chicken in the microwave to thaw. She would *not* let herself think how Eli was growing up and needed her less every day. "My baby has grown up," she said with a sigh as she removed the chicken and began to prepare a stuffing of bread cubes, sage, and onion.

"Don't start feeling sorry for yourself," she said. "You're not dead yet. You could meet a man, fall madly in love, and have three more kids." Even as she said it, she laughed. She wasn't a heroine in a romance novel. She wasn't drop-dead gorgeous with a figure that made men's hands itch with lust. The trouble was that she was an ordinary woman. She was pretty in a dimpled sort of way—an old-fashioned prettiness, not the gaunt-cheeked style that was all the rage now. And she was—well, face it, about thirty pounds overweight. Sometimes she consoled herself that if she'd lived in the seventeenth or eighteenth centuries men would have used her as a model for a painting of Venus, the goddess of love. But that didn't help today, when the most popular models weighed little more than ninety pounds.

As Randy settled down to prepare a meal for her absent patient, she tried to forget the loneliness of her life, to forget that her precious son would soon be leaving her to go to school and she would be left with no one.

Two hours later she had a lovely fire going in the big stone fireplace, a stuffed chicken roasting in the never-before-used oven, and some vegetables simmering. She'd filled a bowl full of wildflowers from the side of the cabin and put a dry pine cone on a windowsill. Her unpacked duffel bags were by the bed the man didn't appear to use; her sweater was draped across the back of the chair, and she'd put an interesting rock on one end of the stone mantel. The place was beginning to look like home.

When the cabin door was flung open and the man burst in, Randy almost dropped the tea kettle. He was *not* old. There was some gray at the temples of his black hair and lines running down the sides of his tight-lipped mouth, but the virility of him was intact. He was a *very* good-looking man.

"Who are you and what are you doing here?" he demanded.

She swallowed. Something about him was intimidating. She could see that he was a man who was used to giving orders and being obeyed. "I'm your nurse," she said brightly, nodding toward his arm, which was in a cast nearly to his shoulder. It must have been a bad break for such a cast, and he must have great difficulty doing even the smallest tasks.

Smiling, she walked around the counter, refusing to be intimidated by his face. "Miranda Stowe," she said, laughing nervously. "But you already know that, don't you? Sandy said you had the medical reports with you, so maybe if I saw them I'd know more about your condition." When he didn't say a word, she frowned a bit. "Come and sit down, supper's almost ready and—here, let me help you off with those boots."

He was still staring at her, speechless, so she gently tugged on his uninjured arm and got him to sit on a chair by the dining table. Kneeling before him, she started to unlace his boots while thinking that sharing a cabin was going to be a lonely experience if he never spoke.

When he started to laugh, she looked up at him, smiling, wanting to share whatever was amusing him.

"This is the best one yet," he said.

"What is?" she asked, thinking he was remembering a joke.

"You are." Still smiling, he cocked one eyebrow at her. "I must say you don't *look* the part of—what was it you called yourself? A nurse?"

Randy lost her smile. "I *am* a nurse."

"Sure you are, honey. And I'm a newborn babe."

40

Randy quit unlacing his boots and stood up, looking down at him. "Exactly what do you think I am?" she asked quietly.

"With those"—he nodded toward her ample bosom—"you could be only one thing."

Randy was a softhearted woman. Wounded butterflies made her weep, but this tall, good-looking man, nodding toward her breasts in that way, was more than she could take. She was strong from years of making beds and turning patients, so she slapped him hard on his shoulders and pushed. He went flying backward in the chair, reaching for the table to keep from falling, but his right arm, encased in plaster, was on the side of the table so he went sprawling to the floor.

Randy knew she should have waited to see if he was all right, but instead, she turned on her heel and started for the cabin door.

"Why you—" he said, then grabbed her ankle before she could take another step.

"Let go of me!" she said, kicking out at him, but he pulled and she pulled in the opposite way until she fell, landing hard on him and hitting his injured arm. She knew the impact must have hurt him, but he didn't so much as show his pain by a flicker of an eye.

With one roll, he pinned her body to the floor. "Who are you and how much do you want?"

Puzzled, she looked up at him. He was about forty years old, give or take a few years, and his body felt as though it was in perfect condition. "For this job I receive about four hundred dollars a week," she said, her eyes narrowed at him. "For *nursing.*"

"Nursing," he said in a derogatory way. "Is *that* what you call it?"

She pushed against him angrily but couldn't budge him.

"So how did you find me? Simpson? No, he doesn't know anything. Who sent you? The Japanese?"

Randy stopped struggling. "The Japanese?" Was the man's injury *only* in his arm?

"Yeah, they weren't too happy when I won on that last deal. But microchips are a dead item. I'm going for—"

"Mr. Taggert!" she said, interrupting him, as he seemed to have forgotten he was lying full length on top of her. "I have *no* idea what you're talking about. Would you please let me up?"

He looked down at her, and the color of his dark eyes seemed to change. "You're not like the women I usually have, but I guess you'll do." He gave her a lascivious, one-sided smirk. "The softness of you might make for a nice change from bony models and starlets."

At that remark, made as though he were in a butcher's shop poking chickens for tenderness, she brought her knee up sharply between his legs, causing him to roll off of her in pain. "Now! Mr. Taggert," she said, standing up and bending over him. "Just what is this all about?"

He was holding himself with one hand, and as he rolled to one side his injured shoulder hit the table leg. Randy's heart *almost* went out to him.

"I'm a . . ."

"A what?" she demanded.

"A billionaire."

"You're a—" She didn't know whether to laugh or kick him in the ribs. "You're a . . ." She couldn't conceive of the amount of money he was talking about. "You're rich, so you think I came up here to . . . to get your money?"

He was beginning to recover as he pulled himself up to sit heavily on a chair. "Why else would you be here?"

"Because you asked for a nurse," she shot at him. "You *hired* me."

"I've heard *that* story before."

She stood looking down at him, glaring, more angry than she'd ever before been. "Mr. Taggert, you may have a great deal of money, but when it comes to being a human being you are penniless."

She didn't think about what she was doing, that she was in the Rocky Mountains and had no idea how to get back to civilization. She just grabbed her sweater from the back of the couch and walked out of the cabin.

She followed a bit of a trail, raging in her anger, but she didn't look where she was going.

Not even Leslie had ever made her as angry as this man just had. Leslie lied to her and manipulated her at every chance, but he'd never accused her of being indecent.

She went uphill and down, unaware of the setting sun. One minute it seemed to be sunny and warm, and the next moment it was pitch dark and freezing. Putting on her sweater didn't help at all.

"Are you ready to return?"

She nearly jumped out of her skin when the man spoke. Whirling about, she could barely see him standing hidden amid the trees.

"I don't think I will return to the cabin," she said. "I think I'll go back to Denver."

"Yes, of course. But Denver is that way." He pointed in the direction opposite to the way she was walking.

She wanted to keep some of her pride. "I wanted to . . . to get my suitcase." She looked from one side to the other for a moment, then charged straight ahead.

"Ahem," he said, then pointed over his right shoulder.

"All right, Mr. Taggert," she said, "you've won. I haven't a clue where I am or where I'm going."

He took two steps around her and parted some bushes with his hand, and there, about a hundred yards in front of her, was the cabin. Light glowed softly and warmly from the windows. She could almost feel the warmth of the fire.

But she turned away, toward the path leading to Denver, and started walking.

"And where do you think you're going?"

"Home," she said, just as she stumbled over a tree root in the trail. But she caught herself and didn't fall. With her back straight, she kept walking.

He was beside her in moments. "You'll freeze to death out here. If a bear doesn't get you first, that is."

She kept walking.

"I am ordering you to—"

She stopped and glared up at him. "You have no right to order me to do anything. No right at all. Now, would you please leave me alone? I want to go *home*." To her horror, her voice sounded full of tears. She'd never been able to sustain anger very long. No matter what Leslie did to her, she couldn't stay angry for more than a short time.

Straightening her shoulders, she again started walking.

"Could I hire you as my cook-housekeeper?" he said from behind her.

"You couldn't pay me enough to work for you," she answered.

"Really?" he asked, and he was right behind her. "If you're poor—"

"I am *not* poor. I just have very little money. You, Mr. Taggert, are *very* poor. You think everyone has a price tag."

"They do, and so do you. So do I, for that matter."

44

"You must be very lonely if you think that."

"I've never had enough time alone to consider what loneliness is. Now, what can I offer you to make you cook for me?"

"Is *that* what you want? My pot roast?" At this thought there came a little spring to her step. Maybe she *did* have something to offer. And maybe she wouldn't have to spend the night running down a mountain chased by a bear.

"Five hundred dollars a week," he said.

"Ha!"

"A thousand?"

"Ha. Ha. Ha," she said with great sarcasm.

"What then? What do you want most in the world?"

"The finest education the world has to offer for my son."

"Cambridge," he said automatically.

"Anywhere, just so it's the best."

"You want me to give your son four years at Cambridge University for one week's cooking? You're talking thousands."

"Not four years. Freshman to Ph.D."

At that Frank laughed. "You, lady, are crazy," he said, turning away from her.

She stopped walking and turned to look at his back. "I saw wild strawberries up here. I make French crepes so light you can read through them. And I brought fresh cream to be whipped and drenched in strawberries, then rolled in a crepe. I make a rabbit stew that takes all day long to cook. It's flavored with wild sage. I saw some ducks on a pond near here, and you would not believe what I can do with a duck and tea leaves."

Frank had stopped walking.

"But then you're not interested, are you, Mr. Billionaire? You could toast your money on a stick over the fire and it would no doubt taste just dandy."

He turned back to her. "Potatoes?"

"Tiny ones buried under the fire coals all day so they're soft and mushy, then drizzled with butter and parsley."

He took a step toward her. When he spoke, his voice was low. "I saw bags of flour."

"I make biscuits flavored with honey for breakfast and bread touched with dill weed for dinner."

He took another step toward her. "Ph.D?"

"Yes," she said firmly, thinking of Eli in that venerable school and how much he'd love it. "Ph.D."

"All right," he said, as though it were the most difficult thing he'd ever said.

"I want it in writing."

"Yes, of course. Now, shall we return to the cabin?"

"Certainly." With her head held high, she started to walk past him, but he pulled aside a curtain of bushes. "Might I suggest that this way would be quicker?"

Once again, not a hundred yards away, was the cabin.

As she walked past him, her nose in the air, he said, "Thank heaven your cooking is better than your sense of direction."

"Thank heaven *you* have money enough to *buy* what you want."

She didn't see the way he frowned at her as she continued walking. If the truth were told, Frank Taggert wasn't used to being around women who didn't fawn over him. Between his good looks and his money, he found he was quite irresistible to women.

But then he usually didn't have anything to do with women like this one. Most of the women he escorted were the long-legged perfect sort, the kind who wanted sparkling baubles and nothing else from him. He'd found that if he grew bored with one of them, if he gave her enough jewelry, she soon dried her tears.

But this one had had a chance at a great deal of

money and she'd asked for something for someone other than herself.

As he watched her walk back to the cabin, he wondered about her husband. What was he like to allow his wife to go alone into the mountains to take care of another man?

Once he was inside the cabin, he sat down hungrily at the table and waited while she reheated the meal she'd cooked, then served it to him. Then she made herself a plate and took it into the living area, put it on the heavy pine coffee table, sat on the floor, and began to eat as she watched the fire.

Annoyed, and with great difficulty because he was one-handed, he picked up his plate and flatware and moved it to the coffee table. He'd no more than sat down when she lifted her plate and took it to the table.

"Why did you do that?" he asked, greatly annoyed.

"The hired help doesn't eat with Mr. Billionaire."

"Would you stop calling me that? My name is Frank."

"I know that, Mr. Taggert. And what is *my* name?"

For the life of him, he couldn't remember. He knew she'd told him, but, considering the circumstances under which she'd told him, it was understandable that he didn't remember. "I do not remember," he said.

"Mrs. Stowe," she answered, "and I was hired as your *nurse.*"

She was behind him, seated at the dining table, and when he twisted around, causing pain to shoot through his shoulder, he saw that she had placed herself with her back to him. Frowning in annoyance, he again moved his place setting so he could face the back of her.

"Would you mind telling me who hired you?" he asked. The chicken was indeed delicious, and he thought a week away from canned food was going to

47

be worth sending some kid to school—well, almost, anyway. Maybe he could write off the expense as charity. This could be advantageous taxwise if he—

"Your brother."

Frank nearly choked. "My *brother* hired you? Which one?"

She still refused to look at him, but he could see her shoulders stiffen. They weren't fashionably square shoulders, but rather round and soft.

"It seems to me, Mr. Taggert," she said, "that a rather unpleasant joke has been played on you. I would hate to think that you had more than one brother who would have such animosity toward you as to perpetuate such a joke."

Frank well knew that each of his brothers would delight in playing any possible trick on him, but he didn't tell her that.

After her remark about his brothers he didn't speak again but tried to give his attention to the food. She wasn't going to put his French chef out of business, but there was a comforting, homey flavor to the food, and the proportions were man-sized. In his house in Denver, his apartment in New York, and his flat in London, each of his chefs served calorie-controlled meals to ensure Frank's trim physique.

She finished eating, then silently cleared her place, then his, while Frank, feeling deliciously full of food, leaned back against the coffee table and watched the fire. He'd never been a man who smoked, but when she served him a tiny cup of excellent coffee, he almost wished he had a cigar. "And a plump woman to share my bed," as his father used to say.

Relaxed, drowsy, he watched the woman as she moved about the room, straightening things, and then—

"What are you doing?" he demanded as she drove a nail into the wall between the two beds.

"Making separate rooms," she answered. "Or as close as I can come to it."

"I assure you, Mrs. Stowe, that that is not necessary. I have no intention of imposing myself on you."

"You have made yourself clear as to your thoughts of my . . . of my feminine appeal, shall we say?" She drove another nail, then tied a heavy cotton rope from one nail to another.

Aghast, Frank watched her drape spare blankets over the rope, effectively creating a solid boundary between the two beds. With effort, he raised himself from the floor. "You don't have to do this."

"I'm not doing it for you. I'm doing it for me. You see, Mr. Billionaire, I don't like you. I don't like you at all, and I'm not sure anyone else in the world does either. Now, if you'll excuse me, I'm going to take a bath."

7

RANDY STEPPED INTO A TUB OF WATER SO HOT IT MADE her toes hurt, but she needed the warmth, needed the heat to thaw her heart. Being near Frank Taggert was like standing near an iceberg. She wondered if he had ever had any human warmth in him, whether he'd ever loved anyone. She'd like to think he was like one of her romantic heroes: wounded by some callous woman, and now his cold exterior protected a soft, loving heart.

She almost laughed aloud at the idea. All evening he'd been watching her speculatively; she could feel his eyes even through her back. He seemed to be thinking about where she belonged in the world. Rather like an accountant would try to figure out where an expense should be placed.

"At least Leslie had passion," she whispered, lying back in the tub. "He lied with passion, committed adultery with passion, made money with passion." But when she looked into this Frank Taggert's eyes she saw no passion for anything. *He* would never lie to a woman about where he'd spent the night because he'd never care enough whether or not she was hurt by his infidelity.

All in all, she thought, it was better not to think at all about Mr. Billionaire. With longing, she thought of Eli and Chelsea, and wondered what they were doing tonight. Would Eli eat properly if she weren't there? Would he ever turn off his computer and go to bed if she weren't there to make him? Would—

She had to stop thinking about her son or she'd cry from missing him. It suddenly dawned on her that whoever had played a joke on Frank Taggert had also inadvertently played a joke on her. Obviously, someone thought that sending a plain, ordinary woman such as she to spend a week with a handsome, sophisticated, rich man like Mr. Taggert was the most hilarious of jokes.

Getting out of the tub, she dried off, then opened her night case to get her flannel gown and old bathrobe. At the sight of the garments within, she felt a momentary panic. These were not her clothes. When she saw the Christian Dior label on the beautiful pink nightgown she almost swooned. Pulling it out, she saw that it was a peignoir set, made of the finest Egyptian cotton, the bodice covered with tiny pink silk roses. The matching robe was diaphanous and nearly transparent. It didn't take a brain like Eli's to see that this was not something a woman who was merely a housekeeper should wear.

Wrapping a towel about herself to cover the beautiful gown and robe, she rushed out of the room, past the bed on which Frank Taggert sat, scurried behind the blanket partition, and began to rummage in her unpacked suitcase for her own clothes.

"Is there a problem?" he asked from behind his side of the blanket.

"No, of course not. What could be the problem?" She went through her bags frantically, but nothing was familiar. If a 1930s-era movie star were going to spend a week in the Rockies, these were the clothes she would have worn. But Randy had never worn clothes made of cashmere and silk and wool so soft you could use it as a powder puff.

Randy knew herself normally to be a soft-tempered person. She had to be to put up with Leslie's shenanigans. But this was enough.

Throwing aside the blanket room divider, three cashmere sweaters in her hand, she pushed them toward Frank Taggert. "I want to know exactly what is going on. Why am I here? Whose clothes are these?"

Sitting on the side of the bed, Frank was unlacing his boots. "Tell me, Mrs. Stowe, are you married?"

"Divorced."

"Yes, then I understand. I come from a large family that is constantly reproducing itself. I believe they have decided I should do the same."

"You—" In shock, Randy sat down on the edge of her bed. "They have . . . You mean, they want us to . . ."

"Yes. At least that's my guess."

"Your . . . guess?" She swallowed. "At this point,

I'd decided your family had sent me here because the idea of a woman like me with a man like you would be very entertaining to them."

He didn't pretend to misunderstand her. While she'd been speaking, he'd been working at untying his boot laces with one hand. So far he'd not managed to even loosen the knot.

Not even thinking about what she was doing and certainly not what she was wearing, Randy knelt before him and untied his laces, then removed his boots. "I don't mean to pry," she said, pulling off his socks and giving each foot in turn a quick massage, just as she did for Eli and used to do for Leslie, "but why would they choose someone like *me?* With your looks and money, you could have anyone."

"They would like you. You look like a poster illustration for fertility."

She had her hands on his shirt collar as she began to unbutton it. "A what?"

"A symbol of fertility. A paean to motherhood. I'm willing to bet that this son of yours is your whole life."

"Is there something wrong with that?" she asked defensively.

"Nothing whatever if that's what you choose to do."

She was pulling his shirt off. "What better life is there for a woman than to dedicate herself to her children?"

"You have more than one child?"

"No," she said sadly, then saw his eyes as he seemed to say, I knew it. "So your brother sent me up here in the hope that I would . . . would what, Mr. Taggert?"

"From the look of your gown, I'd say Mike did this, since his wife, Samantha, is the personification of a romantic heroine."

"A romantic heroine?"

"Yes. All she wants out of life is to take care of Mike and their ever-growing brood of children."

"You have not been reading what I have. Today, the heroines of romance novels want a career and control of their own lives and—"

"A husband and babies."

"Perhaps. Stand up," she ordered and began unfastening his trousers. She'd undressed many patients, and she was doing so now without thinking too much about the action.

"How many heroes have you read about who said 'I want to go to bed with you but I don't want to get married and I never want children?'" he asked her.

"I see. I guess normality *is* a requirement in a hero."

"And to not want marriage and children is abnormal?"

She smiled coldly at him. "I've never met anyone like you, but I assume you are not married, never want to be, never will be, have no children, and if you did, you would only visit them by court order."

She had him stripped to his undershorts and T-shirt and he was certainly in fine physical form, but she felt nothing for him, anymore than she'd have felt for a statue.

"What makes you think I have no wife? I could have married many times." He sounded more curious than anything else.

"I'm sure you could have, but the only way a woman would marry you is for your money."

"I beg your pardon."

Maybe it was rotten of Randy, but she felt a little thrill at having upset his calm. "You are *not* what a woman dreams of."

"And what does a woman dream of, Mrs. Stowe?"

Smiling dreamily, she pulled back the blankets on his bed. "She dreams of a man who is all hers, a man whose whole world revolves around her. He might go out and solve world problems and be seen by everyone as magnificently strong, but when he's at home, he puts his head on her lap and tells her he couldn't have accomplished anything without her. And, most important, she knows he's telling the truth. He needs her."

"I see. A strong man who is weak."

She sighed. "You don't see at all. Tell me, do you analyze everything? Take everything apart? Do you put everything into an account book?" She gave him a hard look. "What are you making your billions *for?*"

As she held back the covers, he stepped into bed. "I have many nieces and nephews, and I can assure you that my will is in order. If I should die tomorrow—"

"If you should die tomorrow, who will miss you?" she asked. "Who will cry at your funeral?"

Suddenly she was very tired, so she turned away from him, pushed the blanket partition aside, and went to her own bed. She had never felt so lonely in her life. Perhaps it was Eli's talk of going away to college, or maybe it was this man's talk of her looking as though she should have many children. When Eli left home she would be alone, and she didn't think some man was going to come riding up to her front door on a black stallion and—

She didn't think anymore but fell asleep.

She didn't know how long she'd been asleep before a man's voice woke her.

"Mrs. Stowe."

Startled, she looked up at Frank Taggert, wearing just his underwear, his arm in a heavy cast, standing there looking at her, his dark eyes serious. Only the fading firelight lit the room.

I'll bet this is how he looks when he makes one of his million-dollar deals, she thought, and she wondered what he could possibly want of her.

"Yes?"

"I have a proposition to put to you. A merger of sorts."

Pushing herself upright, she leaned against the back of the bed, unaware that the gown showed every curve of her upper body. But Frank didn't seem to notice, as his eyes were intense.

"Ordinarily," he began, "the things you said to me would have no effect on me. My relatives have said everything you have said and more. However, it seems that when a man reaches forty and—"

"A billion," she interrupted.

"Yes, well, there does come a time when a man begins to consider his own mortality."

"Midas," she said, referring to the story of the man who turned everything, including his beloved child, into gold.

"Just so." He hesitated, glancing down at her bosom for the briefest second. "Contrary to what people think, I *am* human."

At that Randy pulled the covers up to her neck. She was *not* the one-night-stand type of person. In fact, she wouldn't even read romances in which the heroine had a multitude of lovers. "Mr. Taggert—" she began.

But he put up his hand to stop her. "You do not have to concern yourself about me. I am not a rapist."

She let the covers go. She could not see herself as a woman who drove men to uncontrollable acts of lust. "What is it you are trying to say to me?"

"I am trying to ask if you'd consider marrying me."

8

MARRIAGE?" SHE ASKED, HER EYES WIDE. "TO ME?"

"Yes," he said seriously. "I can see that you're shocked. Most men of my wealth marry tall, statuesque blondes who train horses and wear couture. They do not marry short, unmanicured, plump—"

"I understand. So why aren't *you* married to one of these horsey women who spends her life trying on clothes?"

Her cattiness was acknowledged with a tiny bit of a smile. "I expect to be the man in my own household, and besides, it's as you say—they care only for my money."

"Mr. Taggert," she said, looking at him hard, "I'm not interested in your money *or* you."

He gave an ugly little smile. "Surely there are things you want that money can buy. I would imagine you live in a house with a mortgage and I doubt that your car is less than three years old. Does your ex-husband pay you any support? You're the type who would never take a person to court for nonpayment of debt. How long has it been since you've had any new clothes? There must be many things you want for your son."

That he'd described her life perfectly made her very angry. "Being poor is not a social disease. And since slavery was outlawed some years ago, I do not have to sell myself to get a new car."

"How about a white Mercedes with red leather interior?"

She almost smiled at that. "Really, Mr. Taggert, this is ridiculous. What's the *real* reason you're asking me to marry you? If you still are, that is."

"Yes. Once I make up my mind I never change it."

"I can believe that about you."

Again he gave her a bit of a smile, making her wonder if any of the tall blondes in his life had ever contradicted him. "My life is too perfect," he said. "It is beginning to bore me. It is perfectly in order. My servants are the best money can buy. There is never so much as a hairbrush out of place in any of my houses. For some time now I've thought it might be pleasant to have a wife, someone familiar to me. I like familiarity. The contents of each of my houses are exactly the same."

Blinking, she thought about this for a moment. "Same towels, same—"

"Same clothes in exactly the same arrangement, so that no matter where I am I know what is where."

"Oh my. That *is* boring."

"But efficient. Very efficient."

"Where would *I* fit into this efficiency?"

"As I said before, I have considered a wife, but the ordinary sort for a man of my wealth would be as perfect as my life already is."

"Why not marry several of them?" she asked helpfully. "One for each house. For variety you could change hair color, since I'm sure it wouldn't be natural anyway."

This time he did smile at her. Not an all-out

teeth-showing smile but a smile nonetheless. "If wives were not so much trouble I would have done so years ago."

She couldn't suppress her own smile. "I think I am beginning to understand. You want me because I'll add chaos to your life."

"And children."

"Children?" she asked, blinking.

"Yes. My family is prolific. Twins, actually. I find I want children." He looked away. "Since I was a child I have been very aware of my responsibilities. As the oldest of many siblings, I knew I would be the one to run the family business."

"The crown prince, so to speak."

"Yes, exactly. Fulfilling my obligations has always been uppermost in my mind. But about two years ago I met a boy."

When he said nothing more, Randy encouraged him. "A boy?"

"Yes, he was at my brother's offices, skulking around from desk to desk, pretending to play but actually listening and looking at everything. I spoke to him, and it was like looking into my own eyes."

"And he made you want to have children of your own, did he? Sort of a wish to clone yourself, is that right?"

"More or less. But the boy changed my life. He made me see things in my own life. We have corresponded since that time. We have become . . ." He smiled. "We have become friends."

She was glad that he had at least one friend in the world, but he couldn't marry a woman and hope she would give him a son just like the boy he'd met. "Mr. Taggert, there is no way *I* could produce the kind of son you want. *My* son is a sweet, loving boy. He is the personification of kindness and generosity. He would die if he knew I told anyone this, but I still tuck him in every night and read aloud to him before he goes to sleep." She was *not* going to mention that she usually read advanced physics textbooks to him because that would have ruined the story.

Turning his head to one side, Frank said, "I would rather like my children to be a bit softer than I am."

It was beginning to dawn on Randy that this man was serious. He was coldly, and with great detachment, asking her to marry him. And produce children. For a moment, looking at him, she couldn't quite picture him in the throes of passion. Would he perhaps delegate the task to his vice president in charge of production? "Charles, my wife needs servicing."

"You are amused," he said.

"It was just something I was thinking about." She looked at him with compassion. "Mr. Taggert, I understand your dilemma and I would like to help. If it were only me I might consider marrying you, but others would be involved. Not others. Children. My son would be exposed to you, and if you and I did have—well, if we did have children, I'd want them to have a real father, and I can't imagine you reading fairy stories to a two-year-old."

For a moment he didn't move; he just sat on the edge of the bed. "Then you are saying *no* to me?"

"Yes. I mean *no*. I mean, yes, I'm saying *no*. I can't marry you."

For a few seconds he stared at her, then he stood up and silently went to his own bed.

As Randy sat there, she wondered if she'd dreamed the whole thing. She'd just turned down marriage to a very wealthy man. Was she terminally stupid? Had she lost all sense? Eli could have the best the world had to offer. And she could—

She sighed. She would be *married* to a man who wanted her so she could add chaos to his life. How amusing. Plump little Miranda walking about in circles in her attempt to leave the cabin. Daffy Miranda being stupid enough to fall for an elaborate joke played on a cold, heartless billionaire.

It was a long while before she fell asleep.

The next morning Randy was silently making strawberry waffles while Frank sat before the fire staring at the pages of a book on tax reform. He hadn't turned a page in fifteen minutes, so she knew he was thinking rather than reading.

No doubt I'm the first company he's tried to buy and failed, she thought. What will he do to win me over? Send candy to Eli? A man like Frank Taggert would never take the time to find out that Eli would like to have a new CD-ROM for his computer more than all the candy in the world.

As she watched him, she felt sorry for him. The feeling of isolation he projected surrounded him like an impenetrable glass bubble.

It was while she was making a sugar syrup for the strawberries and thinking how she'd like to see a little fat around the middle of Mr. Trim Taggert, that she heard the helicopter. Frank was on his feet before she was, and to her consternation, he flung open a door hidden in the log wall and withdrew a rifle. "Stay here," he ordered.

"Okay," she whispered, feeling a bit like a heroine in a Western movie.

Seconds later he was back; he put the rifle away, then went to the table. "Is breakfast ready?"

She heard him only by reading his lips, because the sound of the 'copter overhead was deafening. Maybe his curiosity wasn't piqued, but hers was. Quickly, she flung waffles and strawberries onto a plate, sloshed coffee into a cup by his hand, then was out the door.

The helicopter was directly overhead. A couple of duffel bags had already been lowered, and now a tall blond man wearing a dark suit, his briefcase in hand, was descending, his foot hooked into a loop of rope. Randy couldn't help smiling at this version of Wall Street calmly coming down through the tall trees, the mountains in the distance. As he got closer she started laughing, because she could see that while holding onto the briefcase and the rope, he was also trying to eat an apple.

He landed in front of her. He was quite good-looking: very blond, very white skin, blue eyes so bright they dazzled. Holding the apple in his mouth, he motioned the helicopter to go away, and Randy saw that the briefcase was handcuffed to his wrist.

"Hungry?" she asked, as he stood there smiling.

"Starved." He was looking at her in a way that made her feel quite good about herself, and she smiled back warmly.

"You here with Frank?" he asked.

"Not *with* him. I was hired as his nurse, but that turned out to be a joke. I'm just here until— Wait a minute. Maybe I could have returned on the helicopter." With her hand shielding her eyes, she watched the helicopter disappear over the horizon. She looked back at the man.

"Mike. Or was it Kane?"

"I beg your pardon?"

"If a joke was played on Frank, it would have to be either Mike or Kane." When she didn't respond, he smiled, then held out his hand. "I'm Julian Wales. Frank's assistant. Or actually, glorified go-fer. And you are?"

She let her hand slide into his large warm one. "Miranda Stowe. Randy. I'm the nurse, but mostly I'm the cook-housekeeper."

He gave her a look that made her blush. "Perhaps I'll find myself becoming ill and have need of your services."

Perhaps she should have told him she wasn't *that* kind of woman, but, truth was, his admiration made her feel good. Yesterday a marriage proposal and today a very nice flirtation.

She withdrew her hand from his—after two tugs. "Mr. Taggert is in there, and I have strawberry waffles for breakfast."

"Gorgeous, and you can cook too. You wouldn't like to marry me, would you?"

Feeling like an eighteen-year-old, she laughed. "Mr. Taggert's already asked." She was horrified that she'd said that. "I mean . . ." She had no idea what to say to cover herself, so she went back to the cabin while Julian, his eyes wide in disbelief, stared after her before following.

Frank didn't bother with greeting him, and Julian had learned not to expect any. Frank showed his gratitude for Julian's years of dedication with a large six-figure salary and many perks.

Without a word spoken between them, Julian removed the briefcase from his wrist, unlocked it, and turned it over to Frank.

"Unfortunately," Julian said, "I arranged for the copter to pick me up two days from now. I planned to stay and do a little fishing. But I didn't know you had a guest. If it's not suitable for me to stay, I can walk out."

Buried in the papers, Frank didn't look up. "Take the couch."

"Yes sir," Julian said, then winked at Randy as she started to put a plate of hot waffles in front of him.

"Have you had breakfast, Randy?" Julian asked. When she shook her head no, he said, "How'd you like to join me outside? A morning like this is too beautiful to waste inside."

Smiling, plate in hand, she followed him out the

door, and when she turned back, she saw Frank staring after them. "I'll just close this so we won't disturb you," she said, rather pleased that he was frowning.

Julian had put his plate on a stump and was removing his suit jacket and tie. "Hallelujah!" he said, unbuttoning the top of his shirt. "Two days of freedom." Sitting on the stump, the plate on his lap, he looked up at her. "There's room for two."

Maybe she shouldn't have, but she sat beside him, parts of her body warm against his.

"Did Frank actually ask you to marry him?"

She nearly choked. "I shouldn't have told you that. I have a complete inability to keep my mouth shut. It wasn't a *real* marriage proposal, just sort of a business arrangement."

Julian cocked one blond eyebrow. "I see what he gets, but I can't see what you get. Except the money, of course."

"Children. He seems to think he and I could, well, produce children."

At that Julian laughed. "Ol' Frank said that? Do you know him very well?"

"Not at all. Except he makes me cold even being near him."

"Ah yes. Many people feel that way, but don't underestimate him: He's as hot as anybody."

"For making money, maybe, but he doesn't exactly get my vote for lover of the year."

"You've been to bed with him then?"

"No!" she said with her mouth full. "Certainly not! I like there to be hearts and flowers and—Good heavens! I don't know what I'm talking about. Mr. Wales, I am not some romantic heroine to be fought over by two gorgeous men. I am rapidly approaching middle age, I'm overweight, I'm a single mother, and

63

I'm sure that suit you have on cost more than I earned last year. If any other woman on earth were here I'm sure neither of you men would notice me."

He was smiling at her. "Randy, you know what you are? You're *real*. I knew it the moment I saw you. Usually the women near Frank are so perfectly beautiful they look as though they were manufactured. And you know that if he lost his money they'd never look at him again."

"Really, Mr. Wales, I—"

"Julian."

"Julian. I am a perfectly ordinary woman."

"Oh?" He took a big bite of waffle. "Ever been married?" When she nodded, he said, "When you divorced your husband, did you take him to the cleaners?" He didn't wait for her answer. "No, of course not. Looking at you, I'd say you 'understood' his need to run off with some empty-headed Barbie doll."

She looked down at her waffle, now growing cold. "You seem to be rather good at figuring out people."

"That's what Frank pays me for: to look into people's eyes and keep the deadbeats and con artists away from him."

At that moment, the cabin door opened and Frank appeared holding a fishing rod. "Actually, Julian, I've been meaning to do some fishing myself. Shall we go?"

Randy stood up. "I think Julian should change his clothes, and I'll need to pack you both a lunch. You can't leave without something to eat."

"You will come with me and cook our fish. Julian, sort out what is needed and follow us," Frank said, then he started walking down the trail away from them.

Randy wasn't about to obey what sounded like an order so she turned back to the cabin, but before she was through the door she knew she wasn't going to cut off her nose to spite her face and miss what sounded like a lovely day fishing. Julian stood where he was, staring open-mouthed after his boss. He'd worked with Frank Taggert for over ten years, and although during that time Frank had never once told Julian—or anyone else for that matter—about himself, Julian had been able to piece together a great deal. He knew his boss very, very well.

"He's in love with her," Julian whispered. "By all that's holy, he's madly in love with her. Only deep love could make Frank leave corporate merger papers and go fishing." For a moment Julian stared at his boss's back as it disappeared down the trail. Of course Frank knew so little about women that he'd mess this up—as he'd destroyed every relationship he'd ever had with a woman. Julian had to admit that Frank had never thought any woman was worth missing a meeting for or even postponing a call. And it was Julian who had the task of telling the women to get out. He'd had dishes thrown at him and heard curse words in four languages as he removed women from wherever Frank was at the moment.

It was this part of his job that was beginning to make him discontented, beginning to make him wonder if there was more to life than just doing whatever Frank Taggert wanted done.

Julian turned to look into the cabin, where he could see Randy putting food and utensils into a backpack. But now Frank had asked a woman to *marry* him. And knowing Frank, he'd presented the proposal as he would present something to a corporate board. No passion, no fireworks, no declarations of undying love. Just "I have a proposition to make you: Will you marry me?"

Julian grabbed his bags from the ground and changed into jeans and a sweater where he was, thinking all the while. No one knew Frank as he did.

Too many people, like Randy, thought he had no heart, but Julian knew he did. Frank just kept rigid control over himself, but his loyalty was unbreakable. When Julian had smashed a Ferrari, it was Frank who'd flown in doctors from London and New York. When Mrs. Silen's husband had nearly taken her children away from her, it was Frank who'd silently and secretly stepped in and reversed the decision of the court. Frank often helped people; he just hated people knowing he did it. He liked his image of ruthless negotiator.

In his dealings with his employees and his relatives, he was always fair. Perhaps never warm, but fair. It was just with women that Frank seemed to be incapable of human feelings.

But two years ago something had changed Frank, and Julian didn't know what it was. And now this broken arm seemed to have changed him even more. He'd been playing handball as fiercely as he worked at business and he'd slammed against the wall, pinning his right arm under him. It was a nasty break, and Frank had been two hours in the operating room. Julian had been there, along with most of the Taggerts, the next day. They were a loud, happy family, exactly the opposite of Frank with his cool reticence. They teased him mercilessly about his being human just like other people.

As far as Julian knew Frank never so much as flinched from pain, but something seemed to have happened inside him because days later Frank cancelled some very important meetings and announced that he was retreating to his cabin high in the Rockies and he was not to be disturbed. Julian didn't dare ask Frank why, but his brother did, and Frank had said he'd wanted to heal and to think.

9

RANDY KNEW SHE'D NEVER HAD SUCH A WONDERFUL DAY in her life as she did fishing with Julian. Everything he did or said seemed to be funny. He flirted with her, teased her, put his arms around her to show her how to bait a hook. He made her giggle and squeal like a girl again.

But throughout the day, Randy stole glances at Frank, who was standing alone, quietly and unobtrusively reeling in one fish after another. With his arm in a sling he must have been in pain as well as experiencing enormous difficulty, but he never showed any emotion.

"Interested in him?" Julian asked after she'd glanced at him for the thousandth time. Frank stood apart from them, almost as though he were unaware of them.

"Certainly not. I'm not a woman who wants a man for his money."

"Ah, I see. And what *do* you want from a man?" he asked with a false leer.

"Great love. Deep love. I want to be *sure* of him. I want undying loyalty." She smiled. "And a big house set among acres of fruit trees."

"Don't be fooled by Frank. He's the most loyal person I know. Once he takes you under his wing, he protects you."

She looked at Frank again. He was tall and broad-shouldered, and those dark eyes of his were intriguing, but . . . But he was so very odd, one day asking her to marry him, then the next not so much as looking at her.

"A penny," Julian said.

"I was just thinking that he doesn't know I'm alive."

At that Julian laughed. "Frank *hates* fishing. The only reason he's here is to see that I don't touch you."

She blinked at him in disbelief. "But he's catching fish. He must like it."

"Frank is good at everything in life except women."

Randy stared at the rapidly moving mountain stream for a moment, then picked up the thermos of hot coffee and went to offer Frank some. "Having fun?" she asked as he drank.

"Marvelous. And you?"

She could see a muscle working in his temple. "The best. Julian is a truly wonderful man. Funny, happy, laughing. A woman could easily fall in love with him." Randy was watching him so hard she didn't blink. In spite of his coolness, she found herself drawn to him, as what woman isn't drawn to a man who asks her to marry him? Say something, she thought. Maybe even kiss me.

But Frank said nothing as he handed the empty cup back to her and looked at the water. "Julian is a fine man. Very good worker."

"He must have a thousand women friends with his looks and talents and charm." Randy knew she was pushing him, but she wanted some reaction out of him—if he felt anything at all for her.

"I have no idea of his private life." Turning, he looked away from her.

Randy moved closer to him. "And what about you? Lots of women in your life? Do you give out lots of marriage proposals?"

"Only one," he said softly.

Randy could have kicked herself. She was being rude and careless of another person's feelings. She put her hand on his arm. "Mr. Taggert, I—"

She broke off because he turned glittering eyes on her. "You what? Wanted to laugh at me?"

"Why no, I didn't."

"Then what? What is it you want from me?"

"I . . . I don't know."

Abruptly, he turned away from her. "Let me know when you figure it out."

Confused, embarrassed, Randy turned from him and headed down the trail toward the cabin. When Julian tried to stop her she told him she wanted to be alone, so he went back to stand beside Frank, who was pretending to be fishing, but he hadn't remembered to bait his hook.

Julian knew his boss—knew when he was angry, as he was now—so he didn't say anything as he set about building a fire. Maybe some of Randy's food, sizzling hot, would warm Frank up.

It was an hour later that the two of them were sitting around a campfire. In all the years Julian had worked for Frank their relationship had been based on business, but now Julian could feel things changing. Things were changing inside himself and inside Frank.

He took a breath. "Have you told Randy you're in love with her?"

Frank didn't say anything.

"You might be able to fool the rest of the world but

you can't fool me. When did you know you were in love with her?"

Frank took a while to answer. "When I saw that she didn't like me."

"Frank, a *lot* of people don't like you."

He gave a one-sided smile. "But they don't like what I stand for or they don't like that I have money and they don't. It's not *me* they dislike."

Julian tossed a pine cone into the fire. "Don't kid yourself, Frank, it's you people don't like. Freezers are warm compared to you."

Frank smiled. "Women don't think so."

"True. Women do make fools of themselves over you when they first meet you. I've always wondered why."

"Money and power equal sex, and I have an excellent technique in bed."

"Go to school to learn it, did you?"

"Of course. How else does one . . ." He stopped, not wanting to say more.

"Randy is different, isn't she?" Julian waited for Frank to answer. Would he answer such a personal question?

"She is everything that I am not. She is warm where I am cold. She loves easily while I find it difficult to love. If Miranda were to love a man she'd love him unconditionally, with or without money. She'd love him always. I need that . . . that security. Women change toward a man. They love him today, but if he forgets her birthday she withdraws her love."

"Randy wouldn't like a man to forget her birthday."

"If I forgot it on the true date I'd take her to Paris a week later and she'd forgive me."

"Yes, she would. But Frank, how would someone like Randy fit in with your life? If I remember

70

correctly, your last love interest had a doctorate in Chinese poetry and spoke four languages."

"She was a bore," Frank said with contempt. "Julian, something's happened to me in the last two years. I've had a change of heart. I know, lots of people think I don't have a heart but I do, or maybe I've just discovered that I have one. Many people have asked me what I'm earning money for, but I've never had an answer. I think it's been the challenge and the goal. You above all people know I haven't wanted to buy anything. I've never wanted a yacht that costs a hundred grand a day to run. I've just wanted to—"

"To win," Julian cut in, bitterness in his voice. Maybe it was jealousy, but sometimes he was sick of seeing Frank win.

"Yes, maybe so. Maybe that was it."

"What happened two years ago?"

"I met a kid. A boy named Eli, and it was like looking into my own eyes. He was so ambitious, so hungry for achievement." Frank chuckled. "He steals office letterhead and writes letters to people on it."

"Illegal."

"Yes, but he does it to help people. I looked at him and thought, I wish I'd had a son just like him. It was the first time in my life I ever wanted a child of my own."

"The Taggert bug," Julian said. "Bitten at last."

Frank smiled. "Ah yes, my prolific family. They seem to be born with the urge to reproduce themselves."

"But not you. At least not until now. Not until you met Randy."

"Yes. Randy. A real woman. I don't want the mother of my children to be anything but a mother to them."

"And a wife to you, I take it."

71

"Yes. I . . ." He took a deep breath. "When this happened"—he nodded toward his arm—"I had some time to think and to remember. If I'd broken my neck not one of those billion dollars I own would have missed me. Not one of them would have cried in misery at my death. And worst, when I got out of the hospital, there wasn't a woman, a soft, sweet woman whose lap I could put my head on and cry."

At that Julian raised one eyebrow in disbelief.

"I *could* have cried that day. Do you want to know what the Chinese poetry lady wanted to know? She asked me, Was breaking my arm and being in that much pain exciting? Was my pain sexually exciting?"

"Tell her," Julian said fiercely. "You *must* tell Randy what you feel."

"Tell her what? That I have been looking for a woman like her, someone so soft and sweet and loving that she'd get on a horse and ride into the middle of nowhere to nurse a man who's hurt? As far as I can tell she asked no questions. She was told she was needed, so she went. For a ridiculously low sum of money."

"Then tell her you need her."

"She'd never believe that. What do I need her for? I have a cook. Sex is easy to come by, so what else do I need?"

"Frank, no wonder women come to hate you."

"Women hate me when I refuse to marry them and make them part of my community property."

"You *don't* have a heart." They were silent a moment, then Julian spoke again: "If you don't tell her, you'll lose her."

"Julian, you know how I make money? I make money because I don't care. I don't care whether I win or lose. If there is a deal I really truly want, then I step out of it. You can't be ruthless if you care."

"Then you're saying that you want Randy too much to make an attempt to win her?"

Frank looked at Julian, and for just a moment he saw past the coolness that was always there, and what he saw made him draw in his breath. "If I tried and lost, I couldn't go on living."

"You love her that much?" Julian whispered.

The mask returned. "I don't know why I . . . care for her, but I do."

"Therefore you will do nothing to try to win her."

"That's right," Frank said, staring into the fire.

Julian was quiet for a moment. "In spite of what you say, some women have genuinely cared for you. You, not your money. But without exception you have dropped them. Maybe when you started to care for them you got out. I don't know the reason, but I do know that I've always been the one to have to listen to them, calm them down and endure their rages after you've dropped them. Randy isn't one of the women on the circuit, some woman who's had affairs with a hundred men. She's just an ordinary, middle-class woman, and she likes you. She may say she doesn't, but I see it in her eyes. Today I did my best to get her attention onto me, but she was only interested in you. A nudge from you and she could love you."

He turned to look at Frank. "I don't want to have to try to explain you to Randy. I don't want to try to dry her tears with a box full of emeralds." He paused. "In fact, I don't want to do any of it anymore."

Julian gave Frank plenty of time to reply, but when he was silent, Julian stood up after a moment. "Frank, I've worked with you for ten years. I've admired and respected you and at times envied you. But at this moment I feel nothing but pity for you." As he turned away, he halted. "You know, I'm tired of not caring. I'm tired of buying and selling and never having a life of my own. This weekend I had a date with a wonderful woman, then you called and told me to bring you the papers. You didn't ask; you just told. So

I left a message on her machine and came here. I doubt now that she'll ever speak to me again."

"I pay you well enough to do what I want."

"Yes, you do. You pay me so well that I don't need to work anymore. I could retire on what I've never had time to spend." Julian smiled. "And I think I'm going to do that. You will have my resignation on Monday."

For a moment Julian hesitated, waiting for Frank to call him back, but Frank said nothing, so Julian kept walking.

10

RANDY WAS STANDING BY THE SINK, FURIOUSLY GRATING carrots, when Julian returned. One look at his face and she knew not to say anything. To her surprise, he went to a blank log wall to the right of the fireplace, pushed a knot, and a door opened. Anger in every step, he disappeared inside the room.

Curious, carrot in hand, she went to peer inside the room. In contrast to the rugged, almost primitive cabin, the room was ultra modern, its walls painted a hard gloss white. Along three walls were tables, each covered with machines: computer, fax, television with the stock market playing on it, telephone, as well as machines she couldn't even identify.

Julian grabbed a microphone and in minutes he'd

radioed for a helicopter to pick him up. "Wait a minute," he said, then turned to Randy. "Do you want to return with me?"

There was a slight emphasis on the word "me." For a moment Randy's heart seemed to stop beating. Even with anger in Julian's eyes, there was also interest. He hadn't just been flirting with her. This gorgeous man was actually interested in *her*.

But something held her back. "No, I'll stay," she heard herself whisper and couldn't understand what she was doing.

"Sure?" he asked, and she nodded.

Minutes later Julian was jamming clothes into his duffel bag. "He's not worth it. You know that, don't you? I should tell you what he said. He said—"

"No!" she said sharply. "I don't want to know what went on between you two. That's your business. He's injured and he needs me."

"No he doesn't. He doesn't need anyone. I thought he did, but—" He stopped. "It's not him, it's me. *I* need someone. Actually, what I need is a life of my own." At the cabin door, he paused. "Don't let him break your heart. A lot of women have tried to melt him but they couldn't. He . . ." Julian paused. "Look, this isn't about you. It's between Frank and me. He's in love with you."

"What? I know he—"

"He loves you. Which is why he'll never try to win you. Don't expect anything personal from him. Money, yes, but nothing else."

"But—" she began, a thousand questions swirling about in her head.

"I've said too much already. Take care," he said, then he was gone.

When she was alone in the cabin, Randy plopped down onto one of Frank's boring gray couches. "My goodness," she said aloud. "A lifetime of no adventure, and now everything is rolled into a couple of days."

An hour later Frank appeared at the door, and for a split second he looked startled to see her. "Why didn't you leave with Julian?"

Truthfully, she didn't know. "You owe me a Cambridge education," she said.

"Ah, yes, of course."

That wasn't the real reason she'd stayed, because who could charge thousands of dollars for a week's work; but then she didn't know the real reason she'd stayed. She stiffened her spine. "Do you want me to leave?"

"I want—" he began, then cut himself off. "I want you to do whatever suits you."

It was not what she'd hoped for. Had Julian been telling the truth when he said Frank Taggert loved her? Since she didn't love him, what did it matter? But there was something in his eyes. Something deep down in them that made her feel that he was lonely, maybe as lonely as she was when she thought of Eli going away to college and leaving her.

She wasn't sure what to say. "Have you eaten?" was all she could think of, and she was rewarded by the tiniest smile from him.

"You are going to make me fat."

It was the first personal remark he'd made—other than asking her to marry him, that is. "You could use a little fat on you. I have some I could lend you."

His eyes twinkled. "I'd like for you to keep all of yours. It's in the right places."

Blushing, she turned away to serve dinner, and when she turned back, he had his nose buried in the papers Julian had brought and he didn't say another word to her throughout the meal.

The light teasing between them seemed to have turned off something inside Frank, for he didn't speak again the rest of the evening. When he went outside to gather logs for the fire, Randy could see the nearly impossible task was hurting him, but when she offered to help he told her he needed no one.

Cursing herself for not having left with Julian, Randy took a bath, put on the seductive nightgown—the only one she had—and went to bed. "Wasted on him," she muttered, and she went to sleep immediately.

Thunder loud enough to split her eardrums woke her up. As she sat up, lightning lit the cabin, and she gave an involuntary scream. She was not used to such storms.

Frank was beside her instantly, just sitting there, not touching her, but at the next flash of lightning she flung herself into his arms.

She had forgotten how good a man could feel. His big, hard, strong body enveloped her, and before she could breathe he pulled her head back and kissed her.

It was not a kiss from a cold man, and in that moment she believed what Julian had told her: that Frank did love her.

He was kissing her neck. The cabin was lit with lightning and the roar of the thunder seemed to echo within her.

"Yes," she whispered as his hand went to her breast. "Yes, please make love to me."

Gently, he took her face in his hands, his eyes searching hers. "I have no protection with me."

For a moment she held her breath. She felt sure he didn't have a communicable disease. "I would like the consequences," she said, meaning how very much she'd like to have another child, to feel life growing within her, as she had with Eli.

"Yes," was all he said, then he was on her.

He was as hot in bed as he was cold out of it. She'd never seen him leering at her as men did, but he seemed to have noticed all of her body and to want her very much. Her gown was off her body in seconds and his hands were everywhere, caressing her, touching her, as though he wanted to memorize her.

Never had Randy enjoyed sex as much as she did with him. He seemed to know what she liked, seemed to find places she didn't know she wanted to be touched.

Somewhere during the night she thought she heard him say "I love you," but she wasn't sure. For herself, she was too taken away with touching Frank to think any words. Leslie had always been a man who rushed sex, always in a hurry to get onto the next task. Or the next woman, Randy had often thought.

But Frank seemed to have all the time in the world. When he entered her, she was nearly screaming with desire. She held him inside her for a moment, loving how he filled her. When he began the velvet strokes in and out, she thought she might die with the pleasure.

Watching her, he seemed to know when she was ready to peak, then he thrust into her until she thought she might faint. "Baby," she whispered, not sure if it was a word she was calling him or a wish she wanted fulfilled.

Later, shaking in the aftermath, she snuggled in his arms and went to sleep, feeling safe and secure and at home.

But when she awoke the next day, she could tell by the light that it was afternoon and Frank was gone. She thought that perhaps he was outside, but he wasn't. There was no note, nothing. Only his unmade bed showed he'd been there at all.

An hour after she woke, Sandy appeared with the horses and said he'd been instructed to take her home.

11

*T*HE OUTSIDE OFFICES WERE DECORATED FOR CHRIST-
mas, and in the distance was the sound of laughter
and glasses clinking at the annual party at the
Montgomery-Taggert offices. But inside Frank Taggert's office there were no decorations, no lights, just
Frank sitting alone, staring unseeing at the papers on
his desk.

In the last two months he had lost weight and there
were dark circles under his eyes. And in the last
months he seemed to have lost his edge in the business
world; he seemed to have lost his hunger.

"Hello," said a tentative voice from his doorway,
and he looked up to see Eli. He hadn't seen him in two
years, not since that first meeting; they had conducted
their friendship entirely by letters, Frank sending all
his letters to Eli care of a P.O. box in Denver.

"Eli," was all that Frank could say, and the first hint
of a smile in a long time appeared on his face. "Come
here," he said, holding out his hands.

Closing the door behind him, shutting out the
sounds of the other people, Eli walked around the
desk to stand in front of his friend.

"You look as bad as I feel," Frank said. "I guess
you're too big to hold on a man's lap, aren't you?"

Eli would have died before he admitted it, but part of his anger at his father was defiance, telling himself that he didn't need a father. "No, I'm not too big," Eli said, and he found himself swooped into Frank's arms and pulled onto his lap like a child. Eli was quite tall but Frank was taller, and Eli found how much he had missed the solid male touch of a father.

Much to his horror, Eli found himself crying. Frank didn't say a word, just held him until Eli stopped, then offered him a clean white handkerchief.

"You want to tell me about it?"

"My mother is going to have a baby."

"I didn't know she got married."

"She didn't."

"Oh. That's a bit of a problem. You need money?"

"Always. But she needs a man to take care of her. I'll never be able to go away if she doesn't have someone to take care of her."

"Any money you need—"

"No!" Eli said sharply. "I don't want you to give me money."

"Okay." Frank pushed Eli's head back down to his shoulder. "What can I do?"

For a while Eli didn't speak. "Why haven't you written me for two months?"

"I don't think you'd understand."

"That's what adults always say. They think children are too stupid to understand anything. My mother thinks I won't understand about the baby and why she's not married to the baby's father."

"You're right. We adults do tend to put children into situations then mistakenly think they can't understand them. Maybe we're trying to protect you."

Frank took a deep breath. "I did a very stupid thing: I fell in love. No, don't look at me like that. I guess it was all right to fall in love, but I was afraid and I ran away."

"Why did you run away? Why were you afraid? I love my mother, but I'd never run away from her."

"It's not the same as loving your mother. With this woman I had a choice." He pulled Eli closer. "I don't know how to explain it. In all my life I've never needed anyone. Maybe it was because I had so many people around me. I grew up in a huge family and I had a lot of responsibility from the first. Maybe I just wanted to be different and separate. Maybe I didn't want to be like them. Can you understand that?"

"Yes. I am different from other kids."

"You and I are misfits, aren't we?"

"What about the woman?" Eli urged. "Why did you leave her?"

"I loved her. I don't know how to explain it, since it makes no sense. I just looked at her and loved her from the first. I thought she was something other than what she was, and that made me angry at first, but then I saw that she was a sweet, gentle woman." He smiled. "Well, not too gentle."

He paused. "You know what I liked best about her? She judged me on my own merits, not on my money or even on my looks. She just told me she didn't like me and didn't want to be near me. She even ran out the door of the cabin and tried to go back to Denver."

"She has no sense of direction."

Frank looked surprised. "That's true, but how did you know that?"

"My mother has none and Chelsea has none," Eli said, covering himself.

"Better not let any woman hear you make such a generalization. Anyway, I wanted her to stay and cook for me, so I offered her money, a great deal of money. But do you know what she asked for?"

"Something for someone else," Eli said.

"Exactly. That's just what she did. How did you guess?"

Ignoring the question, Eli said, "What did she ask for?"

"An education for her son at the finest school in the world, from freshman to Ph.D."

"Yes," Eli said softly. "She would." He spoke louder. "But what happened?"

"We, ah, we . . . Later we . . ."

"I've learned a lot about babies in the last two months," Eli said in a very grown-up voice. "What happened later?"

"I left her. Radioed for a 'copter to pick me up and for someone to come on horseback and get her."

Eli could feel his body stiffening. "You just went off and left her there. Did she . . . love you?"

"I don't know. She's the kind that if she goes to bed with a man, she—I mean, she takes things seriously and falls in love with any man she . . . spends time with."

"But you *loved* her?"

"Yes. I loved her a lot after that night, and it frightened me so much I left. I got on a plane and I haven't been off since. I think I wanted to run away. Or maybe I just wanted time to think."

"What did you think about?"

"Her. How I wanted to be with her. She has a way of seeing the truth of any situation. She told me she wasn't poor, she just didn't have any money."

"My mom says the same thing."

"Smart mother. Very smart if she had you."

"What are you going to do now? About this woman you love, I mean."

"Nothing. There's nothing I can do. I'm sure she's forgotten me by now."

Eli lifted his head to stare earnestly at Frank. "I don't think she has. What if she cries every night for you the way my mom does for the man whose baby she's going to have?"

Frank raised one eyebrow. "I don't think so. A woman scorned, that sort of thing. I found out a long time ago that if you leave women, they never forgive you. They might say they have, but they get you back in other ways."

"But what if she's not like that? What if she loves you too and she would understand if you explained to her that you were frightened and a coward?"

"You make me feel worse. Okay, so maybe I was a coward. I've been thinking that I should try to find her. If I checked the hospitals they'd know where she was. I asked my brother Mike, but he's not speaking to me." Frank swallowed. "And after what his wife said to me, I wish she weren't speaking to me either."

"What are you going to *do?*" Eli demanded. "What are you going to do when you find her?"

Frank grimaced. "I'd like to think that I'd fall on my knees and declare my undying love for her, but I can't actually imagine myself doing that. Anyway, I've already asked her to marry me, but she turned me down."

"She what! You asked her to *marry* you?"

"Yes." Frank leaned back to look at Eli. "Why are you so interested in this?"

"It's my mother and that man she is going to have a baby with. I wish he'd marry her."

"If he's a good man."

"He is. I know he is."

"It's not your father, is it?"

"No!" Eli almost shouted, then calmed himself. "No, of course not. It's just . . . ." He trailed off, not knowing what else to say.

"All right," Frank said, "let's change the subject. What do you want for Christmas? Computer equipment?"

"No," Eli answered. "I haven't done much work

lately. I may have to get a job after school to help with the baby."

"Like hell you will!" Frank said. "I'll give you a check that will cover all expenses for a couple of years. And I will not take more of your pride!"

Eli knew he should have said no, but he couldn't. "Will you do me a favor?"

"Anything. Want a trip somewhere for you and your mom?"

"I want something for my mom, yes." Eli took a deep breath. "Can you ride a horse?"

"Rather well, actually."

"Do you own a black one? A big black stallion?"

Frank smiled. "I think I can find such an animal. I didn't know you liked horses."

"It's not for me. My mother was paying the bills last week, and she said that we had to face the facts: no handsome man was going to ride up to the front door on a big black stallion and rescue us, so we'd have to make ends meet another way."

"And you want *me* to ride up on a black horse and present a check to your mother?"

"Cash would be better. She'd never cash a check; she has a very strong conscience."

Frank laughed. "A black stallion, eh? And I guess you want me to do it tomorrow on Christmas Day, no doubt."

"Are you busy with your family on that day?"

"Somehow I doubt they'll miss me." For a moment he sat still, holding Eli and thinking. "All right, I'll do it. Shall I wear a black silk shirt, black trousers, that sort of thing?"

"Yes, I think my mother would like that."

"Okay, tomorrow at ten A.M. Now that that's settled, what do you want for your birthday?"

"The password to tap into the Montgomery-Taggert data banks."

At that Frank laughed harder than he had in months. "Come on, let's get something to eat. And I'd have to adopt you before I let you tap into that, and somehow I don't think your mother would like to share you."

As Frank was escorting Eli out of the office, he said, "Would you like me to hire private detectives to find the man who did this to your mother? I could have his taxes audited."

"Maybe," Eli said. "I'll let you know the day after Christmas."

12

ELI," RANDY SAID, EXASPERATED, "WHY ARE YOU SO nervous?" Since early that morning, while Randy was up to her elbows in cranberry sauce and pumpkin pie, Eli had been going back and forth to look out the window every few minutes. "If you're searching for Santa Claus, I don't think he remembers where this house is."

She'd meant to make a joke, but it fell flat. She couldn't afford much in the way of gifts this year, and she was constantly worried about how she was going to support the two of them in the coming months. And then there would be three of them, and she didn't know—

She stopped herself from thinking of the bad things, such as about money and where and how. She also wouldn't allow herself to think of Frank Taggert, the rotten—

Calm down, she reminded herself. Anger was not good for the baby, nor for Eli either, for that matter.

"Is Chelsea coming over?" she asked.

"Not now. Later—" Eli broke off as his face suddenly lit up in a grin. In fact, his whole body seemed to light up. Then he gained control of himself, and, doing his best to appear calm, he went to sit on the sofa and picked up a magazine. Since the magazine was *Good Housekeeping,* Randy knew something was up.

"Eli, would you mind telling me what is going on? All morning you've been looking out that window and—" She stopped and listened. "Are those hoof-beats? Eli, what are you up to? What have you and Chelsea done now?"

Eli gave her his best innocent look and kept staring at the magazine.

"Eli!" Randy said. "I think that horse is coming onto the *porch!*"

When her son just sat where he was, his head down but looking as though he were about to burst into giggles, Randy smiled too, knowing that she was going to open the door to find pretty little Chelsea on her pony, hair streaming down her back, a Christmas basket in her hand. Randy decided to play along with the game.

Wiping her hands and putting on her best stern face, she went to the door, planning to look surprised and delighted.

She didn't have to fake the look of surprise. Shock would be more like it. She didn't see Chelsea's pony but an enormous black horse trying to fit itself onto her front porch. A man, dressed all in black, was on its back, trying to get the animal under control without tearing his head off on the low porch roof.

"You have any female horses around here?" the rider shouted above the clamor of the horse's iron-shod hooves on the wooden porch.

"Next door," she shouted back, thinking that she knew that voice. "Could I help you find your way?" she asked, stepping back from the prancing hooves.

After a few powerful tugs on the reins and some healthy curses muttered under his breath, the man got the horse under control, then leaned over to withdraw a fat envelope from his saddlebag.

"Mrs. Harcourt," he said, "I present to you—"

He didn't say any more as he looked at her. "Miranda," he whispered.

Randy could say nothing. One minute she was watching a man dressed in black trying to control a black stallion on her front porch, and the next she was inside the house, bolting the door.

Frank was off the horse in seconds, not bothering to tie the animal but leaving it where it was and going to the closed door. "Miranda! Please listen to me. I need to talk to you."

Randy stood with her back to the door and squinted at her son, who was bent over the magazine on the coffee table as though it were the most interesting thing he had ever seen. "Eli! I know you are somehow involved in this and I demand to know what's going on."

Outside, Frank wasn't sure what to do. He was confused as much as anything. He'd expected to meet Eli's mother, but instead here was Miranda, the woman he loved, the woman who had haunted him for the last two months.

Leaning back against the wall for a moment, he

suddenly put everything together. Eli had coordinated with his brother Mike to get Miranda up to the cabin, then he and Miranda had taken it from there. For a moment Frank felt like a fool for having been so thoroughly duped, but the next moment he was smiling. How much better did he want life than this? The child he loved was the son of the woman he loved, and Eli had said that his mother was going to have a baby—*his* baby.

"Miranda," he said through the glass-paned door, "I must talk to you."

"Over my dead body," she shouted back. "And get your horse off my porch!"

Randy looked at her son. "When I get through with you, young man, you are going to be very sorry." She too had just put together the cabin and this man with Eli and Chelsea's eternal snooping.

Eli tried to seem more closely bent over the magazine, but he was actually fascinated by what was going on around him, and strained to hear every word that was being said.

Maybe it was the clothes, maybe it was because it was Christmas, or maybe it was because Frank was sick of doing things the proper way, but he picked up a flower pot from the porch and threw it through the glass of the door, then reached inside and opened the lock.

"How dare you!" Randy said when he was inside. "I'll call the police."

He caught her before she reached the telephone. He was sure there were words he should say, but he couldn't think of them. He just remembered making love to her that night, the most satisfying lovemaking he'd ever experienced. Without thinking, he grabbed her in his arms and kissed her. When he stopped and she started to speak, he kissed her again.

When he stopped kissing her, Randy was leaning back in his arms, her full weight borne by him. "Now listen to me, Miranda, I may not know how to be a hero out of a book, but I know that I love you."

"But you left me," she whispered.

"Yes, I did. My feelings for you were too strong for me to handle. I'd heard about this falling-in-love but I didn't know it was so horrible or so strong. I thought that being in love was something nice."

"No," she whispered, and he kissed her again.

"Now," he said, "I want you to listen to me: I love you and I love Eli. I have for a long time. I even told you about him at the cabin."

"Eli?"

"Yes, Eli. And I love our child you're carrying, and I mean to be the best possible father to it. I may not be any good at being a father or a husband, but I'll do my best and that's all I can promise. And I—"

Suddenly all the bravado left him, and he clutched her to him. "Marry me, Miranda. Please, please marry me. I'm sorry I left you that day. Everything happened to me too suddenly. I thought I could forget you, that maybe it was the moonlight and the trees and your strawberry waffles."

"What was it?"

"I don't know. Just you. I just love you. Please marry me."

Before Randy could say a word, Eli jumped up and yelled, "Yes! Yes, she'll marry you. Yes, yes, yes."

"I can't—" she began, but Eli, behind her back, started kissing the back of his hand, and Frank was so fascinated with this that he almost didn't understand what the boy was trying to tell him to do.

Frank took Eli's suggestion and didn't let Randy say another word but kissed her again. "Think of the children," he said.

"But I'm not sure—"

He kissed her again. "I love you. Don't you love me some?"

Randy smiled. "Yes, I do. You don't deserve it, but I do." She leaned back away from him. "What about Julian? You weren't very nice to him."

"My first taste of jealousy. He was bored to death after six weeks without me, so I hired him back at half again his salary. Miranda, marry me, please."

At that moment a siren went off in the next block and scared the horse, which ran inside the house for safety. Ran into Frank, Randy, and Eli, who all tumbled into a startled heap on the floor.

"Stupid animal," Frank muttered as the horse nudged his pockets, looking for apples.

"Whose idea was the horse?" Randy asked.

"Mine," the two males said in unison.

And it was that unison that made Randy know what to do. From the beginning Frank had reminded her of someone, and now she knew who it was: Eli.

"Yes," she said, her arms going around his neck. "Yes, I'll marry you."

Eli put his arms around both of them. "I got what I wanted for Christmas and my birthday," he said. "And I'd rather go to Cambridge than Princeton." But his mother and Frank didn't hear him because they were kissing again.

Smiling, Eli untangled himself from the two adults and the horse and ran to his room to call Chelsea and tell her the news.

Robin and Marian Les Jeunes had struck again.

JUDE DEVERAUX is the author of thirty-one *New York Times* bestsellers, including *Always, Forever and Always, Forever . . ., The Mulberry Tree, The Summerhouse, Temptation,* and *A Knight in Shining Armor.* She began writing in 1976, and to date there are more than thirty-five million copies of her books in print. Ms. Deveraux lives in North Carolina with her son, Sam.

JUDITH MCNAUGHT

Miracles

1

THE ROAR OF MUSIC AND VOICES BEGAN TO RECEDE AS Julianna Skeffington fled down the terraced steps of a brightly lit country house in which 600 members of Polite Society were attending a masquerade ball. Ahead of her, the formal gardens were aglow with flaring torches and swarming with costumed guests and liveried servants. Beyond the gardens, a large hedge maze loomed in the shadows, offering far better places to hide, and it was there that Julianna headed.

Pressing the hooped skirts of her Marie Antoinctte costumc closer to her sides, she plunged into the crowd, wending her way as swiftly as possible past knights in armor, court jesters, highwaymen, and an assortment of kings, queens, and Shakespearean characters, as well as a profusion of domestic and jungle creatures.

She saw a path open through the crowd and headed for it, then had to step aside to avoid colliding with a large leafy "tree" with red silk apples dangling from its branches. The tree bowed politely to Julianna as it paraded past her, one of its branches curved around the waist of a lady decked out as a milkmaid complete with bucket.

She did not have to slow her pace again until she neared the center of the garden, where a group of musicians was stationed between a pair of Roman fountains, providing music for dancing couples. Excusing herself, she stepped around a tall man disguised as a black tomcat who was whispering in the pink ear of a petite gray mouse. He stopped long enough to cast an appreciative eye over the low bodice of Julianna's white ruffled gown, then he smiled boldly into her eyes and winked before returning his attention to the adorable little mouse with the absurdly long whiskers.

Staggered by the abandoned behavior she was witnessing tonight, particularly out here in the gardens, Julianna stole a quick glance over her shoulder and saw that her mother had emerged from the ballroom. She stood on the terraced steps, holding an unknown male by the arm, and slowly scanned the gardens. She was looking for Julianna. With the instincts of a bloodhound, her mother turned and looked straight in Julianna's direction.

That familiar sight was enough to make Julianna break into a near run, until she came to the last obstacle in her route to the maze: a large group of particularly boisterous men who were standing beneath a canopy of trees, laughing uproariously at a mock jester who was trying unsuccessfully to juggle apples. Rather than walk in front of their line of vision, thus putting herself in plain view of her mother, she decided it was wiser to go around behind them.

"If you please, sirs," she said, trying to sidle between the trees and a row of masculine backs. "I must pass." Instead of moving quickly out of her way, which common courtesy dictated they should, two of them glanced over their shoulders at her, then they turned fully around without giving her any extra space.

"Well, well, well, what have we here?" said one of them in a very young and very inebriated voice as he braced his hand on the tree near her shoulder. He shifted his gaze to a servant, who was handing him a glass brimming with some sort of liquor, then he took it and thrust it toward her. "Some 'freshment for you, ma'am?"

At the moment Julianna was more worried about escaping her mother's notice than being accosted by a drunken young lord who could barely stand up and whose companions would surely prevent him from behaving more abominably than he was now. She accepted the glass rather than make a scene, then she ducked under his arm, walked quickly past the others, and hurried toward her destination, the drink forgotten in her hand.

"Forget about her, Dickie," she heard his companion say. "Half the opera dancers and the demimonde are here tonight. You can have most any female who takes your eye. That one didn't want to play."

Julianna remembered hearing that some of the Ton's high sticklers disapproved of masquerades—particularly for gently bred young ladies—and after what she'd seen and heard tonight she certainly understood why. With their identities safely concealed behind costumes and masks, members of Polite Society behaved like . . . like common rabble!

2

*I*NSIDE THE MAZE, JULIANNA TOOK THE PATH TO THE right, darted around the first corner, which happened to turn right, then she pressed her back into the shrubbery's prickly branches. With her free hand, she tried to flatten the layers of white lace flounces that adorned the hem of her skirts and the low bodice of her gown, but they stood out like quivering beacons in the breezy night.

Her heart racing from emotion, not exertion, she stood perfectly still and listened, separated from the garden by a single tall hedge but out of sight of the entrance. She stared blindly at the glass in her hand and felt angry futility at her inability to prevent her mother from disgracing herself or ruining Julianna's life.

Trying to divert herself, Julianna lifted the glass to her nose and sniffed, then she shuddered a little at the strong aroma. It smelled like the stuff her papa drank. Not the Madeira he enjoyed from morning until supper, but the golden liquid he drank after supper— for medicinal purposes, to calm his nerves, he said.

Julianna's nerves were raw. A moment later she heard her mother's voice come from the opposite side of the leafy barrier, making her heart hammer with foreboding.

"Julianna, are you out here, dear?" her mother called.

"Lord Makepeace is with me, and he is most eager for an introduction . . ."

Julianna had the mortifying vision of a reluctant Lord Makepeace—whoever he was—being dragged mercilessly by the arm through every twist and turn, every corner and cranny, of the twisting maze and torchlit gardens by her determined mother. Unable to endure the awkwardness and embarrassment of one more introduction to some unfortunate, and undoubtedly *unwilling,* potential suitor whom her mother had commandeered, Julianna backed so far into the scratchy branches that they poked into the pale blond curls of the elaborate coiffure that had taken a maid hours to create.

Overhead, the moon obligingly glided behind a thick bank of clouds, plunging the maze into inky darkness, while her mother continued her shamelessly dishonest monologue—a few feet away on the other side of the hedge.

"Julianna is such a delightfully adventurous girl," Lady Skeffington exclaimed, sounding frustrated, not proud. "It is just like her to wander into the gardens to do a bit of exploring."

Julianna mentally translated her mother's falsehoods into reality: *Julianna is an annoying recluse who has to be dragged from her books and her scribbling. It is just like her to hide in the bushes at a time like this.*

"She was so very popular this Season, I cannot think how you haven't encountered her at some tonnish function or another. In fact, I actually had to insist she restrict her social engagements to no more

99

than ten each week so that she could have enough rest!"

Julianna hasn't received ten invitations to social events in the past year, let alone in a single week, but I need an excuse for why you haven't met her before. With a little luck, you'll believe that rapper.

Lord Makepeace wasn't that gullible. "Really?" he murmured, in the noncommittal voice of one who is struggling between courtesy, annoyance, and disbelief. "She sounds an odd—er . . . unusual female if she doesn't enjoy social engagements."

"I never meant to imply such a thing!" Lady Skeffington hastened to say. "Julianna enjoys balls and soirees above all things!"

Julianna would rather have a tooth extracted.

"I truly believe the two of you would deal famously together."

I intend to get her off our hands and well wed, my good man, and you have the prerequisites for a husband: You are male, of respectable birth, and adequate fortune.

"She is not at all the sort of pushing female one encounters too often these days."

She won't do a thing to show herself off to advantage.

"On the other hand, she has definite attributes that no male could miss."

To make certain of it tonight, I insisted she wear a costume so revealing that it is better suited to a married flirt than to a girl of eighteen.

"But she is not at all fast."

Despite the low décolletage on her gown, you must not even try to touch her without asking for her hand first.

Lord Makepeace's desire for freedom finally overcame the dictates of civility. "I really must return to the ballroom, Lady Skeffington. I—I believe I have the next dance with Miss Topham."

The realization that her prey was about to escape—
and into the clutches of the Season's most popular
debutante—drove Julianna's mama to retaliate by
telling the greatest lie of her matchmaking life.
Shamelessly inventing a nonexistent relationship between Julianna and the most eligible bachelor in
England, she announced, "It's just as well we return to
the ball! I believe Nicholas DuVille himself has
claimed Julianna's next waltz!"

Lady Skeffington must have hurried after the retreating lord because their voices became more distant. "Mr. DuVille has repeatedly singled our dear
Julianna out for particular attention. In fact, I have
reason to believe his sole reason for coming here this
evening was so that he could spend a few moments
with her! No, really, sir, it is the truth, though I
shouldn't like for anyone but you to know it. . . ."

Further down the maze, the Baron of Penwarren's
ravishing young widow stood with her arms wrapped
around Nicholas DuVille's neck, her eyes laughing
into his as she whispered, "Please don't tell me Lady
Skeffington actually coerced *you* into dancing with her
daughter, Nicki. Not *you,* of all people. If she has, and
you do it, you won't be able to walk into a drawing
room in England without sending everyone into
whoops. If you hadn't been in Italy all summer, you'd
know it's become a game of wits among the bachelors
to thwart that odious creature. I'm perfectly serious,"
Valerie warned as his only reaction was one of mild
amusement, "that woman would resort to anything to
get a rich husband for her daughter and secure her
own position in Society! Absolutely anything!"

"Thank you for the warning, chérie," Nicki said
dryly. As it happens, I had a brief introduction to
Lady Skeffington's husband shortly before I left for
Italy. I have not, however, set eyes on the mother *or*

the daughter, let alone promised to dance with either of them."

She sighed with relief. "I couldn't imagine how you could have been that foolish. Julianna is a remarkably pretty thing, actually, but she's not at all in your usual style. She's very young, very virginal, and I understand she has an odd habit of hiding behind draperies —or some such."

"She sounds delightful," Nicki lied with a chuckle.

"She is nothing like her mama, in any case." She paused for an eloquent little shudder to illustrate what she was about to say next. "Lady Skeffington is so eager to be a part of Society that she positively grovels. If she weren't so encroaching and ambitious, she'd be completely pathetic."

"At the risk of appearing hopelessly obtuse," Nicki said, losing patience with the entire discussion, "why in hell did you invite them to your masquerade?"

"Because, darling," Valerie said with a sigh, smoothing her fingers over his jaw with the familiarity of shared intimacies, "this past summer, little Julianna somehow became acquainted with the new Countess of Langford, as well as her sister-in-law, the Duchess of Claymore. At the beginning of the Season, the countess and the duchess made it known they desire little Julianna to be welcome amongst the Ton, then they both left for Devon with their husbands. Since no one wants to offend the Westmorelands, and since Lady Skeffington offends all of us, we all waited until the very last week of the Season to do our duty and invite them to something. Unluckily, of the dozens of invitations Lady Skeffington received for tonight, mine was the one she accepted—probably because she heard *you* were going to be here."

She stopped suddenly, as if struck by a delightful possibility. "Everyone has been longing to discover how Julianna and her obnoxious mama happened to become acquainted with the countess and the duchess, and I would wager *you* know the answer, don't you! Gossip has it that you were *extremely* well acquainted with both ladies before they were married."

To Valerie's astonishment, his entire expression became distant, shuttered, and his words conveyed a chilly warning. "Define what you mean by 'extremely well acquainted,' Valerie."

Belatedly realizing that she had somehow blundered into dangerous territory, Valerie made a hasty strategic retreat to safer ground. "I meant only that you are known to be a close friend of both ladies."

Nicki accepted her peace offering with a slight nod and allowed her to retreat in dignity, but he did not let the matter drop completely. "Their husbands are *also* close friends of mine," he said pointedly, though that was rather an exaggeration. He was on friendly terms with Stephen and Clayton Westmoreland, but neither man was particularly ecstatic about their wife's friendship with Nicki—a situation that both ladies had laughingly confided would undoubtedly continue "until you are safely wed, Nicki, and as besotted with your own wife as Clayton and Stephen are with us."

"Since you aren't yet betrothed to Miss Skeffington," Valerie teased softly, pulling his attention back to her as she slid her fingers around his nape, "there is nothing to prevent us from leaving by the side of this maze and going to your bedchamber."

From the moment she'd greeted him in the house, Nicki had known that suggestion was going to come, and he considered it now in noncommittal silence. There was nothing stopping him from doing that. Nothing whatsoever, except an inexplicable lack of interest in what he knew from past trysts with Valerie would be almost exactly one hour and thirty minutes of uninhibited sexual intercourse with a highly skilled and eager partner. That exercise would be preceded by a glass and a half of excellent champagne, and followed by half a glass of even better brandy. Afterward, he would pretend to be disappointed when she felt obliged to return to her own bed "to keep the servants from gossiping." Very civilized, very considerate, very *predictable*.

Lately, the sheer predictability of his life—and everyone in it, including himself—was beginning to grate on him. Whether he was in bed with a woman or gambling with friends, he automatically did and said all the proper—and improper—things at the appropriate time. He associated with men and women of his own class who were all as bland and socially adept as he was.

He was beginning to feel as if he were a damned marionette, performing on a stage with other marionettes, all of whom danced to the same tune, written by the same composer.

Even when it came to illicit liaisons such as the one Valerie was suggesting, there was a prescribed ritual to be followed that varied only according to whether the lady was wed or not, and whether he was playing the role of seducer or seduced. Since Valerie was widowed and had assumed the role of seducer tonight, he knew exactly how she would react if he declined her suggestion. First she would pout—but very prettily; then she would cajole; and then she would offer enticements. He, being the "seduced," would hesitate, then evade, and then postpone until she gave up, but he would never actually refuse. To do so would be unforgivably rude—a clumsy misstep in the intricate social dance they all performed to perfection.

Despite all that, Nicki waited before answering, half

expecting his body to respond favorably to her suggestion, even though his mind was not. When that didn't happen, he shook his head and took the first step in the dance: hesitation. "I should probably sleep first, chérie. I had a trying week, and I've been up for the last two days."

"Surely you aren't refusing me, are you, darling?" she asked. Pouting prettily.

Nicki switched smoothly to evasion. "What about your party?"

"I'd rather be with you. I haven't seen you in months, and besides, the party will go on without me. My servants are trained to perfection."

"Your guests are not," Nicki pointed out, still evading since she was still cajoling.

"They'll never know we've left."

"The bedchamber you gave me is next to your mother's."

"She won't hear us even if you break the bed as you did the last time we used that chamber. She's deaf as a stone." Nicki was about to proceed to the postponement stage, but Valerie surprised him by accelerating the procedure and going straight to enticements before he could utter his lines in this trite little play that had become his real life. Standing on tiptoe, she kissed him thoroughly, her hands sliding up and down his chest, her parted lips inviting his tongue.

Nicki automatically put his arm around her waist and complied, but it was an empty gesture born of courtesy, not reciprocity. When her hands slid lower, toward the waistband of his trousers, he dropped his arm and stepped back, suddenly revolted as well as bored with the entire damned charade. "Not tonight," he said firmly.

Her eyes silently accused him of an unforgivable breach of the rules. Softening his voice, he took her by the shoulders, turned her around, and gave her an affectionate pat on the backside to send her on her way. "Go back to your quests, chérie." Already reaching into his pocket for a thin cheroot, he added with polite finality, "I'll follow you after a discreet time."

3

*U*NAWARE THAT SHE WAS NOT ALONE IN THE CAVERNOUS maze, Julianna waited in tense silence to be absolutely certain her mother wasn't going to return. After a moment she gave a ragged sigh and dislodged herself from her hiding place.

Since the maze seemed like the best place to hide for the next few hours, she turned left and wandered down a path that opened into a square grassy area with an ornate stone bench in the center.

Morosely, she contemplated her situation, looking for a way out of the humiliating and untenable trap she was in, but she knew there was no escape from her mother's blind obsession with seeing Julianna wed to someone of "real consequence"—now, while the opportunity existed. Thus far all that had prevented her mother from accomplishing this goal was the fact that no "eligible" suitor "of real consequence" had declared himself during the few weeks Julianna had been in London.

Unfortunately, just before they'd left London to come here, her mother had succeeded in wringing an offer of marriage from Sir Francis Bellhaven, a repulsive, elderly, pompous knight with pallid skin, protruding hazel eyes that seemed to delve down Julianna's bodice, and thick pale lips that never failed to remind her of a dead goldfish. The thought of being bound for an entire evening, let alone the rest of her life, to Sir Francis was unendurable. Obscene. Terrifying.

Not that she was going to have any choice in the matter. If she wanted a real choice, then hiding in here from other potential suitors her mother commandeered was the last thing she ought to be doing. She knew it, but she couldn't make herself go back to that ball. She didn't even *want* a husband. She was already eighteen years old, and she had other plans, other dreams, for her life, but they didn't coincide with her mother's and so they weren't going to matter. Ever. What made it all so much more frustrating was that her mother actually *believed* she was acting in Julianna's best interests and that she knew what was ultimately best for her.

The moon slid out from behind the clouds, and Julianna stared at the pale liquid in her glass. Her father said a bit of brandy never hurt anyone, that it eased all manner of ailments, improved digestion, and cured low spirits. Julianna hesitated, and then in a burst of rebellion and desperation, she decided to test the latter theory. Lifting the glass, she pinched her nostrils closed, tipped her head back, and took three large swallows. She lowered the glass, shuddering and gasping. And waited. For an explosion of bliss. Seconds passed, then one minute. Nothing. All she felt was a slight weakness in her knees and a weakening of her defenses against the tears of futility brimming in her eyes.

In deference to her shaky limbs, Julianna stepped over to the stone bench and sat down. The bench had obviously been occupied earlier that evening, because there was a half-empty glass of spirits on the end of it and several empty glasses beneath it. After a moment she took another sip of brandy and gazed into the glass, swirling the golden liquid so that it gleamed in the moonlight as she considered her plight.

How she wished her grandmother were still alive! Grandmama would have put a stop to Julianna's mother's mad obsession with arranging a "splendid marriage." She'd have understood Julianna's aversion to being forced into marriage with anyone. In all the world, her father's dignified mother was the only person who had ever seemed to understand Julianna. Her grandmother had been her friend, her teacher, her mentor.

At her knee Julianna had learned about the world, about people; there and there alone she was encouraged to think for herself and to say whatever she thought, no matter how absurd or outrageous it might seem. In return, her grandmother had always treated her as an equal, sharing her own unique philosophies about anything and everything, from God's purpose for creating the earth to myths about men and women.

Grandmother Skeffington did not believe marriage was the answser to a woman's dreams, or even that males were more noble or more intelligent than females! "Consider for a moment my own husband as an example," she said with a gruff smile one wintry afternoon just before the Christmas when Julianna was fifteen. "You did not know your grandfather, God rest his soul, but if he had a brain with which to think, I never saw the evidence of it. Like all his forebears, he couldn't tally two figures in his head or write an intelligent sentence, and he had less sense than a suckling babe."

"Really?" Julianna said, amazed and a little appalled by this disrespectful assessment of a deceased man who had been her grandmother's husband and Julianna's grandsire.

Her grandmother nodded emphatically. "The Skeffington men have all been like that—unimaginative, slothful clods, the entire lot of them."

"But surely you aren't saying Papa is like that," Julianna argued out of loyalty. "He's your only living child."

"I would never describe your papa as a clod," she said without hesitation. "I would describe him as a muttonhead!"

Julianna bit back a horrified giggle at such heresy, but before she could summon an appropriate defense, her grandmother continued: "The Skeffington women, on the other hand, have often displayed streaks of rare intelligence and resourcefulness. Look closely and you will discover that it is generally females who survive on their wits and determination, not males. Men are not superior to women except in brute strength."

When Julianna looked uncertain, her grandmother added smugly, "If you will read that book I gave you last week, you will soon discover that women were not always subservient to men. Why, in ancient times, we had the power and the reverence. We were goddesses and soothsayers and healers, with the secrets of the universe in our minds and the gift of life in our bodies. We chose our mates, not the other way around. Men sought our counsel and worshiped at our feet and envied our powers. Why, we were superior to them in every way. We knew it, and so did they."

"If we were truly the more clever and the more gifted," Julianna said when her grandmother lifted her brows, looking for a reaction to that staggering information, "then how did we lose all that power and respect and let ourselves become subservient to men?"

"They *convinced* us we needed *their* brute strength for *our* protection," she said with a mixture of resentment and disdain. "Then they 'protected' us right out of all our privileges and rights. They *tricked* us."

Julianna found an error in that logic, and her brow furrowed in thought. "If that is so," she said after a moment, "then they couldn't have been quite so dull-witted as you think. They had to be very clever, did they not?"

For a split second her grandmother glowered at her, then she cackled with approving laughter. "A good point, my dear, and one that bears considering. I suggest you write that thought down so that you may examine it further. Perhaps you will write a book of your own on how males have perpetrated that fiendish deception upon females over the centuries. I only hope you will not decide to waste your mind and your talents on some ignorant fellow who wants you for that face of yours and tries to convince you that your only value is in breeding his children and looking after his wants. You could make a difference, Julianna. I know you could."

She hesitated, as if deciding something, then said, "That brings us to another matter I have been wishing to discuss with you. This seems like as good a time as will come along."

Grandmother Skeffington got up and walked over to the fireplace on the opposite wall of the cozy little room, her movements slowed by advancing age, her silver hair twisted into a severe coil at her neck. Bracing one hand on the evergreen boughs she'd arranged on the mantel, she bent to stir the coals. "As you know, I have already outlived a husband and one son. I have lived long, and I am fully prepared to end my days on this earth whenever my time arrives. Although I shall not always be here for you, I hope to compensate for that by leaving something behind for you . . . an inheritance that is for you to spend. It isn't much."

The subject of her grandmother's death had never come up before, and the mere thought of losing her made Julianna's chest tighten with dread.

"As I said, it isn't much, but if you are extremely thrifty, it could allow you to live very modestly in London for quite a few years while you experience more of life and hone your writing skills."

In her heart Julianna argued frantically that life without her grandmother was unthinkable, that she had no wish to live in London, and that their shared dream that she might actually become a noteworthy writer was only an impossible fantasy. Afraid that such an emotional outburst would offend the woman, Julianna remained seated upon the footstool in front of her grandmother's favorite overstuffed chair, inwardly a mass of raw emotions, outwardly controlled, calmly perusing a book. "Have you nothing to say to my plans for you, child? I rather expected to see you leap with joy. Some small display of enthusiasm would be appropriate here in return for the economies I've practiced in order to leave you this tiny legacy."

She was prodding, Julianna knew, trying to provoke her into either a witty rejoinder or an unemotional discussion. Julianna was very good at both after years of practice, but she was as incapable of discussing her grandmother's death with humor as she was with impersonal calm. Moreover, she was vaguely wounded that her grandmother could talk of leaving her forever without any indication of regret.

"I must say you don't seem very grateful."

Julianna's head snapped up, her violet eyes sparkling with angry tears. "I am not at all grateful, Grandmama, nor do I wish to discuss this now. It is nearly Christmas, a time for joyous—"

"Death is a fact of life," her grandmother stated flatly. "It is pointless to cower from it."

"But you are *my* whole life," Julianna burst out because she couldn't stop herself. "And—and I don't like it in the least that you—you can speak to me of money as if it's a recompense for your death."

"You think me cold and callous?"

"Yes, I do!"

It was their first harsh argument, and Julianna hated it.

Her grandmother regarded her in serene silence before asking, "Do you know what I shall miss when I leave this earth?"

"Nothing, evidently."

"I shall miss one thing and one thing alone." When Julianna didn't ask for an explanation, her grandmother provided it: "I shall miss you."

The answer was in such opposition to her unemotional voice and bland features that Julianna stared dubiously at her.

"I shall miss your humor and your confidences and your amazing gift for seeing the logic behind both sides of any issue. I shall particularly miss reading what you've written each day. You have been the only bright spot in my existence."

As she finished, she walked forward and laid her cool hand on Julianna's cheek, brushing away the tears trickling from the corner of her eye. "We are kindred spirits, you and I. If you had been born much sooner, we would have been bosom friends."

"We *are* friends," Julianna whispered fiercely as she placed her own hand over her grandmother's and rubbed her cheek against it. "We will be friends forever and always! When you are . . . gone, I shall still confide in you and write for you—shall write letters to you as if you had merely moved away!"

"What a diverting idea," her grandmother teased. "And will you also post them to me?"

"Of course not, but you'll know what I have written nonetheless."

"What makes you think that?" she asked, genuinely puzzled.

"Because I heard you tell the vicar very bluntly that it is illogical to assume that the Almighty intends to let us lie around dozing until Judgment Day. You said that, having repeatedly warned us that we shall reap what we sow, God is *more* likely to insist we observe what we have sown from a much *wider* viewpoint."

"I do not think it wise, my dear, for you to put more credence in my theological notions than in those of the good vicar. I shouldn't like for you to waste your talent writing to me after I'm gone, instead of writing something for the living to read."

"I shan't be wasting my time," Julianna said with a confident smile, one of their familiar debates over nonsense lifting her spirits. "If I write you letters, I have every faith you will contrive a way to read them wherever you may be."

"Because you credit me with mystical powers?"

"No," Julianna teased, "because you cannot resist correcting my *spelling!*"

"Impertinent baggage," her grandmother huffed, but she smiled widely and her fingers spread, linking with Julianna's for a tight, affectionate squeeze.

The following year, on the eve of Christmas, her grandmother died, holding Julianna's hand one last time. "I'll write to you, Grandmama." Julianna wept as her grandmother's eyes closed forever. "Don't forget to watch for my letters. Don't *forget.*"

4

*I*N THE DAYS THAT FOLLOWED, JULIANNA WROTE HER DOZ-
ens of letters, but as one lonely month drifted into
another, the empty monotony of her life provided
little worth writing about. The sleepy little village of
Blintonfield remained the boundary of her world, and
so she filled her time with reading and secret dreams
of going off to London when she received her inheritance at eighteen. There she would meet interesting
people and visit museums while she worked diligently
on her writing. When she sold some of her work, she
would bring her two little brothers to London often,
so they could broaden their knowledge and share the
wonders of the world beyond their little village.

After a few attempts to share this dream with her
mama, Julianna realized it was wiser to say nothing
because her mother was horrified and annoyed by the
whole idea. "It's beyond considering, dear. Respectable, unmarried young ladies do *not* live alone, particularly in London. Your reputation would be ruined,
completely ruined!" She was no more enthusiastic
about any mention of books or writing. Lady
Skeffington's interest in reading material was limited
exclusively to the Society pages of the daily papers,
where she religiously followed the doings of the Ton.

She considered Julianna's fascination with history and philosophy and her desire to become an author almost as appalling as Julianna's wish to live on her own in London. "Gentlemen do not like a female who is too clever, dear," she warned repeatedly. "You're entirely too bookish. If you don't learn to keep all this fustian about philosophy to yourself, your chances of receiving a marriage offer from any truly eligible gentlemen will be ruined!"

Until a few months before the masquerade ball, the subject of a London Season for Julianna had never been discussed as a possibility.

Although Julianna's father was a baronet, his ancestors had long before squandered whatever modest fortune and lands that went with the title. His only legacy from his forebears was a thoroughly amiable and placid disposition that enabled him to ignore all of life's difficulties and a great fondness for wine and spirits. He had no desire to leave his favorite chair, let alone the secluded little village that was his birthplace. He was, however, not proof against his wife's determination, nor her ambitions for their little family.

In the end, neither was Julianna.

Three weeks after Julianna received her inheritance, as she was writing more letters of inquiry to the London papers about lodgings, her mother excitedly summoned the entire family to the salon for an unprecedented family council. "Julianna," she exclaimed, "your father and I have something thrilling to tell you!" She paused to beam at Julianna's father, who was still reading the newspaper. "Don't we, John?"

"Yes, my dove," he murmured without looking up.

After an admonishing look at Julianna's two young brothers, who were arguing over the last biscuit, she clasped her hands in delight and transferred her gaze to Julianna. "It is all arranged!" she exclaimed. "I have just received a letter from the owner of a little house in London in a respectable neighborhood. He has agreed to let us have it for the rest of the Season for the paltry amount I was able to offer! Everything else has been arranged and deposits paid in advance. I have hired a Miss Sheridan Bromleigh, who will be your lady's maid and occasional chaperone, and who will help look after the boys. She is an American, but then one must make do when one cannot afford to pay decent wages.

"Dear heaven, your gowns were expensive, but the vicar's wife assures me the modiste I hired is quite competent, though not capable of the sort of intricate designs you will see worn by the young ladies of the Ton. On the other hand, I daresay few of them have your beauty, so it all works out quite evenly. Someday soon you will have gowns to go with your looks, and you will be the envy of all! You'll have jewels and furs, coaches, servants at your beck and call. . . ."

Julianna had felt a momentary burst of elation at the mention of inexpensive lodgings in London, but new gowns and a lady's maid had never been in the family budget, nor were they in her budget. "I don't understand, Mama. What has happened?" she asked, wondering if some unknown relative had died and left them a fortune.

"What has happened is that I have managed to put your small inheritance to grand use—and in a manner that will pay excellent returns, I am sure."

Julianna's mouth opened in a silent cry of furious protest, but she was incapable of speech for the moment—which Lady Skeffington evidently mistook for shared ecstasy.

"Yes, it is all true! You are going to London for the Season, where we will contrive a way for you to mingle with all the right people! While we are there, I have every confidence you will captivate some eligible gentleman who will make you a splendid offer. Perhaps even the Earl of Langford, whose estates are said to be beyond compare. Or Nicholas DuVille, who is one of the richest men in England *and* France and is about to inherit a Scottish title from a relative of his mama. I have it from several unimpeachable sources that the Earl of Langford and the Earl of Glenmore— which is what DuVille will be called—are considered to be the two most desirable bachelors in Europe! Just imagine how envious the Ton will be when little Julianna Skeffington captures one of those men for a husband."

Julianna could almost hear the sound of her dreams splintering and crashing at her feet. "I don't *want* a husband!" she cried. "I want to travel, and learn, and write, Mama. I do. I think I could write a novel someday—Grandmama said I am truly talented with a pen. No, don't laugh, please. You must get the money back, you must!"

"My dear, foolish girl, I wouldn't even if I could, which I cannot. Marriage is the only future for a female. Once you see how Fashionable Society lives, you'll forget all that silliness your Grandmother Skeffington stuffed into your head. Now," she continued blithely, "when we are in London, I will contrive to put you in the way of eligible gentlemen, you may depend on it. We are not common merchants, you know—your papa is a baronet, after all. Once the Ton realizes we have come to London for the Season, we will be included in all their splendid affairs. Gentlemen will see you and admire you, and we will soon have eligible suitors lined up at our door, you'll see."

There was little point in refusing to go there, and no way to avoid it, so Julianna went.

In London, her mother insisted they browse daily in the same exclusive shops in which the Ton shopped, and each afternoon they strolled through the same London parks where the Ton was always to be seen.

But nothing went as Lady Skeffington had planned. Contrary to all her hopes and expectations, the aristocracy did not welcome her with open arms upon discovering her husband was a baronet, nor did they respond at all well to her eager efforts to engage them in conversations in Bond Street or accost them in Hyde Park. Instead of being given an invitation or invited to pay a morning call, the elegant matrons with whom she tried to converse gave her the cut-direct.

Though her mama seemed not to notice that she was being treated with icy disdain, Julianna felt every insult and rebuff enough for both of them, and every one of them savaged her pride and cut her to the heart. Even though she realized her mother brought much of the contempt on herself, the entire situation made her so miserable and self-conscious that she could scarcely look anyone in the eye from the moment they left their little house until they returned.

Despite all that, Julianna did not regard her trip to London as a total loss. Sheridan Bromleigh, the paid companion whom her mother had employed for the Season, proved to be a lovely and lively young American with whom Julianna could talk and laugh and exchange confidences. For the first time in her eighteen years, Julianna had a friend close to her own age, one who shared her sense of humor and many of her interests as well.

The Earl of Langford, whom Lady Skeffington had coveted for her daughter, threw a final rub into her plans by getting married at the end of the Season. In a quick wedding that shocked London and antagonized Lady Skeffington, the handsome earl married Miss Bromleigh.

When Julianna's mother heard the news, she went to bed with her hartshorn and stayed there for a full day. By the evening, however, she had come to see the tremendous social advantage of being very personally acquainted with a countess who had married into one of the most influential families in England.

With renewed confidence and vigor, she focused all her hopes on Nicholas DuVille.

Normally Julianna could not think about her disastrous encounter with him that spring without shuddering, but as she sat in the maze, staring at the glass in her hand, the whole thing suddenly seemed more amusing than humiliating.

Obviously, she decided, the horrid-tasting stuff she'd drank actually did make things seem a little brighter. And if three swallows could accomplish that, then it seemed logical that a bit more of the magical elixir could only be of more benefit. It was in the spirit of scientific experimentation, therefore, that she lifted the glass and took three more swallows. After what seemed like only a few moments, she felt even better!

"Much better," she informed the moon aloud, stifling a giggle as she thought about her brief but hilarious encounter with the legendary Nicholas DuVille. Her mama had spied him in Hyde Park just as his curricle was about to slowly pass within arm's reach of the path they were on. In her eager desperation to point him out and effect a meeting, Julianna's mama gave her a light shove that put her directly into the path of his horse and curricle. Off-balance, Julianna grabbed at the horse's reins for balance, yanking the irate horse and its irate owner to a stop.

Shaken and frightened by the animal's nervous sidestepping, Julianna clung to its reins, trying to quiet it. Intending to either apologize or chastise the driver of the curricle for not trying to quiet his own horse, Julianna looked up and beheld Nicholas DuVille. Despite the frigid look in his narrowed, assessing eyes, Julianna felt as if her bones were melting and her legs were turning to water.

Dark-haired, broad-shouldered, with piercing metallic-blue eyes and finely chiseled lips, he had the sardonic look of a man who had sampled all the delights the world had to offer. With that fallen angel's face and knowing blue eyes, Nicholas DuVille was as wickedly attractive and forbidden as sin. Julianna felt an instantaneous, insane compulsion to do something that would impress him.

"If you wish a mount, mademoiselle," he said, in a voice that rang with curt impatience, "may I suggest you try a more conventional means of obtaining one."

Julianna was spared the immediate need to react or reply by her mother, who was so desperate to accomplish an introduction that she violated every known rule of etiquette and common sense. "This is such an unexpected pleasure and privilege, my lord," exclaimed Lady Skeffington, oblivious to the ominous narrowing of his eyes and the avidly curious glances being cast their way by the occupants of the other carriages who had drawn to a stop, their way blocked. "I have been longing to introduce you to my daughter—"

"Am I to assume," he interrupted, "that this has something to do with your daughter stepping in front of me and waylaying my horse?"

Julianna decided that the man was rude and arrogant.

"That had nothing to do with it," she burst out, mortified by the undeniable accuracy of his assessment and by the belated realization that she was still holding on to the rein. She dropped it like it was a snake, stepped back, and resorted to flippancy because she had no other way to salvage her pride. "I was practicing," she informed him primly.

Her answer startled him enough to stay his hand as he started to flick the reins. "Practicing?" he repeated, studying her expression with a glimmer of amused interest. "Practicing for what?"

Julianna lifted her chin, raised her brows, and said in an offhand voice what she hoped would pass for droll wit rather than stupidity, "I'm practicing to become a highwayman, obviously. By way of an apprenticeship, I jump in front of innocent travelers in the park and waylay their horses."

Turning her back on him, she took her mother firmly by the arm and steered her away. Over her shoulder, Julianna added a dismissive and deliberately incorrect, "Good afternoon, Mr. . . . er . . . Deveraux."

Her mother's exclamation of indignant horror at these outrageous remarks muffled a sound from the man in the carriage that sounded almost like laughter.

Lady Skeffington was still furious with Julianna later that night.

"How could you be so impertinent!" she cried, wringing her hands. "Nicholas DuVille has so much influence with Society that if he utters one derogatory word about you, no one of any consequence will associate with you. You'll be ruined! Ruined, do you hear me?" Despite Julianna's repeated apologies, albeit insincere, her mother was beyond consolation. She paced back and forth, her hartshorn in one hand and a handkerchief in the other. "Had Nicholas DuVille paid you just a few minutes of attention in the park today, where others could see it, you'd have been an instant success! By tonight we would have had invitations to every important social function of the Season, and by the day after, eligible suitors would have been at our door. Instead, you had to be insolent to the one man in all London who could put an end to my hopes and dreams with a single word." She dabbed at the tears trembling on her lashes. "This is all your grandmother's fault! She taught you to be just like her. Oh, I should be *horsewhipped* for allowing you to spend so much time with that dreadful old harpy, but no one could oppose her will, least of all your father."

She stopped pacing and rounded on Julianna. "Well, I know more of the *real* world than your grandmother ever did, and I am about to tell you something she never did—a simple truth that is worth more than all her fantastical notions, and that truth is this—" And clenching her hands into fists at her sides, she said in a voice shaking with purpose, *"A man does not wish to associate with any female who knows more than he does!* If the Ton's gossip mill finds out how bookish you are, you'll be ruined! No gentleman of consequence will want you! You . . . will . . . be . . . ruined!"

5

A TRILL OF FEMININE LAUGHTER PULLED JULIANNA'S thoughts back to the masquerade, and she listened to the sounds of adults behaving like naughty children, wondering how many feminine reputations were being "totally ruined" out there tonight. Based on what Julianna had gathered from her mother's frequent lectures, it seemed there were countless ways to be ruined, but there were two different and distinct kinds of ruination. Mistakes made by the female alone, such as appearing too intelligent, too clever, too bookish, or too glib, could "ruin" her chances of making a splendid match. But any mistake she made that involved also a gentleman resulted in "*total* ruin," because it eliminated her chances of making any kind of match at all.

It was very silly, Julianna decided gaily as she reflected upon the myriad ways of blundering into "*total* ruin."

A female could be "*totally* ruined" by allowing any gentleman to be alone with her in a room, or allowing him to show a partiality for her, or even allowing him a third dance with her.

As Julianna contemplated all this, she realized she would have been far, far better off if she had done only one of the countless things that could "totally ruin" a female's chances of making any match. If she *had* been totally ruined, she realized with a sudden flash of new insight, she would not now be facing a repulsive marriage to Sir Francis Bellhaven!

The thought of him banished her momentary mirth and made the moon waver as her eyes filled with tears. She reached for her handkerchief, realized she didn't have one, and sniffled. Then she had another sip of her drink, trying unsuccessfully to buoy her plummeting spirits.

For several minutes after he had finished his cigar, Nicki remained where Valerie had left him, deliberating about turning to his right and returning to the garden or turning left and walking deeper into the maze until he came to a path that, he knew, led around to the side of the house and ultimately to his bedchamber.

He was tired, and his bedchamber had an enormous and very comfortable bed. If his mother hadn't specifically asked him to stop here on his way from London and to give her regards to Valerie's mother, he wouldn't have come. According to his father's note, his mother's health had taken a sudden and precarious turn for the worse, and Nicki did not want to do anything, no matter how minor, to disappoint or distress her. Turning, Nicki walked along the convoluted path that led out of the maze and into the garden, ready to fulfill his social obligation this night and his filial obligation on the morrow.

6

JULIANNA WAS QUITE CONVINCED THAT TOTAL RUINATION
would cause Sir Francis to withdraw his offer, though
she had no idea how she would survive if her parents
disowned her for ruining herself. Sniffling again, she
bent her head, closed her eyes tightly, and decided to
resort to prayer. She asked her grandmother to help
her find a way to ruin herself. Deciding that it might
be wise to appeal to an even higher authority, Julianna
took her problem directly to God. It occurred to her,
however, that God might not approve of such a
request, let alone consider granting it, unless He was
fully apprised of her dire plight. She sniffled again,
closed her eyes even tighter, and began explaining to
God the reasons she wished to be ruined. She was just
to the part about having to marry Sir Francis
Bellhaven, and crying in heartbroken little gulps,
when A Voice spoke to her out of the darkness—a
deep, rich, male voice filled with quiet authority and
tinged with sympathy: "May I be of assistance?"

Shock sent Julianna surging to her feet, her heart
thundering, then leaping into her throat as her widened eyes riveted on a shadowy cloaked figure that
materialized from the inky darkness and began moving forward.

The apparition stopped just beyond reach of a pale moonbeam, his face in shadow, his features indistinguishable. He raised his arm slowly, and something white seemed to float and flutter from his fingertips even though there was no breeze.

Her senses reeling from shock and brandy, Julianna realized he was holding the white billowing thing out toward her. She stepped forward hesitantly and reached for his extended arm. The object that came away in her hand turned out to be an earthly, though still very soft and fine, handkerchief. "Thank you," she whispered reverently, giving him a teary smile as she dabbed at her eyes and nose.

Not certain what she was now expected to do with it, she held it out to him.

"You may keep it."

Julianna snatched it back, clutching it safely to her heart. "Thank you."

"Is there anything I can do before I leave you?"

"Don't leave! Please! Yes, there is something I need, but I should like to explain." Julianna opened her mouth to finish explaining to God why she was praying to be ruined when two things struck her as a little odd. First, this celestial being who had evidently appeared in answer to her prayers seemed to have a slight accent—a French one. Second, now that her eyes had adjusted to the pool of darkness that concealed him, she noticed a small detail that struck her as more sinister than heavenly. Since she had been praying to be ruined, it seemed not only prudent but imperative to make certain the *wrong* sort of mystical being hadn't decided to pay her a visit in answer to that prayer.

Fighting against the dulling effects of the brandy, Julianna fixed him with a cautious stare. "Please do not think I am questioning your . . . your authenticity . . . or your taste in fashions," she began, carefully injecting as much respect into her voice as she possibly could, "but shouldn't you be wearing *white* rather than *black*?"

His eyes, visible through the slits of his half mask, narrowed at such an impertinent suggestion, and Julianna braced herself to be struck down by a bolt of lightning, but his tone was mild. "Black is customary for a man. Were I to appear here in white, I would draw too much attention to myself. People would begin trying to guess my identity. They would note my height first, then my other features, and begin trying to guess my identity. If they did, I would forfeit my anonymity and then my freedom to do the sort of things one expects to do on nights like tonight."

"Yes, I see," Julianna said politely, but she wasn't completely convinced. "I *suppose* that's not as extraordinary as I thought."

Nicki thought their entire meeting thus far had been a little "extraordinary." When he first saw her, she had been weeping. In a matter of moments, that expressive face of hers had already exhibited shock, embarrassment, awe, fear, suspicion, and now uncertainty . . . even apprehension. As he waited for her to screw up the courage to explain whatever it was she wanted of him, Nicki realized there was nothing ordinary about her. Her pale blond hair seemed to glisten with silver in the moonlight when she moved her head, and her large eyes actually appeared to be a lavender blue. They dominated a delicately molded face with smooth milky skin, winged brows, and a lovely mouth. Hers was a subtle beauty, easily overlooked at first glance. It came from a purity of features and a candor in those large eyes, rather than from vibrant coloring or exotic looks. He couldn't assess her age, but she looked quite young, and there were certain things about her that did not quite fit.

She drew in a deep breath, pulling his thoughts back

to the matter at hand, and he quirked a brow at her in silent inquiry.

"Would you mind," she said, very, very politely, "taking off your mask and letting me see your face?"

"Was that the favor you wanted to ask of me?" he asked, wondering if she were addled.

"No, but I cannot ask it until I see your face." When he showed no inclination to move, Julianna implored in a shaky, desperate voice, "It's *terribly* important!"

Nicki hesitated, and then sheer curiosity made him decide to comply. He pulled off the mask and even walked out of the shadows to give her a good look at his face, then he waited for a reaction.

He got one.

She clamped her hand over her mouth, her eyes as round as saucers. Nicki stepped forward, thinking she was going to swoon, but her sudden shriek of laughter checked him in midstride. That was followed by great gales of mirth as she sank onto the stone bench and covered her face with her hands, her entire body shaking with hilarity. Twice she peeked out at him from between her fingers, as if to ascertain that she had seen correctly, and both times the sight of his face made her laugh even harder.

With a supreme effort, Julianna finally managed to compose herself. She lifted her face to his, her eyes still sparkling with mirth as she stared in disbelief at the one face in all England that had made her heart pound. And now, as her shock subsided, that face was beginning to have the same effect on her that it had had on her last spring. Only this time there was a difference. This time there was a slight smile touching that chiseled mouth, and his eyes weren't cold and hard, they were merely . . . speculative. All in all, his expression was noncommittal but definitely interested.

That was flattering and encouraging enough to raise

her spirits, bolster her confidence, and make her certain that she had made the right decision a few minutes before. She had prayed to be totally ruined, and it was going to happen at the hands of the most sought-after bachelor in Europe, Nicholas DuVille himself! That made it so much better—it gave it a certain flair, a style. In return for sacrificing herself to total ruin to avoid Sir Francis, she was going to have sweet memories to treasure. "I'm not demented, though it must look it," she began, "and I do have a favor to ask of you."

Nicki knew he ought to walk away, but he was as strangely captivated by her infectious laughter, her entrancing face, and her astonishing reactions as he was completely bored with the prospect of returning to the ball. "Exactly what is this favor you're hoping I'll grant you?"

"It's a little difficult to discuss," she said. He watched her reach for whatever it was she'd been drinking. She took a sip of it as if she needed it for courage, and then she raised those large candid eyes to his. "Actually, it's *quite* difficult," she amended, wrinkling her pert nose.

"As you can see," Nicki responded, suppressing a smile and giving her a gallant little bow, "I am completely at your service."

"I hope you still feel that way, after you hear what I would ask of you," she murmured uneasily.

"What may I do?"

"I would like you to ruin me."

7

Until that moment, Nicki would have wagered a fortune that nothing a woman said could truly surprise him anymore, let alone reduce him to his current state of speechlessness. "I beg your pardon?" he finally managed.

Julianna saw him struggle to hide his shock, and she suppressed another siege of unacceptable giggles. She wasn't certain whether her urge to laugh came from nervousness or the wondrous, evil-tasting potion that men imbibed to make them feel so much more optimistic. "I asked if you would be willing to ruin me."

Stalling for time, Nicki studied her from the corner of his eye while he reached into his pocket and took out the last of the two cheroots he'd brought with him. "What . . . specifically . . ." he queried cautiously as he bent his head and lit the cheroot, "do you mean by that?"

"I mean, I wish to be ruined," Julianna repeated, watching him cup his hands around the flame, trying to get a better look at his features. "I mean, I wish to be made undesirable to any and all men," she clarified. "Rendered unmarriageable. Left on the shelf."

Instead of reacting, he propped a booted foot on the

stone bench beside her hip and eyed her in thoughtful silence, the thin cigar clamped between even white teeth.

"I—I really don't think I could possibly make it any clearer than that," she said anxiously.

"No, I don't think you could."

She leaned a little closer to his leg and tipped her head back, peering up at his unreadable face as he gazed off into the distance. "You do understand what I meant?"

"It would be difficult not to."

He did not sound very enthusiastic, so she blurted the first inducement that came to mind: "I would be willing to pay you!"

This time Nicki was able to suppress his shock though not his smile at her ability to cause the reaction. "That makes twice," he murmured aloud. "And in one night." Realizing that she was waiting for a reply, he lowered his gaze to her upturned face, bit back a wayward grin, and said gravely, "That's a very tempting offer."

"I would cooperate completely," she promised, leaning forward and looking at him with earnest, hopeful eyes.

"The incentives are becoming more irresistible by the moment."

Nicki let her wait for his decision while he gazed into the distance, analyzing the situation and the intriguing young woman seated on the bench beside his leg. He still wasn't certain how old she was, but he had known she was no gently bred debutante long before she'd asked him for a "favor." The clues had all been there from the first, beginning with the fact that she was alone in a dark, secluded area with a man to whom she'd never been properly introduced, and she'd made no effort to correct either situation.

Furthermore, the gown she was wearing was enticing in the extreme, seductively low cut to show off her swelling breasts and tightly fitted to emphasize her narrow waist. No respectable Society matron alive would have permitted her innocent daughter to appear in such a gown. It was a gown for a daring married woman—or a courtesan. She was not wearing a marriage ring, which left only the latter possibility. That conclusion was reinforced by the fact that it had become quite the thing, especially among the wealthy young bucks, to escort their lightskirts to masquerades as sort of a joke. Some of London's most beautiful and sought-after courtesans were in evidence at this masquerade, and Nicki assumed the angelic-looking one beside him had quarreled with whomever had brought her here. After crying her heart out, she was now looking for a replacement. He knew damned well she'd been "ruined" long before and often since, just as he knew she had absolutely no intention of paying him, but the latter approach was so marvelously creative that he was impressed. She was not only entrancingly lovely, she was unique. And extremely entertaining. With her looks and imagination, her soft, cultured voice, she was not going to have to look very far or very long for a new protector. In fact, if she proved to be half as entertaining in his bed tonight as she'd been thus far, he'd be sorely tempted to volunteer for the role.

In an agony of suspense, Julianna stared at his firm jaw and unreadable expression as he gazed off into the distance, his hands thrust into his pockets, his cloak thrown back over his shoulders. His eyes were creased at the corners, and it seemed almost as if he was smiling a little bit, but that may have been caused only by the way he was holding the cheroot clamped between his white teeth.

Unable to endure the wait any longer, Julianna said shakily, "Have you decided yet?"

He shifted his gaze to her face, and Julianna felt the full impact of the lazy, devastating smile that swept across his face. "I would not come cheaply," Nicki joked.

"I haven't a great deal of money," she warned, and Nicki bit back a chuckle that erupted into a shout of laughter when she actually started digging into her little reticule, searching for money.

Extending his arm to her, he said, "Shall we find a place more conducive to . . . ah . . ."

"My ruin?" she provided helpfully, and he sensed a slight hesitation that was gone before it materialized. Standing up, she squared her shoulders, put up her chin, and, looking like a queen going bravely and determinedly, announced, "Let's be at it, then."

He led her deeper into the maze, guided by a long-ago memory of the time when Valerie and he had been lost inside it for hours because they'd missed the secret path. It occurred to him as they walked along at a leisurely pace that introductions were in order, but when he mentioned this, she told him that she already knew who he was. "And you are?" Nicki prompted when she showed no inclination to volunteer him the information.

Somewhere in Julianna's hazy mind, tangled up in the dreamy unreality of the night and the moon and the handsome, desirable man at her side, caution finally asserted itself. Trying to think of a false name to give him, she glanced down at her gown. "'Marie,'" she provided after a momentary pause. "You may call me 'Marie.'"

"As in 'Antoinette'?" Nicki mocked, wondering why she was lying.

In answer, she threw up her left arm in exuberation and called cheerfully, "Let them eat cake!" A split second later she stopped dead. "Where are we going?"

"To my bedchamber."

Julianna mentally recounted the possibilities for ruination. Three dances with the same man. Allowing a man to show partiality. And being alone in a room with a man. Room. Bedchamber. She nodded agreeably. "Very well, I suppose you know more about it than I."

I doubt it, Nicki thought dryly.

They strolled along in companionable silence, and Nicki liked that about her too. She did not feel a need to talk incessantly. When she finally broke the silence, even her timing was right, although her topic was another stunning first in his vast experience with females. She'd been looking down at the ground when she lifted her head and said very solemnly, "I often find myself wondering about worms. Do you?"

"Not as much," Nicki lied drolly, swallowing back a laugh, "as I used to do." He couldn't remember laughing this much in an entire week.

"Then consider this and see if you can think of an answer," she suggested in the grave tones of a puzzled scientist. "If God meant for them to crawl about on the ground as they do, why don't they have knees?"

Nicki stopped dead, his shoulders shaking with helpless mirth as he turned fully toward her. "What did you just say?"

A heavenly face lifted to his, eyes shining, breasts swelling invitingly above her bodice, generous lips forming words: "I asked why worms don't have knees."

"That's what I *thought* you said." Grabbing her shoulders, he hauled her abruptly into his arms and surrendered to the uncontrollable impulse to smother his laughter against the soft lips that had caused it. He let her go as quickly as he'd grabbed her, uncertain whether her expression was one of shock or reproof. Deciding it was unnecessary and undesirable to discuss either one with someone who was going to share

134

his bed in return for payment, he stepped back and turned away.

Despite that, he couldn't stop himself from glancing at her several times in the dark to assess her reaction, and he relaxed when he saw the bemused smile touching her lips.

He was not completely certain he'd made all the right turns until they rounded the last corner and he found the secret exit that led around to the side of the house. Knowing in advance that they were going to be in plain view of the revelers for a few paces—albeit at a reasonably safe distance—Nicki carefully stationed himself on her left, between the house and her. "Why are we walking faster?" she asked.

"Because we happen to be in view of the guests from here," he cautioned.

She peered around him to see for herself. "Let them eat cake too!" she announced cheerfully with another wave of her arm. Raising her voice, she called out, "All of you have my permission to eat cake!"

Nicki felt his shoulders shake with silent, horrified, helpless laughter, but he said nothing to encourage another outburst.

8

In his bedchamber, Julianna sat upon a small sofa upholstered in rich gold brocade, feeling as if she were in a dream, as she watched him slowly strip off his coat and loosen his snowy-white neckcloth. A thousand warning bells were clanging madly in her head, making her feel extremely dizzy. Or perhaps it was the memory of his mouth crushed to hers that made her head swim.

She lowered her gaze, because that seemed like the right thing to do, and then became preoccupied with what she saw.

Divested of his coat and neckcloth, Nicki loosened the top of his shirt and walked over to the polished table where a tray of glasses and decanters had been left. Pulling the stopper out of the brandy decanter, he glanced over his shoulder to ask if she wanted anything, but what he saw made him frown with concern and turn fully around. She was seated on the sofa, but bending as far forward at the waist as she could, looking at something on the floor. "What are you doing?" he asked.

She answered without looking up. "I don't have any toes."

"What do you mean?" Nicki demanded irritably as it began to occur to him that nearly everything she'd done and said in the maze that had seemed shocking or hilarious at the time, including her request to be ruined, could very likely be the result of intoxication or an unbalanced mind. His voice was intentionally sharp. "Can you stand up?" he snapped.

Julianna stiffened at his tone and slowly straightened. Transfixed by the change in him, she stood up as commanded, scarcely able to believe the forbidding man standing there was the same one who had joked with her and . . . and kissed her.

She looked completely dazed, Nicki realized. Dazed and disoriented. With an anger that was heightened by disappointment and self-disgust for his own naïveté, he said scathingly, "Are you capable of uttering anything at all that could convince me you are capable of intelligent thought at this moment?"

Julianna flinched from that all-too-familiar voice. It had the same clipped, authoritative tones, the same contemptuous superiority that had humiliated and antagonized her in the park. Tonight her reaction was slowed by brandy and shock, but when she did react it was just as instinctive and just as effective, although more restrained. She wanted this to be a night to remember, to cherish. "I think I am," she said softly, lifting her chin, her voice trembling only slightly.

"Shall we begin with Greek philosophy?" Clasping her hands behind her back, she turned sideways, pretending to study the painting above the fireplace, as she continued: "Socrates had some interesting observations about knowledge and ethics. Plato was more profound. . . ."

Julianna paused, trying desperately to clear her head and remember what else she knew of philosophers, ancient or otherwise. "In modern times . . ."

she tried again, "Voltaire is a particular favorite of mine. I enjoy his wit. But of all the modern . . ." Her voice trailed off as Julianna heard him coming up behind her, then she made herself go on: "Of all the modern philosophers, the one I am best acquainted with was a woman. Her name was Sarah."

He stopped so near to her that she could actually feel him standing at her back. Shaking with uncertainty, Julianna said, "Shall I share Sarah's favorite theory with you?"

"By all means," he whispered contritely, his warm breath stirring the hair at her temple.

"Sarah's theory was that females were once considered superior to males, but that males, in their deceitful arrogance, found a way to—"

Julianna's entire body tensed as his hands curved around her shoulders, drawing her back against his full length. "Males found a way to convince us, and themselves, that women are actually birdwits and—"

His warm lips touched a sensitive place behind her ear, sending shivers racing down her entire body. "Go on," he urged, his voice like velvet, his mouth against her ear. Julianna tried, but her breath came out in a shuddering sigh. She was losing control again, letting the brandy soothe her and convince her this was right. It was either this or Sir Francis Bellhaven: sweet, forbidden pleasures with memories to cherish . . . or life with a man who sickened her. Surely she was entitled to a few more moments, she decided.

Nicki felt her heart racing beneath his hand as he slid it over her midriff, taking his time before he let himself touch the full, tantalizing breasts that were within his reach. He slid a kiss over her smooth temple and trailed another down the silken skin of her cheek. She smelled like fresh air and flowers, and in his arms she felt like . . .

Wood.

She was breathing as if she were running, her heart was thundering from . . .

Fright.

Nicki lifted his head and wordlessly turned her around. In disbelief, he stared down at the hectic color on her cheeks and eyes, eyes that had darkened to violet pools, eyes that watched him in uncertainty. The color in her cheeks deepened with embarrassment as he inspected every feature of that elegant face, looking for something, anything, to indicate that this wasn't new and terrifying for her. He wanted to discover one thing that indicated experience.

And all he could find was innocence.

This was her first time.

She had *not* done any of this before.

He wanted her despite that. No, he realized with disbelief, he wanted her three times more *because* of that. She was there for the taking, she had asked him to do this, had even volunteered to pay him to do this. And still he hesitated. Taking her chin between his thumb and forefinger, he forced her to meet his gaze. In a voice that was devoid of anything except reassuring neutrality, Nicki asked, "Are you absolutely certain you want to be here . . . to do this?"

Julianna swallowed audibly and nodded slightly. "It's something I have to do—to get it over and done with."

"You're completely certain?"

She nodded, and Nicki did what he'd been longing to do all along. Except that as he bent his head, he had the disquieting thought that he wasn't merely despoiling a virgin, he was destroying an angel. He seized her mouth with violent tenderness, forcing her to respond and then pushing her harder until she was moaning in his arms and his hands were clamping her to him, then moving forward, sliding up to cup her trembling breasts.

"No!" She broke free with such suddenness that she caught Nicki off guard. "I can't! I can't! Not that!"

She shook her head wildly, and Nicki stared at her in frowning disbelief. One moment she'd been kissing him back, her arms twined sweetly behind his neck, her body molding instinctively to his. The next, she was running across the room, leaving him there, jerking the door open and racing. . . .

Straight into Valerie, and another woman who was raving about her daughter being abducted and demanding a search of the house for her. As if in a dream, a nightmare, he saw the woman who had accosted him in the park wrap her arms protectively around the girl who had been his a moment before.

Only the older woman was different now. She wasn't groveling about what a pleasure it was to meet him, she was looking at him with triumphant hostility all over her face, saying, "After I have put my daughter to bed and summoned my husband, we will discuss this privately!"

9

"JULIANNA?" HER MOTHER'S NORMAL SPEAKING VOICE sounded like a screech. Julianna's head hurt so terribly that even her teeth seemed to ache in their sockets. In all the world, the only thing that wasn't awful this morning was her mother. Her mother, who should have been livid, who Julianna had thought would disown her for less than what she'd done last night, was the soul of gentle understanding.

No questions, no recriminations.

Curled up in a tight ball of misery against the door of the coach, Julianna watched the house where it had all happened sway and pitch and lunge from view. "I'm going to be sick," she whispered.

"No dear, that wouldn't be at all pleasant."

Julianna swallowed and swallowed again. "Are we almost home?"

"We aren't going home."

"Where are we going?"

"We're going right . . . here," her mother said, leaning to the side and searching for something with narrowed eyes that widened suddenly with delight.

Julianna made an effort to see where "here" was and saw only a pleasant little cottage with her papa's carriage in front of it, and another carriage with a crest painted on its side. And then she saw the chapel. And in the yard of that chapel, ignoring her father and watching their coach draw up, was Nicholas DuVille.

And the expression on his dark, saturnine face was a thousand times more glacial, more contemptuous, than any she had seen in the park.

"Why are we here?" Julianna cried, feeling faint from shock and nausea and headache.

"To attend your wedding to Nicholas DuVille."

"My what?! But why?"

"Why is he marrying you?" her mama said dryly as she opened the door. "Because he has no choice. He is a gentleman, after all. He knew the rules, and he broke them. Our hostess and two servants saw you running out of his bedchamber. He ruined the reputation of an innocent, well-bred young lady. If he didn't marry you now, you would be ruined, but he could never again call himself a gentleman. He would lose face among his peers. His own code of honor requires this."

"I don't want this!" Julianna cried. "I'll make him understand!"

"I didn't want this!" Julianna was babbling a quarter of an hour later as she was shoved roughly into her new husband's coach. He had not spoken a word except in answer to his vows. He spoke now: "Shut up and get in!"

"Where are we going?" she cried.

"To your new home," he said with scathing sarcasm. *"Your* new home," he clarified.

10

*H*UMMING A YULETIDE MELODY AS SHE SAT BEFORE THE
dressing table in her bedchamber, Julianna tucked
tiny sprigs of red holly berries into the dark green
ribbon that bound her heavy blond hair into curls at
the crown.

Satisfied, she stood up and shook the wrinkles from
her soft green wool gown, straightened the wide cuffs
at her wrists, then she headed for the salon where she
intended to work on her new manuscript in front of a
cheery fire.

In the three months since her husband had uncere-
moniously deposited her in front of this picturesque
little country house a few hours after her wedding, and
then driven off, she had not seen or heard from
Nicholas DuVille. Even so, every detail of that hide-
ous day was burned into her mind with such vivid
clarity that it could still make her stomach knot with
shame.

It had been an obscene parody of a real wedding, an
eminently suitable ending for something that had
begun at a masquerade. Far from condemning
Julianna's breach of conduct the night before, her
mother actually regarded it as a practical and ingen-
ious method of snaring the Ton's most desirable

bachelor. Instead of offering maternal advice about marriage and children before her daughter walked down a short aisle to become a wife, Julianna's mother was advising her on the sorts of *furs* Julianna ought to insist upon having.

Julianna's father, on the other hand, obviously had a clearer grasp of the real situation, which was that his daughter had disgraced herself, and her groom had participated in it. He had dealt with that by anesthetizing himself with at least a full bottle of Madeira before he walked her unsteadily, but cheerfully, down the aisle. To complete the gruesome picture, the bride was clearly suffering from the aftereffects of extreme inebriation, and the groom . . .

Julianna shuddered with the recollection of the loathing in his eyes when he was forced to turn to her and pledge his life to her. Even the image of the vicar who had performed the ceremony was branded into her brain. She could still see him standing there, his kindly face a mirror of shocked horror when, at the end of the ceremony, the groom responded to his suggestion that he kiss the bride by raking Julianna with a look of undiluted contempt, then turning on his heel and walking out.

In the coach, on the way here, Julianna had tried to talk to him, to explain, to apologize. After listening to her pleading in glacial silence, he had finally spoken to her. "If I hear just one more word from you, you will find yourself standing on the side of the road before your sentence is finished!"

In the months since she had been dumped here like a piece of unwanted baggage, Julianna had learned more about the agony of loneliness—not the kind that comes after losing someone to death, but the kind that comes from being rejected and despised and defiled. She had learned all that and more as the gossip about Nicki's flagrant affair with a beautiful opera dancer raged through London before the firestorm of gossip about his abrupt wedding had even gathered real force.

He was punishing her, Julianna knew. Publicly humiliating her in retaliation for what he believed—and would always believe—had been a trap set by Julianna and her mother. And the worst part of it was that when Julianna put herself in his place, and looked at things from his point of view, she could understand exactly how he felt and why.

Until last week, his revenge had been completely devastating. She had wept an ocean of tears into her pillow, tormented herself with the recollection of the hatred in his eyes on their wedding day, and written him a dozen letters trying to explain. His only response had been a short, scathing message delivered to her by his secretary, which warned that if she made one more attempt to contact him, she would be evicted from the home she now occupied, and cut off without a shilling.

Julianna DuVille was expected to live out the rest of her days, in solitude, doing penance for a sin that had been almost as much his as hers. Nicholas DuVille had five other residences, all very grand and far more accessible to company. According to the gossip she read in the papers and what she gathered from the bits of information she pried out of Sheridan Westmoreland, he gave lavish parties at those houses for his friends, and intimate ones for two, Julianna was certain, in his bedchamber.

Until last week, her days had dragged by in an agony of emptiness and self-loathing, with nothing to give her relief except what little she found by pouring out her heart in letters to her grandmother. But all that had changed now, and it was going to improve more every day.

Last week, she had received a letter from a London

publisher who wished to buy her new novel. In his letter, Mr. Framingham had compared Julianna in glowing terms to Jane Austen, he had commented on her humor and her remarkable subtlety in dealing with the arrogance of Society and the futility of trying to belong where one can never truly belong.

He had also enclosed a bank draft with the prediction of many more to come, once her first novel was published. A bank draft was independence, it was validation, it was release from the bondage her wedding to Nicholas DuVille had placed her in. It was . . . Everything!

She was already daydreaming of a place to live in London, something cheerful and tiny, in a respectable area . . . just the way she and her grandmother had always planned she would live when she received her inheritance. By the end of the coming year, she would have enough money to leave this silken prison to which she had been banished.

Her dreams at night were not so comforting. In the defenselessness of sleep, Nicki was there, exactly as he had been in the maze. With a booted foot propped on the bench beside her, he gazed into the distance, a thin cheroot clamped between his teeth, smiling a little as he listened to her outrageous request that he ruin her. He teased her in those dreams about expecting to be paid. And then he kissed her, and she would wake up with her heart racing and the touch of his mouth lingering on hers.

But in the morning, with sunlight streaming in the windows, the future was hers again and the past . . . She left the past in her bedchamber on the pillows. Now more than ever, her refuge was her writing.

Downstairs in the salon, Larkin, the butler, was already placing a breakfast tray containing a pot of chocolate and buttered toast on a table beside her desk. "Thank you, Larkin," she said with a smile as she slid into her chair.

It was late afternoon, and Julianna was completely engrossed in her manuscript when Larkin interrupted her, his voice taut. "My lady?"

Julianna held up her pen in a gesture that asked him to wait until she finished what she needed to write down. "But—"

Julianna shook her head very firmly, telling him to wait. Nothing of urgency ever occurred here, and she knew it. No unexpected callers arrived for cozy chats in this remote countryside, no household matter arose that couldn't wait. The small estate ran like a well-oiled machine, according to its owner's demands, and the staff only consulted her out of courtesy. She was merely a houseguest, though she sometimes had the feeling the servants sympathized with her plight, particularly the butler. Satisfied, Julianna put her pen aside and turned around. "I'm sorry, Larkin," she said, noting that he looked ready to burst from the strain of waiting for her attention, "but if I don't write down the thought while I have it, I often forget it. What did you wish to say?"

"His lordship has just arrived, my lady! He wishes to see you at once in his study." Shock and impossible hope had already sent Julianna to her feet before Larkin added, "And he has brought his valet." Unfamiliar with the travelling habits of the wealthy, Julianna looked at him in confusion. "That means," Larkin confided happily, "he will be staying overnight."

Standing at the window of the study, Nicki stared impatiently at the same view of the winter landscape that used to seem so pleasing from here, while he waited for the scheming little slut he had been forced to wed to answer his summons. The night of the masquerade was no longer fresh in his mind, but his wedding day was. It had begun with a breakfast tray delivered personally by Valerie, along with several pointed and sarcastic references to his having been the only "fish" in London who'd been stupid enough take the bait provided by Julianna and land in her mother's net. Before he ejected her from his bedchamber, she had done a good job of adding to his doubts about Julianna's innocence in the whole thing, and *still* he had refused to believe that Julianna had intended to entrap him.

He had clung to the comforting delusion that it had been an accident of timing and circumstances.

With a streak of naïveté and self-delusion he didn't know he possessed, he had actually managed to concentrate only on how adorable she'd been, and how perfectly she'd fit in his arms. He had even gone so far as to convince himself that she would suit him perfectly as a wife, and he had clung to that conviction while he waited for her at the chapel. If he hadn't been so infuriated with his nauseating future mother-in-law, he'd have chuckled at the way Julianna looked when she alighted from the coach.

His little bride had been positively gray from the effects of the night before, but not so ill she couldn't chat about furs with her mother, not so ill that they couldn't stand in the back of the chapel and gloat about snaring themselves a rich husband. He had heard it all while he waited outside.

She would try some sort of play while he was here, Nicki knew. She was not only clever, she was intelligent—intelligent enough to know she could never convince him of her innocence. Based on that, he rather expected a confession, a claim that she had been coerced by her mother.

He turned away at the sound of the door opening, fully expecting to see her looking only slightly better than the last time he had seen her, and every bit as forlorn, perhaps more contrite. In that, he instantly realized, he was wrong.

"I understand you want to talk with me?" she said with remarkable poise.

He nodded curtly toward the chair in front of his desk, a silent command to sit down.

The brief flare of hope that had ignited in Julianna a minute ago when she learned he was here had already died the instant he turned and looked at her in that insolent, appraising fashion. He hadn't softened, she realized with a sinking heart.

"I'll come directly to the point," he said without preamble as he sat down behind his desk. "The physicians tell us my mother's heart is weakening and that she is dying." His face and voice were carefully blank, Julianna noted, completely devoid of all emotion, so much so that she instantly concluded the feelings he did have were extremely painful. "She will not see another Christmas."

"I'm very sorry to hear that," Julianna said softly.

Instead of replying he stared at her as if he thought she were the most repugnant form of human life he'd ever beheld. Unable to resist the need to try to convince him she was at least capable of compassion, Julianna said, "I was closer to my grandmother than anyone in the world, and when she died, I was desolate. I still confide things to her and think of her. I—I even write her letters, though I know it's odd . . ."

He interrupted her as if she hadn't spoken, "My father also informed me that she is deeply troubled by the state of our so-called marriage. Because of all that, it is my father's wish and my decision that her last

Christmas is going to be a happy one. And you are going to help insure that it is, Julianna."

Julianna swallowed and nodded. Driven by the same desperate eagerness she'd felt the day she encountered him in the park to say or do something to please him, she added softly, "I'll do whatever I can."

Instead of being pleased or even satisfied with her, he looked completely revolted. "You won't need to exert yourself in the least. It will be very easy for you. All you need do is pretend you're at another masquerade. When my parents arrive tomorrow, you are going to 'masquerade' as my tender and devoted wife. I," he finished icily, "have the more difficult task. I have to pretend I can stomach being in the same house with you!"

He stood up. "My valet and I will remain here until my parents leave in a sennight. Unless we are in their presence, I expect you to stay out of my sight."

He got up and walked out, his strides long and swift, as if he couldn't stand to stay in the same room with her another moment.

11

WITH THE EASE OF LONG PRACTICE, NICKI STOOD AT THE mirror, tying a series of intricate knots in his neck-cloth, bracing himself to go downstairs. He had expected to dislike the time he spent here with Julianna, he had not expected it to be a week straight out of hell.

Thankfully, the ordeal was almost over; all he had to endure was the opening of Christmas presents tonight. Tomorrow his parents were leaving and he intended to be no more than a quarter of an hour behind them.

At least he had the satisfaction of knowing he had made his mother happy. There was no mistaking the fact that her eyes lit up whenever she saw evidence of affection between himself and Julianna, which had left him no choice except to make certain they gave her plenty of evidence.

To give Julianna credit, she cooperated. She looked at him with soft eyes, smiled back at him, laughed at his jokes, and flirted openly with him. She took his arm when they went in to supper, and walked close to his side; she sat at the foot of the table, glowing with candlelight and wit. She dressed as if pleasing her husband were her first concern, and she could fill out a gown as well as any woman he'd ever known.

She graced his table as well as any properly trained socialite could have done, but more naturally, and with more wit. Christ, she was witty! The dining room rang with laughter when she was present. She was also a wonderful conversationalist, attentive and willing to contribute. She talked of her writing when asked, and even of her grandmother, who'd evidently been closer to her than her mother.

If he didn't know what a fraud she was, if he didn't despise her, Nicki would have been incredibly proud of her. There were times—too many times—that he forgot what she really was. Times when all he could remember was the enchantment of her smile, the kindness she showed his parents, and the way she made him laugh. Twice, he had actually walked past her and started to bend down and press a kiss on her temple because it seemed so natural and so right.

All that, of course, owed itself to the unnatural situation he was in right now, with his mother bringing up names for grandchildren that were never going to exist. The Ton's efficient gossip mill had provided her with most of the information that led up to his marriage to Julianna, but despite that, his mother had insisted on drawing her own conclusions. She liked Julianna tremendously, and she made it abundantly clear. She'd actually brought little paintings of Nicki when he was young to show her. She knew she had little time left to spend with her new daughter-in-law and she was evidently determined to make the most of every moment, because she wanted Julianna there— and, of course, Nicki—with her whenever she was downstairs, which seemed to be nearly all the time.

Last night, Julianna had been sitting with her hip on the arm of his chair, her trim derrierre practically on his arm. His mother was describing some childhood antic of Nicki's and the whole family was laughing. Julianna laughed so hard she slid sideways into his lap, which made her blush gorgeously. She got up quickly enough, but Nicki's traitorous body had been reacting to the temptation of her before that, and there was little chance she hadn't noticed his erection when she squirmed off his lap.

He hated himself for his body's reaction to her. If he'd have been able to keep his hands off her in the first place, he wouldn't be in this untenable situation. Finished with the neckcloth, Nicki turned as his valet held up his wine-colored velvet evening jacket. He shrugged into the sleeves, bracing himself for the last—and hopefully easiest—of the nightly ordeals as a "family."

It hit him then, that there would never be another family Christmas, not for him, and he stiffened his shoulders against the hurt of that knowledge.

At least by putting on this act with Julianna, he had made his mother feel reassured. She completely believed that he was happily married, sleeping with his wife, and diligently attempting to get heirs.

By this time tomorrow, he would be on his way to his house in Devon.

"Nicki will be on his way somewhere else as soon as our coach is clear of the drive," Nicki's mother told his father, as they dressed to go downstairs for supper.

In answer he pressed a kiss atop her head as he fastened a diamond necklace around her throat. "You cannot do more than you have, my dear. Don't vex yourself, it isn't good for your heart."

"It isn't good for my heart to know that, after years of associations with an endless string of unsuitable females, Nicki has managed to marry a female who is perfect for him, and for me, I might add—and he won't share a bed with her!"

"Please," he teased, sounding scandalized, "do not tell me you've stooped to asking the servants."

"I don't have to ask," she said sadly. "I have eyes. If he were sleeping with Julianna, she would not be watching him with that look of helpless longing in her eyes. That young woman is in love with him."

"You cannot make Nicholas feel something for her."

"Oh, he feels something alright. When he forgets he hates her, he is thoroughly delighted with her, you can see that. She's beautiful and enchanting," she added as she slowly stood up, "and I would make you a wager that he found her to be all those things, and more, the night of that dreadful masquerade."

"Perhaps," he said noncommittally.

"You know he had to have done! Nicholas may have a long history of defying propriety in his personal life, but there has never been a breath of scandal that involves anyone else. He would never have taken Julianna to his bedchamber when he was a guest in someone's house unless he were thoroughly besotted with her."

Since he couldn't argue that logic, her husband smiled reassuringly. "Perhaps everything will work out, then."

His wife's shoulders sagged. "I've thought of saying something to Julianna to encourage her efforts, but if she knew I was aware of her situation, she'd be mortified." She placed a hand upon his arm. "It would take a miracle to bring them together."

12

ALONE IN HER BEDCHAMBER, JULIANNA STOOD AT HER dressing table, the box of letters she'd written to her grandmother in her shaking hands, the Christmas presents she'd received that night on the bed. Nicki intended to leave tomorrow, he'd told her that the day he arrived, and the butler had inadvertently confirmed it yesterday.

Nicki and his parents had been very generous to her, though Nicki's gifts were completely impersonal and only for appearances. He had given his parents their presents as if they came from Julianna as well, but it wasn't the same. And when the moment came for Nicki to open his gifts, there had been nothing there from Julianna—a fact which he'd explained away by saying she wanted to give it to him later. He'd even managed to imply with a smile that she wanted to be private with him when she gave it to him.

But the truth was, Julianna had given no gifts to any of them, because she had nothing to give . . . nothing except the contents of the box she was holding. She had that to give to Nicki. In the last week, she'd heard him called "Nicki" so much that she'd even started to think of him in that way. She'd also done everything she could think of to make him notice her, to make him see her in a different light. She'd flirted outrageously, spent ages on her hair, and deliberated for an hour over what she ought to wear. And there had been a few times, when she thought she caught him watching her . . . times when he looked at her in the same way he'd done when he took her to his bedchamber that long ago night . . . as if he wanted to kiss her.

She was in love with him, she'd learned that during this wonderful, agonizing week with him. She'd learned other things, too, that made it seem essential to make one more attempt to heal the breach between them. First and foremost, according to Nicki's mother, Nicki loved children and doted on his nieces. He wanted children, she said, while Nicki's mother was hoping specifically for a grandson to carry on the family name. As things stood now, all that was impossible. Because of Julianna. She had caused this nightmare, and if there was any way to repair the damage she would do it. The scandal of a divorce would taint the whole family, not merely Julianna. Besides, there had only been a handful granted in the last fifty years anyway, so they were married for life.

An *empty childless* life, unless she did something, and there was only one thing left that she hadn't already done. She had not shown him the letters. They were the only "evidence" she could offer Nicki that she hadn't planned their meeting at the masquerade, nor schemed to trap him into marriage.

The problem was that she could not let him see the evidence without simultaneously letting him see all of herself . . . Everything she had been and wasn't and wanted to be. It was all in there, and once he read it, she would be more nakedly vulnerable than she had ever been in her life. It was still fairly early, and she could hear Nicki moving about. Uttering a fervent prayer that this would work, Julianna walked over to the adjoining door that connected both suites and knocked.

Nicki got up and opened the door, took one look at what she was wearing and nearly slammed it shut in self-defense. Clad in a cherry velvet dressing robe with a deep oval neck and her hair tumbling about her shoulders like molten gold, Julianna Skeffington DuVille was almost irresistible. "What is it?" he snapped, backing up.

"I—I have something to give you," she said, moving toward him in a halo of shimmering hair, alluring skin, and rich velvet. "Here, take it."

Nicki glanced at her and then at it. "What is it?"

"Take it, please. Just take it."

"Why in hell should I?"

"Because it's—it's a present—a Christmas present from me to you."

"I don't want anything from you, Julianna."

"But you do want children!" she said, looking almost as stunned by that announcement as he felt.

"I don't need you in order to sire children," he said contemptuously.

She paled at that, but persevered. "Any others wouldn't be legitimate."

"I can legitimize them later. Now get out of here!"

"Damn you," Julianna choked out, tossing the box that contained her heart and soul onto the table in front of the sofa. "I did not set out to trap you at the masquerade. When I asked you to ruin me, I thought you were someone else!"

A slow, sarcastic smile crossed his saturnine face. "Really," he drawled in a scathing voice, "who did you think I was."

"God!" Julianna burst out tearily, so miserable and so insane about him that she almost stamped her foot.

"I thought you were God! The proof is in that box, in the letters I wrote to my grandmother. My mother had them sent to me here."

She whirled on her heel and fled. Ignoring the box, Nicki fixed himself a drink, carried it over to the sofa, and picked up the book he'd left lying there when he answered her knock. He opened it to the first page, then glanced at the box of letters. Out of sheer curiosity to see what ploy his clever and imaginative young wife had concocted this time, he decided to read one of the letters instead.

The one on top was dated last spring, and he presumed he was supposed to start there, though he'd never set eyes on Julianna Skeffington as long ago as that.

Dear Grandmother,
   I met someone in the park today and made such a cake of myself, I can hardly bear to think of it. There's always so much gossip about gentlemen in London—about how handsome one of them is supposed to be, and it's always such a disappointment when you see them. And then I saw Nicholas DuVille . . . He was beautiful, Grandmama . . . so beautiful. Hard, too, and cold, at least on the surface, but I think he laughed at what I said when I walked away. If he did, then he can't be hard at all, merely cautious . . .

Two hours later a log fell from the grate and crashed in an explosion of orange sparks as Nicki laid the last letter aside, then he picked up the one that he had already read twice, and he read the same lines that had filled him with self-loathing.

   I know how ashamed you are of me, Grandmother. I only meant to dance those three dances

158

with him, so that Sir Francis would withdraw his offer . . . I knew I shouldn't let him kiss me, I knew it, but if you'd ever been kissed by Nicholas DuVille, you'd understand. If you'd ever seen his smile or heard him laugh, you'd understand. How I yearn to see his smile and hear his laughter again. I long to make things right somehow. I yearn and I yearn and I yearn. And then I cry . . .

With her hip perched on the window seat, Julianna stared into the frosty night, her arms wrapped around her midriff as if she could keep out the chill that spread deeper and deeper as each moment passed and he didn't appear. Lifting her finger to the cold pane, she drew a circle, and another inside that one. As she began the third one, an image moved slowly into the center of it—a man in shirtsleeves, his hands shoved into his trouser pockets, coming toward her, and Julianna's heart began to pound in deep, painful beats.

He stopped close behind her and Julianna waited, searching his face in the window because she was afraid of what she'd see—or not see—if she turned and saw it clearly.

"Julianna." His deep voice was rough with emotion.

Julianna drew a shaking breath and slowly turned her head, watching a somber smile twist his lips as his gaze met hers and held it.

"When you were thinking I was God, and then the devil, would you like to know what I was thinking about you?"

Julianna swallowed over a knot of unbearable tension and nodded.

"I thought you were an angel."

Unable to move or breathe, she waited for him to indicate how he felt about her *now*.

Nicki told her. Holding her gaze, he said solemnly, "I yearn, too, Julianna."

Julianna stood up, took one step forward, and found herself crushed against him, his arms like iron bands around her. His mouth seized hers with gentle violence, his hands shifting over her back and sides in a possessive caress, pressing her ever tighter to his chest and hips and legs. Slowly, tantalizingly, he coaxed her lips to part, and when they did, he deepened the kiss. He kissed her until Julianna was breathless and leaning into him, fitting her body to his rigid length, her arms wrapped around his neck to hold him closer. When he finally broke the contact, he kissed her cheek and the corner of her eye and her temple, then he laid his jaw against her hair. "I yearn," he whispered tenderly. "I yearn."

Against her cheek, his chest felt warm and hard. Julianna waited for him to kiss her again. Shy and uncertain, she set about to make it happen again by sliding her own hands along his spine, and when that only made him hold her closer, she took a more direct means.

Tipping her head back, she gazed into his heavy-lidded, smoldering eyes and slowly slid her hands up his chest in an open invitation, watching the banked fires in his eyes begin to burn.

Nicki accepted the invitation by sliding his fingers into the hair at her nape, holding her mouth within his reach as he lowered his head and whispered gruffly, "God, how I yearn . . ."

Epilogue

THE SILK-UPHOLSTERED WALLS OF THE GRAND SALON AT Nicholas DuVille's stately country house near London were lined with priceless paintings by the great masters and furnished with treasures that had graced palaces. It was occupied at the moment by its owner and his four closest friends—Whitney and Clayton Westmoreland and Stephen and Sheridan Westmoreland. Also present on this momentous occasion were the owner's parents—Eugenia and Henri DuVille. The seventh guest was the Dowager Duchess of Claymore who, in addition to being a particular friend of the senior DuVilles, had the honor of being the mother of both Clayton and Stephen.

On this particular day, the guests themselves were seated in two distinct groups in the vast room. One group was comprised of the older parents, namely Eugenia, Henri, and the Dowager Duchess. The other group was comprised of Nicholas DuVille's four friends, who were also parents, but, of course, younger ones.

The seventh occupant of the room, Nicholas DuVille, was not seated with a group, because he was not a parent.

He was waiting to become one, momentarily.

161

His two male friends, who had endured and survived this nerve-wracking wait were rather enjoying watching him suffer. They were enjoying it, because Nicholas DuVille was famous among the members of the elite aristocracy for his incomparable ability to remain supremely unruffled, and even amused, in situations that made equally sophisticated gentlemen sweat and swear.

Today, however, that legendary self-control was not in evidence. He was standing at the window, his right hand absently rubbing the tense muscles at the back of his neck. He was standing there because he had already paced across the carpet often enough to make his own mother laughingly tell him that she was becoming exhausted just watching him do that.

Since her heart had been so weak a year ago that she could not walk up a few stairs, and since no one understood how that same heart was now strong enough to allow her to do that and much more, her restless son ceased his pacing at once. But not his worrying.

His two friends eyed his taut back with amusement and sympathy—more of the first and less of the latter, actually—because Nicholas DuVille had once been vastly admired by their own wives for his supreme nonchalance. "As I recall," Stephen Westmoreland lied with a wink, "Clay had a meeting with some business associates while Whitney was in childbed. Afterward, I think we went over to White's for a few hands of high-stakes whist."

Clayton Westmoreland looked over his shoulder at the silent-father-to-be. "Nick, would you like to run over to White's? We could be back by late tonight or early tomorrow."

"Don't be absurd," came the short reply.

"If I were you, I'd go," Stephen Westmoreland advised with a grin. "Once I spread the word that you paced like a caged lion and behaved like an ordinary lunatic, you won't be able to show your face in White's. The management will pull your membership. A pity, too, because you used to add a certain style to the place. Shall I use my influence and see if they'll let you sit in the window now and then, just for old times sake?"

"Stephen?"

"Yes, Nick?"

"Go to hell."

Clayton interceded, his tone deceptively solemn. "How about a chess game? It will help pass the time."

No reply.

"We could play for stakes that would keep your mind on the game. That Rembrandt over there against my son's most recent drawing of Whitney wearing a bucket on her head?"

Whitney and Sheridan, having failed to silence their husbands, got up in unison and walked toward the father-to-be. "Nicki," Whitney said, "it takes time."

"Not this long, it doesn't!" he said shortly. "Whitticomb said it would be over two hours ago."

"I know," Sheridan put in. "And if it's any consolation, Stephen was so upset when our son was born three months ago, that he called poor Dr. Whitticomb an 'incompetent antique' for not being able to do something to help me get it over with sooner."

That information caused Clayton to give his brother a look of amused censure. "Poor Whitticomb," he said. "I'm surprised at you, Stephen. He's an excellent physician, but you can't predict childbirth to the moment. He was with Whitney for nearly twelve hours."

"Really?" Stephen mocked. "And I suppose *you* thanked him very much for not rushing things along, and letting you wait downstairs hoping to God you still had a wife."

"I said something like that to him, yes," Clayton said, looking at the glass in his hand to hide his smile.

"You certainly did," Dr. Whitticomb agreed, startling everyone as he walked into the room, smiling and drying his hands on a white cloth. "But several hours before you said that, you threatened to throw me out on my—er—nether region and do the midwifing yourself."

He sent a reassuring smile at Nicki who was searching his face with narrowed eyes. "There are some very tired people upstairs who had a bit of a difficult time of it, but they would very much like to see you—" He stopped talking and grinned as the new father strode past him without a word and bounded up the stairs, then he turned toward the new grandparents who were waiting to discover whether the new arrival was boy or girl.

Somewhere far above and beyond the world where all this had taken place, Sarah Skeffington smiled down upon the proceedings, pleased with the way she had used the three small miracles each new arrival in her world was granted. There were limits and parameters on the use of these miracles, which were set by the true Maker of Miracles, but He had approved each one, including the restoration of Madame DuVille's health so that she could see her grandson.

Unaware of all that, Julianna sat propped upon her pillows, writing a letter to her grandmother.

* * *

My dearest Grandmother,

Five days ago, our son was born and we have named him John. Nicki is so proud of him, and he is utterly besotted with John's twin sister.

We have named her Sarah, after you.

You are always in my thoughts and in my heart . . .

JILL BARNETT

Daniel and the Angel

For Emma,
the only angel I've ever known

1

IT WAS THE PERFECT DAY FOR A MIRACLE.

The shimmering sky above Heaven was as gold as Gabriel's trumpet, and the distant sound of canticles filled the celestial air. Clouds, puffy and white as spring goosedown, created the holiest of firmaments —a place where no angel feared to tread.

Standing just outside the Pearly Gates was a novice angel named Lillian. She glanced left, then right, and, just for good measure, she cast a quick peek above her.

The coast was clear.

With a look of pure determination, she shoved up the sleeves on her flowing white robe, flexed her fingers, and did exactly what she had been forbidden to do: She tried to create a miracle.

The blast was loud enough to crack Heaven.

A backdraft of near hurricane force sent clouds skittering and bumping every which way. Lilli landed flat on her back. For a stunned moment, she lay atop a bouncing cloud with her arms and legs out like a snow angel.

Slowly the dark smoke from the blast settled around her. She blew a hank of silver-blond hair out of her face and blinked a few times, then found herself staring up into the Heavenly sky. She wiggled her toes first, then moved her arms and legs.

No . . . Nothing broken.

She sat up quickly. Her halo slipped down over her eyes. She shoved it back into place, then quickly tugged down her robe so her bare legs were again covered.

Like falling snowflakes, three pearlescent wing feathers floated in front of her. She looked over her shoulder and frowned down at her crumpled wings. She rolled her shoulders, shimmied slightly, then fluttered her wings to get the kinks out of her feathers.

She heard a muffled squeal and whipped around. "Florida? Is that you?"

There was another muffled grunt.

"Where are you?"

Nearby, two bare feet suddenly popped out from within a dark cloud.

"Oh. There you are."

The feet kicked in the air a few times, then disappeared in the motion of a somersault. Florie's dark head popped into view, and with Lilli's help she crawled out of the dark cloud, kneeling there for a second, her wings tilted downward while she coughed.

Lilli patted Florie's back gently until she stopped coughing and flung her head up. She stared at Lilli from dazed eyes. "What happened?"

"Nothing."

Florida turned back around and froze, staring horrified toward the west. "Oh, no! Something did happen." She pointed. "Look what you've done now!"

Lilli turned around and almost died—again.

"You've broken the Pearly Gates!"

Lilli covered her eyes with both hands and groaned, then slowly opened her fingers and peered through.

Her stomach dropped. To somewhere near her bare toes. Slowly she stood and walked toward her latest disaster, with Florie "tching" and trailing right behind her. She stopped, unable to think, to speak. She could only stare.

The entrance to the most hallowed place in the universe was in complete shambles. The gates hung at cockeyed angles from their twenty-four-karat gold hinges, which had been shattered in half, their golden pins bent like boomerangs.

The gates, which were originally in the shape of an angel's wings, were meant to meet in the center, where a diamond-encrusted lock held them in perfect symmetry.

"Where's the lock?" Florie whispered.

Lilli stared down at her feet, where diamond dust winked like bits of sand amid cracked pieces of precious pearl. Chewing on her lower lip, she pointed. "I think it's there." She had a sick feeling. "Somewhere."

Florie bent down and scraped together the dust.

"That's all that's left?" Lilli gave the small pillar of white dust an uneasy glance.

Florie nodded.

"It looks like Lot's wife."

"Saint Peter's going to be mad enough to spit lightning. And can you imagine"—she leaned closer and whispered—"*His* reaction? You'll get the worst punishment yet. It might even be worse than the time Saint Peter made you polish all those silver linings."

"Well," Lilli said in a rush, "He can't punish me if He doesn't know who did it." She spun around, gripping her long gown in her fists. "Come on! Follow me!" And she took off at a full run.

"Wait!"

"Hurry, Florie!" Lilli called out over her shoulder. "Or He'll think you did it!"

All the color drained from Florida's face. Quick as a wink, she fluttered after Lilli.

Wings shimmying, they leapt from one cloudbank to another, until Lilli found the perfect hiding spot deep inside a plump cumulus cloud, where glittering icicles framed a silver lining. She grabbed Florie's hand and dragged her inside.

Florie glanced around with an uncertain look. "Do you think Saint Peter will find us?"

"Of course not. This is the perfect place. I found it when I spent those months silver polishing. No one thinks there's a lining in this cloud."

"You're certain?"

"I hid in here the last time."

"Oh." Florie paused, then gave her a knowing look. "The time you were trying to fly and ran headfirst into Jacob's ladder."

Lilli hung her head. "If only all the archangels hadn't been standing on it at the time."

"Gabriel still has a tweak in his halo."

"I know. I've never been able to look him in the eye again." Lilli looked at her friend and after a quiet moment admitted, "Well, you know . . . that wasn't exactly the time I was talking about."

She stared at Lilli with suspicious eyes. "What else have you done?"

"You promise never to tell?"

Florie nodded solemnly.

"Cross your heart and hope to die?"

"I already am dead."

Lilli squirmed for a second, then said, "So am I, but if they ever find out about those ancient scrolls . . ."

"You lost the scrolls? The sacred scrolls?"

She nodded.

"How could you lose the scrolls?"

"Well, I didn't exactly lose them."

Florie just stared at her.

"I dropped them," Lilli admitted.

"Where?"

Lilli's face took on a sick look. "Deep in the Dead Sea."

Florie's mouth hung open.

"I just wanted to move them . . . out of the way. Then I tripped." After a long silent second, Lilli raised her chin, a hopeful look on her face. "But someone will find them . . . someday."

Florie gave her a skeptical glance, then shivered. She craned her neck around the long frosted icicles that framed the entrance and looked outside. "You're certain no one can see us in here?"

Lilli patted her friend's hand reassuringly. "Trust me. Look: See how our wings blend with the sparkling ice and silver? And our robes are white. My hair is so light blond that it won't show."

She looked at Florie's dark hair and frowned. "Well, in your case, just keep your head down." She shoved Florie's head under her wing.

A moment later Florie sneezed. She sniffed and rubbed her nose.

"Are you that cold?"

"No. It was just one of these." She held up one of Lilli's wing feathers.

Lilli's face fell a little.

Florie gave Lilli's wing feathers a reassuring stroke. Four more feathers fell out. "You can't help it if you're the only angel with a molting season."

Lilli rested a chin in her hand and her wings drooped.

"I believe that's why you have so much trouble flying."

Lilli gave a huge sigh. "But I can't blame molting feathers for the reason I can't sing one heavenly note, or play the trumpet, or perform a miracle."

There was a long lapse of telling quiet, until, in the distance, came the lovely lyrical sound of harp music. It grew louder and louder. And closer.

Florie gasped, and both angels ducked down.

"Glo . . . oh-oh-oh . . . oh-oh-oh . . . oh-oh-oh . . . *ria!* In ex-cel-seees dey-ohhh," sang a group of clarion-clear voices.

"Shhhh!" Lilli raised a finger to her lips as they huddled closer together. "It's a chorus of archangels."

There was a loud *clunk* and the angels stopped singing right in front of Lilli's hiding spot. Both novices were so still they barely breathed.

There was another *plunk,* then a sharp *boing!*

A tall regal archangel named Mesopotamia flinched and looked over her shoulder. "Are those your harp strings breaking, Israfel?"

Another shorter angel nodded, frowning at her golden harp. "Four of them have broken just this moment. Look."

The archangels stared at the harp. One by one, five more harp strings snapped.

There was a long pause, then Mesopotamia glanced around. "If I didn't know better, I'd think that Lillian was around here somewhere."

All the archangels scanned the surrounding clouds while Lilli and Florie huddled in frightened silence.

A second later there was a huge crash of lightning. Then another.

Everyone froze.

"My gates!" Saint Peter's thunderous roar echoed through Heaven. "My *gates!"*

There was an eternal moment of silence. Then . . . *"Lillian!"*

Lilli blanched.

"Lill-lee-UNN! Come here! Immediately!"

"Uh-oh," Florie whispered.

"Shhhhh. He can't possibly find us."

Saint Peter shouted her name again. And again. Louder.

An icicle broke, landing with a tinkle at Lilli's feet. For a brief moment there was utter stillness.

A burst of light flashed through Heaven, so strong, so brilliant it made the sun dim. The walls of Jericho didn't hit the ground as quickly as Lilli and Florie tumbled onto the cloud floor, their arms over their heads. All around them, icicles shattered like broken glass.

A moment later, the entire cloud dissipated.

In unison, Lilli and Florida both uncovered their heads and looked up, right into the censorious and knowing eyes of Saint Peter. Taller than the tree of life, he stood before them, glowering, his arms crossed and one gold-sandaled foot tapping impatiently.

Her lip between her teeth, Lilli raised one hand and waved her fingers. "Hello, sir."

He was rigidly silent.

"You know," she said, sitting up quickly, "I was just thinking about you . . ."

His eyes narrowed.

"In fact, I had just said to Florie, 'Florie?' I said, 'I'll bet Saint Peter is looking for us, and he'll *never* find us.' Didn't I?" She jabbed Florie with an elbow, and wide-eyed Florie nodded her head like a woodpecker.

She raised her eyes to meet his. "How did you find us?"

Saint Peter held up a handful of her molting feathers and let them spill from his hand. He watched her from eyes too intelligent for comfort. "Someone has destroyed the gates to Heaven."

"You mean while we were in here, the Pearly Gates—your Pearly Gates, those precious Pearly Gates—were actually broken? How in the name of Heaven could that have happened? Stray lightning? Celestial phenomenon? The Big Bang theory?"

Saint Peter reached out and plucked something from her tangle of blond hair. He held it out in front of her.

It was a piece of pearl. She winced.

Saint Peter clasped his hands behind his back and began to pace. "You have been forbidden to attempt any more miracles." He turned quickly and pinned her with a dark and knowing stare. "I assume that is what you were doing."

She nodded.

He paced again. "I thought as much. Angels are supposed to protect, guard, and educate the human race." He paused in front of her. "Not . . . wipe it out of existence."

Lilli stared at her toes and whispered, "I didn't try to make it rain again. Not after all that lightning . . ." She shuddered. ". . . And the fire in Rome." She slowly raised her face and looked him in the eyes. "I would never do that again."

He was silent for so long she almost couldn't bear it. She needed him to believe her. He had to believe her. She meant no harm. She never meant to do any harm. She stared at her bare toes again.

After eternal minutes he took a deep breath.

She waited to hear her punishment.

"I'm afraid there is nothing I can do for you this time."

Lilli's head shot up. "Nothing?"

"Nothing," he said.

Florie gasped, "No!"

All the archangels began to whisper and mutter. Lilli stood there, stunned, unable to move, unable to speak.

"Please sir," Florie begged. "She didn't mean to do it. Please."

Saint Peter shook his head. "There's nothing I can do."

The light of Heaven dimmed and with it her naive and foolish sense of invincibility. The clouds grew suddenly dark and gray. Lilli looked at the surrounding darkness and knew that she had no hope. No chance. She had nothing but an empty feeling in her heart and the shameful sting of tears in her eyes.

Saint Peter stood up to his full height. "From this day forward . . ." He paused and looked at her. "Lillian is no longer welcome in Heaven."

Lilli slowly raised her head. Everything before her was a painful blur. She heard a *clank*.

Her halo disappeared.

There was a loud and shrill whistle.

Her wings were gone.

Saint Peter gave a direct look. "You will return to Earth."

She could hear Florie sobbing.

He raised his right hand and touched her head. "To a time and place where angels fall."

2

All God's angels come to us disguised.

—James Russell Lowell

New York City
December 1886

ALL HE HEARD WAS THE SCREAM.

"She ran right in front of the carriage, Mr. Stewart. I swear it."

D.L. Stewart stared at the crumpled woman lying so still in the middle of Madison Avenue. A second later he was kneeling on the icy street, feeling for a pulse.

"One minute the street was empty, sir, then suddenly she was just, just there. I—I—"

"She's not dead, Benny." D.L. scooped the woman into his arms. "I'll carry her to the house. Take the carriage and get a doctor. Quickly." He turned and crossed to the wide sidewalk, where streetlights spilled yellow gaslight onto the ice and mucky snow.

He heard his carriage rattle past him, but it was a distant sound, as if the world had fallen away, leaving only himself and the woman in his arms. So foreign was the feeling that he looked down at her.

There were no answers in her features. Her skin was almost as pale as her blond hair, a sharp contrast to the dark blood that trickled from the corner of her mouth and from the red scratches on the side of her face.

Her scarlet hat hung over his arm, still tied beneath her chin with black velvet ribbons that were shredded on one side, the same side on which her dress and jacket were torn from skidding over the rough brick pavement.

Her breathing was labored, short and tight, but she made no sound, no moan of pain, nothing. The faint scent of lemon seemed to drift around her, and it struck him as odd, very odd for a woman to smell of lemons, to smell clean rather than cloying.

A moment later he was in front of the stately marble mansion that served as his home. He ran up the stairs and kicked hard on the front doors.

Nothing happened. He cursed, then awkwardly leaned down and pressed the door handle with an elbow. The massive door clicked open.

An instant later D.L. was inside and he called out, "Gage!"

The butler's name echoed up three open stories to the gallery above.

Gage came running into the foyer, then stopped at the staircase, gaping.

D.L. pinned him with a hard stare. "Gage!"

The man recovered. "Sir?"

"I pay you a bloody fortune to open doors." D.L. gave the library doors a pointed look.

"Yes, sir." Gage shot over to the doors, then paused. "Mr. Wallis is waiting in the library."

"Good. Perhaps," D.L. muttered as he looked down, "he'll know what the hell I should do about this."

Her head was killing her. Almost as badly as the time she had flown headfirst into Jacob's ladder. And one side of her face burned terribly.

Someone touched her shoulder, and pain shot up her neck. She heard an anguished moan. It sounded like her.

She could feel the presence of others—standing over her, around her—but she couldn't quite find the will to open her eyes. It seemed an effort to breathe.

"She's coming around," a man said in a gentle tone.

"Find out who she is." There was no gentleness in this second voice. It was the dark, strong voice of a man in command.

"God?" she whispered. "I know that voice. You are God."

Someone behind them laughed. Someone new. "She called that right. D.L. Stewart, the Money God." Someone cynical.

She felt the tension again and opened her eyes then, but she saw only darkly blurred images. She licked her lips, which felt dry and swollen, then whispered, "My face . . ."

"Yes, my dear?"

"It burns."

"I'm certain it does, but you'll be fine. Just a few scratches. I'm a doctor." A rough but gentle masculine hand touched hers. "Can you tell us who you are?"

"Lillian."

"That's good, Lillian." The kind man shifted away, then said, "It appears she has no serious injury. She knows who she is."

"Lillian who?" came the strong voice.

"Just Lillian. Lilli."

"Where are you from?"

"Heaven."

There was a bark of sharp laughter again, and the cynic said, "At least we know she's not from New York."

"Shut up, Karl."

"Only trying to add a little levity to a tense situation, D.L."

"I fell," she mumbled.

"No, my dear. You were hit by a carriage." The kind man gave her hand a squeeze of reassurance.

"No. No . . . you don't understand. I've fallen." She could feel the tears coming, feel the horror. The shame she carried. "I didn't mean any harm. I didn't."

"It wasn't your fault, my dear. Only an accident."

"No! I just wanted to be like everyone else. They all do it so easily. I'm so ashamed." She felt the tears spill from her eyes, drip over her temples and into her hair. "No more angels," she said, hearing her voice catch. "No wings. No halo. Such a beautiful halo. It's gone." Her voice was little more than a whisper. "My wings . . . everything." She began to sob.

"She's hysterical."

She could barely catch her breath between sobs. "All of it is gone. Everything wonderful. Gone. I've fallen . . ."

Someone else stood over her. She could feel him, could feel the tension. The air seemed to swell with his very presence.

"You will stop crying, Lillian. Now."

Her shoulders shook. She couldn't help it.

"Stop it."

She tried to stop and took a labored breath.

"Stop!"

"Mr. Stewart, shouting at her isn't going to help. I suggest we get her into a bed and I'll give her something to calm her down, then clean the scrapes on her face and shoulder. She needs sleep. Sleep is the best thing."

She felt two strong arms slide beneath her. She opened her eyes and saw a tall dark image bending over her. Only the image of him through her tears. A second later he lifted her into his arms and turned.

She gave a slight moan.

He stilled immediately.

She blinked, and her vision cleared. She looked into a face so harsh she lost her voice.

He was no god. In fact, he looked like the Devil himself.

His hair was short and slicked back from a broad stern forehead. Like his hair, his thick brows were black as the River Styx, and his skin was rough, his jaw covered with a dark shadow.

As a whole, his features were nothing but sharp angles and firm ridges—a hewn-from-granite look that was rare in Heaven, a place where beauty was light and soft and gossamer, not dark and hard and glittering.

But there was harsh beauty in this face. A dark beauty that seemed fathomless. He stared down at her from eyes blacker than onyx. And in those eyes she caught one brief flicker of a soul that was lost.

As if he too had gauged her measure in that one look, he turned with her in his arms and strode from the room, her weight seeming no more a burden to him than a feather.

With the doctor following behind, he carried her up a never-ending staircase. He looked down at her once, his expression stern and hard, so hard that she sensed he was hiding behind it. She cocked her head slightly, but he fixed his gaze ahead of them.

He took her to a room where the door opened quickly, efficiently, when they were but a few steps away. She caught a quick glimpse of a gray-haired servant, but then she was inside, and he laid her down on an elegantly draped bed.

She winced and instinctively gripped his hand for strength.

"Did I hurt you?" His voice was gruff.

"No."

He stared oddly at their joined hands.

She watched his eyes change, flicker with something indefinable, then she whispered, "But I think you will."

He stiffened and shifted away.

She released his hand.

He gave her a long unreadable look, then without a word he turned and left the room.

D.L. leaned a shoulder against the doorjamb, crossed his arms, and just watched her sleep. He didn't know why he felt compelled to do so, but he did.

Sleep had escaped him. That in itself was not unusual. Of late he slept little, his mind unable to rest. His work drove him, and he cared for little else. Did little else. He suspected he worked now because it was something that kept him busy.

Weak as it was, there was still a thrill he could eke from closing a deal. The profit meant little anymore, except that money gave one power. He had enough of a fortune to be omnipotent.

But he took this small moment for himself—for some reason that probably bordered on sheer nonsense. He shoved away from the door and crossed the room, standing at the bedside.

Moonlight spilled through the windows by the bedstead and shone upon the pillow where her silver-blond hair fanned outward like an angel's halo. He wondered how long it had been since he'd noticed moonlight, and if he had ever paid a bit of attention to a woman's hair.

He reached out and touched a strand of it, ran a finger along it, slowly. He didn't know what he had expected to feel: coolness from the icy color or smoothness from the silk of it. What he felt was the insane urge to bury his hands in it.

"Why are you looking at me like that?"

He hid his surprise. Something that was natural and instinctive. Just as feeling any emotion had, over time, become a foreign thing to him. It wasn't often that someone could surprise him. She had.

He looked directly into her green eyes, where frank curiosity stared back at him. "You are supposed to be asleep."

"I've never done what I was supposed to."

He leaned over a night table and picked up a glass still almost filled with a pinkish liquid. "You didn't drink the medicine."

She shook her head.

"I see." He set the glass down. "A rebel."

"More of a disaster, I think. That's why I'm in this fix."

He searched her face, trying to decide why she would admit something like that to him, a stranger. She didn't look like a fallen woman.

"Doing what is expected is so . . . I don't know." Her expression told him she had trouble finding the right word. Finally she gave a small sigh and looked up.

"Boring?"

"Yes! That's it exactly! It would have been extremely boring, for example, if I had slept through your visit." She sat up slowly. "Then we wouldn't be having this chat."

"You would have never known I was here."

"True. But you would have known."

He didn't know how to answer her, so he just watched her—this woman who would be bored by convention. He had been bored until he came into the room. Not that he cared to admit it.

"So, Mr. Stewart. What does the 'D.L.' stand for?"

She reached out and grabbed another pillow, then placed it behind her and settled back for what appeared to be a long chat.

"'Daniel Lincoln.'"

"A famous lawyer and a president."

"I hate to burst your bubble, but I was named after my two grandfathers."

"Oh. That's not as romantic, is it?"

"I suppose 'Romeo' would be more to your liking."

"No," she said very quietly, looking up at him from the most sincere face he'd ever seen. "I didn't mean to make you feel badly about your name. 'Daniel' is a perfectly wonderful name."

She thought she had hurt his feelings? How strange, to worry about hurting someone over something as silly as a name. He made no comment, but she didn't seem to notice. Not more than an instant later, she lifted the covers in one hand and peered under them.

"What am I wearing?"

He could see her wiggle her toes beneath the covers. "A shirt."

"Yours?"

"Yes."

"Silk?"

"Yes."

She dropped the covers and folded her hands on top of them, then looked up at him with a small smile. "Nice."

"I need to contact your family."

"That would be impossible."

"Nothing is impossible."

"Contacting my family would be nothing short of a miracle."

He crossed his arms and watched her. "Not for me."

"Oh. I see you haven't a problem with confidence."

"No, I haven't."

She gave a huge sigh and stared at her folded hands. "I don't have much confidence."

"It has been my experience that having enough money can make one confident about any number of things."

She looked up. "What an interesting philosophy. So . . . you think you have to be rich to be confident?"

"It helps. Money can buy anything."

"I don't think so." She shook her head.

"Name something money can't buy."

"People."

He laughed then, at her naiveté. "I buy people every day."

"Do you really? Hmmm." She frowned, then mumbled, "I had thought slavery was illegal."

He wasn't certain if she'd just cut him purposely or not. Before he could comment, she continued: "Okay then. How about love? Money cannot buy love."

"For a small part of my fortune there are at least a hundred women, perhaps a thousand, who would be happy to *love* me."

The sparkle left her eyes and she gave him a long pensive look that made him feel uneasy. "Memories," she said so quietly that he wasn't certain he'd heard her right. "You can't buy memories. You have to make them."

"It takes money to do things that make memories."

"No it doesn't," she said, with a certainty that jarred him.

"Nothing in this world comes free."

"I assume from this conversation that money is important to you."

"At one time it was." He shrugged. "Now it's a means to an end."

"I see. So what do you do with all this money? Set up charities? Help the sick and poor?"

"No."

"Did you ever hear the expression 'You can't take it with you'?"

"Of course."

"Where I come from, wealth doesn't matter."

"Then it's probably a place I'd rather not visit."

She looked away and muttered, "I don't think that will be a problem." After an awkward silence, she began to pluck at the coverlet.

"Tell me where to find your family."

"I can't." She stilled. "You can't find a family that doesn't exist. I have no family."

He didn't know why he tensed inside, but he did. Something in her manner, something in the way she couldn't look him in the eye, said she was either lying or ashamed. He changed tack. "Where do you live?"

She was quiet. Too quiet. She was going to lie to him, and that angered him more than he cared to admit. He didn't want her to be like every other woman he'd known. He wanted her to be different. "Are you going to answer me?"

"I don't know."

He leaned over her, placing one hand on either side of her hips, and brought his face closer to hers. He looked right at her, just a few inches away. It was intimidation at its best. "I insist."

"No, you don't understand." She returned his look with one so innocent he almost fell for it. "I *am* answering you. I don't know where I live."

He straightened. "How convenient."

She stiffened as if he had slapped her. "You don't believe me?"

"No. I don't believe you."

"I'm sorry."

"I don't want apologies, just answers."

"I wasn't apologizing. I'm sorry for you."

"Don't be." He turned and walked to the door and opened it. "I have everything I could ever want. I don't need anything."

"Except more money," she muttered.

He froze, then turned very slowly, scowling. "Tomorrow, Lillian, you will tell me the truth." Just before he closed the door, he added, "And drink the damn medicine."

She didn't drink the medicine. A short time later, she tiptoed down the dark staircase, her leather half boots in one hand, the other using the thick, smoothly polished banister to steady herself. She was still a little light-headed from the accident.

But not light-headed enough to stay here even another few hours.

She reached bottom and slowly made her way across the dark foyer until she felt the wood of the front doors. Leaning against them, she pulled on her boots, then, as quietly as possible, opened the door, blanching when the handle made a loud click in the eerie stillness of the mansion.

She stood frozen and listened. She heard nothing, then carefully opened the door a little wider and stepped outside.

It was freezing, colder than the highest and stormiest cloud in Heaven. She shivered and stared at the bleak darkness for an uncertain moment, then pulled her short woolen jacket even tighter around her. She took a deep breath and watched it turn to frosty mist in the night air.

Lilli closed her eyes and said a quick prayer, then ran down the front steps. In less time than it took a tear to fall, she had disappeared into the winter darkness of New York City.

3

Angels keep their ancient places,
turn but a stone, and start a wing!
'Tis ye, 'tis your estranged faces,
that miss the many splendoured thing.

—Francis Thompson

Wʜᴀᴛ ᴛʜᴇ ʜᴇʟʟ ᴅᴏ ʏᴏᴜ ᴍᴇᴀɴ, sʜᴇ's ɢᴏɴᴇ?" D.L. stood up and threw his napkin down on the breakfast table. He glared at his butler.

Gage stood just inside the double doors of the morning room, awkwardly holding the white silk shirt—the one she'd been wearing. "She's left, sir."

"Damn." He should have poured the medicine down her throat. He looked at the shirt. Or hid her clothes. He glanced up. "Find out if anyone saw or heard her leave. Check the entire block. Let me know immediately if you find out anything."

His butler turned to leave.

"Gage."

The man turned back. "Sir?"

"I'll take that." He nodded at the shirt. Gage looked at the shirt oddly, then handed it to him and left.

His attorney, Karl Wallis, removed his glasses,

189

polished them with a handkerchief, then put them back on and watched him curiously.

D.L. didn't care. He stared at the shirt. It carried the subtle tang of lemons.

"You need to find her, D.L."

He tossed the shirt onto a nearby chair and walked across the room, where he stood at the long windows, his hands in his pockets. He watched the snow falling lightly on the street corner below. "I know."

"About the release? Yes, well, that's good."

D.L. turned. "What release?"

"You need to have her sign a document of release." Karl began shuffling through some papers on the table. "I have it here somewhere. I was going to give it to you after we finished with the details of these contracts. Here it is." He waved a paper at him. "It releases you from any liability for the carriage accident."

"I am liable."

"Good God, man, never say those words to your attorney. You pay me a fortune to make certain that no matter what, you are never liable for anything."

He turned back around. "Odd," he said quietly. "I hadn't thought she was one to run away."

"What?"

He shook his head. "Nothing. Just an observation."

Outside, snow drifted down on the few pedestrians who hurried along the slushy sidewalk. His mind flashed with the image of a woman with pale skin and even paler blond hair. A fragile, angelic-looking woman who was crying because she had lost everything. A woman huddled on the street with snowflakes sticking to her shivering form, as if each one were a small increment of the burden she carried.

A woman with no one. Some old, time-buried part of him seemed to understand the devastation of that kind of loneliness.

He suddenly felt his exhaustion. He hadn't slept at all after he'd left her. Every time he'd closed his eyes he saw her expressive face looking up at him with disappointment—a look that said he had ripped the stars from her eyes.

"D.L. Have you heard anything I've said?"

"You said I need to find her."

"Yes. Get this release signed, then she can go wherever she wants. And you won't find yourself in the middle of some legal action a year or so from now. We need her signature for you to be free and clear."

"Fine," he said in a clipped tone.

"My advice would be to pay whatever it takes to get it. She seemed a bit of a lost lamb, so I doubt it would cost you very much."

D.L. turned back around and strode over to the table. "Let's get these finished." He sat down but found that he listened to the terms of the deal with only half an ear. He couldn't rid himself of the niggling feeling that this woman might cost him much more than either he or Karl could imagine.

She had spent most of the day on a park bench, watching the world go by. Somehow, with all that had happened, she'd forgotten it was the Christmas season. But once the sun came up, New York City had awakened.

Horsecars decorated with Christmas greenery filled the streets and storefronts opened, festooned with lush ropes of cedar and laurel. Cheery red ribbons were the color of the season, and they trimmed the greens and windows of businesses and residences alike.

Lilli had taken refuge inside a large department store, because it was warm and sheltered from the light snow. But once inside, she had been caught up in the spirit of the season—the smiling faces in the crowds, greetings of "Happy holiday to you" and "Merry Christmas."

There were magic lanterns and fancy dolls, new-fangled electric trains that *chugged* and *chooed* and circled the store Christmas tree. It was festive and joyous and alive.

By the time the storm had stopped, she was smiling when she wandered to the park. Snow-covered trees and plants looked as if they'd been sprinkled with sugar. Ponds that had iced over took on the quality of frosted mirrors, and the fountains and birdbaths stood like stiff snow soldiers.

Before long the air sang sweetly with laughter and the jingle of brass and silver sleigh bells. She smiled, rather sadly, at the sound of the bells. *Every time a bell rings, an angel gets its wings.*

For most of the afternoon the sleighs dashed by, their runners whizzing on the fresh white snow and knocking down KEEP OFF THE GRASS signs. She laughed at snowball fights and gave a misty little smile at a group of children, skates in hand, running for the skating pond with dire threats that the last one there would be a rotten egg.

But by evening, she was alone and the last one to leave the park. She felt like a rotten egg.

She was little more than an aimless wanderer in a foreign land. She had found a small bit of joy in the laughter of others, which had gotten her through a very long day, but by the time the sun had set, she had no idea what she was going to do. She huddled against the cold.

It was difficult to believe that one could be cold with all the clothes she wore. She took a deep breath, something that was nigh on impossible laced into this corset contraption. Her mortal underwear was the closest thing to Purgatory she'd ever come across.

The air was colder than the frostiest cloud, and she

could feel the chill right through to her bones. She pulled her jacket even tighter and looked around.

The streets were edged with snow, and ice covered the curbside gutters. A delivery wagon rattled past, and a hansome cab was parked just a few steps away. Near the corner, a small boy hawked newspapers to the passersby. Everyone looked as if they had a place to go and were hustling to get there now that night had fallen.

She stopped and just stood there for a moment, feeling so lost and alone, aware that she had no place to go. She stepped back and looked upward, instinctively turning toward the Heaven that had been her home.

There were buildings all around her, so tall—as tall as seven stories, and she could barely see the stars twinkling in the night sky. She wanted to see those stars, wanted to reach out and touch them, to wish on them and hope that they would show her the way back to Heaven.

Finally she looked down, staring bleakly at the snow. The tears just fell until she had no more tears left. She wiped her eyes and cheeks, then took a deep breath.

Squaring her shoulders, she turned, then made her way toward a different area of the city, where immigrants, foreign and homeless as she was, were huddled on street corners or around small weak fires in alleys and on stoops.

She wondered how many of them were like her—fallen angels.

Cold, tired, and hungry, she finally stopped and leaned against a brick building where the scent of German sausages made her mouth water and her stomach growl. A group of families swarmed nearby, taking shelter under an awning over a side door in the alley.

The children, bundled in thin blankets and knit mufflers, watched her from frightened eyes and pale faces. A baby wailed. It had a hungry sound.

Hunched over a meager fire, a woman was cooking. She turned and looked up at Lilli. Something passed between them, something female. Something spiritual.

The woman reached over and poured steaming liquid into a dented tin can. She turned back to Lilli and held it out.

With tears in her eyes, Lilli shook her head. "Feed your children."

The immigrant woman frowned, then with a pride and determination that belied her circumstances, she walked up to Lilli and pressed the can into her hands. *"Fröhliche Weihnachten.* Merry Christmas."

Lilli thought she might cry, but she managed a weak smile and to choke out a "Thank you." The woman rushed back to her children and meal.

A few minutes later, huddled on a chilly stoop where damp snow drifted down and stuck to her clothes, Lilli sipped the sour German soup that was so warm and welcome she felt as if it had spilled from God's own table.

She gave a prayer of thanks. Watching the snow drift before her eyes, she sat there, a little lost, very cold, and so weary of heart, of mind, and fast getting weary of spirit.

Then she heard them. Bells. Church bells, ringing out like a chorus of archangels—clear and clean and calling to her.

There was no one near the church when she arrived. She walked up the steps, almost afraid to try the closed doors, afraid they'd be locked to her as Heaven was.

But the doors opened easily and she entered the

massive church, where candlelight, warmth, and peace welcomed her. She walked toward the altar, stopping a few feet away. She sat in the center of the second pew.

She closed her eyes, seeking some small part of what she'd had. Here, in God's house, she felt some distant tie to Heaven, so here she sat.

A minute or so later, her eyes grew unbearably heavy. She untied the ribbons on her bonnet and removed it, letting her hair fall free and loose. Then exhaustion and cold and hunger finally took their toll.

Lilli lay down and fell asleep.

"Pssst!"

She was warm and tired, so very tired.

"Pssst!"

A pesky fly, she thought. Still half asleep, she swatted at it.

"Lilli! Wake up!"

"Florie . . ." Lilli muttered, then snuggled deeper into her clothing.

"Lilli! Wake up!"

She opened her eyes, fully awake, then sat up quickly and shoved the hair from her eyes. "Florie? Is that you?" She reached out to hug her friend, but her arms held thin air. She blinked at Florie's image, then sagged back against the hard pew. "I forgot. I'm mortal now. I can't touch you."

The same emotion glistened in both their eyes.

"I can't hug you."

"I know."

"Florie." She looked down at her hands. "I'm so scared."

"Wait. Don't you see what's happening? I'm coming to you in a dream. You know, the angel coming to you in a dream thing? Lesson 103?"

"I remember. I never could get that right either."

"Wait! Give me a moment. Okay. Now watch." Florie took a deep breath, then fluttered her wings until she was hovering above Lilli. "Here goes . . . Behold! I bring you tidings of great joy!"

Lilli burst out laughing.

Florie stopped fluttering and lit onto the back of the front pew; her wings rippled for a second, then drooped as she dangled her legs over the edge and gave Lilli a small smile. "I suppose that's been overused, hasn't it?"

"I miss you."

"I miss you too." Florie sat up a little straighter, then smiled brightly. "But I do have good news! Well, I think it's good news," she said, chewing a nail.

"What?"

"Saint Peter has relented."

"I get to come back?"

"Well, not exactly. At least not right now. But he said that if you can perform a miracle—just one—here on Earth, then you can come back to Heaven."

"But I can't create a miracle in Heaven. How can I make one here?"

"I don't think that in your case, Lilli, it would make any difference where you were."

"I suppose that's true. Now I must think of a miracle," Lilli said thoughtfully.

"Actually, that's not necessary."

"Why?"

"Saint Peter's decision was based on a more specific sort of miracle."

Another chance. She had one last chance. Lilli gripped the edge of the pew and leaned forward. "Anything. I'll do anything, Florie, if it means I can go back."

"That's good."

"So. Tell me. What's the miracle?"

"It's a lesson. You have to teach a mortal to give from his heart."

She thought about that for a moment, then remembered the kindhearted German woman who'd given her the soup. There were people like her, many of them, in a place like New York City. She looked up at Florie and grinned. "I can do that."

Florie was suddenly quiet.

Lilli looked at her. "You look as if there's more to this specific miracle."

"There is."

Lilli waited. Florie looked uneasy.

"I'm not going to like it, am I?"

Florie shook her head.

"Why?"

"Saint Peter has picked the mortal."

"From your tone, I suspect it might be easier to convert the Devil than teach this person a lesson."

"You can do it, Lilli. I know you can."

"Who is my miracle?"

Florie stared at her bare toes. "The financier D.L. Stewart."

Lilli's mouth dropped open. "Mr. I-Buy-the-World-and-Money-Is-My-Life Stewart?"

Florie nodded.

She groaned and stared at the altar. "You were right. This is the worst punishment yet."

"He can't be that bad."

Lilli snorted.

"Besides, look at the reward. It's the only chance you'll have. I pleaded and begged for you. Please, Lilli, just try."

She looked up to Heaven, then took a deep breath and raised her chin a notch. "I'll try. But this is truly difficult. I was joking when I said converting the Devil

197

would be easier, but Florie," she said, sighing, "that's exactly what Saint Peter has asked me to do."

It took him a day and a half to find her.

He sat in his carriage, parked at the curb, and he watched her standing in front of the church doors. From her manner, she looked as if her burden had only increased, tenfold. Her shoulders weren't squared with determination, and in one gloved hand, her red hat dangled as if it were forgotten. She had the bewildered look of a bird that had fallen from its nest.

Then she saw him. Her face drained of color for the briefest of moments.

He walked up the steps toward her.

She swung her hat on her head and spent a long time tying the ribbons, looking everywhere but at him.

"Lillian." He tipped his hat.

"Mr. Stewart." She raised her chin and took a step.

One could have heard the rip a block away.

She froze, and her eyes grew wide as silver dollars. She looked over her shoulder.

He peered past her. Her dress was caught in the church doors. "Allow me." He opened the door and released her dress.

"Thank you." Nose purposely and humorously high, she descended the steps, her ripped hem dragging like a train behind her.

He watched her, biting back the sudden and foreign urge to smile. He moved to her side, his pace identical with hers.

She said nothing.

"Nice weather," he commented.

"If you like snow."

"I do."

"So do I."

He stopped at his carriage and opened the door.

She gave him a puzzled look.

"Get in."

"No, thank you."

"I wasn't asking."

"I could tell."

He took a deep breath, then gritted, "May I offer you a lift?"

"No. I wouldn't want to keep you. Time is money."

He said nothing but got inside and sat down, feeling suddenly disarmed. He pinned her with a stare meant to make her feel as uncomfortable as he did. To his surprise, something interesting passed between them: a challenge.

After a moment, she turned and sauntered away.

He tapped on the driver's box. "Follow alongside her, Benny."

The carriage moved right next to her, maintaining a slow pace that matched her stride perfectly.

She never made eye contact.

He slipped open the window and settled back against the carriage seat. "I've been looking for you."

"Why? No one for sale today?"

He wouldn't rise to that bait. "It's early yet."

"I would think that looking for me isn't very profitable."

"I have some spare time." He checked his gold watch. "It's ten A.M. The banks have been open for an hour. I've made nearly two thousand dollars in interest already today."

She tugged on her glove but never missed a step. "How nice for you."

"Do you want to know why I was looking for you?"

"No."

He watched her silently, tapping a finger against his thinned lips.

After a few more silent steps she stopped, plopped

her hands on her hips in frustration, and looked right
at him. "I don't understand you."

"Don't try."

She pulled her gaze away and stared down at her
tightly clasped hands. "I think I might have to try."

He rested an arm on the window opening. "I have a
proposition for you." He leaned a little closer. "Get in
and we'll talk."

She looked up at the sky, then sighed. "I don't think
I can do this."

"How do you know? You haven't heard my offer."

She shook her head. "I can't explain."

He paused to let the tension build. It was a tactic he
used often. Time ticked by.

She just stood there.

"I'll give you a hundred dollars to get in this
carriage right now."

Her eyes narrowed suddenly and sharply. She
squared her shoulders and began to walk away again.

"Well?" he called out.

"I don't think so."

He watched her pass an alley crowded with immigrants. She said something to a woman holding a
child, then reached into her pocket and handed the
woman a bent tin can. The two of them spoke briefly,
then Lilli turned around and went on her merry way.

He tapped on the carriage roof again. "Stay with
her, Benny." When his carriage was directly beside
her, he leaned back again and counted to five before
he said, "Two hundred."

"No, thank you."

"Five hundred."

She shook her head.

"A thousand."

She ran into a streetlight and stepped back quickly
—as if she hadn't done it.

He did smile. "Two . . . thousand."

She spun around.

He couldn't tell if she was stunned or horrified.

"You're serious?"

"Very serious."

"Two thousand dollars?"

"Yes."

She gave him a direct look. "Cash?"

"Yes."

"Now?"

"Yes."

She walked over to the carriage and held out her hand, palm up.

He opened the door and stepped onto the sidewalk, then peeled some money from a roll of bills and put them into her hand.

"Count it, please."

"What?"

"You need to count the bills into my hand. Just to make certain it's correct. You wouldn't want to make a mistake."

Irritated, he snatched the money from her and counted each bill.

"Thank you."

"Get inside." He held the door.

"Wait just a moment." She hurried past him.

"Now," he called out.

She waved him away, already halfway back to the alley, and stopped in front of a child, who looked up at her with eyes too big in a thin and pale face. She put a hundred-dollar bill in his small hand and closed his fingers around it. She then did the same with each person huddled in the alley. Finally she stood in front of the woman with the baby and handed her the rest of the bills. "Merry Christmas. *Fröhliche Weihnachten.*"

The immigrants gaped at the bills in their hands,

then looked at her as if she were God's own angel. He caught a whisper of a smile on her lips as she spun around and walked back to the carriage.

Standing in front of him, she raised her chin. "Okay, Mr. Stewart. I'm ready now."

He didn't know if he wanted to strangle her or congratulate her. He just stood there, surprised. Again. And he felt a strange sense of satisfaction. Silently, he helped her inside, climbed in, and closed the door.

They sat there measuring one another. Another kind of challenge. She appeared inordinately proud of herself. He could tell by her expression.

He waited a moment, letting her bask in her victory. Casually, he looked out the window, then said, "I would have paid more."

"Would you have?" she asked quietly.

"Yes."

"Interesting." She cocked her head and tugged on her glove. "I thought you needed a lesson on how to treat people." She leaned forward, propping an elbow on her knee and her chin on a fist. She looked right into his eyes. "I'll tell you a secret."

"What?"

"I would have come for nothing."

4

Be not forgetful to entertain strangers,
For thereby some have entertained angels unawares.

—Hebrews 13:2

*L*ILLI SAT IN A LARGE LEATHER WING CHAIR IN HIS STUDY and looked at the paintings, the rich mahogany and brass furnishings, the long windows that looked out over the street two stories below, and the snow that was falling again outside. She looked at everything. Except him.

"Lillian."

She turned.

He didn't look at her. He sat at his desk, his chair turned to the side and his gaze fixed elsewhere. He had all the appearances of a man who did indeed have the world at his feet. There was no denying that D.L. Stewart had power. His stance, his manner, his surroundings, even his voice exuded it.

He picked up a gray-marbled fountain pen and tapped one end on the desk blotter, then absently flipped the pen and tapped its other end. "You said something that caught my attention when you were here before."

She didn't say anything. But she did wonder what

she could have said that would be of interest to such a powerful man.

He continued: "You claim there are things money can't buy."

"There are."

"I don't agree."

She started to say something, but he raised his hand. "Let me finish. I don't agree, but I like challenges."

"I could tell," she whispered.

He gave her a stern look that said he wanted her quiet. She gave him what he wanted.

"I find what you said very intriguing."

"Oh? So what are you saying?"

"I'm giving you the opportunity to prove your point."

"I don't understand."

"You claim that you have no place to go."

She nodded. "It isn't a claim. It's the truth."

"If that's the case, then this is simple. I'm offering you a place to stay. You, in turn, will attempt to prove your theory correct." He swung his chair around and leaned an arm on his desk, pinning her with a dark stare that could intimidate Saint Peter himself. "Prove to me that there are things in this world that money cannot buy."

"Why? Why this? And why me?"

He leaned back with a bored look that she sensed was calculated. "For entertainment."

"But you called this a challenge."

"It is." He raised the pen and twirled it before his eyes. "You see, while you are trying to show me the things that money cannot buy, I, in turn, will show you just exactly what money will buy. Each of us will be out to prove our point."

"What are the stakes?"

He looked surprised, then laughed loudly and genuinely. There was no sardonic tone to his laughter this time. It had a rusty sound, as if he didn't do it that often.

"Name your price."

She shook her head. "You only think in terms of money."

"Name your reward then."

She thought about her circumstances and her goal. This almost seemed too easy, as if his whole plot was playing into her hands.

Perhaps her years in Heaven had earned her a small modicum of divine help.

Perhaps the carriage accident had knocked her senseless.

"Anything?" she asked.

There was something wicked in his eyes when he answered, "Absolutely anything."

"If I prove you wrong, you will—personally, once a week—find and create an opportunity for someone who has no hope. Someone like those people I gave your money to today." She watched for his reaction.

"Fine."

She froze. He had agreed too easily.

"What do you get out of this?"

He said nothing but stared at a legal paper in his hand. He seemed to be thinking deeply.

After a long silence, she cocked her head and said, "Mr. Stewart?"

He looked up.

"You haven't answered me."

He gave the paper another look, then seemed to come to a decision and quickly set it aside. "I'll get companionship." His tone was clipped, and he braced his hands on his desk and stood up quickly, then shuffled some papers. "I have an engagement to attend tomorrow night and another a few days later. You will accompany me." He turned away then, his back to her, and he stared out the window.

She watched him standing there stiffly, unwilling to look at her. "That's it? I just go with you?"

"Anywhere I ask."

She stood up. "Okay. We have a deal."

He tugged on the bellpull and the butler entered. He faced the man, but his gaze was on her. "Show Miss Lillian to the gold suite, Gage."

Lilli had the uneasy feeling that she had just jumped in a lake with her hands and feet tied.

"See that she has anything she wishes." He paused, a silence filled with meaning, then added, "Anything that money can buy."

The gold suite was just that—gold. The bed was gold. The walls had panels that were covered in gold-flecked wallpaper, then wainscoted in gilt. The high ceiling was coffered and painted with a scene that showed a golden sunrise, and rich golden oak flooring was covered with huge imported silk rugs designed in various shades from deep to light golden yellow.

The rug fringe? Golden silk. Lilli bent down and examined more closely the motif in each rug, half expecting the pattern to be interlocking dollar signs. She straightened, somewhat relieved when she saw only an obscure floral design.

She crossed the room and opened a door that led to a dressing room, three quarters of which was paneled in mirrors, all gilt framed. Through another door with golden handles shaped like dolphins was a private bath of pale yellow marble with gold dolphin fixtures and—

"Good heavens . . ." she muttered. "A gold sink!" She stared at it and at the gold-framed mirror above it with a dazed look of disbelief.

Then she saw something reflected in the mirror. Her mouth dropped open and she blinked twice, then spun around.

The water closet was a golden throne.

One second she gaped, the next she burst out laughing, and every time she looked around the room she laughed harder, until finally she had to sag back against the sink.

This had to be a joke. It was too ludicrous not to be.

But as she stood there, she knew that no one could deny the massive amounts of money it must have taken to decorate this suite. Everything was of the highest quality. What had been ridiculously funny only moments before was not funny any longer. It was a sad example of stupid waste and opulence. Worse yet, a cockeyed sense of values.

She straightened and left the room quickly, feeling oppressed, uncomfortable, and suddenly rather pessimistic about her chances of ever being able to teach D.L. Stewart anything.

Once in the bedroom, she just stood there and stared around her. Every piece of furniture, every painting, every bit of the room from the fireplace to the bric-a-brac was coldly flawless. Expensive. Priceless.

The minutes passed, one by one, time revealing what she hadn't understood before. The man who owned this house, this room, needed to learn more than just how to give from his heart. He was so lost, had his values so skewed, that she wondered if he could ever find any joy or happiness in just living. If he even understood the human spirit or the things that truly mattered in the world.

She lay back on the bed, with its plush down bedding, expensive silk drape, and hand-carved posts. She stared up at the canopy with a sense of grief so very deep it touched her in a way nothing had before.

And she began to cry. She turned over and buried her head in her arms, sobbing painfully and pitifully. Not for herself, a fallen angel, but for Daniel Lincoln Stewart, a fallen soul.

D.L. closed his carriage door and looked up. Lilli was watching him from an upstairs window. The drape drifted back and he watched it for a moment longer, then went up the snowy steps, fighting another smile—his second that day.

The front doors swung open wide and early.

Gage must be looking for a raise, he thought, then recalled it was near Christmas—that time of year when every servant, delivery boy, and elevator operator began to fawn, hoping for a large tip.

But to his surprise it was Lillian who met him at the doors. She was wearing her jacket and gloves, her hat tied beneath her chin in a shredded velvet bow.

He frowned and glanced back up at the window. "Weren't you just upstairs?"

She nodded.

He looked down the front steps. There were eight of them. He knew the main staircase had to have at least forty steps. How in God's name had she managed to meet him at the front door?

She was flushed and perhaps a little out of breath.

He shook his head, then gestured to her clothing. "Going somewhere?"

"Yes. We both are."

"I see. Why?"

"You said I'm supposed to prove my theory. Well, I'm ready."

"For what, exactly?"

"Your entertainment."

He gave a her long, pointed look.

She stared back at him from eyes that were a little too red.

"Have you been crying again?"

She looked down. "I had something in my eye."

"Both of them?"

She raised her chin, a sign of defiance. "Yes."

He crossed his arms with equal stubbornness.

Unfazed, she held out an old cloth valise. "Here."

"What's this?"

"It's a surprise."

He took the valise.

She stood there, silently waiting.

He stood there, silently amused.

It began to snow again, and she looked up at the sky. "Come," she said finally, and she threaded her arm through his, all but dragging him down the steps. They reached bottom just as his brougham disappeared around the corner and down the drive to the carriage house.

"Wait here. I'll call for the carriage."

"Oh, no." She tugged on his arm. "We'll walk."

"It's snowing."

She smiled up at him. "I know. That's the best part. Now come along."

A few minutes later he was walking down the sidewalk, valise in one hand, her arm holding his, while she chattered about the snow and the scenery and the sleighs that passed them by. She hummed a Christmas tune and smiled at people, wishing perfect strangers "Happy Christmas."

She grasped his hand and pulled him across the street to the park. Singing about bells and angels, she led him down a snowy path to a clearing, where a pond had frozen and the surrounding trees and bushes were heavy with white snow.

She plopped down on a park bench up a hill across from the pond and patted the spot next to her. "Sit here."

He bent down and dusted off the snow, then sat. "Is

209

sitting on a snowy park bench your idea of entertainment?"

"Of course not." She took the valise from him and set it on her lap, snapped it open, and burrowed inside. A second later she looked up, grinning. She pulled out an old pair of ice skates and dangled them in front of his face. "Yours," she said, then dropped them in his lap.

He stared at them.

She pulled out another pair. "And mine."

"This is the surprise?"

She nodded. "And it's absolutely free."

"Where did the skates come from?"

"I borrowed them. For free," she said smugly. "Now go ahead. Strap them on." She bent down and fit her feet into the skate clamps, then buckled the leather straps. She lifted one foot, examining the skate as if it were a glass slipper. "Not bad."

She stood up and planted her hands on her hips. "You haven't put them on yet. I thought you said you liked challenges."

He bent down and strapped on the skates.

An instant later she was walking down the path to the pond. He glanced up. She sauntered away like a conquering queen. From the way she carried herself, one would never know she still had a large rip in her skirt and that the rear shoulder of her jacket was shredded from the accident.

Funniest thing. For the first time in too many years to count, he wasn't bored.

"Better hurry," she called out over her shoulder in a singsong voice. "The last one there has to give a thousand dollars to the poor!"

And for the third time that day, he smiled.

"What do mean, we have to pay a dime?" Lilli stared dumbfounded at a park official in a blue uniform coat. He stood inside a small toll booth that had been hidden by the trees and bushes.

The man leaned forward from the window in his booth. "The skating pond has a ten-cent toll."

She could hear someone coming down the path. She didn't want to turn around and see triumph in D.L. Stewart's dark face. Directly behind her, she heard his skates crunch in the snow.

"What's the matter?" he asked in that deep voice.

She stared at the ground for a long moment, then finally admitted, "I was wrong. There's a fee to skate."

A second later she heard the sound of coins and looked up.

He held out a hand filled with gold pieces.

She shook her head. "No."

He turned to the official. "How much does this booth take in on a good day?"

The man shrugged. "Fifty dollars. Maybe sixty."

He gave him three twenty-dollar gold pieces, then added a fourth. "Consider this a good day and close the booth."

She started to say something, but he grabbed her arm and was pulling her along. A second later his hands were on her waist, and with a gentle shove he propelled her onto the ice.

Lillian would have protested, loudly, that he'd paid for something she had planned to be free, that they didn't have to do this, that she would find something else they could do.

Except that she'd forgotten one . . . little . . . itsy-bitsy thing.

She had never ice-skated.

5

If I have freedom in my love,
And in my soul am free,
Angels alone that soar above
Enjoy such liberty.

—Richard Lovelace

FOR THE SECOND TIME IN TWO DAYS D.L. STARED DOWN at Lillian. Only this time she was sprawled facedown on the hard ice.

She turned her head and looked up at him. "I've discovered something. Without wings, you can't hang on to thin air."

D.L. squatted next to her. "Are you hurt?"

"Only my pride." She pushed herself up on her hands and knees.

He straightened, grabbed her waist again, and picked her up. He set her carefully on the ice and kept his hands on her waist because it felt right. "I assumed that you could skate."

"So did I." Her blades slipped and she squealed, then wrapped her arms in a death grip around his waist. She peered up at him, her face sheepish. "It looks so easy."

"Turn around."

"I can't without letting go."

"Let go and turn slowly."

"I don't do miracles," she muttered.

He braced his skates and spun her around so her back was to him. He still held her waist.

She blinked at him for a second.

"Keep your ankles together and your back straight. I'll help you."

"You can skate," she said flatly.

His answer was to tighten his hands on her small waist and push off, skating smoothly and keeping her in front of him. He moved them both swiftly around the pond. "You're wobbling, Lilli. Keep your shoulders back."

She placed her hands over his and straightened. "You're right! It is easier."

She looked back over her shoulder as he picked up speed. Her cheeks were flushed pink and she was grinning. "This is fun!" Then she giggled.

He skated faster, until he could feel the cold air on his face. She laughed louder and clearer.

Before long the subtle scent of lemons drifted back to him, and her laughter—well, the sound of it did something queer to him. It made him want more. 'Round and 'round he skated, just to hear that joy.

He looked down at her at the same moment that she looked up. And it was strangely humbling to look into her face and see such honest emotion.

Over time he had come to accept that he was an outsider in a world where, no matter how much he spent or how much he made, he never felt as if he belonged.

For thirty years there had been an emptiness in him somewhere.

And now, for this one brief instant, skating on the

ice with her looking at him as she did—as if he had given her the whole world—he thought that perhaps that emptiness inside him could be filled.

It was astonishing to think he might have seen in her, this odd woman who claimed to be fallen, a small glimpse of that part of him he had thought was lost—the part that could make him complete.

He forced himself to break contact. "Now you try." He gave her a small push, and she screamed for help. He stood there watching her wobble and shuffle her feet, occasionally swinging her arms when she lost her tenuous balance. He cupped his hands around his mouth and yelled, "Keep your back straight!"

She didn't straighten, exactly. She went as stiff as a streetlamp.

In the next few minutes she must have called his name with every breath, half screaming and half laughing, until she was coming toward him at too fast a speed, her arms out and her mouth wide open.

He reached for her. But she whipped past him.

A tree trunk stopped her. She hit it hard, hard enough to make her grunt. Hard enough to shake the tree. Hard enough for the snow to fall in giant globs from the branches.

Onto her.

He laughed. He could do little else. She had snow on her hat, snow on her clothes, in her face. Snow was everywhere.

She let go of the tree and turned, her eyes—what one could see of them through all the snow—were sparkling like new coins.

He turned around but couldn't stop laughing.

After a moment, during which he had found his control, she called out, "Hey Daniel!"

He turned, his Christian name still sounding

214

strange to him even though she had screamed it at least ten times.

"Here's something money can't buy!" She flung a snowball at him. It knocked his hat right from his head.

It was her turn to laugh.

He turned and looked at his hat, then turned back just as another wad of loose snow sped past his nose. He skated toward her, slowly, with purpose. He didn't know he was still smiling.

She stood in the deep fresh snow that edged the pond. "Isn't this fun!" she said and flung another wad of snow.

He had to dodge this one.

She stepped back a few steps and bent down to scoop up more but chanced to look up.

His purpose and his intent hadn't changed.

"Uh-oh . . ." she said, apparently catching the vengeful gleam in his eyes. A second later she ran like hell through the snow.

He shouted her name and chased her into the deeper snow. Her hat fell back and her hair came loose, drifting behind her like the snow she kicked up, like her laughter and her joy.

He tackled her and they rolled in the snow, down a short embankment and under a cluster of low trees. She was still laughing when they stopped rolling, him on top, pinning her to the ground.

Snow sparkled from her face like Tiffany's diamonds. Her hat was crushed behind her and her hair was again spread out as if it were the glow of a halo. Her chest rose and fell with each warm breath that changed to mist in the small space of air between them.

And she smiled at him. For him.

It felt perfectly natural to cup her head in his hands. Natural to lower his mouth to hers. And natural to taste her when she gasped. But what happened after that was as unnatural as she was unconventional.

Daniel Lincoln Stewart heard bells.

She dreamed that night that he hadn't stopped kissing her in the park. She dreamed that he hadn't looked at her so strangely. She knew that look. The archangels had looked at her with the same dazed and befuddled eyes when she had knocked them off that ladder. It was as if they couldn't believe she was real.

And she almost had to wonder if that kiss was real. It was the closest thing to Heaven she'd found on Earth. She stretched and threw back the covers, swinging her bare legs over the side and dangling them.

She still slept in the silk shirt, with the tails that barely brushed her knees. But she wasn't cold, even if frost did edge the windows. There was a fire in the fireplace, compliments of Peg, the same maid who had brought her hot chocolate and loaned her the skates.

Morning light streamed through the bedroom windows. She stood up and pulled back the drape. On the street below carriages moved past—a world outside where yesterday's snow was fast becoming today's pile of gray-brown ice.

She wondered what Daniel was doing now. Probably off to make more money. She shook her head. The man knew how much money he made by the minute.

From this same window she had watched him leave early this morning, before she crawled back into bed and had some odd dream of Daniel, dressed as a nursery rhyme king, sitting in an office in some city tower and counting all his gold. Four and twenty blackbirds wearing hats that looked like giant pie crusts were guarding the doors.

She frowned, then shook her head slightly.

A sharp rap rattled the door. She jumped back in the bed and pulled up the covers. "Yes?"

The door opened slowly and Peg smiled. "Miss Lillian. Your trunks have arrived."

"My trunks?" she repeated stupidly.

Peg nodded.

Lilli leaned to the left of the bed and peered past Peg and out into the hall where trunks and bandboxes, hatboxes, and cases sat in what appeared to be legions.

Peg stepped back. "Your things. Mr. Stewart said they would arrive this morning."

"He did?"

Peg crossed the room toward the dressing room. "I'll run your bath, Miss Lillian, and you can relax while Gage and I bring everything inside."

Lilli took the fastest bath in history. She asked Peg for some time alone, and as soon as the girl had left, she flew into the bedroom, rebuttoning her shirt. She just stood there looking at the incredible number of boxes and trunks, the stacks of packages. She was certain there was enough in this room to clothe all of New York City.

A little while later she was convinced he had bought out all of New York City. Inside a trunk marked REDFERN were walking suits in the finest cashmere, some trimmed with curly lamb or fur, day suits in figured silk with trims of imported lace and beadwork. Boxes wrapped in silver tissue held tea and dinner dresses of silk grosgrain and brocade, sateen and nun's veiling.

Another huge trunk that opened like a closet held cloaks with matching fur hats and muffs, drawers with silk and kid gloves in every color of nature's palette, and more corsets and underwear than she ever cared to see.

There were at least thirty hatboxes stacked along

the wall and almost as many shoeboxes next to velvet drawstring bags with purses to match each pair of shoes. In another corner was a tower of large lace and ribbon-trimmed boxes stamped THE HOUSE OF WORTH.

Lilli grabbed the top one and carried it over to the bed, then crawled up and sat crosslegged. She untied the ribbon and lifted the lid, then broke the seal and pushed the tissue aside.

Her heart stopped for just one precious breath.

Inside was an evening gown of snow-white velvet with a skirt of matching cobweb lace. The velvet was soft and white as a cloud, and the lace on the skirt had a pattern more intricate than the stars in the sky. It was the loveliest thing she had ever seen.

Holding her breath, she pulled out the gown and held it up, looking at it for the longest time. There were little silver threads in the lace that caught the light from the fire and sparkled as bright as the silver lining of a cloud.

The gown was like a little part of Heaven. Her Heaven. Her only memories.

She hugged it to her chest and just sat there for the longest time, misty-eyed and unaware that she wasn't alone.

"I had thought you'd be pleased by this." Daniel stood in the doorway, watching with an edged look that said he didn't understand her.

"They're lovely."

"So lovely you're crying again."

She shook her head and said wistfully, "I was just remembering something I've lost."

Almost immediately he tensed. He looked angry. "Get dressed." His voice was tight.

She didn't understand his anger.

His face had turned hard, and the look in his eyes was as black as his features. "Come downstairs. Quickly."

218

"We're going out?"

"Yes." He paused for a moment, his hand on the door handle. He turned around. "I don't know who did this to you," he gritted. "But I'd like to get my hands on him." And before she could say a word, he shut the door.

She stared at it, completely baffled. She had done this to herself. If he wanted to get his hands on the person who had created her situation, she was right here.

She dropped the white dress and crawled down from the bed, grabbing a navy blue silk brocade suit—there were certainly plenty—as she went to the dressing room.

Once inside, she paused in front of the mirror and stared at her mouth—seeing it differently now that it had been kissed.

Her lips looked fuller. Did one's lips grow after a kiss? She touched them for a moment, then a silly grin spread slowly across her face.

After the kiss in the park, she knew she would be perfectly happy if he wanted to put his hands on her.

D.L. handed Karl the papers and stood up. They left the library and went into the foyer, where he leaned against the newel post and watched Karl stuff papers into his case. He had rushed through his meeting with no mention of Lilli to his attorney and friend.

He had no good explanation why he had wanted her here. No acceptable explanation. Entertainment, challenges, companionship—they all sounded weak and illogical.

What it boiled down to was that he didn't want to explain his motives for keeping a woman who claimed to be homeless, keeping for himself a woman who was fallen. Now, he knew one thing: He didn't care who or what she was. And that wasn't something he could analyze, at least not comfortably. As for the release, it annoyed him. In his mind it reduced her to nothing but a signature on a piece of paper.

Karl paused at the front doors. "I forgot to ask. Did you get that release signed?"

"No."

"I thought you said you had found her."

D.L. felt his hand tighten on the newel post. "I'll take care of it."

"This is important. You need to find that woman."

D.L. felt closed in and anxious for Karl to leave. He took a step toward the door, but near the top of the stairs he caught a flash of dark blue. He looked up with a sense of doom.

Lilli never looked down. He watched, stunned, as she sat on the banister.

An instant later she was sliding down the staircase, singing some silly song about this being better than wings in Heaven. A few feet from the bottom, she saw him and said, "Uh-oh . . ."

That was the last thing he heard before she sailed into him.

He lay on the marble floor of the foyer, trying to catch the breath that was knocked out of him. He blinked, seeing stars first, then her surprised face. He shook his head to clear it.

She lay atop him, her nose just inches away, her body along his.

Her sheepish gaze peered down at him slowly. "You know . . ." she said, shaking a finger in his face, "I was just thinking about you."

"You slid down the banister," he said, unable to believe it.

She shrugged. "You said come down quickly."

He sat upright, holding her to him. She squealed

and grabbed his neck. They shared a look, a private memory of yesterday in the snow, and an instant later they were both laughing.

"Well, D.L. . . ."

Daniel froze. He turned.

Karl was leaning against the front door, an all-too-knowing look on his face. He smiled sardonically. "I guess you found her."

6

Angels descending, bringing from above
Echoes of mercy, whispers of love.

—Fanny J. Crosby

*I*T HAD ALREADY BEEN ONE OF THE LONGEST DAYS HE could remember. After he'd gotten rid of Karl with some weak excuse they'd both seen through, D.L. wanted to buy Lilli something to make her forget the sadness of her past.

So he did the most natural thing—he took her to Tiffany's.

She looked at the diamonds and found them "nice." She agreed with the bald-headed clerk that they did rather look like stars. But D.L. could sense the diamonds wouldn't put the stars back into her eyes.

Sapphires were "okay," the perfectly cut rubies and

221

emeralds were reduced to "those red and green stones," and the pearls . . . God . . . D.L. wondered if he could ever look at pearls again and not picture in his mind the pain he had seen in Lilli's face.

She had looked at the pearls as if they were her shame. She muttered something about the gates to Heaven, then quietly asked every person in the store if they didn't think that pearls looked like angel tears.

Two hours later, while Lilli was across the store peering into another display case, he'd covertly bought the diamonds and some of "those red and green stones," then asked that they be delivered. The jewelry clerk had sighed with relief and went into the back rooms, wiping his shiny head with a handkerchief.

When they finally stepped from the store, she wore a pair of flawless and exquisite diamond earrings set in platinum that would have made a society matron faint from joy. He knew she'd selected them only out of charity. He had tricked her. He'd casually mentioned that the clerk had ten children and worked solely on commission.

And she did wear one other piece—a plain gold pin in the shape of wings. It was the only thing that had caught her eye. And its purchase was what finally made her brighten.

But now it was that night, and they were riding in his carriage to the opera house, where this evening's symphony performance opened the holiday concert season. It was at these functions where D.L. actually did most of his business. They weren't obligatory. They were necessary.

Lilli sat across from him, extraordinarily quiet, but looking as if she had just stepped from the pages of a fairy tale. A snow queen—in the white Worth gown and a fur-lined silk cape, her pale blond hair piled

regally high on her head, where silver combs caught
the carriage light. At his request, she was wearing the
diamonds.

The tension in the carriage was thick as gold bars
and seemed almost as impenetrable. He, a man who
had dealt with the most difficult men in the business
world, could not seem to deal with one woman named
Lillian.

He had the feeling that he could do little right where
she was concerned. The day had been nothing but
tension. He felt as if he kept doing and saying exactly
the wrong thing.

She had taken his breath away when she'd come
down the stairs—walking, not via the banister. And
he'd complimented her. He had thought compliments
made a woman feel better about herself.

Lilli had looked as if she might cry, or throw
something.

Now, as the carriage moved through the damp and
icy streets, she just stared out the fogged window,
oddly silent and with no light in her eyes.

"You're still unhappy."

She looked at him sadly, then shook her head. "Not
really."

"I don't understand. I've sat here for the last few
minutes trying to figure out what the hell is wrong."
He could hear the edge of anger in his voice. He
thought to soften his words and added, "I meant what
I said."

"When?"

"Tonight. When you came downstairs. I told you
how you looked."

"Yes." She turned back to the window again. "I
remember. You said I wear wealth beautifully."

From her tone, one would have thought he'd told
her she had a wart on her nose. He felt so damned

awkward. All day, no matter what he did, he couldn't do anything to please her. It annoyed the hell out of him.

The next moment the carriage stopped where the street ended and the opera house reigned. He shoved open the door and silently helped her down, holding her arm as he led her along the sidewalk. Just ahead of them, New York society crowded outside and on the steps like cattle hungry for hay.

On the walks and along the neighboring buildings were spectators, out to get a glimpse of Vanderbilts and Rockefellers. And beggars, out to get what they could. The indigent lined the sidewalks, clinging to worn woolen mufflers and rusty tin cans.

Lilli took one look at them and stopped as if she had suddenly grown roots. She pulled her arm from his grip and walked away from him toward the line of poor, her face showing every emotion she felt.

"Lillian."

She ignored him.

He watched, horrified, as she unscrewed an extremely expensive diamond earring and made to toss it into the nearest tin can.

"What the hell are you doing?" he shouted, grabbing her hand.

She looked up at him with surprise, then concern. She looked at the beggars, then back at him.

"Someone has to help them." She placed her hand on his arm.

He looked at her for a very long time. God . . . had he ever been that kind and innocent?

"No matter how solitary your world is, Daniel, not everyone is strong enough to make it all alone."

He knew he'd lost.

Her voice became even smaller. "They could be fallen angels."

He dug into his pocket. His voice was more gruff than he'd have liked when he said, "Put the earring back on." He held out a handful of money.

An instant later he received a gift worth more than any fortune.

Lilli's smile.

It was the longest night she could remember.

She must have met a hundred people like Daniel. Women stared at her jewelry with covetous eyes. Men talked money and business while they looked at her—not her jewelry—with those same covetous looks. Two of those same men pinched her when Daniel had his back turned.

She'd lost count of the number of people who said "Worth? How lovely," never meaning a word they said.

She wondered if Hell was in truth one big New York society party.

And Daniel. From the moment they walked inside, he had kept her close, his hand on her arm. When he looked at her it was from a dark gaze that bordered on obsession, as if she were something necessary to him, desperately necessary.

It caught her off guard, because when he looked at her that way she sensed a vulnerability in him that she hadn't actually seen before.

His grip would tighten, and he would turn and look at her as if he thought she might not be there.

It made the night tense and difficult for her. She supposed she should have been grateful that the long night had been cut short.

There had been a harp solo.

Lilli sat in the balcony, her forehead resting on one hand, when . . . one by one . . . every harp string broke. A series of *boing! Boing! Boing!*

There were some things that were the same whether she was in Heaven or on Earth. Either that, or God had a strange sense of humor.

But now, over an hour later, she stood in the *gold* suite, dressed in Daniel's silk shirt—the one she loved to sleep in—and looked out the window at a world she didn't understand. In a moment of unexplained whimsy, she reached out and drew a heart in the frost on the window.

The moment she finished, she sensed that she was no longer alone. She turned.

Daniel stood in the room, half turned away, his hand just locking the door behind him. He turned back and leaned against the doorjamb, his arms crossed.

He studied her as if he wasn't going to stop looking for a long time. He was still in his dress shirt and black pants, but his tail coat and white tie were gone, and two of the onyx and diamond studs near the collar of his shirt were undone.

As casual as he appeared standing there, she knew that some part of him wanted to intimidate. It was protection. It was how he hid his vulnerable side—the side that held on to her because he was afraid she would leave him.

She saw the rigidness in his square jaw, the tension in his neck, the raw need in his black eyes. She moved to the bed and sat in its center, not knowing exactly why he was there and feeling small and overwhelmed.

She cocked her head and looked in his face, searching for answers before she asked her question.

He shoved off from the wall and moved toward her.

"Why do you always look at me that way?"

He stopped at the foot of the bed, looking down at her from an intimidating height. "What way is that?"

"As if you're hungry."

She had startled him.

He gave a quiet, sardonic laugh that said the joke was on him. "It's that obvious? I must be losing my poker face."

There was a force of some kind between them. There had been from the first moment she'd ever seen him. Now that force was so strong she could feel the pull of it closing in, even the small space that separated them.

He placed one knee on the mattress, his hand reaching out to cup her cheek, then slide through her hair, holding her head in his palm. He pulled her to him gently—too gently for a man with such power.

With a touch as soft as the brush of a snowflake, he kissed her. His hands moved to her waist and lifted her, then he sat down on the bed, pulling her into his lap as he filled her mouth with his tongue and tasted her.

The stars in Heaven were with her suddenly in a wealth of emotion that confused her. His fingers traced her jaw and he pulled his mouth away, only to kiss her face and eyes, her cheeks and ears.

"Let me make you forget the past, Lillian. Forget the man who ruined you."

She cupped his rough chin in her hands. "No one ruined me, Daniel. I ruined myself."

His eyes narrowed, and he ran a thumb over her bottom lip. "You're too generous. It takes a man to make a fallen woman."

Stunned, she sat back, dropping her hands. "What?"

"I know what happened to you. You cried about it after the accident."

"You think I'm a fallen woman?" She felt the kernel of a smile.

227

He gave her that direct look of his. "You admitted it, Lilli. You said you were fallen and ashamed. You won't tell me where you are from. I assumed that's because you've been disowned."

She laughed, just a small laugh, but a laugh just the same.

His black expression said he didn't think this was funny.

"I'm not a fallen woman. I'm a fallen angel."

7

But strength alone though of Muses born,
Is like a fallen angel; trees uptorn.

—John Keats

CALL IT WHAT YOU LIKE, LILLIAN. FALLEN WOMAN. Fallen angel. Soiled dove. I don't really care." D.L. grabbed her by the shoulders. "Your past is not my concern."

"No." She shook her head. "I am an angel. Or at least I was one."

He looked at her, thinking she was making a joke.

"Truly. I had a halo and wings, but I couldn't perform any miracles so—"

He felt his pride and the deep wound to it. He tensed, then stood up abruptly. "If you aren't interested . . . say so. Don't make these ridiculous excuses."

"It's the truth."

"You expect me to believe that you are an angel."

"A fallen angel."

He crossed his arms and leaned against the bedpost. "Prove it."

"I don't know how I can prove it. You tell me how to make you believe me."

"I don't know. You're the heavenly being." His voice dripped in sarcasm and he waved his hand angrily. "Ask for divine guidance. Hell . . . sprout wings and fly around the bloody room."

"Why are you so angry? I can't help what I am."

"Then why are you making up this stupid tale? I told you. I don't care what you are, or even what you've been. But don't—don't lie to me."

"You won't believe me."

"You tell me you're an angel and then expect me to believe you?" He ran a hand through his hair and paced in front of her. "God, that's rich!"

She gave him that look—the one that said more than words that he had let her down. "I'm not surprised that you'd use such a phrase."

He froze. "What's wrong with it?"

"Do you want me to answer that? Honestly?"

"You're the angel." He heard the cruelty in his laugh. "You tell me."

"Okay. You want truth, I'll give you truth. The painful truth. You think *only* in terms of money. Everything is money with you. You offer me money to listen to you, to get in your carriage. You try to buy everything. Everyone."

He stood there, just watching her, listening to her tell him things he didn't care to hear, especially from her.

"You can't even give a woman a compliment,

Daniel. Did you say 'Lillian, you look lovely'? No. You said 'You wear wealth beautifully.' "

She made him sound incredibly pompous.

"Don't you know there are things more important than money or fortunes or gold?"

He was stiffly silent, yet deep inside him he flinched at the sincerity in her voice.

"Is it truly that hard for you to understand? People shouldn't be bought. They should be respected. Even the most ragged and beggarly person in New York is still a human being. Can't you find it in your heart to help them, even one of them, all on your own?"

He was still silent, his jaw tight, his chin raised.

"And look at your house."

"What's wrong with my house?"

"You collect things."

"You make it sound as if that's a criminal act."

"Not criminal. Sad. Look at this room." She waved her hand around.

He gave it a cursory glance. There was nothing wrong with the room. It was the best his money could buy. "Yes?"

"It's filled with collections. Priceless art, perfect porcelain, but nothing . . . alive. And the color."

"What about the color?"

"Look around you. Open your eyes. Everything is gold—as if gold, wealth, is the most important thing in the world. This is not a home you live in. It's a temple to the almighty dollar."

He didn't look at the room. He looked at her. "You criticize my house because I won't believe this foolishness that you're an angel."

"No! You don't understand."

"You're the angel. Work a miracle and make me understand."

She began to pace alongside the bed. Grabbing the bedpost, she stopped and looked at him again. "Okay.

It's Christmas. What is the first thought that comes into your mind when I say the word *Christmas?"*

Tipping, he thought, but he'd be damned if he'd admit it.

"Ah-ha!" She pointed a finger at him. "You thought of money just then."

"You're guessing."

"I'm certain. The gleam of avarice in your eyes was hard to miss. Nowhere in this entire house is there any sign of Christmas. No greenery. No tree. Nothing. And what about your servants?"

"What about them?"

"Do you give them special holidays to be with their families?"

"They'll be compensated."

"Money again." She walked over to him and, placing her hands on his chest, looked up at him as if she expected him to be something he wasn't—something he didn't understand.

"Can't you understand? Can't you at least try?"

When she looked at him that way, he almost thought that perhaps he could be different. But he didn't know if he could give her what she wanted, what she asked. Because he didn't understand it, and it scared the hell out of him.

His gaze moved to her mouth, because he had to look at her. His look wandered slowly down the shirt and her legs. His anger turned to want, the need that seemed to consume him since that first night when she'd caught him looking at her.

He wanted her now, but his pride reminded him that he had for so many years had everything on his own terms. He made the rules.

"Please don't look at me like that."

"Why not? I paid for the privilege."

She flinched as if he had hit her.

Silently he stood there, part of him wanting to take

the words back, and another part of him—pride and anger and rejection—not allowing him to move or speak. Everything was all mixed up in his head and his heart.

She stepped away, raising her hand as if to fend off a demon, her expression half horror, half hurt. "I can't do this," she said under her breath. "I can't."

She looked ready to bolt.

He grabbed her then. "Don't leave. Lilli, don't leave."

She watched him for a long time. "Daniel," she whispered. "What is it? What are you so afraid of?"

He shook his head. "Promise me. You won't leave like you did before."

"Why?"

He let go of her and ran a hand through his hair. "I'm sorry." He turned away, feeling vulnerable and open, naked in her eyes. He just left her standing there because he needed to think and he couldn't think with her looking at him that way. He crossed the room and opened the door.

"Daniel?" Her voice was so soft he wasn't certain he'd heard it.

He paused and took a deep breath.

"I'll stay."

He exhaled and loosened his death grip on the door handle. He nodded, because he couldn't find his voice, and he left, closing the door behind him.

He leaned against it for a moment, then had an insane thought: Perhaps she *was* an angel.

Lilli stood at the window and watched Daniel's carriage pull away from the house. He'd left later this morning than normally. She'd been waiting and watching. She threw on a dark red cloak and tied on a matching bonnet.

She walked to the bedroom door and stopped

suddenly, snapping her fingers. She ran back and grabbed a purse that was sitting on a chair, then she went back to the door, where she listened to make certain no one was in the hallway.

Cracking the door a smidgen, she peered out. The coast was clear. She left the bedroom and hurried to the gallery that ran next to the stairs. Her hands on the gallery railing, she looked down into the foyer.

It was empty.

She moved to the top of the stairs and started to tiptoe down. She paused, then sat on the banister and slid to the bottom, landing perfectly and quietly.

A minute later she was running down the steps and away from the house, and she never looked back.

D.L. stood at the window of his office, his hands in his pockets, as he watched the traffic on the street below. A delivery boy in a blue coat with gold epaulets and a gold-brimmed hat came running through the crowd outside his building.

A few minutes later he heard the chain hoist on the elevator. He stood there, tense and tight, as he waited. The door burst open and the boy rushed inside.

"I went as fast as I could, Mr. Stewart!" The lad was out of breath, which D.L. thought appropriate, since he himself was holding his.

"I spoke to your butler, and he said to tell you Miss Lillian was still asleep."

D.L. closed his eyes and sagged back against the windowsill. He felt the tension he'd been living with all morning drain away. He suddenly remembered himself and straightened, then shoved a hand in his pocket and pulled out a ten-dollar gold piece. "Fine." He flipped it to the boy.

The boy snatched it out of the air. "Thank you, sir." He turned to leave.

"Willy?"

The boy paused and turned back. "Yes, sir?"

"Where's your family?"

Willy's mouth gaped open, then he suddenly snapped it shut. "Hoboken, sir."

D.L. nodded, then turned around and looked out the window. "If one wanted to buy some Christmas greenery and perhaps a tree, where is the best place to go?"

"The freshest greens are at the Washington Market, near the docks on the North River. Most of the freight barges dock there, sir."

"I see," D.L. said, lost in thought.

A few minutes passed, and then Willie cleared his throat.

D.L. turned back.

"Is that all, sir?"

"Yes." He reached into his pocket and pulled out a handful of gold pieces. He stared at them for a moment. He looked at Willy and said, "Take off the two days before Christmas and spend them with your family."

"But sir—"

"With pay. Consider it payment for information."

Willie grinned. "Yes, sir!"

D.L. watched the door close, then heard a loud *whoop* echo down the hallway. His lips twitched slightly as he reached for his topcoat and hat, and he was smiling when he left his office. A few minutes later his carriage pulled away from the Stewart Building, headed for the Washington Market in lower Manhattan.

D.L. strolled through the marketplace, where Christmas greens were piled like cordwood along the walks and twined up awning posts and around storefront windows. Booths were made up of barrels with rising latticework that looked like arbors. And from

234

them hung festoons of every shade and thicket of greenery from Maine to the Catskills.

Three ropes of greenery hung from around D.L.'s neck, and in one hand was a basket filled with holly, red roses, and rolls of ribbon. And the purchase he was most proud of, a large bouquet of snow-white lilies.

He walked along, breathing in the tangy clean scent of pine and trying to picture Lilli's face.

It wasn't difficult. She was standing just a few feet away.

She was bent over a little boy, who was looking up at her with serious wide eyes. He held a tin whistle in one hand, and under the other arm was a mechanical cow with a brass bell around its neck.

D.L. moved closer and listened.

"Yes, Alfred, it's true," Lilli was saying. "Didn't you know that?"

The boy shook his head.

"I have a rhyme to help you remember. Do you want to hear it?"

He nodded.

Lilli squatted down until she was at eye level with the boy, and she said, "Every time a whistle sounds, an angel falls to the ground." She paused, frowning dramatically and shaking her head.

The boy giggled.

"And every time a bell rings, an angel gets its wings." She smiled and nodded vigorously.

The little boy looked at the whistle, then at the cow. He put the whistle down and ran off to tell his mother he wanted the cow instead.

Lilli straightened, then bent down again to pick up a basket of greenery. Smiling, she turned and froze the moment she saw him.

D.L. didn't move. "I thought you were still asleep."

"I thought you were at your office."

They said nothing else. The night before was still too fresh a memory, and it made the moment awkward and tense.

She looked at his neck and then gave a small smile. "Shopping?"

He glanced down, then shrugged. "Yes."

She held up the basket. "Me too."

He then remembered that he'd never given her one red cent. He felt stupid. But after the lecture she'd given him he wasn't certain how to ask her how she had paid for this. He eyed her basket a moment, then said, "I'm not certain I should bring up this subject after last night, but I have neglected to give you any money."

She looked everywhere but at him. Finally she sighed and said, "I pawned the gold pin."

"The wings?"

She nodded, and he groaned. He took her arm. "Where is the pawnshop?"

She pointed. "Down the street a few blocks."

"Come on." He headed down the street, Lilli by his side.

"You should have pawned the earrings."

"I couldn't do that."

"Why the hell not?"

"Because they don't mean as much as the pin does."

He stopped and looked at her. "That makes sense."

She gave a small smile.

"It shouldn't make sense. Don't ask me why. But for some hare-brained reason it does!" He turned and pulled her down the street.

Half an hour later they stood beneath the three white globes that hung above Murry's Pawnshop and D.L. pinned the wings onto Lilli's dress. She touched them when he finished. "Thank you."

Uncomfortable, he shoved his hands in his pockets and looked away. "Would you like a tree?"

Her smile was bright enough to melt the snow.

Two hours later, when the carriage left the market, a lush tree was strapped to the roof and the boot was stuffed with greenery. Baskets filled with flowers and fresh cranberries were on the seats by Lilli. In her hand she held a cornhusk doll in the shape of an angel. "Isn't it just wonderful?"

He looked at her. Only at her. "Yes. Wonderful."

She looked up, then something caught her eye and she gasped. D.L. turned just as they passed a German bakery, its windows filled with a fairyland of gingerbread castles.

He banged on the roof. "Stop here, Benny." He jumped out, then helped her down.

She almost ran to the window, where gaslights made the holiday display sparkle. Intricate castles and houses had snow icing on the roofs. Gingerbread soldiers in full uniform rode horses with trappings and full manes of sugary white. There were gingerbread women and children dressed in costume and carrying baskets of miniature marzipan candy in the shapes of pears and peaches, sausages and hams, little dolls and animals.

Three gingerbread men later, they left the bakery, and Lilli handed Benny a cookie shaped and decorated like a queen's carriage. She always thought of someone else before herself. She didn't want wealth or diamonds. She wanted so little. D.L. wondered if there was anything she truly wanted just for herself.

Then she saw the puppies. Small light brown canine heads with floppy ears and wagging tongues and bright red bows tied around their necks poked out of a street vendor's basket. A squeal of delight and she rushed toward the pups like a Vanderbilt to Tiffany's.

"Daniel, look!"

And he did look. But not at the puppies that were

licking her chin and cheeks. Nor the kittens and the rabbits as she moved from one basket to another.

He looked at the joy on her face and wished that he could give her that kind of happiness every single day of his life.

Lilli. Who preferred puppies to diamonds. Kittens to pearls. Rabbits to . . .

He looked down at her and scowled. "No rabbits, Lilli. Puppies . . . yes. And kittens too. But no rabbits."

8

Unless you can love as the angels may
    With the breadth of Heaven betwixt you;
Unless you can dream that his faith is fast
    Though behoving and unbehoving;
Unless you can die when the dream is past
    Oh never call it loving!

—Robert Browning

*T*HE RABBITS WERE CHEWING ON DANIEL'S SHOELACES.

Lilli sat in a chair in the open parlor, her lap full of wiggling puppies, while purring kittens crawled on the arms and wings of the chair. She was stringing cranberries and smiling at Daniel.

He was on his hands and knees in front of a brass bucket filled with wet sand, muttering and turning the trunk of the Christmas tree. It was his third attempt to get the tree straight.

"It looks fine to me," she told him.

He backed out, scowled down at the two brown and white rabbits, then shifted away, eyeing the angle of the tree. "A little more to the right."

Lilli rolled her eyes and tied a knot in the string of deep red cranberries. The formal parlor was a disaster. A huge bowl of popcorn sat in the center of a Savonnerie carpet, a trail of plump kernels leading to the tree, where the rabbits nibbled the crushed popcorn from the soles of Daniel's shoes.

Scraps of colored paper and string had been scattered by tumbling puppies and playful kittens until the center of the room, where settees by William Kent formed a conversation area, looked like the aftermath of a parade. Next to embroidered pillows once owned by Marie Antoinette were stacks of greens, and in giant piles around the room were spools of red ribbons next to twigs of laurel and cedar.

The entire lower floor of the Stewart mansion was filled with the fresh scent of Christmas. By the time the mantel clock struck eleven the tree was decorated, and greenery hung throughout the front of the house. Tied with red ribbons, cedar and laurel, pine and holly hung from pictures and mirrors and wrapped around the bases of candelabra.

Besides the candles, tables held vases of red roses and the most exquisite white lilies she had ever seen. And the rabbits, puppies, and kittens were tucked into their baskets beneath the tree, exhausted after an evening of chasing string and cranberries—and Daniel's shoes.

"Now it looks like Christmas," she said, putting her hands on her hips. She turned just in time to catch the look on Daniel's face.

He stood next to her, silent and looking at the tree.

His expression was naked and open and for one brief instant filled with such desolation that she was unable to breathe.

She reached out and touched his arm. Because she had to. Because she sensed he needed touching now as he relived some memory.

"Daniel," she whispered his name.

He didn't respond, didn't move, until finally he looked at her as if he had just noticed she was there.

She searched his face for answers and saw nothing but a shuttered look that she sensed hid pain and fear and other emotions so personal that he couldn't bear to let anyone see. "What's wrong?"

He shoved his hands in his pockets, a move she was beginning to recognize. She suspected that his hands were tight fists.

Daniel had, over the years, learned to hide his emotions from the world.

"I haven't had a Christmas tree since I was thirteen." He didn't look at her. He stared at the tree.

She watched him with this horrid sinking feeling. "Do you want to get rid of it?"

"No." He shook his head. "It's not the tree. I never had the time for one. I was working too hard, and then when I did have the time . . ." He shrugged. "I didn't care anymore."

"Do you want to talk about it?"

"No." He laughed without humor, then turned to her.

"I think perhaps you should."

He leaned back against the edge of the pocket door and crossed his arms. "Why?"

She could be as stubborn as he could. She mimicked him, crossing her arms and raising her chin. "You tell me."

He didn't look her in the eye, but he turned and took two strides into the room, his face hidden in the shadow of the doorway. His back was to her. "I wasn't born into wealth. I've earned every cent I have. What you said the other night made me think about what I am, Lilli. Why I am. Whether I have put money before everything else in my life." He turned back to her then. "I think it's true.

"My father died in an accident on the job. My mother was killed two weeks later. She was looking for a job and was murdered. No one ever knew what happened, except the police thought it might have been a robbery attempt.

"I lived with my grandfather for a while, but he had a stroke. No matter how hard any of them worked, no matter how much they tried, there was never much money. I don't have a lot of childhood memories, except that everyone I cared for I lost, and that we had little time together because they were always working so hard." He looked around the room, his gaze stopping on each priceless piece of art that adorned the walls.

"I remember thinking, when I buried my grandfather, that someday I would have so much money that I would never have to live like they did." He gave a droll laugh.

She looked at him.

"I realized this morning that I had done exactly what they had. I have spent almost every minute of my life working. The only difference is, I made money, more money than I could ever spend or need in my lifetime and theirs put together."

"Daniel. I'm sorry I said those things."

"Don't be. They needed to be said."

She stood there, feeling awkward because she wanted to run to him, but she was afraid.

"Can we start over? No challenges, no bets, no deals. And no questions. You can stay here as long as you want to, Lilli."

She didn't know what to tell him.

"Will you stay?"

Every person he had ever cared about left him in one way or another. Perhaps she understood that look. She understood him.

She couldn't leave him. Not now. Not when she was so confused and fast feeling as if Daniel were part of her. And deep inside her, she didn't want to leave him. She looked up and nodded. "I'll stay."

There was a flash of relief in his eyes. He gave her a slow and lazy smile, then looked pointedly above her.

She followed his gaze to where a giant ball of mistletoe, almost two feet wide, hung from the crystal chandelier directly above her.

Two steps and he had closed the distance between them. He lowered his mouth to hers and kissed her softly, tenderly.

She slid her hands around his neck and returned his kiss, his taste. He groaned and his arms held her tightly, lifted her to him.

The kiss lasted forever and an instant. He pulled back. Her head was against his chest, and he rested his chin on her head, his breath a little fast, his heart pounding in her ear. "Whenever I kiss you, it's the strangest thing. I could swear I hear bells."

She smiled into his shirt and said, "Then perhaps you should kiss me more often."

"Perhaps you should go to bed before I do and then can't stop." He released her and stepped back, his look only for her.

She smiled and went up the stairs, feeling his gaze warm her all the way to the top. She stopped at the landing and turned. "Daniel. You know what they say about bells. Every time a bell rings—"

He smiled and finished, "An angel gets its wings."

* * *

The next two days were theirs alone.

They went back to the park and skated again. Well, he skated. She fell. They joined the throngs of uptown shoppers who milled along Broadway from Union Square and along all the uptown avenues where, this close to Christmas, the stores were open until eleven at night to handle the crowds of people who were too busy to shop during the workday.

With hundred of others, they watched as a huge Christmas tree lit with two hundred gas jets was rolled into the Trinity Church sanctuary. Every branch of the tree was laden with gifts for children from a nearby orphan asylum, compliments of D.L. Stewart.

But the best Christmas gift Lilli received came in the form of laughter.

Lilli met Daniel at the top of the stairs one evening.

He stopped. "Go on down to dinner. I forgot something."

She walked down the stairs, humming "O Holy Night," a kitten tugging at her skirt and two puppies yapping in her arms. She reached the bottom step.

There was a loud *whoop*.

An instant later Daniel slid down the banister, off the newel post, and sailed into the foyer just as Gage opened the front door.

Daniel kept going.

He bounced down the icy marble steps until something on the sidewalk finally stopped him.

His attorney, Karl Wallis.

"I'm not certain I'll ever be able to sit again," D.L. said, wincing as he crossed the library and handed Karl a drink.

Karl took the drink. "You weren't at the Van Cleves' dinner party last night.

D.L. took a swig of Scotch. "No."

"Prescott was there."

"I'll call and set up a meeting with him sometime next week."

"I've never known you to miss an opportunity like this. The man has a fortune to invest."

D.L. didn't respond.

"Have you gotten that release signed?" The look Karl gave him spoke volumes.

"I said I'll take care of it, and I will."

"Tell me something."

"What?"

"What is she to you?"

"I don't know what you're talking about."

"You damn well know what I mean, D.L."

"Stay out of it, Karl."

"I've never seen you act this way about a woman."

"She's different. I don't know how to explain it." He'd known the night he took her to the concert. She looked lovely, but she'd been too quiet and out of place in that crowd—like fine silver exposed to the harsh elements. She had lost her luster. He felt some odd need to protect her from anything that would or could hurt her, anything that would steal her laughter.

Karl got up and set his glass down. "I'm not here to pass judgment. I was concerned, both as a friend and as your attorney."

"Don't be. I can handle this."

"Will I see you at the club?"

He shook his head. "Not until after Christmas."

Karl went to the door and opened it, then paused. "I hope you know what you're doing."

"I'm fine. Everything will be fine," D.L. said, but he wasn't certain if he was talking to Karl or himself.

A clock down the hall struck two.

Daniel didn't move, didn't even take a breath.

She stood by the light of her bedroom window, the

moon shining down and making her look like the angel she claimed to be.

"You can't sleep either," he said.

She shook her head. "No."

She hadn't looked at him, but he could see that she had known he was there. It didn't surprise him. There was something between them, some elusive chain that bound them together.

Whenever he was near her he could feel it, as if it were a live, animated thing, this acute awareness that she was the other half of him—a side that had been lost or perhaps had never existed until he found her.

He crossed the room and stood behind her. She didn't step away but just slowly looked up at him.

He reached out and swept a hank of hair from her face, then cupped her cheek in his hand. Her skin was so soft and pale, and it made him even more aware of how fragile she was.

He trailed his fingers down her cheek and caressed her jaw, tilting her head up. He had never in his entire life touched a woman this way. Never had he run his fingers across her features, memorizing them with his hands.

But with Lilli it was a sensory need he had to fill.

His mouth touched hers once, the barest of touches —the brush of an angel's wing. Moments later their kisses were dizzying and deep and felt as necessary as air. He craved her flavor, the same way he craved her scent, the sound of her voice, the brightness of her smile.

His hands floated down to her breasts, skimmed them and cupped them, brushed the tips and felt them react to his touch.

"Daniel." Her whisper was dreamy and wanton, and it made him want her more.

She was dressed in his shirt and nothing else. A slight touch here, a button undone there, and the shirt floated to her feet. She was sleek and pale and perfect, her skin flushed.

His own clothes fell away and they stood there bathed in moonlight and love. His hands on her waist, he picked her up, lifting her high so his mouth could worship her breasts, her belly, and lower.

She gasped, her breath coming in hard shocks, and her hands clutched his shoulders. He tasted heaven. Her fingers threaded through his hair and his name was a prayer on her lips.

He laid her on the bed and kissed her legs, her calves and ankles, then held a foot in each hand and slowly moved his hands up her legs, inch by slow inch, until his thumbs met, then he kissed her again, light feathery touches of his mouth—a kiss so intimate that it was theirs alone.

Tears of passion fell from her eyes. He moved up her body, touching her and kissing her. His hand cupped her womanhood and stroked her over and over. Touching her was everything. Watching what his touch did to her was more than everything.

They spoke in half-finished phrases, desire and passion stealing their words.

"Please, Daniel . . ."

"Lilli, my Lilli, let me . . ."

And he shifted, poised to touch something finer than Heaven. He slowly sank into her.

She gasped and stiffened. Tears shimmered from her eyes.

"My God . . ." He froze. Time stopped. He tried to focus on her face, then groaned, "You couldn't have fallen very far."

She said nothing but gripped his shoulders and slowly opened her eyes.

He saw his future and his heart. "Easy, love, easy." He slid a hand between them and lit her passion again.

A gift for what she had given him. Soon his touches had her body crying tears too.

"Hold on to me, love, tightly," he whispered thickly, then buried his tongue in her mouth.

She gripped his upper arms and lifted her hips, seeking extra caresses that would send her over the edge he craved. He gave her those touches and more, feeling her ecstasy hit fast and pulsing.

Then he thrust home. She groaned and twisted. He stilled, afraid he would give her more pain. "Lilli. Look at me."

She slowly opened her eyes.

"Are you okay?"

She nodded, then reached up and ran her fingers over his mouth, unspeakable emotion in her eyes.

"Tell me if I hurt you." And he moved slowly, very slowly, for long minutes, watching her until her eyes drifted closed and she was meeting each of his thrusts and moving with him, catching an intimate rhythm of their own.

It went on forever, an eternity within this woman that showed him more than words ever could about life and love and his reason for being. He felt release coming hard and fast, from his mind to his heart and on to parts more elemental, hotter and faster and stronger than anything ever before. He slowed for control, wanting to take her with him, needing the first time to be them, together, completely them and nothing else.

He felt the rise in her, the heat run through him. He shifted and moved faster; their motion and drive changed too. Because they were reaching for something impossible, something that a primal sense told them was only a moment away.

The passion came hard and powerfully. Their breathing, like their bodies, became one.

He clung to her, consumed with an emotion that was wild and loose and free. And when every bit of physical passion drained away, what he felt for her was still there.

He tenderly cupped her head in his hand and told her then what he now knew had been there from almost their first moment together: "You are my heart, Lilli. God in heaven, how I love you."

Her face crumpled with emotion too. She shook her head, her breath a cry and a whisper. "Oh no . . . please."

But it was too late.

Daniel had found in her a miracle, and he had already given her his heart.

Lilli stood by the bed and watched Daniel sleep. He had fallen asleep before she'd whispered "Oh no."

The house was quiet. Still. There were embers in the fireplace, but the chill she felt had nothing to do with the air. It seemed that her life in Heaven had been everything wrong. Here everything was right. Even her miracles.

There was a kind of cruel and wry irony in the fact that the one thing she could never do in Heaven she had managed to do here. A miracle. Daniel's miracle.

She wondered if she would go back to Heaven now. Could there be such cruelty? With all of her earthly being she hoped not. But if she must go, she had a brief glimpse of how painful eternity would be now that it no longer meant anything to her. Because Daniel loved her.

And what about him? She covered her mouth with one hand and tried to catch a shuddering breath that wouldn't be caught. Her mind became images of his pain should she leave him, this man who had lost every person he'd ever cared for. Dear Lord, she'd carry that pain for him too, would carry it throughout all eternity.

For his sake, she prayed to stay, knowing her prayers were lost before she even said them. She prayed again, and again, litanies of prayer, until finally she sank to her knees. Her hands were folded tightly. She stared at them, not knowing if she clasped her hands so tightly to try to hold on to this earthly life or to help insure that her prayers might by some chance be answered.

But prayers and folded hands and words were not helping. She could feel it. It was as if she were slowly fading away, after only this brief glimpse of Heaven on Earth.

I want to stay. Please . . . please . . .

She buried her face on her folded hands and sobbed silently.

Somewhere in the distance, a church bell rang.

And a second later, Lilli disappeared.

9

Her angel's face
As the great eye of Heaven shined bright,
And made sunshine in a shady place.

—Edmund Spenser

*S*OMEWHERE IN THE DISTANCE A CHURCH BELL RANG and woke him. He opened his eyes, then reached out and touched the sheet where she had been. It was empty.

He listened for her sounds in the bathroom but heard nothing. He wanted to go to her but thought perhaps she needed some privacy. He locked his hands behind his head and stared up at the canopy, a sense of profound peace surrounding him.

One night wouldn't be enough.

He had never thought of marriage for himself. But he lay there now, knowing that he wanted Lilli with him for a lifetime. He smiled at the contentment he felt, the fullness of knowing and loving Lilli. He closed his eyes and waited for her to come back to bed.

He didn't know how long he'd slept. Five minutes? Five hours? Time had given birth to uncertainty and fear.

He threw back the covers and stood up, then looked

in the dressing room. The bathroom door was open. The room was dark.

His stomach turned over.

He rushed inside, stepping around baskets of sleeping puppies, kittens, and rabbits. She wasn't there.

"Lilli?" he called, tearing back into the bedroom. There was no sound but the sleepy meow of a kitten, the whimper of a puppy.

"Lilli!" he shouted again, pulling on his clothes.

He threw open the doors and ran down the hall. He stopped at the top of the stairs. "Lilli!" he yelled. Her name echoed mockingly through the gallery.

But at that moment he knew that she wouldn't answer him. In his heart he knew, because that magical feeling—the one he'd felt since the first moment he had looked at her—was gone.

As quickly as if God had snapped His fingers. It was gone.

He stared at his hand, white-knuckled as it gripped the banister, then he sagged down on the top step. He didn't move for the longest time. Everything he was, and every joy he had, drained away until he felt as if he were nothing but emptiness . . . human emptiness.

He rested his head in his hand and took a couple of deep breaths.

"Lilli . . ."

He said her name that one last time. It was barely a whisper.

"Dammit, Karl! Just forget about the release!" D.L. spun around and glared at his attorney. "I don't care about it! I just don't care about it." He heard his anger and the desperation in his voice. His panic.

Time was going by. A whole day. He couldn't find her. No one could find her. No one had seen her leave. No one had heard a thing.

"I wish she would come back and sue the hell out of

me." He spun around in his chair and stared at nothing. "At least then I'd know where she was."

Karl rose from his chair, picked up his case, and snapped it closed. He stood there for an awkward second, then said, "I'm sorry, D.L."

Daniel didn't respond. The door clicked closed, and a minute or so later he heard Karl get into his carriage and leave.

He just sat there staring at the white storm outside. And he relived his memories: Her standing under a tree with so much snow on her she looked like a snowman. Her face looking up at him, her eyes sparkling, the way she crinkled her nose at something, the delight in her eyes when she saw the bakery, and the animals.

He remembered mistletoe. A sweet kiss. Christmas greens. A cornhusk angel atop a tree. And another angel. The only angel he'd ever known.

He stood up and slowly went upstairs, his hand dragging absently along the banister. When he reached her bedroom, his hand paused on the doorknob. Some last remnant of hope made his breath still as he opened the door.

His hope died. She wasn't inside. He stepped into the room, because he had to, then closed and locked the door.

Four puppies, three kittens, and two rabbits greeted him. He crossed the room and stared at the bed. His shirt was lying where she had lain only hours before, when his world had been everything wonderful, when he had been alive in his heart as well as in his mind and body. When love had been there for an instant.

Now there was just his silk shirt, nothing more. He reached out and touched it, foolishly expecting it to disappear too.

But it didn't disappear. He picked it up and walked over to a chair, where he sat down, staring at it.

Her scent was there with him. Lemony and real. But she wasn't.

A puppy jumped into his lap, then another and another. One of them was chewing something, and he took it from its mouth. It was the gold pin. Her wings. He held it tightly in his fist, as if by doing so he could bring her home to him.

Fly home to me, my angel.

The kittens crawled up the chair and the rabbits chewed on his shoelaces. He looked at them, at the pin, then at the white silk shirt clutched in his hands.

A moment later he buried his face in the shirt and cried.

"Lilli's watching him. Constantly she watches him."

Saint Peter stopped pacing and looked at Florida. "Has she stopped crying?"

Florie shook her head.

He sighed, then moved across the clouds with Florie fluttering in his wake, until he stood near where Lillian knelt, clutching the rim of a cloud in tight hands and peering intently over the edge. Her halo had no glow and her wings drooped downward like the wilted petals of a broken rose.

She raised her head and looked up at Saint Peter, the tears she couldn't seem to stop streaming down her face. "He's at the park, calling my name."

Saint Peter looked down. "So I see."

She bit her lip and watched Daniel, his head bent, his hands shoved in his coat pockets and snow falling all around him as he walked despondently from the park. "He's alone and lost. Can't I help him? Can't you or someone help him? He's lost everyone."

"Some people have a harder road to travel, Lilli."

She looked up at him. "I never really knew what Heaven was until I found Daniel."

Saint Peter looked at Florida, who was crying silent tears of her own. He shook his head and waved her away.

Lilli's shoulders shook and she hiccuped as she looked downward. "He's at the church now, praying. Hear him?" She paused. "I can hear him."

Saint Peter sat down on the rim of the cloud. He looked down at the world below, then watched one man in particular—the dark and empty shape of a man.

Saint Peter was quiet, then he looked at Lillian for the longest time. After an eternal minute, he cleared his throat and said in a gruff voice, "So. Lillian. Tell me about your young man."

Daniel had searched everywhere. He went back to the German bakery and stood by the window, watching and hoping, until hope felt like it was nothing more than a fantasy. He sat on the same bench in the park for hours, wanting to see her running in the snow, her hat flying behind her, wishing to once again hear a little of that joyous laughter. All he found was the world going on without him.

Scouring the Washington Market had done no good either. He had rung bells and asked children if they'd seen her. She seemed to be as elusive as Saint Nicholas. He went into churches, every church, and he prayed, prayers that seemed to have no answers.

By midnight on Christmas Eve he had walked all the way to the opera house, not caring about the cold or the snow. There was a performance of Handel's *Messiah* scheduled. He wandered through the crowds until most had gone inside. He dug into his pockets and dropped coins and bills into every dented and rusty tin can along the way.

The snow began to fall harder and faster. He tossed

a gold coin into an old dented enamel bowl sitting by a blind man dressed in rough homely clothes, then he paused and said, "The storm is picking up. Do you have somewhere to go?"

"I live near Grand Street, east of the Bowery." The old man tried to get up but his hands were old and gnarled and he had no gloves to protect him from the elements.

Daniel helped him, then bent down and picked up the bowl and placed it in the man's gnarled hands. He turned and hailed a hansom cab with a sharp whistle.

He opened the door. "I've paid the driver to take you home," he told the old man, helping him inside. He paused and looked into the old man's creased eyes, eyes that showed every hard year he had lived. Without a thought, he pulled off his gloves and placed them in the man's hands, closing his bent and aged fingers around them. "Merry Christmas," he said, then closed the door. "Merry Christmas."

For the longest time he just stood there, watching the cab disappear down the snowy street. He turned, stuck his icy hands in his coat pockets, and walked toward home, his mind in a place of loss and emptiness.

He passed a Salvation Army bell ringer near the corner and reached into his pants pockets. He'd used the last of his money for the cab.

He started to walk on but stopped and pulled out his gold pocket watch. He looked at it for a moment.

Time didn't matter to him anymore. Without Lilli, nothing mattered.

He walked back and tossed the watch into the collection bucket, then he turned and walked away.

He realized with a sudden sense of panic that the woman had stopped ringing the bell. He froze, his shoulders hunched against the cold in his heart more than the cold outside. "Don't stop ringing that bell. Please. Keep ringing, because . . ." His voice dropped to a tight whisper and he stared sightlessly at the snow-covered walk. "Every time a bell rings . . ."

"An angel gets its wings," she finished.

"Lilli?" His head shot up. He spun around, then reached out and pushed back her bonnet. A pile of silver-blond hair tumbled loose. "Lilli!"

"Daniel . . ."

And she was in his arms.

"God, Lilli. It's really you!" He held her so tightly, afraid to let her go lest she disappear again.

"I'm here now. I'm here." She must have read the look on his face because she said, "And I'll not leave you. It's for a lifetime."

"My God, I thought I'd lost you." He held her face and kissed her over and over. "I've searched everywhere. Been everyplace we were, looking and hoping." He held her face in his hands and just took a moment to look at her, to memorize her face, that smile. "I've given away more money than you could fathom. Everything. Anything. Nothing matters but you."

Tears streamed down her cheeks.

He held her so damn tightly and whispered, "My angel."

She touched his lips with her fingers. "Daniel? Your angel?"

"My fallen angel. You've come home to me."

She smiled up at him, then fixed an odd look up at Heaven. She winked, then she was looking at him again, her smile only for him. She leaned back in his arms. "Maybe, just maybe, Daniel . . . all you had to do was whistle."

Epilogue

It is said by those who ought to understand such things,
That the good people . . . are some of the angels
Who were turned out of Heaven,
And who landed on their feet in this world.

—William Butler Yeats

AND TEN YEARS AFTER THAT CHRISTMAS, DANIEL STILL heard bells whenever he kissed his wife. They still lived in the huge house on the corner, but inside the house had changed.

Gone were the priceless art and porcelains. Gone were the collections. Instead, the walls of the Stewart home held simple drawings from children's unskilled hands and portraits of Lilli with his daughters and his sons.

She had named their eldest daughter Florida, the twins Cherubim and Seraphim—Cheri and Sera, for short—and then his sons Peter and Gabriel, saying she was naming them after old friends, very, very old friends, to whom she owed a debt.

Gone now were the French antiques and stiff-backed chairs. Comfortable and colorful furniture filled every room, some of it nicked and snagged from children and pets. But it was warm and welcoming and real, and it made Daniel's house a home.

There was not a whistle in the entire place. But there were bells everywhere, on tables, near doorways. There were dinner bells and sleigh bells, breakfast bells and door bells, chimes and clock bells, tea bells and Chinese gongs. Jingle bells tingled from toddlers' shoes and puppies' collars. A cow bell called the family together.

At a place of honor on a table in the foyer was a set of glass bells. Whenever someone slid down the banister they rang one of them.

For you see, Daniel and Lilli Stewart had given their children a wonderful gift: the ability to believe in things magical and whimsical and heavenly, to believe in people and, most of all, to believe in things that can't be proven—to know in their hearts that every time a bell rings . . .

An angel gets its wings.

JILL BARNETT is the author of fifteen acclaimed novels and short stories. Her work has appeared on many national bestseller lists and has been published in fourteen languages. She is a recipient of the PERSIE Award for Literature and the National Waldenbooks Award.

ARNETTE LAMB

Hark! The Herald

For Jake,

a little guy, who came with love and
joy and a great big heart,
and left with a bite out of mine

Scottish Lowlands
November, 1308

HARK! THE HERALD OF THE KING OF SCOTLAND!"

In a swirl of gold and scarlet Bruce livery, the herald of King Robert I glided into the common room of Douglas Castle and wound her way through the tangle of benches. Seated near the hearth, across a gaming table from his brother Drummond, Randolph Macqueen forgot the dice in his hands and stared in rapt fascination at the unusual messenger.

Drummond nudged his arm. "A woman?"

"More woman than the rumors say," Randolph mused, thinking of the stories he'd heard about her.

"'Tis an occasion," Drummond said, "seeing you gawk at a female like a lovestruck lad."

Randolph couldn't see her face, but she carried herself with poise, and in her wake, she left a sea of admiring men and pinched-mouthed women. He blew out his breath. "'Tis plain to see why so many correspond with the king of Scotland."

"Who is she?"

"Elizabeth Gordon, the most intriguing woman in our land."

"If women are summoned into service as royal

messengers, Scotland has changed more than I thought."

For seven years Randolph's brother had been imprisoned by the English, who named a Scotsman guilty of treason for defending his own home. A stipulation of Drummond's pardon prohibited him from traveling above the Highland Line. Another stipulation had stripped him of the title of chieftain of Clan Macqueen.

Randolph spoke from the heart. "A pity you cannot come home to the Highlands and see the changes for yourself."

"I am free, and I prosper in the Debatable Lands." Contentment made a vow of Drummond's words. "Worry not, Brother."

Years ago, Randolph had given up hope of seeing his brother again. Now, on the brink of the most special of seasons, they were eye to eye across a table in Douglas Castle. Praise the saints, Randolph thought, and drape the halls with holiday ivy.

"Tell me about the herald," Drummond said.

Randolph laughed. " 'Tis clear the subject of our conversations has not changed."

In a thick voice, Drummond said, "As lads we talked of little else, save women and politics."

Old bonds tightened, and they were young siblings again, making silent judgments and unspoken vows of loyalty. "Aye, only now we can discuss them at once. 'Tis said that Elizabeth Gordon is the most honorable lass in this land or any other. She ferries Bruce's messages to the king of England."

Both men looked to the head table, where Edward II held forth. His father, Edward I, had vanquished the Scottish Lowlands. This Edward now visited his loyal vassal, Red Douglas. While here, the king would bestow the traditional Christmas gifts of tunic, surcoat, and mantle.

"Then you must become a confidant of Scotland's king."

Unlikely, Randolph thought, so long as Robert Bruce refused to participate in the first Christ's Mass of unity to be held in the Highlands. But Randolph would not voice his opinion with so many Lowlanders to hear. When they were alone, he would speak frankly with Drummond.

His interest seriously engaged by the herald, Randolph followed her progress to the head table.

Her floor-length cape billowing behind her, a floppy velvet cap sitting at a jaunty angle and shielding her face, she halted before the king of England. With her back to the crowd, she removed her hat, revealing a coil of braids as colorful as an autumn fire. With fluid grace, she went down on one knee and, bowing her head, awaited the notice of Edward Plantagenet.

For balance in the awkward position, she splayed her gloved fingers on the cold stone floor.

The rumble of male appreciation grew so loud the minstrels gave up their effort. From across the cavernous room, a brash youth whooped and yelled, "A Gordon! A Gordon! To me, a Gordon!" A loud smack silenced him. Female laughter trilled until a sharp shush put an end to the woman's amusement.

Every pair of eyes, save two, were trained on the Scotswoman showing obeisance to a foreign king.

Not with a nod, not even with a glance, did Edward Plantagenet acknowledge her presence. Rather he continued his conversation with his longtime favorite and newly ennobled earl of Cornwall, Piers Gaveston.

Randolph listened to the English monarch's condemnation of the Highland clans, but his eyes stayed fixed on the magnificent woman who wore leather trews, fine boots, and a cape lined with fox fur. The fiery color complimented her hair, and he pondered the shade of her eyes. Would they glow like rare blue jewels or sparkle with the amber hue of whiskey?

His answer would come the moment she turned around.

"Know you what a Highlander's Christmas wreath is fashioned of?" Edward asked his friend.

Piers Gaveston pretended to consider the subject. "Haggis?"

The English king roared. "And thistles too. They'd sooner wage war on each other than bow their heads in tribute to the Christ child."

The weak beer grew sour in Randolph's stomach. For years, the wars of Edward I had taken a heavy toll on the Highlands. Only his death in July of last year had stopped the destruction. The Christmas past, the Highlanders had been too busy surviving the winter to celebrate with more than a blessing from their priests. Not this year. A glorious holiday season awaited all of the upland Scots.

Drummond tapped Randolph's arm. "I wonder what message our king sends to the English monarch."

Randolph hoped it did not concern the Highlands; as the only Highlander in the room, he felt conspicuous. Since his arrival a few hours earlier, he'd received enough wary stares to last a lifetime. He'd come to the Lowlands for two reasons, and aside from admiring Elizabeth Gordon, a reunion with his brother was his primary concern. For now.

"Bother the message," he replied lightly. "'Tis the messenger I'm after. For her, I would swear off other women."

"You? Be true to a woman above a night's pleasure?" A wry grin gave Drummond a boyish look, although he was older than Randolph. "I'll believe *that* when England and Scotland unite."

266

Desire for her be damned, Randolph thought; the messenger of Robert Bruce deserved better treatment. "Why does she tolerate the king's rudeness?"

Ever the voice of reason, Drummond said, "She has a choice?"

Randolph seethed. "Will Edward never acknowledge her?"

Drummond huffed and drank deeply from his tankard. "With Piers Gaveston here? Not bloody likely. I'm surprised they've stayed at table so long."

"Shush!" hissed Randolph. Behind his hand, he whispered, "Speak openly in this company of the king's proclivities, and you'll find yourself back in the Tower of London. These people owe no loyalty to the Macqueens. Like you, they are pledged to Edward Plantagenet."

In an expression reminiscent of their father, Drummond scowled. "Pray this Plantagenet contents himself with England, Wales, this piece of the Lowlands, and what the French allow him. If he inherited his father's obsession for Scotland, only the Highland clans can stop him."

In yet another of the stipulations of his royal pardon, Drummond was denied any congress with his kinsmen. When word arrived that his brother had traveled from his property in the nearby Debatable Lands to Douglas Castle, here in the Lowlands, Randolph had made haste for Solway Firth. The long-incarcerated Drummond possessed information vital to the success of the upcoming Christ's Mass of unity.

Under the pretext of paying his respects to the Douglas chieftain, Randolph had left his crew aboard the *Seawolf* and made the journey alone to the Douglas stronghold. He'd pretended surprise at seeing his brother.

Red Douglas had probably seen through the ruse,

but he took the gift of Spanish fruit Randolph offered, welcomed him into his keep, and convinced the English king that Randolph's presence did not violate Drummond's pardon.

The gravest condition of his brother's release involved Drummond's loyalty, and before Randolph's arrival, Drummond had sworn fealty to the English king. Randolph cringed at the thought of a kinsman bending a knee before a Plantagenet. Watching Elizabeth Gordon, a noble Scot who was privy to the opinions of Robert Bruce, subjugate herself to the enemy was becoming unbearable to Randolph.

Edward's insults went on and on. The crowd laughed when he swore that Scottish chieftains made a practice of sleeping through Christmas Day. "As a precaution," Edward added, "to keep them from killing each other before the Mass can be said. Of a certainty, the pope will never bless their heathen causes."

A misconception, thought Randolph. But let Edward assume the Highland clans still warred among themselves.

"Edward's a boor to ignore her," Randolph grumbled.

"What else do you know about her?"

Randolph sat straighter, his gaze never leaving Elizabeth Gordon. The fingertips of her right hand were still pressed to the flagged floor, and he imagined them growing numb with cold. Damn Edward Plantagenet.

"Stories of her abound. According to the gossips in Edinburgh, when given a choice by her guardian uncle between service to the Church or service to the king, Lady Elizabeth chose Bruce over God."

"She's of noble birth?"

Although he'd just clamped eyes on her himself,

Randolph sent his brother a quelling look. "How can you doubt it after seeing her?"

Properly admonished, Drummond refilled their tankards. "She is bonny. Tell me more of her."

"In Inverness, they believe she's Bruce's mistress and talk of him keeping her in a golden chastity belt."

"Which do you believe?"

At the mere thought of another man touching the beautiful creature, Randolph felt his hands curl into fists. And that was odd; he could not remember the last time he'd been covetous of a woman. But Elizabeth Gordon was different, and his desire for her newly forming. Her alliance with the king of Scotland added intrigue to an already appealing woman.

But if Bruce had sent her on a mission that in any way involved the fledgling Highland unity, Randolph must glean the details. "I believe none of the tales about her. I'm certain she searches for her destiny."

"You think she will find it in you?"

On the table, the flame of the tallow candle wavered. Soon bayberry would scent the wax and fill the hall with the smell of Christmas.

"Aye," Randolph said.

"Does she wear a chastity belt?"

Unwilling to admit he didn't know, he gave his older brother a sly grin.

Duly impressed, Drummond tapped his mug against Randolph's. "I wish you good luck of her, little brother. Why has she chosen to serve as the king's herald?"

"I do not know." But Randolph intended to learn that too.

At last, Edward concluded his insults and glanced down at her, his expression one of pained resignation. Curling his fingers in a beckoning motion, he presented his ear.

Shifting her weight to both knees, she knelt forward and spoke briefly in a tone too low for others to hear.

"Very well." The king rolled his eyes toward Gaveston and murmured something that made his favorite earl smile. Then he rose. When the others at the table moved to stand, he bade them keep their seats and carry on.

Whatever the Scottish king's words, England's monarch would hear them without an audience, for he stepped away from the table and motioned for Elizabeth Gordon to follow him to a corner.

Randolph stood considerably taller than the English king. Overly tall for a woman, the herald stood almost chin to chin with Edward II. A pleasant image came to Randolph's mind. Elizabeth's cheek would fit nicely against his shoulder. No bending down to hear her playful banter or learn the plans of Robert Bruce. No maneuvering to perch her onto a higher step to steal a kiss or a state secret. Standing, he could cuddle her until her eyes turned softly luminous with passion. But what color would they glow?

"Douglas!" yelled the king. "Have you proper quarters for Bruce's herald?"

Their host lunged to his feet and hiked his belt over his belly. "Aye, Your Majesty."

Randolph's heart leapt into his throat; she was staying.

To her, Douglas said, "How long will you bide with us, my lady?"

Edward roared, "Until I give her leave to go!" Then he picked up his tankard and, with Piers Gaveston, disappeared up the steps leading to the private chambers.

Elizabeth Gordon turned around.

Her eyes were cold, stark gray, and they scanned the room with cool efficiency. Some of the occupants ducked, as if to escape her notice. Others squirmed like young bucks eager for the rut. Randolph willed her to look for him.

She did, then spied his brother. She paused and looked again at Randolph.

He felt as if he'd been yanked by a mooring line.

"She casts her eyes on you," Drummond said.

Randolph had told no one of his plans to come to Douglas Castle. "But for what reason?"

Glancing neither left nor right, she moved toward them.

Her nose bore a regal slope and her chin was delicately pointed. A faint pink blush stained her cheeks, but Randolph suspected the ride on a cold night had brought on the color rather than anger at the poor behavior of Edward Plantagenet.

With each step she took, Randolph found something new about her to admire. No freckles marred her complexion, and wisps of spiraling curls framed her face.

His brother nudged his ribs, but Randolph couldn't look away from her.

In a graceful motion, she unclasped her cloak, swept it from her shoulders, and draped it over her arm.

Randolph and Drummond stood up.

He'd been correct about the fit of her cheek against his shoulder, for the top of her head almost reached his nose. When her spicy fragrance drifted across the table, Randolph had trouble swallowing.

"You are Drummond Macqueen," she said to his brother.

They were as alike as two thistles. Randolph felt compelled to say, "How do you know which of us is Drummond?"

She turned, and her keen gaze searched Randolph's face. "Randolph Macqueen. You are now the chieftain of your clan."

"I did not seek the post."

"Nor do you shun it." She turned to Drummond. "Our sovereign lord bids you welcome home and praises God for your release."

So that was her message. Randolph relaxed.

"Home?" said Drummond. "The Highlands are forbidden to me. The only property I am allowed lies nearby in the Debatable Lands."

"Although he would have it otherwise, our king knows you have sworn fealty to the English." The strong words rolled off her tongue as if she were commenting on his preference for hart over pig.

"I had no choice, herald." Drummond's tone grew gravelly with anger. "And the Highlands will not fall to ruin for want of one Macqueen. You may take those words to Bruce."

To divert the potentially dangerous conversation, Randolph stepped aside. "Join us, my lady."

She pointed to the table and the forgotten dice. "I have discharged my duty, and your gaming awaits."

"'Tis boring now." Randolph raked the dice onto the flagged floor. "I have heard it said that you can recall every word of a message as if the speaker were doing the telling again. I would hear the truth from you." He offered her his seat. "While you warm yourself by the fire."

She glanced with longing at the hearth. Then she took the stool he offered and eased her long legs beneath the table.

"Do you truly remember every spoken word?"

She shrugged. "'Tis the work of a herald, remembering conversations."

"You never blunder?"

Her knee brushed Randolph's, but she did not bring attention to it. "Not when kings speak to me."

Enchanted, he wanted that knee back; so he moved his leg. "A scribe aids you."

She made a slow inspection of the space around her and scooted out of his reach. "See you a scribe about, Lord Randolph?"

Only the two men who had just left the room outranked Randolph, and neither of them were Scottish. More outstanding than her incorrect address was the straightforward manner in which she delivered it. "I'm no English lord, and how do you know me?"

A serving maid offered her a steaming tankard. She fished a coin from her pouch and tossed it to the girl. After a quick sip, she said, "I saw you this summer past at Auldcairn Castle."

Located in the northern shire of Elgin, east of Inverness, Auldcairn was the home of Revas Macduff, Randolph's liege lord and friend. "Impossible." Randolph scoffed. "I did not see you there, and I would have remembered."

She chuckled, but more from irony than humor. "'Twas Midsummer's Eve, and the night unseasonably warm. Your host, Revas Macduff, was seated next to John Sutherland, who sat to the left of Sheriff Brodie. Angus Davidson and the earls of Montcrief and Mar were also in attendance. Macduff had just presented warbands to his fosterling, Glennie Forbes. The priest, Father Thomas, was unduly gleeful, even for a Scottish clergyman. He occupied a gaming table with Summerlad, who is your younger brother and an admirer of Serena Cameron. You were there to . . ."

"To celebrate Glennie's achievements." The truth behind the meeting was a Highland matter and the principal reason for Randolph's presence here at Douglas Castle today. But the gathering and the important Christ's Mass it spawned must remain secret for now.

Of a certainty, Randolph must watch his words, for Elizabeth Gordon had correctly named the important men in attendance last summer at Auldcairn Castle. "I am flattered that you remembered me among so much Highland manhood and wisdom."

She whisked off her gloves and laid them on the table. "You were unforgettable that evening."

Drummond nodded sagely. "So say all of the lassies when speaking of my brother."

What had he done, Randolph wondered? And how delightful that this lovely creature wished to discuss it.

Loud enough for her other admirers to hear, he said, "Explain what disguise you wore, dear Elizabeth, for I did not see you."

To his relief, the minstrels began a seasonal lay about a goodly maiden who pined for the return of her true love by Christmas Day, thus saving her from the clutches of a foul-hearted merchant. The occupants of the other tables returned to their revelry.

Elizabeth Gordon wrapped her hands around the steaming tankard. The tips of her fingers were white with cold. Hearthlight shimmered in her hair, glowing first red, then richly gold. By God, she was a prize, Randolph thought, and he pictured her draped in tinsel and sipping yule wine by his hearth.

"I did not hide," she said. "Rather, you were engaged in a weighty conversation with the countess of Nairn. Seldom have I heard a man explaining to a peeress of the realm the finer points of women's undergarments."

"Oh, ho!" said Drummond.

Now Randolph knew why he hadn't seen the herald.

"The widowed countess of Nairn, you see," Elizabeth Gordon continued, "had just concluded her mourning for his lordship."

In actuality, the very young and extremely friendly countess had begged Randolph to guess the color of her smallest clothing, which she confessed to have worn to please him.

His traitorous brother chuckled and said, "Randolph offered his consolation to the grieving widow."

In mock seriousness, the herald touched a hand to the scarlet lilies emblazoned on her tabard. "The last of the consolations, I believe, for she returned to court immediately thereafter."

Under his brother's goading stare, Randolph fought the urge to squirm. On that night months ago, when the countess's teasing had turned carnal, they'd adjourned to a guest chamber. Two mornings later, Randolph and a thoroughly consoled countess had emerged. The herald had already departed.

"That is why you did not see me at Auldcairn Castle," she said with finality.

Randolph sprang to his feet. "Shall we take a walk on the battlements, Lady Elizabeth?"

She tilted her head back. "Nay. I doubt we share a common thought on which to build a conversation."

Moments before she had been friendly; now she was evasive. Dutifully challenged, Randolph raised his eyebrows. "Neither of us is common, and you are known for conversation."

Her mouth twitched beautifully with suppressed laughter. "Absolutely. Resolutely. Never will I walk alone with you on a battlement or anywhere else after the sun has set."

He couldn't stop looking at her lips and the delicate line of her jaw. "Aye, you will." He sat down again. "Shall we make a wager of it, my lady?"

"That I will not be seduced by you?" She shook her head in rueful amusement. "Name your forfeit, Macqueen."

"My ship. And my boon shall be your hand in marriage." Now why had he said that? He'd made a point of disdaining marriage.

Her mouth dropped open in surprise, but she recovered quickly. As direct as a priest dispensing a penance, she looked him in the eye. "First you speak openly of seduction, then marriage, which neither of us truly wants. Even so, I haven't that to give."

"Seduction can be enjoyable for both of us."

She moved to stand. "Your charms are wasted."

He grasped her arm. "I'll decide when my charms are wasted."

She stared at his hand, which looked rough and dark against the velvet sleeve of her tabard. "I have nothing to wager." She sat down again.

He released her arm but held her gaze. "'Tis said the desert horses your uncle bought from the Saracens are worthy of a chieftain's ransom."

"True. But that depends on the *clan* he is chieftain *of.* A Macqueen." She sighed. "I'm not certain the Macqueens . . ."

At the thinly veiled insult, resolve spread through him. *"This* Macqueen will make you forget your pledge to Robert Bruce."

Something flickered in her eyes. Fondness, or perhaps disappointment, but he didn't know her well enough to say. Not yet. But with a certainty he could not explain, Randolph knew she would be his. He liked her confidence, and if he could glean information about the plans of the king of Scotland, his charms would certainly not be wasted.

"The English king spears salmon on the morrow," he said. "We go for boar. I should like to examine your horses for myself. Will you join us?"

"Us?" She looked to Drummond.

"Not I," he said. "I've an elephant and a family to attend."

The subject pleased her, for her eyes twinkled with fondness. "You have the beast from the Tower of London?"

"Aye. We both received a pardon from English captivity."

"A noble gesture, sir. The elephant deserves freedom, as do you." She turned to Randolph. "Does your ship's crew go a-hunting for boar, or have you brought an army of Highlanders?"

She sought an escort to shield her from his advances. Any decent woman would. She couldn't know that a legion of angry Turks couldn't keep him away from her. "My crew awaits aboard the *Seawolf* in Solway Firth. Douglas's huntsmen will accompany us—and your maid of course."

"I will come, but not for the hunt. I require no maid, and you'll find me a poor companion when the kill commences."

He'd won her acceptance, but he did not feel victorious.

The next afternoon, Randolph leaned forward in the saddle of his charging mount, his spear poised and ready. Two lengths ahead, a snorting boar raced for freedom.

Randolph remembered her words. *A poor companion when the kill commences.* On reflection, it sounded like a plea.

He glanced back. She sat atop one of her elegant desert horses. Her expression verged on a disappointment so painful, he did something he'd never before considered. He lowered the spear and reined in his horse. The boar scrambled beneath a patch of bracken and was swallowed up by the underbrush. The huntsmen charged after the beast.

Behind him he heard the rattle of harness. His mount grew anxious, and so did he.

When her white stallion moved abreast of his, she said, "Why?"

"The huntsmen will make the kill." Coloring up his reasons with logic sounded dishonest, so he told her the truth: "I thought to spare you the death cry of the animal."

Her gaze sharpened.

He guided his horse closer to hers. "You are not the only one to correctly remember a conversation."

"'Twas the spirit of my words you recalled. For that, I thank you."

"I need no thanks for sparing you distress. 'Tis the work of a gentleman for a lady." Softer, he said, "Your desert horse exceeds his reputation. I've heard it said he can run a day and a night without losing his wind."

She stroked the animal's neck. "He's worth a fleet of ships."

He imagined her hand caressing him just so. "Shall we have a race?"

She stared into the distance. The proof of her Gordon lineage lay in the high bridge of her nose and the strength of her chin. Beneath the fox-lined cloak, she wore a long woolen surcoat over a bliaud of yellow linen. Even without royal livery, she was no ordinary woman.

"You're mad, Randolph Macqueen."

"But the idea excites you." What the idea did to him didn't bear close scrutiny.

"'Tis another foolish wager on your part." Her gaze moved to his horse. "You cannot win."

If a look from her assured success, he should concede defeat now. But more than a race between galloping steeds was at stake. Politics aside, he leapt at the chance to better know Elizabeth Gordon. She had been friendly during the outing, and the thought occurred to him that she was lonely. The holidays loomed ahead, and he suspected that, because of her position, she held herself apart.

He'd sift through the gossip and separate truth from rumor. "Then you accept the wager and agree to keep my company during our sojourn here?"

Elizabeth hesitated. She liked Randolph Macqueen. From the moment she'd spied him in the common room, she had been drawn to him. Curiosity had made her linger at his table.

He did not pry into the king's business. He did not fawn or act the smitten swain. He did not pepper his conversation with names of influential families or boast of personal wealth.

Since they'd met in the stables after morning prayers, he had been respectful and anything but distant. He seemed honestly interested in her, and he was thoughtful beyond the ordinary.

She felt obligated to say, "The English king may summon me at any moment."

Randolph Macqueen had a reputation for being ruthless in battle, but now the set of his mouth spoke of disillusionment. "Not soon?"

Questions always made her wary, for everyone wanted to know the affairs of kings. To better serve them, she had trained herself to answer with caution. But with Randolph Macqueen, caution wasn't an option but a necessity. "I cannot anticipate the king of England."

"But must you return to Bruce immediately? Can you not bide awhile with me, even if the Englishman replies?"

His Highland speech lent intimacy to the query. She was enjoying herself. Winter already bound the uplands in snow, and no matter where the king sent her next, she'd be forced into crowded common rooms and the company of shallow-minded women and scheming men. Her escorts on this mission were rough fellows, better suited to alehouses and wenching than riding for the joy of it. The English king was inclined to linger.

If Edward were true to his past, he would keep her waiting for as long as he could. When last she'd been sent to London, he'd taken a fortnight to form a reply to Bruce. Once in York, she'd languished for a month before he'd responded to a trivial concern. No matter the wait, Bruce would expect her to return immediately with Edward's reply.

Douglas had given her a private chamber. Her escorts would sleep in the barracks. Randolph Macqueen was both a well-traveled sea captain and a respected swordsman. In his company she need not suffer the unwanted advances of others while awaiting the royal whim. And he was an outsider, same as she.

The ridiculous wager offered a distraction. But if Macqueen ill treated her, she would avenge herself. "If I put up this horse for wager, you *will* forfeit your ship."

He arched his dark eyebrows, and his blue eyes brimmed with invitation. *"If* I lose. After you lie beneath me, I shall demand your stable and all else you possess."

Any such claim was years late in coming. She'd given her word to the king of Scotland, a man pledged to defending their land against English aggression. The maidenly dreams of one woman paled against the greater cause: Scottish autonomy.

"You speak of the forbidden, Randolph. My hand in marriage is not part of this bargain."

"Very well. I'll settle for your heart."

Darkly handsome and dangerously confident, he fairly dripped Highland charm. She'd been raised among men like him, and in all of her missions to the southern courts, she seldom encountered so much gallantry. Romance and marriage were denied her so long as she served as herald to the king. But away from the prying eyes of Bruce supporters and the court gossips, she could do as she pleased—if she behaved with propriety.

Another factor begged consideration. She suspected

that Randolph Macqueen had come to Douglas Castle for more than a reunion with his brother. As a trusted emissary of the king of Scotland, she had a duty to learn why a steadfast Highlander journeyed into what was now enemy land. Especially with the king of England in attendance.

If Randolph Macqueen plotted villainy, she must know.

He posed no threat to her, for she would not fall prey to his seduction. She rather liked the idea of outsmarting a notorious rogue and owning her own ship. "I accept your wager, Randolph Macqueen, but I do not know how to sail. After I win, will you continue being a gentleman long enough to teach me?"

"Oh, aye," he said smoothly, plucking twigs from his mount's black mane. "I'm told I'm the best of tutors."

Thanks to the countess of Nairn, court gossip named him a knave who would not go willingly to the marriage bed. A perfect companion for a woman prohibited from speaking wedding vows.

"How long will you stay here?" she asked.

"Until . . ." He paused and followed the progress of a young doe evading a ready buck. "Until I win the wager or you are called away."

Her question had caught him unaware; yet he lied smoothly. Randolph Macqueen was hiding something. "Then what else shall we do?" she asked, more curious than before.

"Go a-hawking? I promise to shield your ears from the cries of the prey."

She gave him high marks for attentiveness. "I haven't a bird with me."

"Douglas neglects his mews in favor of the burn." He made a sour face and grumbled, "I'm told we're having salmon again tonight."

The companionable statement pleased her, for she

could not remember discussing a meal with a stranger before the food was served. "Will you fast?" she teased.

"With you beside me?" Beneath black lashes a queen would envy, he studied her. "Aye, for by my oath, Elizabeth Gordon, a thought of you robs me of appetite."

She couldn't help chuckling, but she was flattered all the same. "Then what is the point of going a-hawking?"

He gave her a look so blatantly suggestive, she blushed and admitted to herself that she underestimated him.

"I favor quickness in a woman."

Her horse sidestepped. "Even a feeble-minded grandmother could not mistake your meaning."

"And you said we could not build a conversation," he chided. "We speak without words."

A distant and agonized squeal shattered the friendly mood. The boar's end was at hand.

"Come." He kicked his horse into a canter and motioned for her to follow. Pointing, he said, "We'll race to the loch beyond those oaks. Winner names a boon."

With a certainty gained from past experiences with other men, she knew he would demand a kiss. The knowledge disappointed her, for she expected originality from Randolph Macqueen.

As they rode toward a stand of barren hardwoods, the pounding of horses' hooves silenced the boar's death cry. Halfway across the moor, Macqueen veered south and onto a well-traveled wagon road. This was the longer route to their destination, but the safer path. Had he chosen it out of concern for their mounts? She hoped so. Given the added distance, her horse would easily win. Even now, her stallion strained to overtake his stocky Spanish mount.

She pictured Randolph Macqueen on a warhorse and knew he sat a destrier with the same ease and control he exhibited now. Like the other Macqueens, he was sinfully handsome, and he possessed a playfulness and depth of character she had not expected.

In chapel that morning, she'd observed him with his brother and nephew. While other heads were bowed in prayer, Randolph had stolen glance after vulnerable glance at his older sibling. He'd also doted on his nephew, who bore the dark good looks of the Macqueens. Witnessing his familial loyalty had been oddly painful to Elizabeth; until that moment she had not missed the company of her kinsmen.

At the point they entered the forest, the road became a sea of newly fallen leaves that crackled and flew into the air, reminding Elizabeth that the holiday season was nigh.

Her opponent turned and grinned at her. He looked so happy and self-assured, she smiled back and urged her horse into a full gallop. As she breezed past a surprised Randolph, she blew him a kiss and took the shortest path to the finish.

Her nimble-footed mount skirted patches of bracken and clumps of ripening holly. Hares dashed for their warrens. Fat red grouse lumbered into flight. Up ahead, the loch shimmered in the distance. Behind her, the Highlander urged his horse faster. But the animal had spent his strength chasing the boar, and hers was still fresh.

Crouching upon the stallion's withers, she whispered encouragement. The animal answered with a burst of speed that made a blur of the landscape. The sound of thundering hooves thrummed in her ears. The wind buffeted her face and neck. Her mind cast out politics and intrigues. Time and place vanished, taking with them maidenly regrets and selfish yearnings.

For now, Elizabeth Gordon was an unburdened spirit riding a fast white horse on a bright November day. Lightness of heart made her dizzy. She focused on a spot between the horse's ears and held on to her freedom.

Too soon, glaring light pierced her eyes, and she squinted against the reflection of the sun on the loch. As she neared the water's edge, the stallion slowed. She dismounted and, on wobbly legs, lunged to the bank and drank her fill. Then she sat on a fallen log and awaited Randolph Macqueen.

He was far behind, his red-and-black tartan cape a colorful dot amid the barren trees.

According to Red Douglas, Randolph was merely paying a courtesy call—his first. Everyone knew the Macqueens were liegemen of Revas Macduff, an ambitious man who wanted to rule all of the Highland clans.

As always, Elizabeth reminded herself, clans and their chieftains, kings and their consorts, would do as they may. She had stolen a few hours of freedom, and she had won a race. To a woman who made the sovereignty of Scotland her life's work, the respite should have seemed paltry. But times had changed.

Or had she?

When Macqueen reached her, he sprang to the ground and slapped the rump of his horse. The lathered beast trotted to the water and drank. Her stallion cast a wary eye on the newcomer, but his gentle nature prevented aggression.

His chest heaving, Randolph rested his hands on his knees and breathed deeply. "'Tis warm still, here in the Lowlands." He glanced at her horse. "Revas Macduff did not enlarge the tale. Your desert horse is truly fine."

In her uncle's home, she had possessed riches without end. Now she groomed her horses herself, and they were the sum of her wealth. "He's a distance runner. You should have chosen a shorter course."

"Or a faster horse."

"None exists on this island."

"Winning suits you, Elizabeth." His smile faded, and he grumbled, "But your cocky grin spoils it."

She bristled with umbrage. "Had you won, you would have crowed."

He laughed and raked his hands through his overlong hair. "True."

Congeniality filled the moment. "Will you concede defeat to me?"

He flung his arms wide and stared into the sky. "Willingly and completely do I yield to Elizabeth Gordon."

She laughed too. "Your reputation goes before you, so spare me the grovelings of a vanquished rogue."

He pointed a finger at her and said with mock seriousness, "Never have I groveled."

She couldn't help saying, "'Tis well known what *you do*, Randolph Macqueen."

"You speak of court gossip." He picked up a stone and sent it skimming across the loch. "I have not been to court. What do they say about me?"

Best put him in his place and keep their association on friendly ground. "'Tis said that beyond the bed, you have little use for women."

His gaze was sharp, his expression defensive. "Have I tried to kiss you?"

He excelled at frankness, but so did she. "You haven't had the opportunity."

"Perhaps I lured you here apurpose."

"You did—to win a race. Are you disappointed?"

His eyebrows rose. "Are you?"

She knew instinctively he wasn't speaking of fast horses. "Nay, but time will tell. You owe me a boon."

"I could suggest a very pleasant one."

"Pleasant for you, disastrous for me. I have my reputation to consider."

"You are reputed to be Bruce's mistress."

At first the rumor had hurt her deeply; now she used the tale to her advantage. Few men were willing to risk the displeasure of Robert Bruce, who laughed at the story and encouraged her to do the same.

She had a bevy of bold retorts at the ready. "And you would like for me to become *your* mistress."

"What would *you* like, Elizabeth?"

Peace and unity in Scotland. An English king who respected borders. An open court where all of the men looked and behaved like Randolph Macqueen. "I'd like an honest answer."

"Then hear me well, dear Elizabeth: If you are not Bruce's mistress, I can solve no great mysteries for you, save one."

Tossed out like bait, the cryptic statement was meant to lure her into an intimate discussion. Habit ruled her reply. "Give me the answer I seek: Tell me what brings you to Douglas Castle."

The subject displeased him, for his mouth tightened, and he looked away. "Good manners draw me to the Lowlands. I have just come from Spain, where the crops were fruitful. I thought to share the largesse with Douglas and make his acquaintance."

"No other reason?"

"You are very curious."

"You are very evasive."

If he hid another purpose, she'd learn it. Red Douglas and Randolph Macqueen were not allies. Castle servants were always eager to earn an extra coin in exchange for information. If bribery failed, she'd find another way. "'Twas a casual question."

"Not from one who listens to kings." He sat beside her on the log. "Unless you are beginning to like me."

She was. Although his objective was obvious, his

methods were pleasantly surprising. Gossips named him a knave where females were concerned, and Elizabeth understood his success. Were she free to bestow her affections, she might well rush into his arms.

"Confess, Elizabeth," he cajoled, nudging her knee with his own. "You are enjoying yourself. You find me interesting."

Honestly, she replied, "I am not here to make merry with a rogue." That was the mildest of her opinions of him.

"Yet you are. I see happiness in your eyes."

It was true, and she owed him an explanation. "When the English king summons me, I must take his reply to Robert Bruce. Do not expect me to delay my departure to search you out and say farewell."

"If you did, I would offer you my ship for your return to our sovereign. You did express an interest in sailing."

He tried to trick her with words. Bruce awaited near Saint Andrews, a distance traveled quicker by land. But with the English king presently on what was once Scottish soil, she would keep Bruce's whereabouts to herself. "I said I would rather *sail* my ship myself."

"*If* the *Seawolf* falls to you in the wager."

He'd named his ship for the device of the Macqueens, a common practice among the clans. "*When* the *Seawolf* falls to me."

"Either way, rest assured that you may captain my vessel whenever you wish."

How did he manage to distract her and direct the conversation? He had skillfully avoided giving her an answer. She would try again. "Where shall we go a-hawking?"

His sly grin said he wasn't fooled by the change in topic. "'Tis my first visit to Douglas's land. I'll consult the falconer."

She remembered his complaint about the food. "I'll ask the cook to provide a lunch. A salted salmon, perhaps?"

His broad shoulders sagged and his eyes glimmered with mock reproach. "You're cruel, Elizabeth Gordon."

"A haunch of Spanish beef?"

He groaned and looked so forlorn, she patted his hand. He twisted his wrist until their palms touched. The look in his eye turned positively sleepy.

Intimacy crept into the moment, but she did not feel the need to shy away.

He threaded his fingers through hers. "If you enjoy our hunt and the king does not summon you, I would seek your agreement now to celebrate Saint Nicholas's Day with me in the town of Closeburn."

Celebrated on December 6, a fortnight away, Saint Nicholas's Day was a time reserved for children. Puppet shows and mock battles were staged by the castle youth.

"According to the brewer, ghosts perch in the trees there, and trolls rob children of holiday sweets if they are bad."

Elizabeth couldn't help saying, "What if you are bad? What will the monsters take from you?"

"Nothing," he almost purred, "for I intend to be very, very good." With that, he squeezed her hand, then released it.

After the particularly satisfying day in the company of Elizabeth Gordon, Randolph found his brother and broached the subject that had brought him to the Lowlands.

"Where is the relic of Saint Columba?" Centuries ago, Columba had introduced the Scots to Christianity. A piece of the jawbone of the saint was the only holy relic of Clan Macqueen. It had been lost since Drummond's capture by the English.

"Why do you seek it?"

They sat in a corner table in the alehouse. It was the hour of vespers, and most people were at prayers. Several rough-looking fellows occupied a table near the door. A fat yellow candle cast faint shadows on the smoke-stained walls. Across the room, the burly ale-man climbed a ladder and disappeared through a hole in the ceiling.

Quietly, Randolph said, "Revas Macduff is gathering the Highland clans on Christ's Day for a Mass of unity at Elgin Cathedral."

Drummond choked on his ale. "The butcher's son unites the Highland clans at Christmas?"

"Shush!" Even though they were out of earshot of the alewife and other patrons, Randolph spoke softly. "All the clans, save the Macgillivrays, have sworn fealty to him. We solemnize our vows at the Mass."

"I'm wonderfound." Drummond stared at the earthen floor. "Who, outside the Highlands, knows of it?"

"No one."

"Not even Robert Bruce?"

"The king knows. He would have us wait another year to see if Edward continues his father's quest for Scotland."

"Then Bruce errs. The time is ripe, for the English war among themselves."

Randolph had heard that rumor, but with his brother's confirmation he grew more determined to see the Highlands unify quickly. "Revas Macduff has rightly demanded secrecy until the event. A bishop from the Vatican comes to say the Mass to Christ. Before the pope will bless the Highland causes and fill our warchest with holy gold, all of the clans must present their relics and, upon them, renew their vows to God."

"The Church has promised money?"

The ale grew bitter in Randolph's mouth. "Aye, but only if we all attend with our holy relics in hand."

Drummond surveyed the room, then leaned close and whispered, "Then I pray you all do unite and seal your vows before the pope's man."

It was odd hearing his brother speak of the Highland clans in terms of "you" and "your," but Randolph did not debate the point. "'Tis said Edward cannot yet afford to continue his father's war on Scotland, but that will change. He rules a beggared kingdom now. Bruce's support grows from day to day, yet his progress is slow. This Edward will make his march on Scotland, and when he does, 'twill be up to the Highland clans to stop him. If Revas Macduff sits at the helm and flies the pope's banner, we will prevail no matter what King Robert does."

With the same hand he'd used to teach Randolph to arm wrestle, Drummond strummed the table. "The Church demands much ceremony and devotion. How will the chieftains put aside their own causes and kneel before the pope's man?"

The candle sputtered. Hot tallow splattered Randolph's hand, but he did not feel the burn. "'Tis what we all want. We have given our pledge to Revas Macduff. Bruce is busy uniting the isles and wooing back the border lords. He wrongly places little faith in Revas."

"The herald told you that?"

"She did not have to." Randolph sighed, and frustration settled in his gut. "Enough of politics, Brother, I'd rather discuss the woman herself."

"Have you lost your heart to her?"

"'Tis true I lust for Elizabeth Gordon, but she is not a woman to dally with."

"My wife's maid says the herald is cold."

"Nay." Randolph remembered the look of sheer joy on her face when she'd blown him a kiss and ridden the white stallion to victory. "Her heart is warm and friendly."

"'Tis said she seeks the favor of no man."

She had said as much, but the pleasure she took in his company was plain to see. "For the moment, but we are newly met."

A worried frown scored Drummond's forehead. "My son heard it from the chandler's lad that Lady Elizabeth's uncle disowned her when she would not wed his choice of husbands. Where are her mother and father?"

Randolph dredged up a snippet of the Gordon family scandal. They had been blessed with a kinswoman any clan would prize, but her uncle was too selfish to see it. "Some tragedy befell her parents years ago. The titles and her guardianship fell to her uncle."

Drummond sipped his ale. "She tends her own horses."

Now Randolph understood why she had stayed in the stables when they'd returned from the boar hunt earlier in the day.

"The cooper also believes she's Bruce's mistress."

On that dreadful thought, Randolph pounded the table so hard the candle toppled from its holder. "Elizabeth Gordon will be mine. Now, where is the holy relic of Saint Columba?"

"In the hilt of my sword. Come back with me to our chamber and I shall give it to you."

Randolph sagged with relief. "Gladly."

"'Twill be a bonny sight," Drummond said, "the first Highland Mass to Christ. I never thought to see all of the chieftains kneeling in prayer and swearing upon their holy relics."

A truce pledged before God and ordained by the

291

clergy would unite the clans as no signed treaty could. It was also dangerous. If the lone dissenter, Cutberth Macgillivray, caught wind of it, he would bring his army to Elginshire and capture all of the chieftains. Victory would be as easy as spearing fish in a barrel. But the risk was a worthy one. "A pity you will not be there, for we shall miss you."

"I am contented to my soul." Drummond paused. The aleman climbed down the ladder, a keg on his shoulder. When the man was out of hearing distance, Drummond said, "'Tis not yet December. Will you leave immediately?"

"Nay. I've plenty of time to journey to Elgin Cathedral before Christmas, and another matter detains me."

"The seduction of a flame-haired herald?"

"Aye. Tomorrow we go a-hawking at Malcolm's Moor."

"May I join you?"

"Not unless you relish taking a crossbow quarrel in your back. I want Elizabeth to myself."

"She took the wager?"

The door opened, and a group of Douglas clansmen trudged in and shouted for ale. Randolph finished his. "Aye, and she bested me on horseback today."

"They say her horses can fly."

"True, but the rider flees slower by the moment."

"I've heard it said she cannot be seduced."

Randolph laughed. "I've heard it said the earth is round."

Days of rain delayed their plans to go a-hawking. With the relic of Saint Columba secured inside his boot, Randolph relaxed and turned his energy to the seduction of Elizabeth Gordon. He accompanied her to the fuller's shop, where she purchased finely carded wool and ordered it dyed a deep red—a Christmas gift for the king of Scotland, she'd explained. At the chandler's she bought a bayberry-scented candle for her chamber. From the farrier she chose a pair of brass harness buckles, a present for the master of the stables where she kept her other horses.

Randolph purchased a flax-breaker, half a dozen of the new spinning wheels, and paid extra for the merchant to deliver them to the *Seawolf*.

In the evenings, Randolph took his meals with his brother, nephew, and sister-in-law. He asked Elizabeth to join them, but she declined. Several times he saw her at the high table. From the serving maid he learned that at other times Elizabeth dined alone in her chamber.

The citizens and soldiers of Douglas Castle grew more friendly to Randolph, but he suspected the cause was seasonal good will rather than any likeness for a Highlander.

On the next clear day, Elizabeth and Randolph sat on a blanket at the edge of Malcolm's Moor. Sunset was still hours away, and they had a brace of moorhens and a dozen black grouse for their effort. In the course of the outing, Randolph had spoken of his first falcon and she her first horse. She told of learning to swim with her cousins in the river Tweed. He recalled fighting with his brothers for a go at the quintain.

Elizabeth had ridden a mare today, a smaller counterpart to the prancing white stallion.

Randolph turned to her. "Unless you object, I should like to send the falconer and his best boys back to the keep."

Over the rim of her cup, she asked, "Why?"

"Your stallion is a fine beast, but the mare you ride today is magnificent." He stared across the meadow to where her horse grazed. "I should like to ride her through that field of dried heather."

"Without prying eyes."

"You may pry to your heart's content."

"My heart and all else is happy at the moment. I'll ride your mount and go with the falconer. Unless you dally here overlong, you will catch up with us before we reach Douglas Castle. I'll not stay alone with you long enough to give the gossips reason to talk."

"You fear a stain on your reputation."

"I care not what is said about me, but I am a servant of the king. Were I alone with you to the count of fifty, some would say we are lovers."

"Only if the counter were very slow."

"What difference does that make?"

Without knowing it she had declared her innocence, for even a green lad would take more time spending his passion. No man had touched her.

At a loss for words, he murmured, "I cannot say."

He watched her walk toward the others, her hips swaying gently beneath the full skirt. She had no maid, yet her clothes were perfectly tended and her hair tucked neatly beneath a crisp linen coif. A practical woman, she wasted little time on trivialities and less on gossip. She avoided his queries about the intentions of Robert Bruce with the same skill with which she evaded Randolph's attempts at seduction. It wasn't that she lacked feminine attributes, for she was surely the loveliest woman in Scotland. The truth of it was that she governed his moods—no, it was better said that she brought out the gallant in Randolph.

On her return, she snatched up the reins to his horse and whistled for her own. The dainty white mare answered with a musical whinny, then trotted to her side. Elizabeth eyed Randolph from head to toe and adjusted the stirrups on her saddle to fit his longer legs.

"Behave yourself, Majesty," she instructed the horse. Over her shoulder, she said, "She's just bred and always frisky."

"Nay, she's gentle."

"A ploy for the unsuspecting. Keep the reins tight and say her name before you tell her to stop. She knows the command." Like a kitten, the horse nuzzled her.

"What if I do not tell her to stop?"

"You'll find yourself in England by sunrise."

"Truly?"

"Nay. She will not go afar from me, and your horse is known to plod."

Randolph did not take offense; she'd fairly judged his mount. "He is not mine. I hired him in Ruthwell."

She moved to the stallion and stroked his ears. "He's a good animal all the same."

"I'll help you up," Randolph said, reaching for her.

The moment his hands touched her waist, Elizabeth started. When his palms slipped lower, she looked up at him. "What are you about, Randolph Macqueen?"

He gave her a sheepish grin. "You do not wear a chastity belt."

Under normal circumstances the topic would have been judged vulgar, but Elizabeth's life had ceased being normal the day she became Robert Bruce's herald. "Perhaps I should—to protect me from you."

"'Tis said you possess one that is forged of gold. Do you?"

"Aye."

"How can you wear the ghastly thing?"

"When compared to the alternative, the discomfort is minor."

"What alternative?"

She sighed. "For a well-traveled man, you know little of life. I ride the same roads as briganas and frequent courts that teem with knaves. All men do not respect the herald of Robert Bruce as much as Randolph Macqueen does."

There it was again. A simple, flattering statement designed to keep him in his place. Randolph balked. "You're not wearing a chastity belt now."

"Do I need protection from you?"

"Not yet." He touched her cheek. His fingers were rough against her skin, and Elizabeth had to tilt her head back to look into his eyes. They were deep blue and filled with admiration. She had seen the expression in other men, but within Randolph's eyes lurked a tenderness and honesty that were new to her.

He lifted his brows in invitation.

Temptation tugged at her determination to resist him. They conversed easily, so much so that she often revealed too much of herself. Just this morning he'd lulled her into telling him about the tragic fire that had killed her parents.

She glanced beyond his shoulder but did not see the falconer.

Randolph must have sensed her hesitation, for his hands tightened on her waist. Her heart tripped fast, and her mouth went dry. She licked her lips, and he cursed.

Knowing he was about to kiss her and certain she would enjoy it, Elizabeth drew back. A kiss fell far short of seduction, but she would not give him the advantage in the wager. "The others."

"The others will what? Besmirch the reputation of the king's herald because she takes pleasure in my company?"

"Aye."

"The moment will come, Elizabeth, when you must forget what you are and listen to your heart."

She owed too much to Robert Bruce, and Scotland stood on the brink of autonomy.

"What are you thinking?"

Her circumstances were her own concern.

"Tell me, Elizabeth."

He spoke from the heart, but she could not answer in kind. She would not regret pledging her life to a greater cause. She searched for a diversion and found it in a wild hawk sailing overhead. She pointed to the bird. "I was thinking that he's glad to have his hunting grounds to himself again."

"'Twasn't what you were thinking, but I'm a patient man, and you are worth the wait."

Her worthiness, or lack of it, would not come into play.

"A pair of swans inhabit Loch Lanark," he said. "Would you care to see them while you are here?"

She scanned the cloudy sky. "They will have flown south by now."

"Not so. The falconer said the female suffered a broken wing some three summers ago. The male stays with her year after year."

"A male whose heart is engaged. How romantic."

From the top of his head to the flat of his feet, Randolph Macqueen was completely engaged by this bright woman who made lad's work of the business of kings and rode the finest horses in the land. "Do you think the female is smitten with him?"

"The swan?"

"The female."

She tried to suppress a smile but failed. "'Tis your ship I'm after, my lord. You may yield it now."

Her playfulness filled him with joy. Before meeting her, he could not remember wanting to please a woman in small ways. "We were discussing the swans, and you needn't call me 'my lord.' I am chieftain of the Macqueens, nothing more."

She gave him a naughty grin. "'Tis said you own a fleet of merchant ships, and you wield considerable power in the Highlands. The Mackintoshes, Macraes, Mathesons, and Chisholms all swear fealty to you."

His alliances were common knowledge; discussing them and his possessions with a woman who had no interest in marriage was unusual. "I am at peace with my neighbors. My uncles are trustworthy, which allows me to take to the sea—in my only ship."

"You wagered your only ship to me?"

"Had I a fleet, I would have wagered it."

"You gifted Douglas with oranges and figs."

Her clumsy attempt to change the subject only encouraged Randolph more. "I saved the pomegranates for you."

"Are you offering me a ship with a hold full of rotting fruit?"

Light banter came easily to her; he replied in kind. "Not in this cool weather. Still, if you are worried, we can ride to the port now and make a feast of the cargo."

"I thought you wanted to ride my horse through yonder field of dried heather."

He wanted to own the horse and possess the woman, and he would, in good time, for she was beginning to like him. "I do."

"Then help me into your saddle and be about your pleasure."

Elizabeth changed her gown and informed Douglas's steward of both her return and her plans to absent herself from the castle for her planned outings with Randolph Macqueen. In the crowded common room, she was approached by a succession of men eager to make the acquaintance of Robert Bruce's herald.

She tolerated their unoriginal invitations and sugary innuendoes until a man old enough to be her grandfather boldly offered her a choice of residences within his domain. Patience gone, she excused herself and visited the weaver to see if the cloak she had ordered for King Robert was ready.

The shop teemed with activity. Douglas had commissioned for all of his vassals the traditional Christmas gifts of tunic, surcoat, and mantle. Even with the holiday almost a month away, the weavers would be hard pressed to finish on time.

Assured that the garment would be ready in a day or two, Elizabeth climbed the battlement steps to watch for Randolph.

In the inner bailey below, the elephant grazed while a group of children stared in awe at the enormous beast. Randolph's brother Drummond and the Lady Clare stood nearby.

Just as the sun set in a fiery display of orange, red, and purple, the mare emerged from the forest, a splash of white against the evening-shrouded landscape. Randolph kept the horse at a smooth canter—a feat, for Majesty was prone to gallop. He'd removed his tartan cape and draped it over the mare's withers. When he reached the curtain wall, he drew rein and exchanged a greeting with his brother.

Man and horse were an impressive sight, which the captain of the guard acknowledged with a wink. "Masters the lassies as well, or so the gossips say of Randolph Macqueen."

Elizabeth understood.

"For my own part," the man went on, moving closer and dangling a small mirror before her, "'tis better to gift a woman with trinkets to sweeten her mood."

Fearing she could disguise neither her dislike of the soldier's method nor her admiration for Randolph, she went back to the stables. There she fed and groomed her stallion and the Spanish-bred horse.

She smelled Randolph before she heard him address the stable lad. "A brimming bucket of your best oats, lad," he commanded and led the mare into the next stall.

Dried heather coated his hair and stuck to his clothing.

"I've changed my mind," he announced expansively. "Instead of your stallion, I'll take Majesty when I win the wager."

He looked boyishly excited, and she appreciated the joy he felt at riding the swift mare. "You'll take neither." She pitched him the brush she'd used earlier. "Have a care when you touch her hocks. She's prone to nipping."

"'Tis her right." His chest swelled, and he propped his hands on his hips. "By the saints, Elizabeth, this is a fine beast—as fast as the wind and better mannered than my mother's lap dog."

Even oft-spoken, the words of praise always filled Elizabeth with pride. As if she knew they were discussing her, the spritely mare tossed her head. "Her daintiness is a deception. She has strength to spare."

"You'll get no argument from me." He removed the saddle and blanket and gave the mare the attention she demanded. "But I'm surprised your uncle would part with this beauty or the stallion. You must be his favorite."

She stifled a bitter chuckle. "'Tis better said that he wanted my dowry, and he had grown so fat the horses could no longer carry him."

The first of the vespers bells rang out, calling the faithful to evening prayers.

Randolph surveyed both the horses, then her. "You traded your dowry for two horses?"

To escape an unwanted marriage, Elizabeth had given up her wealth and cut her ties with the Gordons. She'd been three and ten at the time, and not once in the ensuing years had she regretted the decision. "For six horses. The mares are fruitful. I now own a score, with another in Majesty's belly."

He scratched his cheek. "An interesting bit of commerce. Had you a choice?"

She attached no sentimental feelings to the estate. A means to freedom better described the property. "'Twas a modest estate from my mother. The land lies on the river Tweed, and my uncle wanted access to the water."

"Why did they allow you to forfeit your dowry? You must have been a child when you made that decision." He stopped and his expression grew grim. "I beg your pardon. 'Tis poor manners to discuss a lady's age."

His politeness banished another of her reservations about him. "I do not regret my decision. I perform a valuable service to the king. I have my horses. The future lies in God's hands." The present was pure luxury, for she stood in a stable with the influential and engaging Randolph Macqueen.

"Still, you must have been a child at the time."

"Now 'tis you who flatters me," she said. "I was three and ten, a most marriageable age, when I gave up any claim to Gordon land. I will be two and twenty on my next birthday."

"Which is?"

He also wanted to put the subject behind them. "A fortnight hence," she said.

"What gift would please you?"

She did not collect trinkets and had few occasions to wear jewels. In a way, his acquaintance was a gift in itself. "Your ship!"

Chuckling, he lowered the candle in the rushlight and examined the mare for scratches and thorns. "Where do you stable your horses?"

"At the baroness of Leith's estate in Edinburgh."

The stable lad returned with the oats, and Randolph gave him a coin. "Do you know my brother, Drummond Macqueen?" he asked the boy.

"Aye." The lad beamed. "He's the one what brought the elephant. Took me 'n' the other lads up on the beast the day he come. I weren't afraid of that elephant."

"That's a good lad. Find my brother and tell him I'll not accompany him to vespers. Then tell the steward I'd like a bath in my chamber."

The boy hurried out. Randolph put the oats before the mare.

Elizabeth said, "Seems a crime to wash. You smell delightful."

He made a funny face and raked a shower of dried and faded heather from his sleeves. "I smell like a woman's clothes chest."

"Which of your women would that be?"

Dwindling patience gave him a lordly air, and his fine blue eyes twinkled with glee. "Never you mind."

"I see. Their numbers are so great, you cannot remember the name of even one. Or do they all prefer the scent of heather?"

"I remember this much, my curious herald: None of them has a tart mouth and prying nature."

She rested her elbows on the chest-high railing that separated them. "You think I do?"

Had he been walking, he would have swaggered. "Aye, unless you are merely verifying my sterling character."

She had reason to inquire. In his company she forgot kings and ransoms and promised treaties that never came to pass. But she knew better than to reveal her feelings. "Your character or lack of it is not my affair. When given a preference, I simply dislike crowds."

"Yet you like me."

As if conceding a major point, she said, "I find you entertaining."

"You flatter me overmuch," he replied, meaning the opposite.

"Then I shall cease altogether."

"You are different, Elizabeth Gordon, and you look bonny in that gown. Green suits you."

She'd brought only two gowns and three bliauds. The king's livery gave her a measure of protection— whether real or imagined, she did not know. One thing was certain: She doubted that a crested tabard and a golden chastity belt would shield her from Randolph Macqueen, not when her heart was engaged.

The second bell rang out, a perfect excuse to leave him. But never had she been dishonest or cowardly. She would not begin now.

He strolled toward her, the gentle odor of heather at odds with his rugged good looks and commanding presence.

"Mischief glitters in your eyes," she said, but did not retreat.

"Have you become a seer?"

"I do not need the sight to know the direction of your thoughts."

He held out his hand. "Shall we be companions, Elizabeth?"

To refuse the friendly gesture smacked of pettiness. He'd forsworn marriage. She would not compromise herself. They were a companionable match. They did not travel in the same circles. Years might pass before she saw him again.

She took his hand. "Aye, we shall."

"Thank you," he whispered, "for letting me ride your horse."

As before he did not mask his admiration for her, but this time Elizabeth basked in it. As always, it felt natural to tell him something about herself. "Even as a child, riding was my passion."

His examination of her face grew intense. "'Tis a distant second for me."

She'd misjudged the situation. "You have more than companionship on your mind."

He feigned a startled expression. "I'm only returning good will. During our first horse race, before you and that stallion left me in a hail of fallen leaves, you blew me a kiss."

Apprehension gripped her. She glanced past him. The stable doors were closed. They were alone. "'Twas a mistake."

"Then I propose we do it properly this time. May I kiss you?"

The request was new; most men of means and title thought it their right. Both yes and no battled to be said. She settled for "Why?"

"You know the answer, and you're too bright to play timid with me."

He took her silence for the agreement it was. Her fingers curled over the wooden rail, and her ears buzzed with anticipation. His mouth was soft, and his manner undeniably appealing. Even with a barrier between them, she could feel the warmth and strength of him, and when he lifted her arms and placed them around his neck, she threaded her fingers through his hair and breathed in the clean smell of seasoned heather.

She'd been kissed before, but never with such finesse and purpose. *We speak without words,* he'd said, and she understood what he meant. As his lips moved gently on hers, he silently encouraged her to put away her doubts and explore the moment of closeness.

Against her mouth, he murmured, "Come nearer still, Elizabeth. By my oath, you are safe with me."

When his tongue grazed the seam of her lips, she knew what he wanted and opened her mouth to deepen the kiss. A manly moan of pleasure was his first response; his second was to twirl his tongue with hers until his breathing grew ragged and her body sang with yearning.

"Heed your conscience and your heart, lass," he whispered.

No groping lad or randy nobleman, Randolph Macqueen kissed her with ease, as if they'd shared a lifetime of such intimacies. The knowledge spurred her to look beyond the physical need, to understand every nuance of the man and the kiss. She felt sheltered, reassured, and enormously curious. As he cupped her cheeks and slanted his mouth over hers, her head began to spin, and she clung to him. He devoured and nourished her at once, and with every beat of her heart, she yearned for more.

Yet when she least expected it, he broke the kiss and wrapped her in his arms. Cheek to cheek, his stubbly, hers flushed with desire, they stood in a stranger's stable, but for the moment it felt like hallowed ground. The tenderness of the embrace seemed at odds with their labored breathing and pounding hearts.

"What thought wends its way through your mind, Elizabeth?"

"Never an intelligent one," she confessed. "And you?"

Against her cheek, she felt him smile. Deep in his throat he growled an agreement. "I am consumed with want of you."

The honest admission sparked confusion. "Yet you master your passion."

He leaned back until their eyes met. "My feelings for you go beyond an evening's dalliance in Red

305

Douglas's stable or a wager over a ship and a fine horse."

Awareness thrummed through her. "You are surprised by that."

A crooked grin gave evidence of his dilemma. "Pleasantly so, and I find myself in the odd position of not knowing what to do next. Such feelings are new for me."

Desire ebbed, and in its place lay a beginning, a wellspring of mutual respect and friendship. Uncertainty made her say, "You could kiss me again and find out what to do next."

"If I kiss you again, I will not stop. 'Twould be best if you step away now, else . . ."

"Else what?"

He swallowed loudly and licked his lips. "Else we'll end up on the ground, and you'll have a chafed bottom from lying naked beneath me in the straw."

The image made her blush; yet with the embarrassment came a truth: Even a flirtation was impossible for a respected herald of the king.

"I will be one horse the poorer."

"And enlightened to a maiden's greatest mystery."

Embarrassment filled her. To avert the conversation, she strove for nonchalance. "'Twas only a kiss."

His gaze hardened. "And I am the king of France." He caressed her cheek and stepped back. "I want more for us than a tumble in yonder stall."

Reality hardened her heart. Not only had she misjudged the situation, she'd underestimated the man and the depths of the feelings that flourished between them. But the responsibility was hers, for she'd all but begged him to kiss her. "There is no more for us. There can never be."

"I'll provide you with a home of your own and a stable a king would envy."

His was not the first offer of its kind, but her refusal was by far the most painful. "You honor me, but I must decline."

Determination hardened his features. "Spare me your honeyed speeches. Speak to me from your heart."

"No matter the source, my answer must remain the same."

"By the will of your uncle or because of your service to the king?"

The purpose behind and the length of her service to King Robert was her own affair. "I will not be your lover."

"Why not?"

Because it wouldn't be enough for her. When she gave her heart it would be to a man who would treasure her and cherish the children of her womb. She could not leave the king's service—not now, when the future of Scottish independence was at stake. To ease her troubled mind, she dwelt on the drawbacks of marriage to Randolph Macqueen. He favored adventure and the sea over hearth and home. She envisioned a Scotland unified from the southern border to the Orkney Islands in the north. His loyalty began and ended with the Highland clans.

"Elizabeth?"

Hopelessness swept over her. "Perhaps you should see to Majesty. She's well-lathered."

"Perhaps you will do me the courtesy of answering my ques—"

She pressed her hand to his lips. His breath felt hot against her fingertips. "Do not spoil our lovely moment," she entreated. "Life holds too few of them."

Stubbornness tightened his mouth. She looked him in the eye and willed him to understand. At length, he kissed her fingers and snatched up hands full of straw.

As he groomed the mare, he spoke of his first warhorse, of his father's stable, and of the trials of growing up with so many siblings. Elizabeth confessed that at eight years old she'd fallen in love with the farrier's son.

"'Tis because you have a weakness for men who share your love of fine horses."

He sounded so worldly, she grew defensive. "'Tis not so."

"Then 'tis me alone you fancy."

"Not above a mere kiss."

He whirled so fast that the mare sidestepped. His eyes blazed with righteous anger. "If you name what passed between us a mere kiss, I'll . . ."

"You'll what?"

"I'll trade my tartan plaid for a monk's robes."

She burst out laughing.

He looked positively insulted.

Eyes narrowed, he shook the brush at her. "Watch yourself, my tart herald, or I'll go a-raiding at the Baroness Leith's stables. We Highlanders are masters at acquiring what we want."

"You cannot have my horses."

Anger left him as quickly as it had come. "Then go with me," he entreated. "And help me find my own. We'll sail to Constantinople and scour every stable until we find other horses as fine as these. A sorrel, a bay, even a wicked black stallion."

"Pure blacks are rare in the desert breed."

"Then I *must* have a black. We'll eat figs and dates and sample all of the heathen delicacies. We'll walk the battlefields of the Great Crusade."

For such a journey she would trade her soul. But she had made a promise to a king, and Scotland needed her. "I regret that I cannot."

"Oh, *Ealasaid.*"

If words could caress, she felt embraced by the tone of his voice and the sound of her name spoken in Scottish. But the man and his adventure were not for her. "When will this quest commence?"

"I cannot go until after Christmas—" Abruptly he stared at his boots. "Better we depart at Hogmanay." Snapping his fingers, he continued, "'Tis a fine way to start the new year. I'll speak to Bruce. Hell, I'll even bargain with your uncle. He is your guardian?"

His brief loss of composure spoke of secrets kept; she knew the practice well. His involved Christmas, a peculiar subject on which to err; Highland Scots placed their first loyalty to their clan, not their religion. For that reason the Holy Church refused to bless their causes and finance their armies.

Yet in their defense, she was forced to admit that life was hard in the Highlands and the weather bitter at Christmas time. The last harvest had been fruitful, but one bountiful season after so many years of war with England would not enable the clans to have a prosperous holiday. For that she pitied them. But Randolph hid a secret.

"You mentioned Christmas, Randolph. I wonder why."

"'Tis simple. I've just come from Spain, where the people pray even as they go about mundane tasks. A man's faith is his own, yet the Spaniards take it to market as if the grocer were a priest."

Precisely her point. Highland priests were Scotsmen first, and pity the sinner who forgot it. If Randolph Macqueen were preoccupied with Christmas, she must learn why. To test him, she said, "I agree to accompany you, but only if we sail before Christmas."

A change came over him. Abject disappointment softened his features. A moment later he typified the term *stern Highlander*.

"Is your business here concluded?" he asked.

Again, she'd underestimated him. Having no answer, she returned his bold stare.

"I tell you my business, Elizabeth, yet you will not show me the same respect."

Randolph had told her nothing but a confusing tale of Spanish faith. "You liken yourself to our king? 'Tis his causes I serve."

"What causes would those be?"

On the surface they appeared opponents at a stalemate. Deeper, their mutual affection and, yes, respect were at stake. She would not risk losing either. "Speak no more of my mission, Randolph, and I will refrain from the subject of Christmas."

He'd get nothing else from her on the subject, but Randolph knew a hard-won concession when he saw it. He wanted the woman herself, and damn the politics that brought them together. The common ground they shared was a place where sweet and joyous subjects reigned. On those he would rely. But he must watch his words, for he had almost revealed the Christ's Mass and placed every Highland chieftain in danger.

He slapped the brush over his heart. "You have my word of honor. Now come and distract this nipping mare while I groom her legs."

Elizabeth moved into the stall. The mare turned puppylike, swishing her tail and demanding attention, which Elizabeth readily gave.

For her affection, Randolph knew he would bargain with the devil himself. He tried to name the precise quality about her that he liked the most, but there were many. He enjoyed the way she laughed at his obvious attempts to flatter her. He loved to watch the sheer joy she experienced in riding her horses. He took pride in her intelligence and imagined a castle full of daughters all as wise and remarkable as

Elizabeth Gordon. He was glad that his life had changed the moment she entered it. A future with her had become his primary concern.

The stable doors opened.

"Good herald!"

Randolph stiffened. It was the king of England. He'd come from the chapel, for his prayer beads were tucked into his belt. Formally dressed, he wore a fur-trimmed tunic and trunk hose beneath a cape lined with beaver skins. Instead of an elaborate crown, he wore a circlet of gold studded with rubies. In the English fashion, his pale beard was long and twisted into curls.

"Still grooming your own steeds, Lady Elizabeth?"

She stepped into the aisle and curtsied. "A small joy to me, Your Majesty."

"I'm certain you have few enough of those."

Even Edward Plantagenet knew more about her than Randolph Macqueen. He moved to her side and bowed to the king, praying all the while that Edward had not come to send her away.

Edward acknowledged him with a nod, and his keen gaze surveyed Randolph, probably looking for a weapon. "Do you attempt to seduce the respected servant of your Scottish king?"

Answering to his enemy rattled Randolph's pride. "My intentions toward Lady Elizabeth are my own affair."

"Randuff," she spoke sternly in Scottish. *"Be silent and have faith in me."*

He hated doubting her, but her first loyalty lay with Robert Bruce. Yet how could Randolph gain her trust without giving his own? He could not. "Aye, *Ealasaid."*

"A pair of Highlanders speaking Scottish." The king looked from one to the other. "What mischief do you plot?"

"No mischief, Your Majesty," she said. "Macqueen stays to pay his respects to Red Douglas and to visit the brother you so generously pardoned."

"You so swear?"

"On my very soul, Your Majesty."

"But why do you meet with Macqueen in a stable?"

Randolph took her arm. "Prior to my arrival here, Sire, I had not made the acquaintance of Lady Elizabeth."

Humor flashed in her eyes. "He travels in different circles than I."

Ruefully, Edward said, "Just so. He is of the Highland breed."

Reluctantly, Randolph offered his own excuse to the enemy. "Lady Elizabeth was gracious enough to let me ride her mare."

"Macqueen is also a suitable escort for me," she said.

Edward sneered. "Where Englishmen are not fit company for you."

She lifted her chin and faced him boldly. "On my last visit to London, you gallantly saved me from the unwanted advances of a determined English peer."

"Westmoreland wants you still."

"I shall go to my grave flattered by his attention and grateful for your intervention."

He shook his head and chuckled. "You've a gentleness and intellect foreign to your kinsmen."

She tilted her head to the side and gave him a little smile. "I serve where I may."

"Pity you served Bruce so well during my father's reign."

"Your sire's hunger for Scotland was great."

Bitterness tainted his fair features. "So great he left me a beggared kingdom for it!"

"Your champions swear you are resourceful where he was not."

Like a comforting hand, her words soothed him, and he sighed. "Pray God I am." He waved a bejeweled hand toward the door. "Take your leave, Macqueen."

Her virtue was safe with Edward Plantagenet, but Randolph bristled at being dismissed by an enemy king. He must know why Edward had sought her out.

Having no choice, he nodded respectfully to the king and lied to Elizabeth. "I'll await you near the sundial." He would hurry to the side of the stable and listen to their conversation.

Elizabeth followed his departure, but even after the door closed behind him she had to work to keep her mind on the conversation to come.

"On the matter of ransom for Lord William Cameron, the Scottish earl of Strath," the king said, broaching the subject that had brought her to Douglas Castle, "the price is fifteen thousand marks."

Elizabeth wanted to curse out loud and blame Randolph Macqueen for the lapse in her composure. Marshalling her wayward thoughts, she stared at the fine golden stitchery on the king's tunic. "As I said upon my arrival, Sire, in exchange for Lord William, my sovereign offers you back the three ships you left at anchor in Tynemouth Harbor."

His eyes bulged and his complexion grew mottled with rage. "I left no ships at Tynemouth. Bruce pirated them away."

Bruce had, and he'd celebrated the occasion by using the cargo of arms to outfit his clansmen. "My sovereign offers you the vessels in exchange for Lord William, who now resides in the Tower of London."

Edward looked from the hay-strewn floor to the beamed ceiling. "What of the ship's armaments?"

The absolute power of both men always amazed her, and with Bruce's influence growing stronger every day, she anticipated many more conversations like this one. To her surprise, the notion failed to excite her. She knew the cause: a rakish Highlander who was very close to winning their wager.

"Herald?"

Her hesitation would be viewed as indecision. She harkened to the matter at hand. "On the subject of armaments, my sovereign says that England has iron aplenty for more swords and shields."

Through tightly clenched teeth, Edward said, "Then tell the Scottish sovereign that his terms are unacceptable. I want money!"

She took a deep breath and braced for the worst. "To that, my sovereign has instructed me to say you insult him by suggesting that he finance your war against his own people."

Held by a thin thread, his dreaded Angevin temper snapped. He made a fist and shook it at her. "I've declared no war!"

Elizabeth swallowed back fear. "To which, my gracious lord bade me say, the English seldom announce their intentions to ravish their brethren in the North."

"For what reason does Bruce think I prepare for war?"

"I relay his messages, Your Majesty. King Robert's thoughts are his own."

He pointed at her. "Then I give you another thought for him to ponder: Tell your king the earl of Strath will rot in the Tower until his ransom is paid or I am offered a worthy exchange."

As always, Bruce had prepared her. "Then my sovereign instructs me to offer you the marshal of Northumberland in exchange for the release of Lord William of Strath."

Quietly, he said, "A peer in exchange for a mere marshal?"

Calm settled over her. "I am instructed to remind Your Majesty that you are godfather to the marshal's children. In all events, King Robert says 'twould be a fair trade."

"What other information have you tortured out of the good marshal, save my commitment to his children?"

"He is unharmed, as we know our own Lord William is safe in your Tower. The marshal willingly gave me the information, along with a message for his lady wife, which I delivered to her personally at harvest time last."

The offer held promise; the king considered it as he stared at the rushlight, which flickered in the drafty stables.

"Soon will you know my answer."

She bowed. "Aye, Your Majesty. Shall I keep close?"

"I give you leave to bide as you will, so long as you continue to tell Douglas's steward of your comings and goings." He chuckled and surveyed her up and down. "I rather think you enjoy keeping the company of Randolph Macqueen."

No answer was required, but even had he demanded one, she would have declined. "I bid you goodnight, King Edward." She moved past him and toward the door.

"Lady Elizabeth?"

She turned. He looked oddly out of place, a regally garbed and handsome Plantagenet king standing in a modest stable.

"Once again, good herald, you perform your office fairly."

It was the strongest compliment he could pay her. She acknowledged it with a formal bow. "Thank you, Sire."

Now that she'd done her duty to Robert Bruce, she

had business with Randolph Macqueen. She found him on a stone bench near the sundial. "I gave the king of England my oath that you are here for honest reasons. If you hide an evil purpose, I shall pay dearly for it."

He slapped a hand over his heart. "On my honor, I do not."

To an extent, she believed him. Still, she would maintain her vigil to learn his secret. And why did he appear out of breath, as if he'd run across the yard?

"Must you return to Bruce?" he asked.

"Eventually, aye. But not soon."

"I recall that you expressed an interest in seeing a devoted swan. Loch Lanark is only a morning's ride away."

"I thought you came here to visit with your brother."

Would she never let the matter drop? Randolph could not tell her about the relic of Saint Columba or mention the Christ's Mass. Much as he hated it, he told her a lie. "I did not know my brother was here. Did you?"

"Nay, and I expected you to prefer his company to mine."

"Then you erred, Elizabeth. But I see him most every day."

In that he spoke the truth, for he attended church with his brother and took his meals with him. When Elizabeth was not invited to sit at the high table, she took her meals in her chamber.

"Will you accompany me to Loch Lanark?" he asked.

"Only if you promise never again to ask me to be your mistress."

Agreement came easily to Randolph, for he'd overheard her conversation with the English king. Her mission here involved only an exchange of prisoners. With the holy relic in his possession, he could concentrate on the future. She had risked her reputation to assure Edward that Randolph was here for personal reasons. The trusting gesture went straight to his heart. He wanted Elizabeth Gordon. He needed her wisdom, craved her passion. But more than his own desire, the Macqueens deserved a woman of honor, especially now.

Never had the clans been offered a better chance at unity. As a chieftain and member of this new order, he must take a strong and dedicated Scotswoman to wife.

At the thought of marriage, he expected his independent nature to rebel. He waited, but the feeling did not come. In place of the old need for freedom, he felt a new yearning that both alarmed and thrilled him.

"What's amiss?" she asked. "You look like a man who's lost his last tartan plaid."

"Nay, I was thinking of that devoted swan," he said.

Elizabeth and Randolph paused at the crest of a hill overlooking Loch Lanark. Unlike the harsher, northern regions, this landscape bore only a thin blanket of snow. Clouds shrouded the sun, and every exhaled breath turned to smoke; yet the stable lad had assured them the day would turn fair.

A gentle breeze filled the air with the crisp scent of pines and reminded Elizabeth of the holiday seasons of her youth. In the distance to the east, a group of tartan-clad soldiers and woodsmen scoured the forest in search of a fitting tree for the yule log. Closer still, a band of children gathered pine cones and hazelnuts. Women sheared boughs of berry-ladened holly and tossed them into a cart driven by one of the local priests.

Below, dried grasses and leaf-bare thistles ringed

the lake. On the rim of the southern bank, a small hut squatted between a pair of evergreens. Nearby sat a grouping of benches. Both the wood and the surrounding area were worn smooth by wear.

"The swans must be sleeping in," Randolph said as he dismounted. "We should approach downwind." He indicated a well-used cart path.

He wore a jerkin of quilted wool dyed a rich blue and trimmed with black cord. A bonnet of sheared beaver, fashioned in the floppy style of the day, added to his roguish good looks.

He lifted her to the ground, and she clutched a sack of grain and stale bread she'd procured from the kitchen maid.

The faint pealing of childish laughter drifted on the wind. "The bairns sound happy," she said.

"Better they should enjoy themselves now," he replied. "After Christmas they'll be trapped inside until the snow melts."

Elizabeth started down the path. "Was it so for you as a lad?"

Randolph moved into step beside her. "Oh, nay. The Macqueen lads were far too rowdy. To save the furniture, the steward often chased us outside and threatened to toss our Christmas gifts down the privy shaft."

"Where did you foster?" Fostering was a common practice. At six or seven years old, lads were sent to the household of a relative or overlord. There they learned to ride, to wield a sword, and to become a man.

"My mother did not approve of fostering."

"She prevailed in the matter?"

"Two of my uncles lived with us at Castle Macqueen. 'Tis a rambling keep with a large village nearby. And Mother is very persuasive."

A trait the woman had passed on to her son,

Elizabeth thought with a smile. "Who taught you to sail?"

"Mother's father. He was a Matheson and plied the Denmark trade. Have you been there?"

"Nay. I've only been to France." The painful memory of the long-ago journey to meet her uncle's choice of husbands for her was easily put aside.

A fat brown hare dashed across the path. Elizabeth almost stumbled. Randolph grasped her arm and did not let go until they'd reached the spot where the path leveled out.

At the opening of the hut appeared an orange bill with a distinctive black knob on top. Like a snake, the swan's long neck curled around the edge of the doorway as the bird spied his guests. A moment later, the head of the smaller female popped into view.

"They're mute swans," Randolph said correctly.

Working open the bag of grain, Elizabeth whispered, "In breed only. According to the milkmaid, they're as noisy as Irishmen on Saint Patrick's Day."

Laughing, Randolph guided her to a bench. At length, he asked, "How did you come to be a herald?"

Which version should she tell him? The casual answer satisfied the oft-asked question. The truth was a private concern. Glancing up at him, she chose the latter. "'Twas my own stubbornness, actually."

"That," he murmured, "I can believe."

Ignoring the friendly jibe, she continued: "Bruce, who was earl of Carrick at the time, was visiting my uncle to enlist support for his claim to the Scottish throne. I had refused to go to bed and watched and listened as they both drank too much. The next day, they argued over vows made in ale the night before. I've always been blessed or accursed with a good memory. So I was summoned to recount their drunken words."

"How old were you?"

"One and ten. Bruce was so impressed, he declared that when he was king he hoped to find a herald with half of my abilities. At three and ten, I refused to marry the Frenchman my uncle had chosen for me. He threatened to give me over to the Church, so I ran away and sought sanctuary with Bruce. He took me in, and on the day he received the crown, he named me his herald."

"Have you ever regretted your choice?"

"Only when I'm deceived by those I trust." He looked sharply at her, and she added, "Or when I am forced to spend Christmas in England."

"Do you anticipate a regrettable holiday this year?"

"I hope to drape my horses in Edinburgh ivy and warm my toes before a hearth blazing with a good Scottish oak. And you?"

He paused, and she saw indecision in his eyes. He took the sack of grain and began pitching kernels. The now-fearless male swan scurried to nibble up the grain, then deliver it to the webbed feet of his waiting mate.

"I expect to hear squeals of delight from the weavers of Lochcarron when they see the spinning wheels I have bought for them."

He had not bought trinkets to entertain his people through the holidays, but rather a practical gift to ease their daily burden all the year long. Still, his clever verbal hedge did not fool Elizabeth.

That evening as they walked to the chapel, they were joined by Randolph's brother and his family. His inquisitive nephew, Alasdair, skipped ahead of them and plied Elizabeth with question after question.

"Are you going to drag my uncle Randolph to the altar?"

"As the king's herald, I cannot take a husband."

Randolph looked pointedly at the lad, who nodded sagely. "'Tis just as well. Mother says the countess of Nairn will not easily give him up. Is that true, Uncle Randolph?"

They passed through the open door of the church, and Randolph heard Elizabeth choke back laughter. Determined to move the conversation to a safer topic, he gave his nephew his most stern glare. "Ill-mannered children must forfeit their Christmas gifts."

The boy grew pensive. "I could be persuaded to drop the matter if you could be persuaded to convince Lady Elizabeth to teach me how to be a herald."

Candlelight glowed on her skin and shimmered in her fiery hair. "Well put, Alasdair," she said. "But I should think you will grow up to be an influential man, one who needs a herald of his own."

Enlightenment gave the boy a comical grin. "I'm to have a new sister in the spring. When she's older, she will ferry my important messages."

The chapel doors closed and the congregation grew quiet. Behind her hand, Elizabeth said to Randolph, "King Edward speared the largest salmon today, and his mood is generous for it. Your brother's pardon prohibits any congress with his kin. Shall I ask King Edward to grant you permission to travel to your brother's home?"

If the king altered the conditions of Drummond's release, Randolph could visit whenever he liked. Her offer was an unexpected gift.

"Shall I approach him on the matter?" she said, her eyes twinkling.

Admiration joined Randolph's other strong feelings for her. "Succeed, and I will build you a stable." He lifted his brows. "Free of obligation."

She fairly beamed with joy. "Swear?"

He tapped his clan badge and winked.

"Done." She turned her attention to the altar. "Above a ship, 'tis what I've always wanted."

If Randolph told her what *he* truly wanted, she'd run from the church.

On Saint Nicholas's Day in the city of Closeburn, Randolph bribed a fortune-teller to predict that Elizabeth would bear him a dozen sons.

Rather than become startled as he expected, she sighed and said she preferred a husband who would give her daughters. Then she asked if Majesty's foal would be a colt or a filly.

"A black colt," the seer swore, "with never a speck of white."

Elizabeth smiled at Randolph. "Are you interested in buying him?"

"For certain, but I'd rather have him as your dowry."

"Impossible, but if we agree on a price, perhaps I'll deliver him to you. I expect to be a master sailor by then."

And he'd be a master husband to her by then. "You are bold tonight, Elizabeth. Must be the effect of the December brew."

As serene as a princess, she took a coin from her pouch and slid it across the table to the fortune-teller. "What does the future hold for my Highland friend?"

Seated between a pair of horn lanterns, the crone screwed up her face. "Give me yer sword hand, m'lord."

More to shock Elizabeth than to confuse the seer, Randolph put both hands on the table, palms up, and addressed the older woman. "Take your pick."

Elizabeth rose. "I'll take my leave and await you at the baker's shop. You're too much man for me."

When they were alone, the fortune-teller grasped

his right hand, the one he favored, and drew it closer to the light. Her fingertips were as soft as swansdown, yet her touch was firm, her gaze knowing. "Your first lass will have hair like her mother's."

"Red, like that one?" He jerked his head toward the door.

"Aye. Your wee lassie will wed a prince with dark hair and green eyes."

"But when will I wed?"

"Ah, that." She folded his fingers and pushed his hand away. "Not afore Whitsunday next, but her heart is given to you now."

As Highlanders go, Randolph was not superstitious, unless it suited him, which it did at the moment. He gave the woman an extra coin and stood up.

"M'lord." Her expression turned solemn, and her tone grew grim. "Have a care, for I see darkness and despair in your future."

A chill passed through him, and he thought first of the upcoming Christ's Mass. If the chieftains were betrayed at the event, the Highlands would again fall into discord.

The walls of the tent closed in on him, and sweat beaded his brow. But the moment he stepped into the cool night air and spied Elizabeth, his spirits rose.

She handed him a thick square of nutcake. He broke off a piece and held it to her mouth. She hesitated, her eyes searching his. Revelers passed them by. The sounds of tinkling bells and merrymaking faded. Her lips parted. The cake touched her tongue. When she closed her mouth and hummed in pleasure, his mind went blank.

"More."

He gulped back a swallow and complied. "Your mouth should be outlawed."

She sent him a playful glare. "Then how would I eat?"

323

Desire pooled in his loins. "'Tis said the sustenance of love is fulfilling."

"Who says?"

He dusted a crumb from her chin when he wanted to lick it off. "The great minds, I'm sure."

"You didn't have any cake."

He could spend a lifetime feasting on her. "Nay, my hunger rages for a different delicacy."

Rather than shy away or chide him, she smiled and, with a quick glance around her, reminded him of their surroundings. "What did the fortune-teller say?"

Mastering his passion, he hooked his arm through hers. Together they strolled the lane, ducking beneath streamers and dodging mud puddles. Parents indulged despotic children, who took seriously their role of leader, as the day prescribed.

"The seer swore that I will soon possess a stable of fast desert horses."

"Given enough gold, she'd swear you were purity itself."

Her laughter reminded Randolph of the trilling of a flute. Caught up in the magic of the evening, he pulled her into the shadows and drew her against him.

Somewhere above them, an owl hooted an eerie cry.

"Do you dance?" he asked.

She flattened her palms against his chest but did not push him away. "I've seen it done, once or twice."

His hands moved to her hips and encountered the ridge of the chastity belt. "From whom do you protect yourself tonight, Elizabeth? Brigands or me?"

"There's a difference?"

Like a beacon in a stormy sea, her voice drew him. He leaned into her until her back met the trunk of a stout pine, and their mouths blended in a kiss that made gospel of the seer's predictions. He tasted sweetness on her lips, and in the next breath he knew the pleasure of her response. When her fingers curled and clutched his tunic, padding the fabric in kittenlike movements, he set free his passions and kissed her with all the love in his heart.

To his delight, her hunger matched his, and they were swept up in the moment and carried on a current of promised bliss that left them breathless and weak with need.

When he tore his mouth from hers and cradled her head into the curve of his shoulder, Elizabeth thought she might fall into her first swoon. The tree felt solid at her back; he felt like heaven before her. What harm could come, she wondered, from loving this man who had sworn to have her?

She could forge new bonds with the Macqueens. His clan was large and prosperous, with alliances throughout the Highlands. He would give her children and the future she never thought to have. But what could she bring to the marriage?

Like a mournful winter wind, the answer saddened her. She possessed only twenty horses and a few commendations from warring kings.

"Whatever you are thinking," he murmured, "I command you to stop it."

The force of his will was strong, but when pitted against the facts, her convictions held sway. "I cannot."

His hands closed around her upper arms, and he shook her gently. "You can. You must."

Sad truths clamored to be said, but she could voice none of them, not when they stood on the brink of the happiest of seasons. To bare her soul would taint the moment; that she would not do. She would take this precious time and hold it to her heart, to cherish always and relive when loneliness visited her.

She hugged him, and as he squeezed her tight, she

willed herself not to cry. "We should return to the lane. Even a lackwit could have counted to fifty by now."

Ignoring her attempt at humor, he stepped back and folded his arms over his chest. "Who is he?"

Caught off guard, she blinked in confusion. "He?"

"The man who holds your heart. Name him."

Exhaustion drained her. Randolph Macqueen thought she had given her heart elsewhere. An escape from this lovers' coil beckoned. She had but to think up a name, toss it into the tense silence, and provide him a target at which to aim his bruised pride.

At his unfair assumption, her own pride bristled. "Why must it be another man?"

"What else could it be? You are not pledged to God."

He did not think her capable of honoring a promise when romance beckoned. Only men were allowed so much integrity. To his mind, women were shallow and incapable of managing their own destiny, let alone playing a part in the future of a nation.

She went still inside. "You put yourself in high company."

He blew out his breath and glanced over his shoulder. Torchlight illuminated half his face, but his anguish was plain to see. "For a truth from you, Elizabeth, I would go down on my knees."

She was tempted to give him what he asked for, but fear and loyalty and soul-deep disappointment held her back. "Let it be, Randolph. Can we not dance and make merry awhile longer? 'Tis Saint Nicholas's Day. The children have commanded us to be of good cheer."

His gaze swung back to her. Shadows again shrouded his face, but she needed no light to see his determination. "I will not give up. You will be mine."

"You wish to possess me, but only on your terms."

He cursed and threw his hands in the air. "'Tis plain to see why God made man superior to woman."

In two steps, she stood nose to nose with him. "Hear me well, *Lord Superior.* I cannot and will not simply walk away from my service to the king."

"I will speak with him."

She despaired. "I'm not a laundry maid to be replaced at a snap of the fingers. I have given my word to our sovereign lord. Negotiations are ongoing."

"What of the promises I wish to make to you?"

She felt like a leaky ship caught in a tempest. Love pitched her one way, doubts pulled her in another. He did not trust her; yet he offered her her heart's desire: children and a life spent languishing in his arms.

"Saints rejoice," he said, watching her, "for I believe you are considering my offer."

When she remained silent, he lifted her chin and gazed into her eyes. "'Tis enough for now."

No. The matter of his secret remained. "Where will Christmas find you?"

"In your arms, I pray." He smiled, but she saw deception in his eyes.

Beginning the next day, Douglas Castle came alive with anticipation of Christmas. Ivy draped the halls and every meal began with cheese and good dark bread and ended with cakes baked with silver coins inside. The children gathered in the church to practice singing the psalms they would perform at vespers on Christmas Eve. Servants and masters smiled as they passed in the lane. Merchants laid out their best wares. Torches were replaced, and candlelight brightened even the meanest hovel.

Edward II did not summon Elizabeth until two days after Saint Nicholas's Day. As she approached his chamber, another door opened, and a familiar messenger stepped into the hall. He wore no heraldic devices, but she knew him as the messenger of Cutberth Macgillivray, the ceremonial king of the Highlands and Randolph's enemy. Through the still open door, she saw Red Douglas sitting in a chair, his head in his hands, his eyes closed.

What business did Macgillivray, a Highlander, have with Red Douglas, a man sworn to the king of England? She thought of Randolph, and wondered if his presence here played a part.

It was yet another concern she would share with Robert Bruce before she told him of her feelings for Randolph Macqueen. Although she still harbored small doubts, she was confident enough. The mere thought of him put a bounce in her step and hope in her heart.

In good spirits, she made her way to the chamber occupied by the king of England.

She found Edward Plantagenet alone and lounging on an ornate throne that dwarfed the guest chamber. Holly and candles scented with bayberry adorned tables that were draped in white linen embroidered with silver thread. Edward wore a long surcoat in a shade of pale blue that perfectly matched his eyes. With a beringed hand, he waved her toward him.

She knelt, and he quickly told her to rise.

"'Tis a bargain struck, good herald," he said. "Lord William of Strath for the marshal of Northumberland. Get you back to Bruce, and say to him the exchange will be made here, a week hence. *You* will deliver my man. The earl of Pembroke will deliver yours."

She wanted to jump for joy. She would return here, and if this king were generous, Randolph would be waiting. "'Tis agreed, Your Majesty, and there is a private matter, of which my sovereign has no knowledge, that I would discuss with you."

He propped his elbow on the arm of the throne and

rested his chin in his palm. "Do you seek a royal favor, herald?"

He would see it that way, and she had reservations, but she'd given her word. "Of a sort, Sire."

"You may speak to me of this personal matter."

She had to fight to keep from blushing. "A thousand thanks. The matter concerns a stipulation of Drummond Macqueen's pardon."

"I'll not allow him above that accursed Highland line—wherever it lies."

"I understand, Your Majesty," she rushed to say. "He thrives in the Debatable Lands and has sworn his oath to you. He expresses no regrets in either. His wife carries another child. He enjoys the son she bore him during his imprisonment—"

"You digress, herald." He chuckled. "A first for you."

She felt like laughing at herself. "I beg your pardon. His brother, Randolph, whom I have come to respect, humbly seeks your permission to journey in peace to the Debatable Lands."

"Randolph Macqueen humbled himself?"

She should have known better. "'Twas my word. He swears to go in peace. Will you give him leave to visit Drummond on occasion?"

"Not at this time, but I will think on it, only because you asked, Lady Elizabeth."

He seldom addressed her in that fashion, and even though he was the enemy, she was flattered. "My thanks, King Edward. I will tell him to await your decision."

"As I will instruct Douglas to extend his hospitality to *your* Highlander. Although I would have preferred that you pick a good Englishman."

"I am a Scot, Your Majesty."

He huffed. "The best of the damned lot, you are."

Complimented to her soul, she went down on one knee.

The door opened behind her.

"A moment, Douglas," said Edward, looking past her. To Elizabeth, he declared, "Rise, good herald, and God grant you a safe journey."

She took her leave, but one glimpse at Red Douglas made a lie of his name, for his complexion was pasty white. She bade him farewell and returned to her chamber. As she packed her belongings, she couldn't stop wondering what news Cutberth Macgillivray's messenger had brought to Douglas and if he would share it with King Edward.

But the moment she stepped into the stables and saw Randolph stroking Majesty's nose, Elizabeth put the concerns of kings behind her.

"Do you sail back to Bruce, or do you concede our wager and leave Majesty with me?"

She'd forgotten the bet. At the beginning it had been a game—entertainment for her stay at Douglas Castle—but that was before she'd fallen in love with Randolph Macqueen. "My horses go with me, but perhaps one day I will sail."

He grinned and held out his arms. "As my wife, my ship and all I have will be yours."

He'd made that offer before; now she could take it seriously. But first she would get the business out of the way. "King Edward will consider allowing you to travel in the Debatable Lands."

"Consider? Then he did not agree."

"Or disagree."

"Do you think he will?"

"Randolph, I cannot speak for the king of England. My stay here is proof that he often takes his time in deliberation. I advise you to keep close. He will ask Douglas to continue to extend his hospitality to you."

"When will I see you again?" he asked.

He had not been honest with her; yet he expected answers to all his questions. Old habits ruled her. "I return when our sovereign gives me leave."

"When will that be?"

"Randolph." Her patience dwindled, but she hesitated to challenge him, for they must part in harmony.

"You will tell him about us, Elizabeth?"

"Aye, but do not forget that I have given my word to serve him." The first Scottish parliament loomed on the horizon, and Bruce would need her. "'Tis for him to release me. What will you do?"

He jerked his head toward the other side of the stable. "I'll take that hired horse back to Ruthwell tomorrow and deliver my cargo of ripe fruit to Glasgow. Then I will return here and remain, unless Edward grants me leave to go with Drummond to his home. 'Tis named Fairhope Tower and lies east of Carlisle."

"I pray you are allowed to go there." When he nodded, she stepped into his arms.

"Come back to me, for as rain to the earth and wind to the sea, I need you, Elizabeth."

The romantic words went straight to her heart, and she cherished them, but she grew sad at the separation to come. A smile from him would ease the pain; she knew the way to get it. "You want my horses."

He blinked in surprise, then his eyes narrowed. "One night soon, you'll learn the particulars of my desire—and discover yours."

They shared a lingering kiss, fraught with regrets, yet filled with hope. His hands traced the curve of her shoulders and the length of her arms. When their palms touched, he threaded his fingers through hers and held on tight. He showered her face with kisses and swayed against her, showing her the extent of his need. He whispered in her ear, "Consider a delay, my sweet."

A fog of desire clouded her thoughts, and her body cried out for the satisfaction he offered. But her obligation was too deeply ingrained. "If I stay we will anticipate our vows."

"Hum." He squeezed her tight. "I prefer the term 'early celebration.' "

"Haste is more to the point."

He relaxed against her. "Then I withdraw the offer, for I intend to love you for hours on end."

She shivered with longing.

"Go with that thought, my love."

Love. As if strolling the clouds, she mounted the mare and waved goodbye to the man she loved.

One week later, with a jubilant marshal of Northumberland riding one of her mares and a dozen Cameron clansmen in tow, an equally jubilant Elizabeth returned to Douglas Castle. Drummond Macqueen had left, for the elephant was nowhere about. When she led her horses into the stables, she faced a puzzle. King Edward's horses were gone. The Spanish stallion occupied the same stall. Randolph had not returned the animal, as he had said he would.

She rejoiced, for her beloved was still here. But, sadly, she concluded that he'd been denied permission to visit his brother's home. Ah, well, she thought, such was the will of kings.

She recalled the recent meeting with Robert Bruce. Upon learning that Randolph had braved the wrath of Edward Plantagenet to see his brother Drummond, Bruce had grown suspicious. When told of the presence of the herald of Randolph's enemy, Cutberth Macgillivray, Bruce fumed.

"Stubborn Highlanders! They'll carry out that Christ's Mass of unity, even if it gets them all killed."

Shocked, Elizabeth asked him to explain.

Bruce's ruddy complexion reddened. "To celebrate

the birth of the savior, we drape our castles in rosemary and laurel. We bake trinkets in sweet cakes for our bairns. Our faith in God and our devotion to his son is never stronger than at Christmas. But what of the future? The children deserve peace and a sure future more than playthings."

Then he told her of the upcoming Christ's Mass.

Elizabeth rejoiced. "Now the Highland clans will use the occasion to present their holy relics to the Church and pledge their support for each other. Is that not the greater gift of which you speak?"

"Of course, Elizabeth, and given another year I would have brought the Macgillivrays into the fold."

She thought of Randolph and his devotion to his clan. "'Tis true, my liege, that the Highland clans are impatient, yet you will benefit from the accord in the north." She would also benefit. Edward II could not defeat a unified Scotland. When peace reigned, she could retire to Lochcarron with Randolph.

"Cutberth Macgillivray lies in wait for Macqueen, and Randolph cannot attend the Mass unless the holy relic of Saint Columba is somehow found."

It was the first she'd heard of a relic. "When was it lost?"

"Years ago, when the older Macqueen was taken by Edward's father."

An ugly possibility occurred to her. "Do you think Drummond will participate in the Mass of unity?"

"I'd sooner believe that you are the lost Maiden of Inverness."

Elizabeth chuckled. The Maiden was a centuries-old and often ceremonial title. "What will you do?"

"I'll send word to Cutberth Macgillivray that he is to keep within his walls at Christmas. Should he disobey me, I'll put him to fire and sword."

Upon hearing the news that he risked being named outlaw and his lands forfeited to the throne, Cutberth

Macgillivray would surely obey King Robert and stay at home.

"Shall I deliver your message, my liege?"

"Nay, lass. 'Tis your birthday, as I recall. Wait here." He went to an adjoining room and returned carrying a new saddle. "For you, Elizabeth."

Tears of joy filled her eyes; he always remembered her birthday. "Thank you, Your Majesty."

Then she told him of her love for Randolph Macqueen.

"My lady!"

Robert Bruce and the conversation were forgotten as the lad in Douglas's stable came rushing toward her, holding out his hands for the reins.

Upon entering the yard, the marshal had fled into the castle, leaving Elizabeth to see to the horses.

She gave the boy a coin. "You've not many horses to care for, lad."

His mouth curled in disappointment. "Alasdair Macqueen's father took his elephant home. I liked the beast."

"When?"

"He left afore the English nobs went back to London."

Drummond had left before King Edward. That surprised her, for she had expected Drummond and Randolph to enjoy each other's company for as long as possible. "When did King Edward leave?"

"The day after you did, my lady. I had to work all night to ready their steeds. Gave me only tuppence for all them weeks' work on a score o' nags. Bleedin' carker." He spat in the straw. "An' 'im a king."

Such was the plight of servants. "Where is Randolph Macqueen?" She indicated the Spanish stallion.

The boy shrugged. "Ain't seen 'im since vespers on the day the Englishmen left."

That was odd; no matter where he'd gone, Randolph couldn't have walked. But where was he and how had he gotten there?

The steward greeted her in the common room, where the good marshal occupied a table with the earl of Pembroke.

"Where is Randolph Macqueen?" she asked the steward.

His gaze slid to the heraldic lilies emblazoned on her tabard. "Not here, my lady."

It was the steward's job to account for guests. "When did he leave?"

"I cannot say for sure."

The evasion spoke poorly of her host's household practices, but it was not her place to judge. So she made her way to Red Douglas's chamber. Seated next to him was Lord William Cameron, the Scottish earl of Strath, and he looked none the worse for his time in the Tower of London.

"You are free to go, my lord," she said, offering a polite bow. "Unless Douglas has other instructions."

The Douglas chieftain rose. "None were given to me. Fare thee well, Lord William."

The earl moved to her side. "My deepest gratitude, Lady Elizabeth."

As always, she fell back on protocol. "'Tis our sovereign lord who deserves the credit. I am but his messenger. Your clansmen await in the yard to take you home."

When the door closed behind the earl, Douglas grew expansive. "How was your journey, Lady Elizabeth?"

He'd barely spared her a word on her last visit. Why was he being so friendly now? Self-importance, she decided, at having had King Edward as his guest.

Again she posed the question that was foremost in her mind. "Where is Randolph Macqueen?"

He frowned and rubbed his rotund belly. "Turned

peevish when the king forbade him a visit to his brother. Took off in a huff, he did."

Something was wrong. She could feel it in her chest and in the sensitive skin at the nape of her neck. But she had no intention of revealing her suspicions to Red Douglas.

She gave him a bland smile. "When would that have been?"

He stuck out his bottom lip and plucked at it with a dirty thumb and forefinger. "I was occupied with the king, you see."

"Then Macqueen left before Edward?"

"Must have, but with all the comings and goings, I cannot rightly say. Look for him in the bed of a willing wench. 'Tis the way of those randy Macqueens."

He was lying. "When did the English sovereign depart?"

"Stayed awhile for the salmon. Left just yesterday."

Douglas did not owe her the truth; the wars of Edward I had taken a toll on many Lowland Scots, and men like Douglas were still pledged to England. In good time, King Robert would take them back or put them to the sword. But for now she must find Randolph.

She stopped first in Ruthwell to return the Spanish stallion and to question the stable master. As befitted his part, he cared only about being paid. He did report that a seaman wearing Macqueen colors had come looking for his captain.

She found the *Seawolf* still at anchor, the cargo rotting and the crew awaiting Randolph's return. Worse, he'd sent no word to the first mate, and the man did not hide his concern.

Next she traveled to the home of Drummond Macqueen. Randolph was not there, and his brother did not expect him. She was careful in her words, saying she'd just come from King Robert, so as not to distress Drummond.

Instinct told her to return to Douglas Castle.

She arrived late, on the night of December 16. The stable lad roused himself in relative good humor. When she opened her palm to reveal a dozen pennies, he fairly beamed.

"I am concerned," she began cautiously, "and in need of someone trustworthy. Someone who can gather information."

He hooked a thumb in his armpit. "'Tis me, my lady, an' my sister tends the hearth in the kitchen."

"Randolph Macqueen has gone missing, but no one else must know that I am troubled over his absence."

The boy yawned and blinked, but his attention stayed fixed on the coins. "Good to me, 'e was, that Highlander."

"Go and ask your sister if she knows of him, but have a care. I'll see to my horse and await you here."

He returned sooner than she'd expected, and his expression boded ill. "Ain't none talkin' 'bout that Highlander, my lady, but there's been some comin' an' goin' in the dungeon. Sorcha, that's my sister, thinks 'tis 'imself down there—since he's gone missing an' you being fretful an' all."

Elizabeth's stomach floated. What had happened? "Are there guards in the dungeon?"

"Dunno, but I can show you the way."

The boy lived here; his safety was a consideration. "Just tell me, and I'll find my own way."

Again he stared at the coins. She handed them over and he told her what she wanted to know.

Moments later, she tiptoed down the circular stone steps leading to the dungeon. No guards were in attendance, and when she found Randolph, she understood why.

Manacled to the wall, he looked near death, his complexion sallow in the yellow glow of the torch-light. He wore filthy trunk hose, a ragged tunic, and scuffed boots. A tattered blanket lay nearby. The stench of neglect made her wince.

With shaking hands, she touched his now-bearded cheek and said his name. No reply.

Carefully, she shook his shoulder. "Randolph."

He moaned, and his eyelids fluttered. "Water," he whispered.

She found a barrel near the stairwell and filled a cup. Hurrying back to his side, she lifted his head and helped him drink. He'd lost a stone's weight, and his lips were cracked and swollen. Fighting back tears of worry and rage, she spoke reassuringly to him.

His head lolled to one side, and he lifted a hand, but the chains allowed him little movement.

"Who did this to you?"

He glared at her. "The archbishop of Canterbury. His altar boys bashed in my face, and a band of angels bruised my ribs."

The absurdity of his reply surprised her; he was too weak to hold up his head, let alone jest.

"I'll be back." Alternately cursing and promising retribution, she retraced her steps. Red Douglas would pay for this villainy, but Randolph was her first concern.

At the top of the stairs, the stable lad awaited her. "Did you find 'im?" the boy asked.

"Aye. I need blankets and bread and some broth. Can you help me?"

He nodded and put a finger to his lips. "Follow me."

With the help of the boy and his sister, Elizabeth returned to the dungeon a short time later. Randolph had not moved.

Her heart ached for him, and she told him so. But

he was too helpless to do more than swallow the food. When he'd eaten all he could, he turned his head away.

"What is the date?" he asked.

"The sixteenth of December." She knew the reason behind the question: the Christ's Mass at Elgin Cathedral, near Auldcairn Castle. But he hadn't trusted her enough to reveal the secret, so she said, "You missed my birthday."

"A thousand pardons, my lady. But I've been indisposed."

She allowed him the sarcasm, and although he did not ask, she told him about visiting the ship and his brother.

"My crew is safe? The *Seawolf* is still at anchor in Solway Firth?"

"Aye, to both. Where is the key to the manacles?"

"Ask Douglas," he murmured before drifting to sleep.

Since she'd come to Douglas's home this time for purely personal reasons and had no excuse to stay, she invented one: She faked a fall in the stables. If Douglas doubted her tale of a twisted ankle, he gave no indication. But he housed her on the upper floor, far from the entrance to the dungeon.

By day she played the invalid; by night she filled the role of healer. The search for the key to the shackles proved successful, but Elizabeth kept the knowledge to herself; Randolph was still too weak to travel. When his strength returned, they would flee.

That afternoon Douglas and his wife paid a courtesy call on their invalid guest. With Randolph's foul mood as example, Elizabeth grumbled to her host and hostess, which cut their visit short.

Not until four days later was Randolph strong enough to sit. His first words to her were always the same.

"What is the day of the month?"

She told him but said nothing more on the subject. Out of fear of being discovered, she brought only a candle with her every night. The flame offered scant light, so she could not see his expression. As a further precaution, they were forced to speak little and in whispers.

"Did anyone come down here today?"

"Nay, save my guardian angel."

Her feelings were bruised from his callousness, and her temper snapped. "What is wrong with you?"

"Other than being chained in a dungeon, I cannot say."

No words of gratitude. No pledges of love. Despair sapped her strength. "Oh, Randolph. Have hope, and cease being so rude to me. You'll be strong enough to travel tomorrow, and all of the arrangements are made."

As usual, silence was his reply, but he'd been brought low, and he was prideful. In the same circumstances, she'd be too embarrassed to utter a word.

The next night, all was in readiness. Earlier in the day, the maid Sorcha had spirited Elizabeth's traveling bag and Randolph's possessions into the stables. By midnight, the lad would have their mounts saddled. Even with the additional weight of provisions, the desert horses could outdistance any in the stables.

Clutching the items she needed, she traced the familiar path into the bowels of the castle. After lighting the candle, she fished the key from her pouch and freed him from his chains.

He sent her a baleful stare. "How convenient. When did Douglas give you that?"

The black beard lent him an evil look, and rather than ask if he had secured the relic of Saint Columba, she stepped back.

He snatched the cloak from her arms and swirled it

340

over his shoulders. "Bother it! Let's away from this hellhole."

Short replies had become the norm. "You ungrateful wretch."

With a hand that felt dangerously strong, he grasped her arm and pushed her toward the stairs. She felt his rage, but it made no sense; he should be jubilant and grateful.

At the top of the stairs, he spat, "Which way?"

Confused and disheartened, she pointed to the door to the buttery. "Through there and into the yard."

Moving with stealth and keeping to the shadows, they made their way to the stables and found the lad waiting, the reins of the horses in hand.

He screwed up his face. "Gor, my lord. Ye smell o' the privy."

Randolph moved around Elizabeth. "I'll ride the stallion."

She placed two gold coins in the lad's hand. "My thanks, and if ill befalls you as a result of our escape, you must flee to Fairhope Tower in the Debatable Lands. Seek sanctuary with Drummond Macqueen."

The boy preened but cast a wary eye toward Randolph. She understood completely.

Randolph held out the reins to the mare. "If you're coming, Elizabeth, mount up."

Second thoughts plagued her, but once they were away, she was certain all would be well.

The assumption proved false. Douglas's men pursued, but their mounts could not keep up the pace. Still, Randolph and Elizabeth pushed the desert horses hard. The December wind cut to the bone, and she pressed close to the mare to gain a little warmth.

When they reached the quay the animals were lathered, and Randolph had not even spared her a glance.

"To me, a Macqueen!" he yelled to the crew of the *Seawolf* as he drew rein.

The seamen scrambled to lower the plank. Randolph dismounted and reached for her. The proof of his imprisonment was all too plain; his hair was matted, his skin dingy, and his clothing soiled to ruin.

In a steel-like grip, he almost dragged her from the horse. "Still wearing your fancy chastity belt, I see."

She jerked free of him. "What is wrong with you? And stop tossing me around like a sack of grain."

He pointed to the startled first mate. "Jamie, secure the horses below and set sail for Elgin's End. Make haste, man, for we must dock before Christmas Day."

"Aye, Randolph."

"Then bring me a bath and something to saw through gold!"

Elizabeth gasped.

Randolph seethed with rage. Taking her arm, he forced her onto the ship. "My cabin's at the foot of that companionway. If you're wise, you'll hie yourself down there now."

"I know where your accursed cabin is," she spat and again pulled free of him.

Too angry to see beyond the degradation that still clung to him, he gritted his teeth and forced her below. Pushing her into his cabin, he took the key and locked the door from the outside.

A shiver of revulsion passed through him, and he squeezed his eyes shut. He heard both the shouts of his crew and the tread of hooves on the deck, but he paid them little mind. Two thoughts ruled him. He was free of that dank dungeon, and the treacherous Elizabeth Gordon was within his grasp.

She had begged him to have faith in her, and like a fool, he had ignored the voice of reason and believed she meant him no harm. He almost chuckled at that, for the pain she'd dealt him went beyond the physical.

His heart ached, as if ripped out. He knew better than to trust a woman, even a respected messenger of the king. Even as he'd been beaten, dragged into the dungeon, and the manacles clamped around his wrists, Randolph had listened in shock. Douglas had admitted that the herald brought the order to imprison Randolph. But Randolph's jailer was a sworn ally of the English. Why would he do the bidding of the Scottish king? And more, why would Bruce send his herald to participate in so low a scheme? He must know that the other Highland chieftains, with the mighty Revas Macduff at the helm, would seek revenge in Randolph's name. Civil war would again reign over Scotland. Divided, their people would be easy prey for Edward II.

The ill logic of it baffled Randolph, and as his mind grew clouded with confusion, his heart spoke loud and clear: Why had Bruce, through Elizabeth, betrayed him? Or had she acted alone, perhaps out of love for some Englishman?

Never, his pride answered.

Bide your time, his conscience pleaded. *You love her.*

It was the truth, Randolph thought with dismay, for he looked for reasons to defend her treachery. With the evidence scarring his wrists and searing his soul, he still wanted to believe her innocent of crimes against him.

Christmas was five days hence. He must hurry to Elgin's End, a distant city on the northern coast of Scotland.

Weary to his soul, he slid to the companionway floor.

Would he make it in time?

Elizabeth couldn't sit still. Wringing her hands, she paced the tiny cabin. A heavy stone brazier sat in the corner beside a stack of peat. She started a fire and huddled beside it, thinking. Had imprisonment crazed Randolph? She'd heard of such madness but had not personally witnessed it. Like the earl of Strath and the marshal of Northumberland, the prisoners she encountered were political pawns and royal captives. They were not chained in dungeons, starved, and beaten.

The ship creaked, then began to move. The motion threw her off balance, and she braced herself. The warmth of the fire soothed her, but at the memory of Randolph's angry threat, she grew frightened again. Why would he treat her so badly? He cared for her—had been relentless in his pursuit of her affections. She knew the work of a rogue when she saw it; Randolph was true at heart. She could only pray that his madness passed. But what if it did not?

A search of the room yielded an arsenal of weapons. Choosing one and hiding the others, she moved to the bed and waited.

Some time later, the door opened. Hoping for the best, she looked up as Randolph strolled into the cabin. He'd bathed and donned a long woolen surcoat. His face was once again cleanly shaven, and his damp hair was raked back. The look in his eye had turned menacing, and in his hand he held a file.

She brandished the dirk. "Keep away from me."

In a voice as cold as the wind outside, he said, "Take off your clothes."

"Why?"

He chuckled and tested the texture of the file with his thumb. "Because I intend to ravish you."

Fear thickened her throat, but she fought it back. She must reason with him. "You love me."

"Call it what you will, but I intend to have you."

He'd tricked himself up. "Then why take my innocence?" she challenged. "Why not spend your rage in beating me?"

"I've ample time for both." He scanned the room, and his gaze rested on the dagger in her hand. "That blade is very sharp."

She could not escape; the cabin was too narrow. Given time, she would change his mind. Words were her tools, not weapons. She pitched the knife to the floor. "Violence is not the way of a lover. Tell me why you accuse the woman who loves you."

Through gritted teeth, he said, "Cease using that word!"

She winced but held her ground. "In your heart you know that I have done nothing wrong. I love you."

"Then why turn me over to the enemy? Betrayal is a poor lover's tool."

"How have I betrayed you?"

He picked up the dagger. "Remove your gown, or I'll cut it to ribbons."

Beneath the fear, her faith was strong. "Terrible acts have been committed against you. You have a right to retribution, but you look for it in the wrong place."

She scooted to the edge of the bed and stood. With trembling hands, she threw off her cloak and removed her overdress. The linen fabric of her bliaud offered little protection from him or the quickly chilling air. "'Tis cold in here."

One side of his mouth tipped up. "That will change."

She must break through to the decent man. "I am a virgin, Randolph."

"That too will change." Spoken plaintively, the words belied the new glimmer in his eyes. "Take it off."

She needed more time. In desperation, she pulled the coif from her hair and uncoiled her braid.

"So." He folded his arms over his chest and leaned

against the cabin door. "You swear your innocence and play the harlot."

She felt the first stirring of anger. "Only harlots let down their hair?"

"In that fashion, aye."

"What are you talking about? I'm cold, and you commanded me to undress."

"Worry not, your discomfort will be short lived."

There it was again; below the anger, he spoke in the tone she remembered. "Then you intend to give me pleasure?"

He squeezed his eyes shut. The tendons in his neck grew taut and his knuckles were white with strain.

She drew off the bliaud, which left her wearing only trunk hose and the chastity belt. Her skin turned to gooseflesh. She shook out her hair and spread it cloaklike over her shoulders.

He opened his eyes, and as she expected, his gaze fell first on her hair, but stopped at her waist. Of finely wrought golden filigree, the chastity belt draped her hips and narrowed to a point over her belly. Attached there, and disappearing between her legs, was a strap of golden chain mail.

He swallowed loudly. "Where is the key?"

"You love me, Randolph."

"Oh, aye," he growled, never looking away from her feminity.

"Tell me how I betrayed you."

"You knew all along why I came to Douglas Castle."

"I know now. You came to fetch the holy relic of Saint Columba so that you can participate in the Christ's Mass of unity."

"You told Douglas about it."

"'Twas not I. Cutberth Macgillivray sent word with his herald to Douglas."

A change came over him. Contemplation robbed

him of that menacing air, and he stared at the brazier. "Douglas spoke of a herald but did not trouble himself to say whose messenger."

Had he ripped out her heart, the pain could not have been greater. "And you thought 'twas me. You thought the worst."

"Cutberth told Douglas to detain me until after Christmas Day."

"I suspect so."

"But how did you come by that knowledge?"

She told him about seeing Cutberth's herald leaving Douglas's room. "Not until I spoke with our king did I learn of the Mass of unity and discover Cutberth's intention of foiling it. King Robert did not think they would look for you in the Lowlands."

"He was wrong, as is often the case in his dealings with his Highland subjects."

"He knows that now and has taken appropriate measures."

"What measures?"

"Even now, royal troops stand guard outside Cutberth's castle. He will not interfere with the Mass."

"You have more faith in Bruce's leadership than I."

Loyalty to her sovereign held her back. But when she saw doubt creeping into Randolph's eyes, she knew she must tell him the truth and more. "Our sovereign plans a Parliament at Saint Andrews in March."

"Parliament?" Randolph blinked in surprise. "A true Parliament, with representatives of all the clans?"

If she believed they could make a life together, now was the time to bare her soul. "Aye, but 'tis not common knowledge. Please understand that I have gone against my king for you."

Caution ruled him. "How?"

"He forbade me to linger at Douglas Castle."

"Why did you disobey?"

"Because I love you, and I promised you I would find you. When you were not there, I came here and spoke with your first mate. Then I rode to your brother's home in search of you."

"How did you find me?"

"The stable lad. Tell me how you came to be in the dungeon."

"Edward left the day after you. Drummond had departed earlier the same morning. Douglas asked me to wait in my chamber and walk with him to vespers. Just as the last bells rang out, his soldiers burst through my door. While everyone else was saying their evening prayers, Douglas's soldiers were pounding me with their fists."

"King Robert attends the Mass. He will want to know what has happened to you."

Randolph's shoulders slumped. "Why did he not reveal his plans to attend?"

"Our sovereign keeps his participation a secret from the English until the Holy Church has blessed our cause."

"We will unite in God's name and celebrate the birth of our savior."

"Aye, and all of Christendom will praise us for it."

He threw away the file and hurried to her side. "Oh, Elizabeth, forgive me for losing my faith in you."

She hugged him and rained kisses over his face. He murmured her name a dozen times, and when their lips met at last, the forgiveness was complete, the joy without bounds. So eager were they to touch and explore each other, their hands kept bumping and foiling the love play.

"I'm clumsy," she confessed.

"You're perfect," he swore.

"You're wearing too many clothes."

He began stripping off his garments. Watching him, she noticed the signs of his incarceration. He was still thinner than he should be, and his wrists bore scars from the manacles. But when he peeled off his trunk hose and she spied his manliness, she swallowed in surprise. Magnificent in form, his desire stood stiff and proud, and her body's reaction seemed in opposition, for she went weak with want of him.

"Which brings us to what you are wearing, my love."

At the sound of his voice, she glanced up, but admiration and anticipation drew her gaze back down. It was her first glimpse at a man's private parts, and an absurd thought flashed in her mind. "Our bodies are very different."

Her words moved him in a physical way. "Delightfully so. Now where is the key to that contraption?"

She shook her head to clear it. "There is none."

"Then how do I get you out of it?"

His sudden impatience made her smile. "Give me your hand."

When he did, she placed his index finger on one of three flowers fashioned into the filigree. With her own hand, she found the other two. "Now we push together."

"A clever way to phrase it, love."

They both applied pressure. A click sounded, springing the hinges, and the belt fell into halves. Randolph tested the weight, and his eyebrows rose. "'Tis not so heavy as I thought."

"It serves the purpose."

He dropped it to the floor. "But its work is done." Then he reached for her hose.

As she watched him kneel and strip away her remaining garment, her heart pounded in anticipation of what was to come. His hands were gentle, yet strong, for he lifted her with ease and placed her in the center of the bed. When he climbed in beside her and slid a leg between hers, she sucked in a breath.

"Shush," he whispered, facing her, then lowering his head until his lips closed over her breast.

A shaft of longing pierced her, making child's play of what had gone before. He drew her nipple into his mouth and alternately suckled, then stroked the throbbing bud with torturously long licks of his tongue.

She grew damp in secret places that yearned for his touch, and her hands and mouth were idle compared to his. "Show me how to please you."

"'Tis simple, my love. Forgive me for doubting you."

Warmth seeped into her bones. "I meant how do I please you in such moments as these."

He took her hand and drew it down until her fingertips touched the velvety skin of his maleness. She curled her hand around him and squeezed, which yielded a moan from him.

"'Tis soft," she said, working her hand up and down. "Yet not at all."

"Keep that up, Elizabeth, and you'll know the meaning of soft."

She chuckled. He did the same, and their laughter vibrated from chest to breast, heart to soul. He touched her in ways that stole her breath and made her shiver with longing, but when his hand moved between her legs and he explored her softness, she gasped and cried out his name.

His breathing grew labored, and his hips moved against her, pushing and pulling in perfect time with the delicious motions of his hand. She trembled and felt as if she were racing on a journey toward some heavenly place. Faster and faster she hurried, taking shallow breaths and drawing strength from the knowledge that he traveled the same path as she.

Then the world burst in an explosion of pleasure so sweet and unexpected, she stiffened from head to toe. He murmured encouraging words and loving phrases, and she clung to the sound of his voice while the joy ebbed and her senses returned.

She swallowed with difficulty and opened her eyes. They still lay side by side, and he smiled at her with so much love, she thought she might swoon. But there was more, she knew instinctively. "Make me yours," she murmured.

He withdrew his hand, rolled her onto her back, then moved over her. Wedging himself into the cradle of her hips, he said, "Spread your legs wide, love."

Now eager, she did as he asked, and felt him push inside her and thrust beyond the barrier of her innocence. Against her will, she tensed at the new fullness, but he soothed her and took her mouth in a deep and stirring kiss.

A moment later he withdrew slightly, only to return, to draw back, and to come into her again. She matched the rhythm he set, and as the cadence quickened she reveled in the harmony and anticipated the pleasure to come. And when it did, she forgot that earlier, singular moment and thrilled at the feel of him throbbing inside her and celebrating his own moment of joy.

In the aftermath of passion, he tucked her to his side and hugged her close. "Thank you for the gift of your innocence."

"'Tis odd," she said, snuggling closer. "We're taught just that—that our virginity is a gift for a man. But on my oath, Randolph Macqueen, you could not have enjoyed our loving so much as I."

He burst out laughing, and it went on for so long, she grew self-conscious. At last he sniffed and said,

"Keep that knowledge to yourself, sweet, else virgins in the marriage bed will go the way of stone privy seats."

Appeased, she reached for the blanket and drew it over them.

"Elizabeth?"

"Hum?"

"If I ever again lose my faith in you," he swore, "I pray you will beat me with a mace."

"Agreed," she said, and fell asleep in the arms of the man she loved.

The voyage was rough, and not until the morning of Christmas Day did they make port in the city of Elgin's End. The horses had also suffered on the journey, and Randolph was forced to walk their mounts for a time before they could begin the overland trek.

They rode hard for Auldcairn Castle, and at every bend in the road they saw evidence of the joyous event to come. Pennons emblazoned with the heraldic symbols of dozens of clans lined the rutted path. Garlands of rosemary and ivy draped the signposts, and at a crossroad, a goodwife offered them mince pies and warmed yule ale.

But the display of Highland unity that awaited them in the common room of Auldcairn Castle surpassed their wildest dreams. The chieftain of the Mackenzies stood shoulder to shoulder with the chieftain of Clan Munro. Mackay befriended Mackintosh, Chisholm laughed with Fraser, Davidson exchanged a holiday gift with Grant.

Seated on a familiar throne at the back of the room was Robert Bruce. A richly garbed bishop flanked the king of Scotland on the left. On his right sat the mighty Revas Macduff, who, along with Randolph, was responsible for the Christmas gathering.

Arm in arm, Elizabeth and Randolph made their way through the crowd. When they reached the dais, they fell to their knees before the king.

"You have abducted my herald," accused Robert Bruce.

"Nay, my liege, for she is soon to be my wife."

The king of Scotland rose and looked from one to the other. "I would speak with you alone, Lady Elizabeth."

As the king drew her aside, Elizabeth saw Randolph do the same with Revas Macduff. Whatever the information Randolph conveyed, Revas Macduff liked it well, for he thrust both arms into the air and cheered.

Ignoring them, Robert Bruce said, "You will take that Macqueen for your husband?"

Elizabeth faced him squarely. "Aye. I love him well—if it pleases Your Majesty."

"So be it, lass. 'Tis truly a day for rejoicing." He glanced past her. "You may say your vows on Whitsunday next."

A masculine groan she recognized sounded behind her. Then Randolph stepped to her side.

"Well, Macqueen?" demanded the king. "As your Christmas joy, I give you permission to wed my ward and the finest herald in the land, Elizabeth Gordon."

Randolph was too disappointed at having to wait until May to respond.

"Have you no words of thanks?" said Bruce.

Randolph took her hand and gazed into her eyes. "I am the most fortunate and patient of men."

That remark was met with a roar of laughter that echoed throughout the room. But between Elizabeth and Randolph passed a silent vow that joined their hearts and sealed their future.

Hours later, at the first ringing of the vesper bells, the chieftains of every Highland clan, save the treacherous Macgillivrays, marched solemnly into the church, their precious holy relics in hand. There, in the place named the Lamp of the North, the greatest leaders of Scotland placed their treasures before the bishop of the Vatican and put their swords at the feet of Robert Bruce, king, at last, of a united Scotland.

In a ceremony of historic proportions, Christmas brought peace and unity to the Highland clans.

ARNETTE LAMB's signature style—fast-paced, witty, and deeply sensual—has won her raves from critics, booksellers, and readers, as well as the coveted *Romantic Times* award for Best New Historical Romance Author. Her wonderfully exciting romances have all been bestsellers, from her sizzling 1991 debut with *Highland Rogue* to her magnificent *Chieftain,* which appeared on the *USA Today* bestseller list.

Pocket Books

proudly presents

ALWAYS

❧ JUDE DEVERAUX ❧

Available from Pocket Books

The following is a preview of *Always* . . .

∗∥∗

CONNIE AND KAYLA WERE ALMOST THE SAME AGE AND about the same size. Even their coloring was nearly the same. But as alike as they were, they couldn't have been more different. Kayla exuded golden blondeness, while Connie looked pale, washed-out. Kayla was statuesque, whereas Connie seemed to tower over people and slumped to keep from doing so. Kayla was a woman no one could overlook, while Connie could stand beside a person and not even be seen.

Connie had been working at Wrightsman's Jewelry Store for six years; Kayla had been there for three weeks. Connie knew everything there was to know about the cut and clarity of jewels. She could tell you the weight and the color number of a diamond at a glance. She knew the provenance of every jewel in the store, knew what was in the safe and who had owned what and why they'd had to sell it.

Kayla asked customers if they liked "the blue ones or the green ones" better.

But in three weeks Kayla had sold more jewelry than Connie had in the last six months. After the first week, Connie had complained to Mr. Wrightsman. "She *models* the jewelry. She wears low-cut dresses, hangs a million-dollar necklace around her throat, then leans over so men can look down the front of her dress." Connie had not been pleased by Mr. Wrightsman's answer. He'd told her to "join the real world."

It was late on Friday when the man approached the store. After having worked at Wrightsman's for so long, Connie was used to the rich and powerful stepping into the store. There was an elegant room in the back where they could sit in private and sell what they could no longer afford to keep. And there was the professionally lit showroom where the customers could show off their wealth by buying something Marie Antoinette had once owned.

Connie had met many politicians, movie stars, and jet-setters, but she'd never seen this man before. He was handsome in a masculine way, with heavy black eyebrows, dark eyes, and an aquiline nose set above lips that had a slight, teasing smile, as though he knew something no one else did.

As Connie looked at the man, she felt her knees start to melt. The only other time she'd felt this way was when Sean Connery had walked into the store. This man was wearing a black leather jacket that she was sure had cost thousands; she could almost feel the softness of the leather under her fingertips. His light-weight tan wool trousers had to have been cut to fit him. As he walked toward the door, she saw that he wore no jewelry and her heart dropped. He was buying for a woman, not himself.

She didn't really think that a man like him would be interested in her, but still she relished the thought of the coming hours of searching through the vaults for just the right jewel. She prided herself on being a good judge of financial position and this man exuded money. Naked, dripping from a shower, she thought, this man would have an aura of wealth about him.

As he pushed the glass door open, Connie nearly giggled at her thought of this beautiful man being wet and naked. Catching herself, she looked across the cases filled with sparkling jewels on blue satin to Kayla, and she was horrified to see Kayla staring at the man with the same expression that Connie was probably wearing.

Connie wanted to scream "Oh no you don't. This one is *mine!*" Men like this one, men who possessed old-world manners—and old-world money—were her reward for putting up with tourists who wanted to see where "Brad Pitt shopped." And with rude rock stars and ego-tripping two-bit actors who wanted the world to know that they bought their jewels at Wrightsman's.

The man entered the store, removed his sunglasses, then stood for a moment as his eyes adjusted. When they did, he looked at Connie and smiled. Yes, she thought. Come to me.

But in the next second he turned his head and saw Kayla—and it was to her that he walked.

Connie had to duck behind the counter to hide her anger. Before Mr. Wrightsman had hired Connie, he'd dumped a pile of diamonds on a velvet tray, then sat there in silence and looked at her. He didn't tell her what he wanted her to do with them. Arrange them in order of size? Clarity? Connie had paid her dues at half a dozen retail stores and two wholesale merchants before she dared to even apply at a prestigious store like Wrightsman's. With no hesitation, she chose one diamond out of the pile, one of the smaller ones. She had no loupe so she couldn't judge it for flaws, but for color, the diamond was nearly perfect.

She set the diamond on the side of the tray, then looked at the old man. The tiniest of smiles appeared at one corner of his mouth. "Monday, nine A.M.," he'd said, then looked back at the ledger in front of him, dismissing her.

In the past six years Connie had brought the old family-owned store into the twenty-first century. She'd put in a computer system, created a website, had arranged for some discreet publicity, and had twice foiled Mr. Wrightsman's youngest son's plans to abscond with the store's profits.

Her life had been nearly perfect until Mr. Wrightsman had, for some unfathomable reason, hired a woman whose only selling advantage was a lot of hair and a lot of bosom.

Now, surreptitiously, Connie watched the man as he bent over the counter in front of Kayla. When she put what Connie called "the tourist tray" before him, she heard the man give a low laugh. His voice was silky, smooth, and deep, a voice that made Connie close her eyes for a moment.

And when she did, she dropped the tray of rings in her hand. Never had she dropped a tray before. Cursing Kayla, cursing Mr. Wrightsman for hiring her, Connie got down on her hands and knees and began to pick up the scattered $20,000 rings. One emerald beauty had bounced under the cabinet so Connie had to bend low to get it—and when she did, she glanced through the glass case just in time to see the man slip a ruby and diamond necklace into his trousers' pocket.

Connie was so taken aback that she sat back on her heels and stared at what she could see of the man through the glass. Surely not, she thought. Slowly, she stood up, then even more slowly, she walked over to where Kayla and the man were standing, keeping her eyes away from him. She mustn't let a pair of sexy eyes distract her.

While Connie had been scurrying to pick up the rings, Kayla had done what she'd been repeatedly told not to do: she'd covered the countertop with merchandise. She'd been told to take one item at a time out so she could keep track of what was where.

It took Connie all of three seconds to see that the molded tray that held the necklace that an empress of Russia had worn was empty and not in the jumble of jewels lying in a heap. Unaware of what the man had done, Kayla had bent down, and was pulling three more trays out of the bottom of the case.

Connie raised her eyes to look at the man and when

her gaze met his, he smiled in a soft, seductive way that made her want to run to the vault and get out the really good jewels. Maybe he'd like a Fabergé egg or two.

But Connie had morals, and wrong was wrong. The man was beautiful, but he was a thief. With her heart pounding in her throat, she smiled back at him while she reached under the counter, opened the little metal door, and pushed the button of the silent alarm. In six years, she'd pushed that button only one other time.

Sitting on the floor, Kayla saw Connie push the button and looked up at her co-worker in disbelief. With her head turned away from the man, Connie gave Kayla a look meant to silence her.

After the button was pushed, there was about five seconds of quiet, then all hell broke loose. Sirens sounded outside and heavy iron bars began to drop down across the front of the store.

For a moment Connie's heart seemed to stop. She locked eyes with the man and she had to fight against screaming at him to run, to try to get away. If he broke a window ... if he pushed open a door ... But no, the glass had high-strength plastic in the middle and the doors wouldn't open because of the gates.

But Connie's feelings of compassion, her desire to see the man get away ended when Kayla stood up. "You mean, spiteful bitch," Kayla said. "You couldn't stand that *I* got him and you didn't."

Flustered, Connie couldn't speak. She hadn't pushed the alarm because she was *jealous*.

"Quiet, little one," the man said to Kayla in his smooth voice, then he picked up her hand and kissed the back of it.

Connie turned away at that and in the next second three policemen were there. "He put a necklace in his pocket," she said, not looking at Kayla.

The police were oddly silent, and when the man held out his hands, they put handcuffs on him and read him his rights. It was almost as if they had been told not to ask questions. As far as Connie could tell, he'd never lost his small smile and she was puzzled by it. Why had he been so stupid? Why wasn't he protesting? After all, until he'd left the store with the necklace in his pocket, he hadn't actually committed a crime. Maybe she'd been hasty in pushing the alarm button.

It was when they reached the door that Connie heard her own thought. Grabbing the empty velvet tray, she ran forward and held it out to the man. "He still has the necklace," she said.

"You know where it is," the man said, so much sex oozing from his voice that Connie could almost see the two of them sitting on a mile of white beach, margaritas in hand.

She couldn't help herself as she reached forward to slip her hand inside the man's front pocket to retrieve the necklace. And when she did, he bent his head and kissed her. Time seemed to stand still. She could feel his warm thigh under her hand, his chest was touching hers, and his lips were . . . She closed her eyes and she could almost hear steel drums, feel soft tropical breezes on her skin.

"Okay, let's break this up," one of the cops said. "Lady! Get your hands out of his pants and your face off his."

This brought guffaws of laughter from the two other policemen. Connie pulled the necklace from his pocket and, her eyes never leaving his, spread it on the tray.

Standing by the window, the tray in her hand, Connie watched them lead the man to the waiting police car. She could still feel his kiss on her lips.

"Is that the right one?" she heard Kayla ask. Reluctantly, Connie pulled her eyes away from the man and looked at the necklace on the tray. It was not an exquisite ruby and diamond creation but a cheap concoction of glass and gold-toned pot metal.

When Connie glanced up, she saw that the man was about to enter the police car. "He still has the necklace!" she shouted, but the thick glass was almost completely soundproof. She banged on the window to get their attention and when the policemen turned to look, the man took that moment to go into action.

His hands were in cuffs, but, standing on one leg, he kicked out to send one policeman spinning, then whirled to plant a foot in the chest of the second one. The third cop pulled his gun but the man knocked it with his cuffed hands, sending the gun flying into the street.

In the next second, the man was running down the street with the speed of an Olympic athlete and she saw him disappear into an alley a block away.

"If he gets caught, it will be *your* fault," Kayla said as she flung the door open and went outside.

For a moment Connie stood alone in the shop, then she thought of what Mr. Wrightsman was going to say when he heard that Connie had allowed the thief to take the necklace. She hadn't even looked at it when she'd taken it from his pocket. She'd been so ensorcelled by his kiss that . . . that she was going to lose her job.

Dropping the horrid necklace, she ran out the door, reaching into her pocket to push the electronic door lock as she ran. She *had* to get that necklace back!

By the time she got to the alley, the three policemen had recovered and were searching inside the Dumpster and behind the garbage cans. She stood back, watching them, her heart pounding from her run. If the man had run in here, unless he was Spiderman, there was no escape. There were twenty-foot-tall brick walls and the few windows were painted over, unused for years. All the fire escapes ended two stories above the ground.

Connie's first impulse was to join in the search, but instead, she stood back and looked. Where could a man hide?

She never would have seen him if he hadn't moved. It was almost as though he wanted to be caught.

There was a tiny ledge on one of the buildings and he was lying flat on it, so still that there were two pigeons on his back. She took a moment to figure out how he'd managed to climb up there. He must have leaped from the Dumpster to catch the bottom of a fire escape, swung upward, crept along the four-inch-wide ledge into the deep shadows where two buildings intersected, then lain flat out, half hidden under the broken remnants of an old iron and concrete balcony.

Why had he moved? she wondered. Why had he *purposefully* let her see him?

One of the cops saw Connie looking up and drew his gun. But before the policeman could do whatever he was going to do next, two cars screeched to a halt at the end of the alley and six men in suits and dark glasses jumped out. They flashed badges at the cops and one man said, "FBI. We've been looking for this guy for a long time. He's ours."

Two minutes later, the beautiful man, still handcuffed, was on the ground, this time surrounded by FBI agents.

Boldly, Connie stepped forward. "He still has the necklace he stole," she said, not looking into the man's eyes. His eyes—and his lips—had the power to make her forget about everything.

"You'll get it back," one of the FBI agents said brusquely as he led the man away.

Standing at the edge of the alley, the three policemen behind her, Connie watched them put the man into the car. He winked at her through the window . . . then they were gone.

Atria Books

proudly presents

HOLLY

❧ JUDE DEVERAUX ❦

Now available in paperback

from Atria Books

The following is a preview of *Holly*...

Prologue

"ARE YOU SURE YOU WANTA DO THIS, DOC?" CARL asked, looking across to the driver's seat at Dr. Nicholas Taggert. "My brother's cabin is a wreck and the only transportation there is his truck, and it isn't street legal so you can't drive it."

Nick looked in his left mirror, signaled, then moved Carl's car into the fast lane. "I told you that all I need is a place to get away to for a few days, and my cousin is going to pick me up. You said there's a grocery within walking distance so I won't need a vehicle for the three days I'm alone there."

"It's just a mom-and-pop store. No caviar or anything." When Nick didn't smile, Carl knew his joke had fallen flat. "Sorry about your girl," he mumbled.

"Over and done with," Nick said tightly, letting it be known that Stephanie Benning was not something he was going to discuss.

Carl looked out the window at the beautiful Smokey Mountain scenery, but he was so nervous he could hardly sit still. What was he, an ambulance driver, doing in a car with a big-deal doctor like Nicholas Taggert? Why hadn't Dr. Nick asked one of the doctors at the clinic if they knew of a cabin to rent? They could have found him a place on five acres, near a movie theater and something called a "bistro."

Carl couldn't figure out why Dr. Nick wanted to stay in a derelict cabin, but he did know why the man wanted to hide out: Stephanie Benning, ol' Doc Benning's youngest—and meanest—daughter.

About nine months ago, long-legged, long-haired Stephanie had come back from some place with a French name, the ink still wet on her divorce papers, taken one look at Dr. Nick Taggert's movie-star good looks, and gone after him like there was no tomorrow. Of course everyone in the office knew that she wasn't after his looks. Her last husband had been the clone of a toad. She knew that Dr. Nick was from money—real money. Big money. He didn't know anyone in the office knew about his family's worth, but they did. Ten minutes on the Internet and the news was out.

More of a secret was what Stephanie Benning was really like. Only the locals in the clinic knew that she'd been a selfish, hateful child and she hadn't changed as she got older. Somehow, she'd managed to fool Dr. Nick for eight whole months before he broke up with her.

Of course Stephanie told everyone in her father's clinic that she'd been the one to break it off. She'd said that Dr. Taggert had used her, then thrown her away like an old handbag. She'd wept so prettily that everyone except the locals believed her. She'd even made a big deal about the yellow diamond Dr. Nick had given her because he'd asked for it back. She'd whined that no gentleman would demand the return of jewels given to a lady.

One of the women in the office said the rock was worth at least a million and belonged to Dr. Nick's family.

"I notice she kept that big dinner ring he gave her," Lucy in reception had snipped.

"And the sapphire earrings," someone else said.

"And the pearl necklace."

"All she had to give back was that big yellow diamond and the key to the ball and chain she'd clamped around him."

Everyone had fallen over in laughter.

But the physicians on the staff at the Benning Clinic had believed everything Stephanie had said about Dr. Nick. Overnight, words like "gentleman," "honor" and "integrity," were overheard—as though Nick Taggert didn't have these qualities.

The locals had tried to defend him, but they couldn't say much. After all, Stephanie's father signed their paychecks.

One of the women tried to get Dr. Nick to defend himself and tell the truth about what Stephanie was like. They didn't know the details of the breakup, but they were sure he'd found out that all she wanted was his money. But Dr. Nick wouldn't defend himself. He bore the looks from the other doctors and the whispered comments without flinching. Even when Stephanie threw one of her spoiled-brat tantrums in front of the entire staff and the waiting patients, he still didn't defend himself.

The locals were split down the middle about his silence. Half said he was an idiot and the other half said he was a hero out of a storybook.

So, three nights ago, when Carl had returned from a late run and Dr. Nick had been alone in his office, Carl hadn't been shocked when Dr. Nick asked if he knew of a cabin to rent, a place to get away for a few days.

But a cabin that would suit the likes of a man with the doctor's pedigree was out of Carl's league.

Carl had just smiled. "The only place I know of is my brother Leon's house. It's fallin' down enough that you could call it a cabin, and it *is* on a lake."

"Sounds great. When will your brother be away so I can rent it?"

"He'll be gone for about twelve more years," Carl said, still smiling. "If he behaves himself, that is. Look, Doc, I was just kidding. You do *not* want to rent Leon's place. It's horrible. The house is a pigsty and it's got a big barn that looks like it's gonna fall down any minute. The truth is, atomic bombs wouldn't hurt that barn, but that's neither here nor there. Now, across the lake, just on the other side, are some really nice houses. I bet if you called a realtor—"

"How far from here is your brother's cabin?"

"A couple of hours. But, Doc—"

"Is it vacant now? Is it furnished?"

"Sort of," Carl said, then got louder, firmer. He needed to stop this *now*. "You can*not* rent Leon's place, Doc, it's awful. My brother has only one interest in his life and that's his truck. He dedicated every penny he could earn, steal, or con somebody out of to that truck. He's in prison now because he robbed three gas stations just so he could buy a spare transmission and a transfer case."

Carl could see that Dr. Nick wasn't listening to him.

"Does the roof leak?"

"No," Carl said patiently. "I look after the place enough that the roof doesn't leak, and I cleaned it up enough that the rats don't tear down the walls to get at the food Leon left lyin' around. Doc!" he said emphatically. "You can't think of stayin' in that house."

Dr. Nick leaned back in his chair and narrowed his eyes at Carl. "Why not? Do you think I'm too much of a priss to get my hands dirty in a house like your brother's?"

Carl had to smile at the word "priss." In the five years Dr. Nick had been at the Benning Clinic, he'd never heard the man use foul language. He'd always been fair and honest to everyone, but, until Stephanie, he'd never been close to any of them, not doctors or staff. He was a good doctor and the only times Carl or anyone else had seen Dr. Nick get angry was when a patient wasn't getting the best of service.

In the end, no matter what Carl said, Nick Taggert had overridden him, and now they were driving through the mountains to Leon's cabin.

As they drove up the weed-infested driveway, Carl relaxed. There was no way anyone on earth would want to stay in this place unless he had to. It was almost with triumph that Carl said, "Watch out for snakes," as soon as they stepped into the waist-high weeds that surrounded the old house.

He walked behind Dr. Nick as he battled through the weeds to the front steps of the house, then up to the porch. There was no reason to lock the house; who'd want to go inside it?

In the living room were three pieces of furniture Leon had found at the dump, the stuffing coming out of the arms. The two end tables, the coffee table, and both lamps were made of beer cans welded together. The dining room had an old table, hidden somewhere under Leon's collection of a couple of thousand old car magazines. The kitchen was the worst, with cracked dishes on the floor, magazines with curled pages, dented aluminum pots, and mouse droppings everywhere. At the back of the house was the bedroom, with an old, stained mattress and a jumble of torn, dirty sheets at the bottom of a closet.

"See what I mean?" Carl said when they were outside on the back porch. In front of them stretched the lake, crystal clear and beautiful. Across the pristine surface, on the other side, were gorgeous houses, each house painted a different color, with a matching boat dock. Some people even had boats painted to match their houses and docks.

When Leon had been arrested, Carl had wanted to sell the lake house to pay for a good lawyer, but Leon had refused. He said that someday the developers would want his place and Leon would make them pay.

"I bet you can get one of those houses over there," Carl said, nodding across the lake.

Nick was leaning on the porch rail and looking across the water. "Lavender," he said.

"What?"

"I don't see a lavender house. There are three shades of pink, but little in the lavender family. What if I paint this house lavender, build a matching boat dock, and get a sailboat with bright purple sails?"

It took Carl moments to realize that Nick was kidding. Laughing, Carl slapped him on the back. "As long as you don't touch the truck, you can do whatever you want to to the place."

Nick stood up and stretched, and Carl could see that, in a way, the doc fit with this place. There was something old world about the man that suited this half-overgrown old house.

Abruptly, all Carl's nervousness left him. The doc would do all right here.

"So where's this infamous truck?" Nick said, stepping back for Carl to lead the way.

Carl took the set of keys out of his pocket as he kicked weeds aside. When Leon had bought the place years ago, Carl had tried to get him to tear down the old barn. He'd said Leon should build a new, secure building of concrete blocks to use for his garage.

"I plan to," Leon said, but Carl hadn't known what he meant. Leon had built a new building inside the barn, camouflaging it so no one would guess what was inside.

Carl unlocked the old barn door, then used a code to unlock the inner steel door. If Dr. Nick was surprised, he didn't show it. When Carl slid the heavy steel door back, the lights inside the garage went on. Carl gave a little smile when, behind him, he heard Dr. Nick gasp. It was an enormous, windowless room, spotlessly clean, with two smaller glass-walled rooms inside, one outfitted with a bath and a full kitchen.

In the main room a two-ton overhead electric hoist system and a bead blasting system sat near a Hollander drill press, a band saw, a puller set, an air compressor, and a parts washer. There were several tall metal cabinets in deep red full of Hollander tools. Always the best for Leon.

In the middle of the room, on a concrete floor that even after six months barely showed any dust, was the truck. The Truck.

Dr. Nick stepped into the shop and stood a few feet back from the truck, looking at it with wide eyes.

"Ever see anything like it?"

"Never," Nick answered. "What, exactly *is* it?"

Carl knew that to the uninitiated the truck looked bizarre. It was a 1978 Chevy half-ton body, with a Chrysler V-10 engine. Nearly everything inside the truck had been removed and replaced by something better, and more expensive, and bigger. As a result, every square inch was filled with machinery.

Since Carl had spent too many weekends helping his brother, he knew a lot about what had been done to the truck, and while Dr. Nick listened in appreciative silence, Carl gave him the full rundown, explaining why the bed of the truck was filled with machines and pipes. When Carl quit talking—not that he'd finished—he looked at Dr. Nick, who was blinking at the truck as though trying to comprehend it.

"So how fast does it go?"